You Light Up My Death

Books by Mary Jane Maffini

Camilla MacPhee Mysteries

Speak Ill of the Dead

The Icing on the Corpse

Little Boy Blues

The Devil's in the Details

The Dead Don't Get Out Much

Law & Disorder

You Light Up My Death

The Charlotte Adams Mysteries

Organize Your Corpses

The Cluttered Corpse

Death Loves a Messy Desk

Closet Confidential

The Busy Woman's Guide to Murder

Death Plans a Perfect Trip

The Fiona Silk Mysteries

Lament for a Lounge Lizard

Too Hot to Handle

The Book Collector Mysteries
(written as Victoria Abbott with Victoria Maffini)

The Christie Curse

The Sayers Swindle

The Wolfe Widow

The Marsh Madness

The Hammett Hex

For Mary Ellen

You Light Up My Death

A Camilla MacPhee Mystery

Enjoy the trip!

by
Mary Jane Maffini

Mary Jane Maffini

OTTAWA PRESS AND PUBLISHING
MYSTERY

Ottawa Press and Publishing
Copyright © Mary Jane Maffini 2022

ISBN BOOK: 978-1-990896-01-9
ISBN E-BOOK: 978-1-990896-02-6

Cover design: Nicolas Fairbank / badduck.ca
Cover photograph: Giulio Maffini
Layout: Patti Moran / Patti Moran Graphic Design
Printed in Canada

This is a work of fiction. All of the characters, names, incidents,
organizations, and dialogue in this novel are either products of the
author's imagination or are used fictitiously.

Library and Archives Canada Cataloguing in Publication

Title: You light up my death / by Mary Jane Maffini.
Names: Maffini, Mary Jane, author.
Description: Series statement: A Camilla MacPhee mystery
Identifiers: Canadiana (print) 20220411069 | Canadiana (ebook) 20220411077
| ISBN 9781990896019 (softcover) | ISBN 9781990896026 (EPUB)
Classification: LCC PS8576.A3385 Y68 2022 | DDC C813/.54—dc23

In memory of Zita MacNeil, beloved auntie

CHAPTER ONE
Pass the air freshener

It would have been the honeymoon from hell, if we'd actually had a wedding. The signs were there: endless road trip, brooding man with quest, and large, smelly dog. I'm sure you can fill in the blanks even before I mention Mrs. Parnell's cat. The silky little calico had hitched a ride for reasons that I won't go into because they will make your head hurt.

And that was just the beginning. Who knew it could get worse? Eloping while in Cape Breton would tick one item off my partner Ray's to-do list. That list also included packing up his recently sold family home in Sydney and disposing of the contents, then catching the best of the Celtic Colours concerts.

Code word for trip: intense.

Never mind. Sergeant Ray Deveau was worth a bit of tension. My sisters—Edwina, Donalda, and Alexa—all insisted Ray was the calmest and most tolerant man they'd ever met. I'm sure you can pick up on the subtext.

For his part, Ray claimed I was the woman for him. All to say at the tender age of forty-nine, I'd committed to tie the knot again. We had given the slip to my omnipresent family, his self-obsessed daughters, and our meddling friends. He called me the anti-bride and maintained he liked me that way.

Don't get me wrong: I was happy. Ray was a good cook and a better lover. He didn't leave his dirty clothes on the floor, and he knew how to run a washer-dryer combo better than I did, although that's not saying much. On one hand, he was a cop and, after years as a Legal Aid lawyer and victims' rights activist, I wasn't a fan of the police. On the other hand, his job as a detective sergeant with Ottawa Police Services kept him from being underfoot all day while I rethought my career. Various agencies and government departments were providing support for victims, although slashed budgets could change that. The same with the cuts to the provincial legal aid system that would mean less access for unlucky clients. It seemed a good idea to decide on my work future before I hit the benchmark birthday.

Of course, I had other stuff to ponder too. I'm not big on weddings and ceremonies. Yet I'd tucked my new red dress and strappy sandals into our oversized duffle bag, along with my computer, work files, and the marriage license we'd ordered online. When we'd left our boutique hotel in Quebec City in the morning, Ray was still lovey-dovey. Hours later, I was stuck with a fiancé snarling about the stinky pets in his one-week-old Ford Escape.

"Until this trip, my vehicle still had its new car smell. Remind me again why we have this dog with us," Ray said.

"I told you. Alvin has a new job—"

"Alvin has a job?"

"Well, not a job per se. It's some kind of quasi-business commitment. I don't have all the specifics. You know that Alvin's younger brother, Jimmy, wants Gussie back, and since we're on our way down East…"

Ray was no fan of Alvin Ferguson, my former employee and arguably the world's worst office assistant. No doubt he was picturing Alvin's long ponytail, vintage leather jacket, nine visible piercings, and the new green tattoos of a pot leaf on each hand.

"Don't grind your teeth," I said. "You know you hate getting dental work."

I decided against telling Ray about Alvin's planned line of artisanal marijuana bath and body products. Ray had been opposed to the legislation to legalize cannabis. Even though the law had passed, and regulations continued to wind their bumpy way through the system, Ray would not find the Garden of Weeden amusing.

The grumbling continued about Gussie. "What in the name of all that's good and holy are you feeding that dog?" He'd fed Gussie last, but pick your battles, as they say.

"As long as it drowns out that Hugo Boss aftershave," I said. The Hugo Boss had been a Father's Day gift from his daughters. They'd bought a variety of scents because they were "so over" his Old Spice. I kind of like Old Spice, but it wasn't my decision.

Ray selected his current favourite music and played Little Miss Higgins' "Restless Heart." He pressed REPEAT and we were able to tune each other out.

I chomped on a granola bar, and gazed at the endless trees fringing the Trans-Canada as we barrelled through New Brunswick. After more than five years together, Ray had picked our pre-wedding trip to unveil his moody side. I considered hauling my files from our duffle bag in the trunk space and doing a bit of work on my pending court case, defending my favourite client Bunny Mayhew on a spurious charge of breaking and entering. I'd ensured Bunny made bail, otherwise I would still have been home. I don't believe in locking people up before they're convicted of minor and nonviolent crimes. Ray and I had agreed to disagree on that principle.

I turned around to see if I could reach the bag while the car was moving. I should have brought my own suitcase with me, but *somebody* had thought with both animals in the back, Ray's hefty rolling duffle would have to do for the two of us. We'd be dragging stuff back to Ottawa from Ray's house and we'd need the room. I'd made the point Gussie would be staying in Sydney but got nowhere.

If Ray hadn't chosen that moment to pull off the highway and park on the shoulder to take an incoming call on his cell—the fifth since breakfast—I might have had a bit of fun, teasing him about feeding the dog. But I bit my tongue until he finished. He didn't use Bluetooth, so I couldn't listen in.

Silence. A grunt. More silence. More grunts. Then, "What the hell. Yeah. Keep me in the loop." Then a snarl, followed by, "'Course I'm in. What choice do we have?"

He shot back onto the highway without a shoulder check. A glance at Ray's pleasant, freckled face and you would have thought someone had died. I figured Ottawa Police Services Human Resources had dropped some bomb. But why would he take a call from HR? What couldn't wait?

I didn't give him the satisfaction of asking.

Ray kept his eyes on the road while doing a steady 140 kilometres an hour. The speed limit was one-ten through New Brunswick. That wasn't like him either. Could HR be messing with his pension?

I turned my mind to the fun part of the trip: Celtic music is one of the few areas in life that Ray and I agree on. We had tickets for five Celtic Colours events. We'd matched the concerts to our honeymoon trip around the trail and booked them as soon as the tickets were available, even before we decided on our quick and quiet wedding. After a few years trying, we'd finally snagged seats for the dinner and candlelight concert in the chapel of Fortress Louisbourg. I couldn't wait.

When we got to Sydney, I'd hustle Gussie to the Fergusons, and Ray would get the house organized, decide what would be taken back to Ottawa, what to store for his daughters, and what to donate to a local refugee support group. He'd already arranged boxes, packers, and cleaners.

By Tuesday, we'd be getting hitched on the beach in Ingonish, in front of our rental cabin. Ray had an old buddy who was authorized to perform marriages. The buddy had promised to bring along witnesses. Aside from that, a few sea birds would watch over the spectacle of us shivering through our vows.

I'd stuffed a wool shawl, plus our puffer jackets and warm hats, into the duffle in case they were needed. And if the weather turned stormy, we had permission to say our vows and sign our papers in the main guesthouse with the beach visible through the big window.

After we sealed the deal, we planned to reward ourselves with beer and fishermen's platters at the Seagull restaurant before we returned to our cozy beachside retreat, where we would have a bonfire on the shore and toast marshmallows.

Our elopement would in no way resemble the proper wedding my sisters would have insisted on: deckle-edged cream invitations, colour-coded napkins, seating plans, control of the invitation list, chairs with covers and bows, dyed-to-match doves, scattered rose petals, and all that crap. They would expect to do up their perfect hair even more stylishly than usual, and I could cover my dark curls with a poufy veil. Not happening.

We had planned the perfect wedding.

Not so perfect was Ray's scowling. I switched back to watching the scenery.

"Boring," I said after a half hour, tired of the scowl and Little Miss Higgins. "Why do they need all these trees? What kind of a province is made up entirely of evergreens? Is it a lack of imagination?"

Ray didn't divert his gaze from the road. "It's the Trans-Canada. You can find plenty of varied scenery off the highway, as you well know, Camilla. Where's your patriotism?"

"Where's my patriotism? Please tell me marriage is not going to lead to a lifetime of stupid questions."

"You never change, Camilla."

"No plans to. Has to be more to Canada than eight gazillion trees. Most of them are plain vanilla evergreen too. Not even many autumn colours."

"Vanilla isn't green," Ray muttered.

I didn't plan to show off my legal training by coming up with a statement to the effect that—under the right circumstances—vanilla *might* be green. Instead, I offered a pleasant suggestion. "Why don't we try some of the secondary roads? If that's where the scenery is, we might get a peek at the ocean."

"Because we're in a hurry, and there is no ocean in the interior of New Brunswick any more than there are green vanilla trees."

"If you say so," I responded, adding a yawn.

"I do. But I saw plenty of colourful leaves on this trip, red, orange, whatever. You could try to enjoy them, instead of bitching."

"Nothing compared to what we'll see in Cape Breton," I shot back. Ray didn't answer.

And by "didn't answer," I mean he didn't react to questions, comments, veiled threats, snide remarks, and sarcasm. All those years of being a cop have made him immune to verbal assault.

I gave up.

Gussie had not given up farting.

Then I had an overdue insight. "Ray, if you're having second thoughts about getting married, don't worry about it."

This time, Ray glared at me. "What are you talking about?"

"No need to yell. And keep your eyes on the road. I'm saying if you want to back out of the ceremony, all you have to do is say so."

He shook his head. "Everything is not about you, Camilla."

All my life, I've been made aware that everything was not about me. I stared at the road, not wanting to make eye contact with him. "True. But I feel our wedding is—at least peripherally—about me. So if you don't want to go ahead with it, consider yourself a free man. By the way, I hate it when you roll your eyes."

I hunched down to endure the rest of the trip in silence.

Ray said, "Oh for God's sake."

People tell me I can be abrasive. Perhaps I'd made a remark that wounded Ray's spirit. But as a rule, major crimes detectives are not the most sensitive flowers. For the past four years, he'd asked me to marry him every Saturday night before the hockey game. Now, when it mattered, he did not say, "Of course, I want to marry you."

I found that telling. And I should add that the trip to Sydney from Ottawa is 1,642 kilometres, not including the detour to Quebec City. We had hours to go.

Did his long silences have to do with his daughters? No doubt they were pissed off about the house sale. The girls were living happy lives in Halifax, so I didn't believe that could cause Ray to change his mind, but human relationships were not my strong point. So what else could explain it?

"Is it because you feel bad about letting the house go? I could understand—"

"What are you going on about now?"

Going on about? I put my hand on top of my head to keep it from blowing off. "I get it, Ray. All those memories of Ashley and Brittany as kids. Skating. Christmas. Summer barbecues. Missing teeth. Trips to the emergency department. Vomiting, diarrhea. Parent-teacher night. The whole enchilada. Painful to think about." I didn't say a word about his wife, Carol, who had died of cancer eight years back. I always sense his sadness when he hears her name.

This time he raised his voice. "The girls have moved on with their lives. Have you forgotten Brittany's doing her PhD and Ashley is finishing her MBA? What the devil has gotten into you?"

"Fine, then. But you're not the only one with a secret." I turned away as we passed another thick wall of spruce.

Ray kept silent.

I didn't push it because I didn't actually have a secret.

Ray barrelled through New Brunswick and into Nova Scotia.

Eloping with a grouchy cop. The fun never ends.

CHAPTER TWO
That didn't go as planned

"Here's a fact you should learn about women, Ray."

He flashed me an irritated glance. Ray thought he knew all about the female of the species. Point of pride.

"It's this: if we gaze at nothing but trees for four or five hours, then we need to stop and go to the restroom. I mean in a facility constructed for that purpose and not in a clearing off the road. So you might want to start planning."

We pulled into a Tim's outside of Antigonish, not far from the causeway, and found a small but clean ladies' room. Next I picked up two double-doubles and a box of eight chocolate glazed plus two plain Timbits to keep our energy up. The dog and the cat appreciated the opportunity to stretch their legs on a patch of grass. I stayed with them and held the cat's leash while Ray paced the parking lot, yapping on the phone. A small drama ensued when the scheming calico slithered out of her collar and made a bid for freedom. Gussie and I earned a few war wounds capturing her.

Back on the highway, wincing from the sting of peroxide I'd found the first-aid kit, I said, "This is a nice tradition, Ray," meaning our routine stops at Tim's on long-haul drives. "The cat scratches have become part of it."

On a regular day, we would laugh together at this, but Ray's cell phone rang, and he snatched it up. He always insisted I had to be hands-free when I drove and yammered on about the law.

This was now the seventh call since we started out and another one-sided conversation, punctuated with "What? Where? When? How?"

And pauses in between. I waited for "Who?" and "Why?"

Ray disconnected without comment. I refrained from asking "How much?"

Seemed that a detective could be tracked down, even if he was on his way to get married.

Cops. What can I say?

He wasn't the only one with unwanted tasks. My three sisters had instructed me to carry gifts to a bewildering number of relatives. Of course, I'd refused, but the box of jams, homemade liqueurs, chocolate truffles, and who knew what else was in back with the duffle. *This batch to our cousin Donald Donnie MacDonald and his wife, Loretta. That batch to Auntie Annie MacNeil in Ingonish. And don't tell me you're too important to make the drive. Annie is almost ninety and getting a bit fragile, although she continued to drive until this summer. She told Donalda that she's hanging on to a car because you never know. She'll be expecting you. If you can't find her, check with Rita Susanne Kelly. Rita Susanne is a practical nurse, and she does home care for Auntie Annie. After all the trouble she's had in her life, the woman's turned into an angel taking care of other people. She treats Auntie like a queen. You could learn a lot from her. I sent her jam too. Don't forget blah blah blah.*

Angels? Queens? Give me a break.

Never mind, the coffee and Timbits improved the air in the car. I ate all the chocolate-glazed ones and ruminated. Gussie ate the two plain ones. Ray and the little calico remained in their own private worlds. Little Miss Higgins sang on.

It had to be a case. In Major Crimes, Ray deals with the worst of humanity. When he doesn't want to talk about an investigation, I've learned to let it go.

By the time we crossed the Canso Causeway, Ray still hadn't said a word. I gazed at the sun sparkling on the frigid waters of the Strait of Canso and the dark, ruined hills that had been blasted sixty years earlier to build the connection from "the mainland." I saluted the sign saying *WELCOME TO CAPE BRETON*, waved at the piper, and settled down for the drive along Highway 104, past blinding fall foliage, verdant hills, and glistening bodies of water. The air smelled of cedar and spruce and tasted of salt. Except for the stony silence from you-know-who, the drive couldn't have been better.

I used the time to anticipate my favourite glimpses of the Bras d'Or Lake—all those annual childhood trips home had left me with a litany of familiar names: Irish Vale, Ben Eoin, Big Pond. My tall, beautiful, blonde sisters would challenge their annoying small dark-haired sibling to predict the next community on Route 4, keeping me busy for the long ride. I called out the names as they flashed into view, for my own amusement. Ray ignored the glittering waters of Bras d'Or, the distant smoky blue hills, and me. Never mind. When each view flashed into sight, it gave me the old thrill.

I started watching for the landmark that always signalled we were getting close to Sydney.

"Ray! The Cape Breton tartan house is right around here. Slow down so I can take a—"

"They painted over it."

Fine. Whatever.

•••

For every occasion you need a cell phone to save your life, a thousand other times you wish people would leave you to hell alone. As we pulled into Sydney, my cell bleated.

"Yes. Edwina. We're arriving this minute."

"No. We haven't seen any of the relatives. As I said, we're getting in now."

"Yes, we have the gifts."

"No, I am not going to deliver them tonight."

"Let me repeat: I am *not* going to deliver them tonight. We're pulling into Ray's driveway now, and it's an emotional moment for him." Emotional enough to leave me in the car with the animals.

I rolled my eyes. "Because this is the house he lived in during his marriage. He raised his children here. The gifts won't go bad."

"Gotta go," I said. "It's my other line."

It was. My sister Donalda with *her* list. Alexa called next. "And don't forget Auntie Annie in Ingonish, Camilla, because—"

I tuned her out and let Gussie and the little cat water Ray's lawn and considered switching off my cell. If I'd had any more sisters, no doubt they would have called too. But I didn't, so that ensured a call from Alvin, former assistant and ongoing pain in the ass. I ushered the pets into the house as the phone played Alvin's special ringtone.

"Argh, I can't deal with Alvin. I'm wiped out by my sisters."

Ray turned around snatched the phone from my hand. "Alvin, Camilla can't come to the phone."

"Never mind why. She can't."

"Because she's about to leap from the second-floor window," I muttered, "to get away from the phone."

"Yes, I'll tell her. I will. Gussie's fine. The cat is fine. Camilla is fine. I am fine. The trip went fine. Don't worry. She'll let you know when she delivers Gussie to Jimmy."

I hoped the molars Ray kept grinding could be built up again by the right orthodontist.

Ray said, "What? Oh. Sorry. How are *you*, Alvin? Well, I'm glad you are also fine."

I made a sound like a strangled duck and Ray said, "You're breaking up, Alvin," and disconnected. This would have been the right time to share a good laugh, but Ray had already stomped upstairs. I almost wished I were still counting trees. I knew the breaking-up remark referred to the phone connection, but the words echoed in my brain.

•••

Ray's house was a twenty-eight-year-old Cape Cod style in the King's Road area, ten minutes away from the Cape Breton Regional Police Headquarters where I had first met him under less-than-ideal circumstances when Jimmy Ferguson had gone missing. The aftermath had yielded Gussie. A long story for another time.

Tonight, the house felt cold, even bereft. Dusty, too. Ray's lousy mood didn't warm it up. I'm not sure why I lugged in the box with the family gifts to be delivered, since it would need to be carted out again, but I wanted to keep busy.

I fed Gussie and the little calico. I stroked the cat's soft ears and then took Gussie for some much-needed exercise. The puss declined.

Gussie and I enjoyed the pleasant stroll up and down hills, the crisp fall evening, and the full moon. Five minutes later, I found Ray staring though the door of the darkened first bedroom. Posters of forgotten boy bands and sports medals covered the walls. The furniture was white, the bedding pink. A forlorn pile of stuffed animals sat on the comforter waiting for a girl who had moved on. A slant of light from the full moon shone through the window, brightening the room but not the man. Ray looked tired and grey. I could smell the loneliness in this house.

"How can I help?"

My heart did a little lurch at his lopsided grin, the one I have come to rely on over the years. Good. Ray was back.

He said, "You could *try* to stay out of trouble."

"What kind of trouble could I get into anyway? I can help you pack up."

"Nope. The packers are booked. Packing's not your best skill, Camilla. And you know you don't take instructions well. I need to make decisions and to remember…"

"I'll keep busy delivering the gifts to my gazillion relatives. How about that?"

"Sounds harmless, although I'm sure it won't be."

Gussie whimpered at my side. Ray reached down to scratch the waiting ears. "I might even miss you, stinky old slug."

"Don't bother lying," I said.

I, on the other hand, was expecting to miss Gussie, although I would have cut my tongue out before admitting it.

•••

The Fergusons were their usual selves. I suppose they couldn't help it. I rang the doorbell of the tall clapboard house—now a deep blue—overlooking Wentworth Park and got no reaction. Of course, the door stood open, revealing a crowd scene inside. The scent of bread baking drifted out. A few junior Fergusons scooted by, chasing each other. I thought I got a glimpse of Alvin's brother Vince and his sister Lisa Marie. Ferguson *mère*'s voice could be heard from the kitchen. I rang again and knocked.

From the next house—painted a fetching purple—my father's first cousin twice removed (or something like that) waved merrily. Daddy always said if Donald Donnie MacDonald didn't know it, it couldn't be worth knowing, even though it might not be worth repeating.

Donald Donnie and his wife Loretta kept watch, smoking their heads off, eyes bright with interest.

"Go right in, dear. Everyone does," Loretta shouted.

Not a chance. I wanted a little ceremony to help Gussie make the transition.

Soon two small children spotted Gussie and stopped in their tracks. They raced off shrieking toward the kitchen, and Lisa Marie Ferguson emerged wearing a serious scowl.

"What's this all about?" she said, shooing the kids back to the kitchen.

"It's Gussie."

She stared.

"The dog." Did she have memory lapses?

"And? What's he doing here?"

"I brought him home. For Jimmy."

"Well, what a spectacularly stupid idea."

"No doubt it is, although it isn't my stupid idea."

She ignored that. "What were you thinking?"

"You mean when I endured a car ride of oh, let's say 1,642 kilometres with a large dog?" I left out smelly. I didn't think it would advance my case. "Well, Lisa Marie, and hello, by the way, I thought Jimmy wanted Gussie to come home."

"Well, I don't know where you got such a ridiculous notion."

For the record, Alvin's sister is a high school principal. I imagine students and staff quake in her presence.

"From Alvin, in fact."

"Ma!"

Mrs. Ferguson popped out of the kitchen.

Lisa Marie said, "You won't believe what that idiot Ally's done." She turned to me. "No way can Ma handle that dog, and Jimmy isn't capable of it. You should goddam well know it too."

I stood, prepared to argue. I am, after all, a lawyer. But I did goddam well know it. It was never in the cards for Gussie to be welcomed with open arms. I decided the Fergusons had waived their rights to Gussie for all time. So not a complete loss, if you get my drift.

CHAPTER THREE
I need a little space

That evening, Ray sat across the table from me at Kiju's, the upscale restaurant on the Membertou reserve. He stared over my shoulder. I loved the place because it showed what good can come out of a great injustice. Ray and I tend not to talk about the unfair murder conviction and subsequent exoneration of Donald Marshall of that same reserve. We were both babies at the time. Years later, the case made its way through the Supreme Court of Canada. Subsequent facts revealed through a Royal Commission shook the Nova Scotia justice system to its core. It became my main motivation for choosing law school and was one of the reasons why I spent so much time working for Legal Aid. It taught me influential people can develop tunnel vision, ignore the facts, twist the truth, and bully witnesses to pervert justice. Police, lawyers, and judges are not immune to bias.

The Donald Marshall story would take two books to tell, but let's say I liked that this Mi'kmaq reserve had become an economic hub in the region.

The dinner here was part of our original plan to enjoy every minute of our trip. We'd planned to scoot downtown after dinner to the opening night concert at Centre 200.

Ray kept fuming about Gussie. "I can't believe we drove for two days with that dog reeking in the back seat of my new Escape, and we paid extra for a pet-friendly hotel in Quebec City, and now those stupid Fergusons don't even want it." He swirled his spoon in his fish chowder. He didn't lift his spoon to his mouth. From where I sat, the chowder smelled too delicious to resist.

"That is what I am telling you." I took a large sip of my Pinot Noir. It was unlike Ray to call anyone stupid.

"And this is because Alvin didn't discuss it with anyone except Jimmy."

"Correct again."

"Jimmy, if I remember, is somewhat developmentally delayed."

"Yeah, well."

"Didn't you have Gussie in the first place because Jimmy became terrified of the dog?"

"Might be part of it." I topped up my glass and made a move toward my haddock taco.

Ray sighed. "I think I might have to kill Alvin."

"Take a number."

Of course, I hadn't wanted to ruin our romantic dinner by bringing up either Gussie or Alvin, but I couldn't hide the results. Ray's cop senses tingled when I returned with the same dog I'd taken to its new home. I was kind of glad to hang on to Gussie but kept that to myself. I figured Mrs. Parnell's cat would be lonesome without Gussie as her sidekick. The cat also continued to reside *chez nous* for complex reasons, and we had achieved a certain détente on matters of food and sleeping quarters over the years. In her nineties, my friend Violet Parnell remained as sharp as ever but was now in a care-assisted home and inclined to tip over even without a snootful of her beloved Harvey's Bristol Cream. How could she keep the cat? I owed Mrs. P. my life, and, of course, the little calico had never lived with her, so what can you do?

But back to dinner. Romantic? Who was I kidding? Before our main course arrived, Ray took yet another work call and stepped out for what he called a few minutes. Why not? The food might have been delicious, but this was no starry-eyed encounter. How could it be with Ray busy packing up the remnants of his former life? I got that. The packers would do their job, but the decisions rested with the man of the house. Toss your adult child's Grade One drawings and Christmas might be ruined for the rest of your miserable life. The girls had been firm. "Don't throw out important stuff, Dad."

I tried hard not to make the situation worse. But it didn't take long to get restless and I ambled down the corridor to the ladies' room, glancing across the parking lot to the Trade and Convention Centre. People were bustling in and out. From the corner of my eye, I watched Ray outside in a vigorous conversation with a large and thuggish guy. His back was to me, and both he and Ray were waving their arms at each other. I'd never seen Ray wave his arms at anyone. Now Ray jabbed the guy in the chest, even though this thug must have had about eight inches and fifty pounds on Ray. I changed position for a better view but couldn't see the big guy's face even as he lumbered away, limping, unless I was mistaken. Ray scowled as he shoved the door open to re-enter the building. I scurried back to my seat and practiced looking bored.

"Who was that guy? Was it someone you arrested when you were on the force down here?"

"No one."

"Pretty big no one. Looked mean too."

"Turned out to be mistaken identity. Hey, here come our mains." Ray greeted the server with relief. I sat sulking and slurping my wine and wondering why Ray Deveau—as a rule too good to be true—had taken up lying his head off. I worked my way through the cedar-planked Nova Scotia salmon in silence, and Ray did the same with his venison. We left without dessert when he announced he had to go out after dinner. Business. None of mine being the subtext.

"What about the opening concert?"

"You go. I'll join you later. Sorry, no choice."

Oh, well. Things happen. After all, what could Ray get up to in Sydney on a fall night with the opening concert the only action?

•••

The fiddles were irresistible, the bows flashing faster than the eye could follow. The stranger to whom I'd given Ray's ticket was clapping to the traditional tunes. My toes kept tapping, and I kept my eyes on the stage and not on the seat next to me. People had come from all over the world to watch this stunning stage full of musicians. The Celtic music that had thrived despite tough lives, rocky soil, and savage seas can get right into your brain and your bones. I could feel the seats quivering as the crowd responded to the ancient tunes. I resolved to enjoy the night, clap, and shout out with my tribe.

The warmth of the concert was followed by a frosty night on the home front. Somewhere around two in the morning, Ray came to bed and muttered, "Sorry."

"Never mind. I can't wait for tomorrow night with the dinner at Fortress Louisburg and then the concert in the chapel." But he was already snoring.

•••

The idea had been for Ray to visit Carol's grave early on Sunday. When I woke up, he was already gone, although there was no sign that he'd showered and not a whiff of the Hugo Boss anywhere. Maybe he planned to shower later. As for me, I didn't have a plan. I thought perhaps I could visit my mother's grave, for the first time. I decided to pick up a potted plant at Sobey's and leave it at the graveside. I had no idea where she was buried, but I knew how to find out. And my sister rises at dawn.

"Stop whinnying, Alexa, and tell me where."

Alexa is the most reasonable of my three sisters, but I thought I could hear her hyperventilating. I heard a scrambling, and my brother-in-law Conn's voice boomed in my ear. "What the hell did you say to Alexa?"

"I asked her where our mother is buried so I can visit her grave. What does she think I'm going to do? Dig up the coffin?"

"Jeez, MacPhee. Did you say that out loud to her?"

"Do you think I'm out of my mind?"

"Don't ask."

"Put her back on, please, Conn. This is important."

But it was not to be.

It took a while before I figured out a way to kill two birds. At 8:00 a.m., I fished out the gift for our cousin Donald Donnie MacDonald and Loretta. Ray hadn't returned with the car yet, so I went on foot and took Gussie with me. The more that dog was in the fresh air, the better. Besides, the sight of us might have been alarming to the Fergusons. That could be a bright spot.

We found Donald Donnie drinking tea on the porch with Loretta at his side. They waved as I approached. As long as I've known them, they've been in the grey zone between seventy-five and eighty, although they could be older or younger. Loretta's startling burgundy hair stood at attention, and Donald Donnie's bald dome looked freshly polished. I carried a tin of Edwina's home baking and a bag with Donalda's blueberry jams and a nice coffee liqueur from Alexa. The liqueur had been intended for someone else, but needs must, as they say.

I figured the extra gifts should be enough to squeeze the right information out of them. I joined them on the porch, smiling like a shark. Gussie wandered across the property to christen the Fergusons' lawn but had the good instincts to avoid Loretta's new Honda Accord.

Loretta and Donald Donnie pointed toward the Fergusons' yard and guffawed, heads back, mouths open, revealing bright new-looking chompers.

Of course, I couldn't come out and ask Donald Donnie or Loretta where my mother was buried. A family scandal would ensue, and I'd be dealing with fallout for years. After an hour of tiptoeing around the real topic, I'd come no closer to ferreting out the answer.

I needed to know so I forged on. "So, where are your parents buried?" Followed by, "Do you visit the graveyard often?"

Loretta leaned over, looked me straight in the eye, and said, "Are you extra tired after your long trip, dear?"

Donald Donnie's kind face creased with worry. "I think you are right, Mum. This girl is exhausted."

I smiled. "To tell the truth, I didn't sleep well, and I'm half-dead. And I'm wondering if I were dead, where I might choose to be buried. Can you find lots of good choices around here?"

They goggled at me, mugs of tea suspended midair.

I carried on. "For instance, would it be better to be stashed with your relatives or cremated and sprinkled over a river? I guess it's nice to have a place where your family can visit and chew the fat. I am planning to go visit my mother's grave when I'm here. I can't remember the exact location."

I imagined them both thinking: *You don't know where your mother is buried?*

I rushed to say, "I was a kid the last time I visited. Do you remember, by any chance?"

Donald Donnie rumbled to his feet, a bit white-faced. "Look at the time, Mum. We're late for the bingo at Membertou. Sorry, Camilla. It's been right nice seeing you again, but we're after having to rush out."

I thought Loretta would faint with relief.

I said, "Isn't it a bit early for—?" But for all I know bingo goes on 24/7 every day of the year and twice as often on holidays.

I watched as they shot out the driveway in their glossy new car.

This is why, in life, we always need a Plan B. Too bad I didn't have one.

•••

Still no sign of Ray when Gussie and I arrived back at the house.

I called Alvin on my cell to enlist his help with my project.

"You don't know where your mother is buried? Your own mother? That's bad even for you, Camilla."

"Hold the commentary for once, Alvin. You know perfectly well my mother died right after my birth, and then our family moved to Ottawa. And you are aware of what my relatives are like. Life is always so fraught."

"Lord thunderin' Jesus, quit whining. And you think the MacPhees have a monopoly on fraught? The Fergusons wrote the book on it."

True. "I'm saying that's why I never visited her grave."

"I guess."

"I have a chance now because I'm here, but first I need to know where she's buried. Alexa got hysterical when I asked, and if I nose around here more than I have already, word will get back to my sisters, and they will be ultra-humiliated by this gaffe. When you find out, call me on my cell phone."

I thought I heard an acquiescent grunt, then, "Why is this important to you after all these years?"

"I'm not sure, Alvin, but deep down there's a damn good reason. By the way, Gussie's coming home again. He'll continue to live with me."

"I already got an earful from Lisa Marie. I wish you'd shown a bit more spine."

Alvin no longer worked for me, so I could hardly fire him, and, anyway, I needed him on the graveyard task. I let it go.

•••

Ray wasn't happy when he got back from wherever. He hogged the house phone, keeping his voice low. He kept glowering whenever I came within earshot. His cell jabbered too. I understood the visit might have been difficult, so I hung out in the living room out of sight, waiting to seize the moment between calls. I heard a click and called out. "How can I pitch in? Get boxes? Take donations? Doughnut run? Tim's?"

Ray stared as if I'd asked to burn the place to the ground. "No. It's all taken care of."

"I like to help," I said.

Come on! Did I merit that particular expression?

"You can help by giving me a little space," he said.

Hey. "You want space? You got it."

CHAPTER FOUR
Quite the headstone

The trouble with dramatic gestures is they have such a short life span. So when Gussie and I stomped out the door for our next stroll, we had to keep going or lose the impact of our actions. I checked my phone and googled the nearest cemetery.

We were close to Holy Cross, an old graveyard meandering between a brook and residential streets. Gussie liked this new territory, although he found the dogs in a nearby backyard distracting. I peered at stones and found some heartbreakingly short lives but no MacPhees.

We continued on, looping around the downtown area and back to George Street. I had a vague memory of another cemetery at the top Hardwood Hill, a steep incline through a neighbourhood of larger and older houses, with mature trees. The hill went on and on, up and up. But it was closer than Resurrection, off somewhere in Sydney Forks. Gussie liked the hill more than I did. About halfway up, my cell rang.

Alvin.

"Out with it," I said.

"Are you panting?"

"It's a long story and a steep hill."

"Fine. What was your mother's name?"

I paused to roll my eyes before saying, "Camilla."

"Lord thunderin'—"

"Lord thunderin' nothing. You know they named me for her."

"Oh, right."

"That it, Alvin?"

"Last name?"

"Um, MacPhee."

"No need to shout."

"She was my *mother*. Married to my *father*. Donald MacPhee. Of course, MacPhee. We are *all* MacPhees."

"Don't get your panties in a twist. Lots of people didn't change their names. My sisters—"

The last topic I wanted was Alvin's unfathomable and dogless sisters. "Let's see. My father is ninety. My sister Edwina is in her sixties. My parents got married right after World War II. So, it's a safe bet her married name was, what is it now? Oh yes, MacPhee."

"Let me finish."

"Hurry up. I'm at Hardwood Hill Cemetery."

"Why do you sound like you swallowed a whistle?"

Hardwood Hill—a long stretch at a forty-five-degree angle—had me gasping. I needed to spend a bit more time in the gym. "You bring it out in me, Alvin. Like being strangled, only less fun." I had no idea why I felt so stressed by this mother situation. I'd grown up without a mother but not without mothering. Until now, it had never bothered me. My sisters were much older, and the three of them had been born with the ability to command armies. They'd dressed me in coordinated outfits, supervised my play, and made sure I did homework to the headache-inducing family standards. With them around, I had homemade cookies for school events, got my Brownie badges—even Housekeeping—and managed to learn a few table manners. As a twelve-year-old, I'd nicknamed them Hitler, Mussolini, and Stalin. That got me grounded for a month. Totally worth it.

All those arguments helped me prepare for a career in the law.

The graveyard visit might have been odd, but it kept me from thinking about Ray and whatever bee buzzed in his baseball cap.

Gussie and I wandered through the old site with the beautiful view down the long hill. I peered at the weathered granite and the faded inscriptions. The graveyard went on for acres. The city had grown up around it. The earliest tombstone I found read 1888, although they might have gone back further. Gussie sniffed the damp ground while I made my way, feeling a shiver down my back as I read the sad stories. Beloved wife. Faithful husband. Cherished son.

The day continued cool and windy, an autumn chill drifting up Hardwood Hill from the harbour a mile or so away. A stooped, white-haired woman wearing a stretched-out black beret glared at me as we rounded the end of one row. She paused in laying some fresh pink carnations in front of a weathered and mossy stone.

"Shame on you," she said. "Bringing a dog into a cemetery! Where's your respect?"

I cut my losses and trudged home with Gussie, wondering how I would have reacted to seeing my own name on a granite slab.

•••

Back at the house, I found no sign of the shiny red Escape or Ray. He must have come and gone, but he'd left the front door unlocked. As I let myself in, the rooms felt even creepier than the graveyard.

I made myself a mug of tea, black, as neither Ray nor I had thought to pick up milk or coffee. I took my time heating the old Brown Betty teapot and waited for the tea to steep, as I had been taught.

Four minutes later, I poured, sipped, socialized with Mrs. Parnell's little calico, and paced for a while.

I washed up Ray's mug and plate in the sink. I'd never known Ray to leave dirty dishes behind. He handled mundane tasks with ease and good humour. Beds were made, laundry put away, garbage trotted to the curb without a fuss. As a rule, Ray left a place a bit better when he headed out the door.

So, he was weirdly distracted, not like himself at all. Of course, packing up the house was hard, but those phone calls had to be the problem.

And who was calling him? Was it that big guy?

My cell trilled, and for once I felt happy to hear from Alvin.

"According to A Billion Graves, your mother is in Resurrection Cemetery."

"A Billion Graves? Is that even a thing?"

"Yes. Here's what you need to know," he said, rattling off directions.

"Okay."

"That's so you, Camilla."

Oops. "Thanks, Alvin. I appreciate your work on this."

"Try to sound sincere. Anyways, I'm off. Our latest crop just came in. And we're testing cannabis body cream recipes. We're calling this one Cream of Weed." One of the line of fine products from the Garden of Weeden.

"Oh man, I see a trademark lawsuit in your future, Alvin."

•••

I had started unpacking the duffle bag when Ray elbowed his way through the door. He had already taken his stack of clothes out and placed them on the chair. I smoothed the covers to resemble making the bed. I fished out a change of clothes, clean underwear, and a fresh pair of jeans and a turtleneck, both identical to the ones I was wearing. I tossed them on the bedspread, along with our tickets for the four remaining Celtic Colours events, when Ray arrived with a muttered greeting, dropped his key fob on the bedside table, and then responded—big surprise—to his phone.

I suppressed the urge to pick a fight. I had places to be. "Going to the graveyard," I yelled on my way out. I left my stuff on the bed, snatched up the fob, and drove out on King's Road to Sydney River. At the Atlantic Superstore, I picked up a potted plant in time to learn at the checkout that I didn't have my wallet. I left the plant and stomped to the car, trying to remember where I'd put it. On the bed? Time for that later. I kept to the speed limit as I made tracks to the "new" Resurrection Cemetery. Alvin had said it was beautiful. Of course, Alvin and I have different views of beauty. Ray had left the radio tuned to some station I wouldn't have chosen, and not merely because of Hank Williams sad-singing "I'm So Lonesome I Could Cry."

"I hear you, Hank," I said.

Resurrection surprised me by being a cheerful place. This was my third graveyard of the day. I preferred them to be morose and even glum. Perhaps the world had changed after 1964. Maybe with all that sixties stuff, cemeteries went all Age of Aquarius. What did I know? I was killing time until I could arrange an exorcism for Ray, and this was the cemetery I'd been dealt. I decided my mother's death merited a bit of melancholy.

Alvin had given me the range, section, and lot number. I'd written them in a small notebook and stuck it in my pocket in case I needed to record details.

I parked a distance away and proceeded along the path. My heart was beating ridiculously fast.

The small, neat marker was made out of glossy, dark-veined marble, like most of the others. No frolicking angels or eternal posies. No décor at all. Suited me.

The sight of my mother's grave caused me to catch my breath. *Pull yourself together*, I told myself. *You need to do this.* The inscription read:

> *Donald Blaise MacPhee 1930–*
> *Camilla Lorranda MacPhee (née Gallivan)*
> *Beloved wife of Donald*
> *1933–1972*

It took a minute for the full impact to sink in.

My mother, Camilla Lorranda MacPhee (née Gallivan) had died a year before I was born.

CHAPTER FIVE
Must be some mistake

Another MacPhee family, perhaps? Even with all the MacPhees around, there'd be a slim chance of another batch with these exact names. And honestly, how many Camilla Lorranda Gallivan MacPhees could there have been?

Ancillary questions: if my mother had died a year before my birth, then who was my mother? If I wasn't Camilla MacPhee, youngest daughter of Donald and Camilla MacPhee formerly of Sydney, Nova Scotia, then who was I? A tornado kept whirling in my brain. Had I been adopted? Why would a widower with three teenage daughters adopt an infant? If I couldn't trust my father and my sisters to tell me the truth about my own identity, who could I trust?

I thought about my sisters: tall, blonde, imperial. Perfectionistic, controlling, bossy. And then me: short, stocky, dark. Stubborn, oppositional, difficult.

I didn't resemble them or my father. I'd always assumed I took after my mother's side. We didn't have much to do with them.

My life growing up had been a long series of mistakes. I'd enjoyed making most of them. Now it appeared others had made mistakes too.

I felt a whoosh of relief. Of course! Mistakes. What if it was the wrong date on the tombstone?

Lucky I hadn't called my sisters to blast them over the big lie.

•••

I drove back to Ray's.

"You'll never believe what happened to me." I dropped the fob on the telephone table in the hall and hollered up the stairs. No answer.

I'd just plunked myself down on the living room sofa to call Alvin when Ray thundered down the stairs and shot out the front door, slamming it behind him.

He must have been pissed off because I took too long with the Escape. So what? He could stomp it out elsewhere. I made the call.

"Alvin. Find out if there can be mistakes on tombstones."

"Hello to you too, Camilla. I'm fine; thank you for asking. And the skin cream is awesome."

"Don't get all princessy. My mother's year of death on her gravestone must be wrong. No doubt an error. I need to know when she died."

After a longish pause, Alvin said, "Check her death certificate."

"Who knows where that document is after fifty years, but it's definitely not in Sydney at Ray's house."

"Call your sisters then. Ask one of them."

"Rather poke a sharp stick in my eye. But *you* could ask them, Alvin. It's important."

"Fine. If it's such a big deal, I'll find out, and I'll call you back. But even if it is a mistake—"

"Come up with a good cover story first."

"Do you think I'm a fool? Of course, I'll think of a ruse, although I am taking time away from my budding business to do you another favour."

"Budding business. Ha-ha. And while you're rubbing in the favours, don't forget to subtract the trip from Ottawa to Sydney with the flatulent dog your family didn't want."

"Make sure you answer your phone when I call."

Did I want my cell ringing when I sidled up to Ray to find out what he'd been up to? "Don't call me. I'll call you."

"Is that a joke?"

"No. And thanks for helping, Alvin."

"But have you considered—"

I disconnected before we could get off on one of many possible tangents.

I thought I had my answer. A grief-stricken widower, eyes closed, three teenage daughters distraught at the loss of their mother. And me, an infant, shrieking up a storm at the cemetery. It would have been so easy for a mistaken date to be overlooked.

But wait, a grave marker would be installed after the interment, maybe months or even years later. I knew that. Once the fresh rush of mourning ended and everyone's thoughts cleared, what were the chances no one would notice the wrong date? My father taught math before he became a school principal. Would he miss such a colossal blooper? Edwina wouldn't overlook a wrong date if she was blinded by tears. Plus she'd never weep in public, a ludicrous idea in my family. If indeed it *was* my family.

•••

I peered out the window at the empty driveway. I made for the kitchen to search for a bite to eat. All those graveyards and not a food concession in any of them. I felt it displayed a lack of entrepreneurial spirit.

Still too soon to call Alvin back. Anyway, I was fed up with wondering what Ray was up to as well as speculating about my origins.

I glowered at the front hall phone, where Ray had been involved in furtive conversations that were none of my concern. My stomach growled in protest, and I stomped into the kitchen and opened the pantry cupboard. If I wanted cream of mushroom soup, this would have been my lucky day. Ray must have found a serious sale. I turned the cans over, checking for best before dates in case any had been five years earlier, but I was in business.

Speaking of business, Ray hadn't yet told me whatever was occupying his mind was none of mine. He'd said he needed space. So, it should have been my business, but he didn't want to discuss it. You have to consider all possibilities, as I learned in my years practicing law. I stared hard at the cans of mushroom soup. But first, a call or two.

I've never been the girliest of girls. I'm not one to call my friends over hurt feelings, real or imagined slights, or what to wear to a party. They call me if they are accused of murder, and even then, we keep it kind of nonemotional.

I decided my old pal, Elaine Ekstein, might have an idea what was going on. If she didn't, I could always chortle at the latest doings in her relationship with retired detective Leonard Mombourquette, Ray's cousin and former partner in the Ottawa police. I'm never sure what she sees in Mombourquette's receding chin, beady eyes and, yes, pink, twitching nose. More of a mouse than a man, in my view.

I lifted the house phone receiver and poised my finger to dial Elaine's number. Instead, my finger decided to press CALLER LIST. Three PRIVATE NUMBERS followed before a name: Pierre Forgeron in 506. Two more PRIVATE NUMBERS next.

Who were these private numbers? What was he telling them or asking them that was none of my beeswax?

I may not be the savviest computer user, and I hate searching stuff on my cell, but even I knew if you use Canada411 in reverse, you can get an address from a phone number if it's listed. I'm not the best with my smartphone, so I hurried upstairs to get my laptop.

My footsteps echoed in the bedroom. I stared at the rumpled bed and the clean clothing I'd left. Where was our duffle bag? I whipped open the closet door. No duffle.

I stepped over to the chair. No sign of the small, neat stack of Ray's clothes. On hands and knees, I checked under the bed, because you never know. A taupe envelope, the thick square kind you find on pricy greeting cards, must have slipped behind the headboard. The envelope was empty. I found no sign of the card it had contained, no way to know whether it was important. I didn't recall seeing any cards or letters for Ray before we left. I glanced out the bedroom window at the driveway and blinked.

The car was gone.

The duffle bag was gone.

Ray was gone.

CHAPTER SIX
What the hell?

I sat on the bed and thought hard. I had my pathetic pile of clothes, but no laptop and no files. I checked around the bed for my wallet. It must have fallen into the duffle. I had no driver's license, no credit card, no debit card, and no cash. My wedding dress was gone too.

Why hadn't I finished unpacking while I'd had the chance? Mind you, I'd had no reason to expect this. After giving myself a little shake, I went hunting for an explanatory note. Ray must have left a message someplace that seemed logical for him. I reminded myself that except for this trip, the man was always predictable.

I thumped down the stairs, rattling the Deveau family photos hanging on the wall. I started at the front door and checked around the porch and mailbox. Back inside, I used my brain. I checked the telephone table and in the small drawer. No luck. There's been a whoosh of air when I opened the door. Perhaps Ray's message had blown off the telephone table and ended up underneath a piece of furniture. I lifted the jumble of old running shoes in the boot tray by the door. I peered under the chairs in the living room and found a couple of dust bunnies.

The rest of the living room yielded no notes: not on the square glass table or under it. Not on the scratched leather sofa or under the cushions or wedged down the sides. I even moved the little calico cat from her spot to check. The bookcase was also a letdown. Gussie followed me, eager to help. I only tripped over him once.

The dining area was clear and clean. No note on a chair, no paper propped up on the piano or in the piano bench. Under the piano: also noteless.

That left the kitchen. I checked the fridge where magnets still held Ashley and Brittany's high school graduation photos. Their framed university grad pictures were on the wall in my own home. For the time being.

I turned my attention to the inside of the fridge, where a lonesome jar of mayonnaise shared space with some matching squeeze bottles of ketchup, mustard, and relish.

The other cupboards were a letdown, as was the clean black chalkboard.

Two bathrooms, three bedrooms, four closets, one basement, and a garage later, I admitted defeat. If Ray had left me a note, no one was ever going to find it.

Then how would he plan to explain his departure? I smacked myself in the head. Of course, my phone! I flipped open my cell and checked for messages. Two from Alvin, at least a half dozen from miscellaneous sisters, and one from "the Captain" telling me that I'd won an all-expenses-paid week on a fabulous cruise. Lucky me, this was the same week I'd won the Dutch national lottery.

No message from Ray.

Not even: *It's not you. It's me. Hope we can still be friends.*

Of course, that didn't make sense, since this was Ray's house, not mine, and if he wanted to break up, he would have bought me a ticket and driven me to the airport. Or he would have rented me a car. Of course, I could have done that myself.

What if he'd forgotten my cell number? We always spoke on the home phone. I'm not good at returning messages from my cell, I'm told. There's a way to call your landline and get your messages, but I'd never bothered to learn it. I broke down and called Alvin again.

"I need you to—"

"Hello, Camilla, how are you?"

"This is not a good time to yank my chain. Just listen."

Alvin muttered "Lord thunderin' Jesus" under his breath. At times of stress, his Newfoundland ancestry shows.

"I need you to go to my place and check my main computer. See if Ray left a message on the home phone. Call me right back with a yes or no. Feel free to swear. The least I can do is to let you vent. I'm sorry I'm being pushy, as you like to call it." Alvin owes me big-time because back in the day, he caused my office to explode, among other transgressions. So even though he sulks, he almost always comes through.

"What's going on, Camilla?"

"When I find out, I'll let you in on it. By the way, can you change your ringtone? I don't want to spend any portion of my life with Cheech and Chong."

"I like *Up in Smoke*. It suits my new business venture. That's why I set it up on your phone. Where's Ray?"

"Don't ask, because I have no idea."

"But I thought you were getting married."

"Who told you?"

"I might have expected you to, but Ray did."

"Ray was mistaken."

No one needed to know Ray had dumped me with no warning, no wallet, cash, or computer. "Do what I ask, please. If you don't get an answer on my cell, call me here at Ray's place."

"But Camilla, we're ready to harvest our—"

Back upstairs, I called Mrs. Parnell.

"Ms. MacPhee," she shouted, "how splendid to hear from you. I hope your trip with the most agreeable Sergeant Deveau is going well."

"The formerly agreeable sergeant is AWOL." Mrs. P. is also a fan of Ray's, but she's my friend first.

I heard a sharp intake of breath. "Hard to believe, Ms. MacPhee." It takes a lot to shock Mrs. P, but I heard it in her voice. "Cold feet?"

"If he wanted out, do you think I'd stand in his way?"

"Of course not, Ms. MacPhee. You would keep your head high and soldier on."

"And I might let the air out of his tires."

"Now?"

"He has vamoosed without a word. Plus, he left with my wallet in his duffle bag, along with my laptop and files, so I now have no choice but to track him down." I didn't point out that my wedding outfit had been what Mrs. P. would call collateral damage. Puffer jacket and hat too.

Mrs. P. cleared her throat.

I said, "And I want to know why. Isn't that a coward's way to break up?"

"I can arrange to e-transfer funds to you, Ms. MacPhee. Leave it with me."

"Thanks. But I have no bank cards or ID to get funds. But I'll get by. First, I need to locate Ray and find out what the hell he's playing at." Through a long pause on the line, I could hear Mrs. Parnell inhaling one of her trademark Benson & Hedges. I figured she'd taken her phone to the small, paved courtyard reserved for smokers at the extreme edge of the property at her new assisted living home. She'd made it this far in life. No point in giving her the gears about the bad habits.

"You took me by surprise, Ms. MacPhee. This is not the man I thought I knew. More to it, do you think?"

"Could be connected with the Ottawa police, some case he's working on. It seems serious."

"That could be an explanation, I suppose, although inadequate. The sergeant is no coward, and he would tell you in person if he wanted to terminate the relationship. You'd never cause a fuss. Aside from the flattened tires."

"Yes."

"And no sign of a problem?"

"Not until our trip down. He's been skulking about on his phone since Quebec City. Says he needs space."

"Perhaps he is under duress?"

I felt a lump in my throat. I loved my old friend's military logic and her lack of drama. "I don't know what kind of duress it could be."

"When people act so out of character, there is often another person in the background, pulling strings."

Pulling strings? "You mean another woman?" This hadn't occurred to me.

"I'd never suggest another woman. We must ask if Sergeant Deveau is completely in control of his actions."

"He's not my prisoner."

"Perhaps," Mrs. Parnell said gently, "it's not about you, Ms.

MacPhee."

Ray had made the same comment.

"If my fiancé vanishes on the eve of our wedding, it *might* be a little bit about me."

I listened to her wheezy chuckle. "Ms. MacPhee, you have coped with much more than this in recent years."

She was right. The wallet and the disappearance were inconvenient. Even a tiny bit heartbreaking, but I'd get over it.

"I need to know he's all right before I let him have it right between the eyes."

"Fair enough. And Sergeant Deveau will be well aware of your reaction."

"And he'll be even more aware when I catch up to him."

"Indeed, Ms. MacPhee. And what does that tell you?"

"Nada."

"As I am trying to convey, when an honourable man begins to act in a way so unlike himself, something is going on. It could be coercion or fear or—"

"Fear? What would he have to fear?" My heart skipped a beat.

Mrs. Parnell inhaled her Benson & Hedges, leaving me to answer my own question. "He'd fear for his health, I suppose." Had Ray been to the doctor or had any symptoms lately? No.

"Might he confide in his daughters?"

"He's the one who holds his family together. He wouldn't want the girls to worry." And of course, their concern was all for themselves.

"Would he tell you?"

"Why wouldn't he? It's not like I'm fragile."

"What else do people worry about? Their employment. Their financial security."

"He had twenty-five years' service in Sydney, and so even if for some bizarre reason his Ottawa position disappeared, he'd still retire with a pension. He's just sold this house. I mean, house prices in Sydney are well below Ottawa's, but he owned it outright. He'll settle an amount on each of his girls to get them started. So, no. Unless, he's picked up a gambling addiction."

"Do you think he might have?"

"I do not."

"Next then, trouble with the law."

"What?"

"We're talking about what a man, or a woman, might fear, Ms. MacPhee. We're being dispassionate about it."

"Fine. But you can't be suggesting—"

"Hypothetical. Might he fear he would be in trouble with the law?"

I sputtered. "He *is* the law. He's a working detective."

"I am aware. What if a criminal wishes him harm and has the means to implicate him?"

Of course, that could happen to a cop. But to Ray? "Not that I can imagine," I said snappishly.

"Everyone has some secrets, Ms. MacPhee."

"Agreed, but I don't believe Ray would have a secret connection to a criminal."

"Coercion then. If not himself, then a threat to someone he loves." I felt my stomach contract as she spoke. "So if he's afraid, who's he afraid for?"

"His daughters. Me."

"There you have it, Ms. MacPhee."

"Huh. Well, as I'm okay—"

"The daughters then."

"I can't buy it, Mrs. P. If there was a threat to the girls, why wouldn't he tell me?"

"Police officers can play their cards close to their chests. Are his daughters all right?"

"I'll call them."

"Excellent, and now on to other theories. We must leave no stone unturned."

Mrs. P.'s at her best when she's in warrior mode.

She said, "Fear for a friend, perhaps?"

I thought I was Ray's best friend. He had buddies at work, but no one close except for Leonard Mombourquette. "I plan to call the retired rodent. He may have an idea."

"Give Sergeant Mombourquette my salutations. I hope retirement agrees with him."

"Sure, lots of cheese."

"I can't imagine why the two of you don't get on better," she said, following a sharp bark of laughter.

"I'll grill Leonard. He'll still have lots of contacts. I'll make sure the girls are all right. And I'll believe myself when I say I'm okay."

"You could check his bank accounts to see if any unusual amounts have been taken out."

As a rule, I'm not a gasper. "I can't, Mrs. P."

"Can't or won't?"

"Both. I don't know how to get into Ray's accounts, and I wouldn't do it if I did know how."

"Understood, but if you change your mind, I'll be happy to facilitate."

Once again, I was reminded my friend had a decades-long and mysterious history in the murkier corridors of government 'communications.' She still had plenty of friends with influence.

"I'll start on those calls."

"You know how to reach me, Ms. MacPhee."

I imagined her teetering back to her room and refilling her favourite Waterford crystal tumbler with Harvey's Bristol Cream, leaving me with plenty to think about.

CHAPTER SEVEN
No reason. Just checking in

I slumped on the bed and stared at the hideous avocado-green wall. What could Ray be involved in? Whatever, it had first raised its ugly presence on our trip. What could have happened between Quebec City and New Brunswick to change his happy, honeymoony mood into grim silence? Each phone call had made him worse. The trouble was, I had no idea what those calls could have been about or who they were from.

It was time to reach out to Ashley or Brittany, although I would have preferred to drink toilet bowl cleaner. I needed a ploy.

I gritted my teeth and called Ashley first. No answer. I left a message: "It's Camilla calling to say hello."

I wasn't sure how Ashley would react. I had never called to say hello before.

Next, Brittany. She did answer.

"Oh hi. This is Camilla." I breezed. "Just checking in."

Silence.

"You know, calling to say hi. See how you and Ashley are getting along with your, um, lives."

"What?"

"And I wanted to know what you'd like done with your old running shoes in the front hall. Should I donate them? Our car is full, and the new owners—"

"Is Dad there?"

"Dad?"

"Yes, Camilla. Dad."

"But first, the posters on your bedroom walls—"

"What?"

"Posters. You know. Pop singers. Do you want them saved? I supposed we could get mailing tubes and send them to you."

"The man you know as Ray, the one we call Dad, put him on please."

"He went out."

"Where is he?"

"Off on an errand. So I thought I'd take this opportunity—"

"Tell Dad to text me when he gets a chance. He didn't respond to my texts today."

"He's been busy with the house move, you know, without any help from the family. I'll tell him to call."

"Text is better." Then, apparently, it was all right for her to hang up.

The call told me Ashley and/or Brittany were still jerks.

That left Ray's work. Had to be work.

He was never one to talk about his job. Fine with me, since my sympathies were never with the police side.

I tried Leonard Mombourquette and Elaine Ekstein on their separate numbers next and didn't leave either one a message, preferring to catch them unaware. Leonard was retired, but he might still be in the know, and Elaine has a way of digging out secrets. It's a social worker skill.

In a reflection of my desperation, I dumped two cans of no-name cream of mushroom soup into a pot, thinned out the gelatinous contents with tap water, stuck the pot on the cooktop, and turned the burner to high. I did singe my tongue a bit, but eventually my stomach stopped growling.

•••

I figured I might regret this next step, but then I'm not much given to regret, so I keyed in a number I knew by heart: the Ottawa Police Services central switchboard, and asked for Ray's partner, Danielle Soublier.

"Soublier." Dani has a brisk, no-nonsense voice that should make a person think twice before trying any bullshit. She was raising four teenagers in her blended family, so she'd trained in the trenches.

"It's Camilla. Ray and I are in Nova Scotia."

"Okay."

"Great," I chirped. "Someone's been trying to reach him about a case he's working on. It's urgent."

"And?"

"This will sound stupid, but he left me a note, and I accidentally spilled mushroom soup all over it."

"What?"

"I can't read it, and I don't know if it's connected with the case. I need to reach him. Can you help?"

"I don't know what case that would be. Ray's earned his break."

"Oh, I agree. No question." What dingbat was speaking these words?

"So, um, is that it?"

I needed to press on. "Well, an old case then. Did he ever talk about a Pierre Forgeron?"

"Pierre's a cop from somewhere down east. If I remember right, he's a little guy. Pretty sure they went to Holland College together."

"Oh man, do I feel dumb. Now I remember Pierre. Sorry to bother you, Dani. It's good to know Ray's not working a case on this trip."

Provocative pauses ticked by before Dani said, "Uh-huh. Well, I guess congratulations are in order. It came as sort of a surprise when Ray told me about, um, it."

I figured 'um, it' was our elopement, but in case she was referring to a different surprise, I said, "Do you mean the—?"

"Right, the wedding. Too bad we didn't know. We could have had a stag for him."

"You may find a few more surprises to come."

Ray would not be happy I'd called his partner. Of course, he'd be nowhere near as unhappy as I was. At least, I believed Dani. She'd think I was a fool for calling, but she wasn't aware of any case or any problem. And she wasn't worried. That was good.

Now what?

•••

Aside from the odd mention of cousins and people he used to work with on the Cape Breton Regional force, we didn't talk much about people from Ray's past. There would have been guys from the old timers' hockey team he played on, but they weren't part of our family life. Okay, so Pierre was a school buddy of Ray's. I'd heard bits about the group of pals from Ray's time at the Atlantic Police College on P.E.I. more than twenty-five years earlier. I didn't know much about any of them. Weird?

I have a ton of colleagues and acquaintances and a handful of close friends. Mrs. Violet Parnell might have been circling ninety, but she was the finest and truest of mine. Elaine Ekstein has been my buddy since we met doing victim support work decades ago, and I can't imagine a week without her and her unruly red curls and neon wardrobe. Green and orange together? No one else would even think about it. I still missed Robin Findlay, who had moved to Niagara to raise her family. And I suppose Alvin could be filed under "friend" on a good day. Aside from a curt nod in court, I didn't keep in touch with most of my classmates.

I had the odd affectionate moment with my sisters, mostly Alexa. And fond relationships with a surprising number of my old clients, like Bunny Mayhew, last seen swearing on his mother's life that he had no idea how that jewellery case came to be in his possession. But back to the Ray problem. It was time to try Leonard Mombourquette once more. Just because he didn't answer didn't mean I wouldn't catch him. He'd know if a Cape Breton connection explained Ray's behaviour. Ray and "Lennie" grew up in a tiny Acadian community on the French shore of Cape Breton near Cheticamp. Ray liked to say he became a cop because of Mombourquette.

No doubt, Leonard would dodge my call, but he'd take one from Ray's number.

"What are you doing in Cape Breton, Camilla?" Elaine snapped when she heard my voice. Answering another person's phone is one of those intimate gestures designed to let everyone know the status of your relationship, in case all those public lip-locks hadn't been a clue.

"You know that Ray's sold his house in Sydney and I'm along for the ride. Also acting as dogsbody to my sisters and trying to repatriate Gussie to the Ferguson family."

She snorted. "How's that working out for you?"

"Why didn't you answer my call earlier?"

Elaine has a big, booming laugh. "Enough with the bullshit, why do you want to talk to Leonard?"

"Advice."

"You want advice from Leonard? Give me an effing break."

"Information might be more accurate."

"The end of the world as we know it. Hang on." Her bellow must have shaken the walls of Mombourquette's tiny yellow house. His Sandy Hill neighbours would have found that Elaine's large, red-haired presence and vivid hues took some getting used to.

"What is it, MacPhee?" Mombourquette said at last. I imagined his whiskers quivering, expecting the cat to pounce.

"Took you long enough," I purred. "Tail caught in the door again?"

"No time to waste."

"Elaine doesn't need to know about this, or you and she will be on her way down here this afternoon."

"I hear you. And?"

"Ray and I are in Sydney. Long, boring story. We drove. Blah blah, lots of trees. He got some unsettling calls. Now he's vanished."

"What?"

"You heard me. He's gone."

"What do you mean, 'gone'?"

I uttered a long sigh. "He left without a word to me, and keep in mind we drove all the way down here to get married—"

Mombourquette's squawk would have made me laugh under normal circumstances.

"Sorry to ruin your day, but he insisted. Now he's disappeared with the car, our luggage, our computers, plus my wallet and the keys to the house." I left out wedding outfit. Too embarrassing.

"Where did he go?"

"If I knew that, Leonard, I wouldn't be irritating both of us with this phone call."

"Well, that's not like Ray. Did he leave you a message? Email?"

"How would I know? He took my computer too."

"Check your phone."

"Wait." I felt a delicious surge of hope. The hope vaporized. "No messages. I'm not sure my email is even set up on the cell. Look, Leonard. I know you'd prefer this to be my fault, but I need to find out where he is. I can't even fly home. I don't have my computer or money. I don't have the house keys. I don't have my car keys."

"Where are they?"

"Thought I told you they were in the luggage he absconded with."

In the pale hope of gaining sympathy, I neglected to add that Alvin and Mrs. P. had access to the house, and my own car keys would be hanging in my kitchen. I knew that without spilling a drop of her sherry, Mrs. P. could arrange an airline ticket and book me an Uber to and from the airports.

Mombourquette said, "He must have had a reason."

"What could be so urgent that he would leave me stranded?"

"Put on your big girl pants, MacPhee."

"I put them on to call you. Any chance you can find out if he's working on a case during this trip?"

"I'm retired, remember?"

"But you're still connected."

"Why don't you call your own brother-in-law? He's more connected than I am."

"Might create a rift between Ray and my family. Face it, my sisters are not people you want cheesed off at you. Anyway, Ray obviously has some kind of problem."

Was that a muffled snort? "Probably wanted to dump you." I thought I heard Elaine chortling in the background. Some friend.

"Any time he wants out of this relationship, he can go. No hard feelings and no need to steal my wallet. But I'll be relieved if it turns out to be urgent police work."

"You're gonna owe me, MacPhee."

CHAPTER EIGHT
Well, who are you?

Doesn't matter what's going on in your life, your dog will have business to conduct. Your cat too. I had escorted the menagerie to the backyard, and when I returned, the phone was ringing. I didn't quite make it in time. I didn't recognize the number. I pressed REDIAL and plunked down on the hard wooden chair by the hall phone.

My redialled call rang on and on, and that gave me time to write down the number.

I was about to hang up when a man's voice answered. "What the hell are you still doing home, Ray? I need you here now. It's worse than we thought."

I channelled my frostiest sister, Edwina. "To whom am I speaking?"

Once again, silence on the line. Then, "You have the wrong number."

"Really?" I said. "This is Ray's phone. How about giving me your name, and we'll take it from there? I'll pass on your message."

It takes more than a dial tone to get rid of me. As I had no computer and my own phone didn't do that trick, I called Mrs. Parnell and asked her to hunt down this 902 number.

The second I disconnected, my cell phone buzzed. Ray's number showed on the screen.

My heart thumped as I answered. I gave myself a shake. I needed to make sure Ray was all right before I killed him. "Where are you?"

"Who's this?" he said.

"Who the hell do you think it is?"

During the silence that followed, I realized it wasn't Ray talking.

An unfamiliar voice said. "I dunno who you are."

"It's Camilla. Who are *you*?"

"I'm the person who found this phone."

Found it? "Where did you find it?"

"On the road. More like in the gutter."

The voice was young, a teenager, I thought. "Where's the gutter?"

"Duh, it's on the side of the road."

"I need to get that phone. Why don't you make it easy for me to find you so I can pick it up? So which road?"

"I'm not sure if you should have it."

"Why would that be?"

"Well, how do I know who you are?"

"You called me. You must have pressed 1, and up comes my number, the number one person in my fiancé's life."

"But it's not your phone."

"And I will give it back to the owner."

"I don't know that, do I? You'd need to give me a gesture of good faith."

"Good faith?"

"You pay me and promise to give the phone back to the owner, and we'll be even."

"Love the math. Tell me where you are."

"We have to agree on how much."

"How much are you asking for it?"

"Five hundred?"

"Dollars?"

"Of course dollars. What else?"

"I don't know. Cents. What makes you think I'll pay five hundred for a phone Ray got for free from his service provider? Use your brain."

"Two hundred?"

"You think you can get two hundred?"

"Okay, fifty."

I didn't want him to think he had a valuable find and hike off to find a higher bidder. "Fine. Tell me where you are now, and I'll come and get the phone."

"How do I know I can trust you?"

"I've agreed to pay fifty dollars for a phone that does not belong to you. You can trust me not to call the police. Let's call your extortionate request a finder's fee."

"What?"

I massaged my temple. "I am glad to get the phone back, and I'm grateful you saved Ray some trouble by giving me a call. I'll pay you the fifty."

"I don't know. You could be a cop."

"I'm not a cop. But you don't want to mess around with Ray, who *is* a cop. Consider me your friend. Where are you?"

"Baddeck Street."

Baddeck Street didn't sound familiar. I hoped I could go on foot as Ray had the car. "I don't know Sydney well."

"Sydney? What would I be doing in that hole? Baddeck Street is in Baddeck. Where did you think it is?"

"Fine. Baddeck. But as I'm in Sydney, it'll take a while. Meet you in, let's say, an hour."

"That's longer than I want to wait."

I tried to remember my last trip to Baddeck. "It takes close to an hour to drive."

"Make it a hundred, or I'll find another buyer. I don't got all day."

"Fine. A hundred. But you have to tell me how you found it."

"Whatever."

"Did you see the guy who dropped it?"

"Might of."

"You don't want that hundred then?"

"I seen him." He actually sounded aggrieved. Not bad for a guy who was ransoming a phone.

"And maybe you stole it."

"He dropped it."

"And you didn't give it back to him?"

"Couldn't, could I? He was jumping into the truck, and they raced down the road like their arses were on fire."

"You mean a red Ford Escape?"

"Na. Not a crossover. This was a Silverado."

"He jumped into a truck, a Silverado?"

"That's what I said, didn't I?"

"You did. And who was driving?"

"The other guy."

"Okay. I'm on my way. Make sure you answer if I call you, or you can kiss your hundred goodbye."

"Ya."

"So what's your name?"

"What's it to ya?"

The second I got my mitts on the phone, I was going to throttle this kid. "Just give me your name and don't be a jackass."

Silence.

I moderated my tone. "If you don't mind."

"You don't need to be ignorant like that."

"Fine, I won't call you a jackass anymore, but why won't you tell me your name? You a crook?"

"I'm not a crook. I found your guy's phone, and I called you."

"Your first name."

"Trevor."

"Okay, Trevor. You can count on a bonus if you don't piss me off. So exactly where will you be?"

"Outside Buns and Bagels."

"Make sure you're there, and it will be worth your effort."

I hung up and called the closest car rental. Of course, there was not a single car available. I called the other one. Ditto.

At least at this one I got an explanation. "Celtic Colours is on, eh? Tons of tourists. Not a spare car to be had on the Island this year."

Right, Celtic Colours. There was next to no chance we'd get to the concert in the chapel at Louisbourg. Oh dear, yet another Plan B needed so soon in the game. I was scratching my head about what form Plan B might take when it ambled right up the front walkway and through Ray's door.

I shot out of the chair when I heard the voices in the hall. I never get used to the habit of people swanning into your house and then announcing themselves. What if you were standing naked getting yourself a snack

from the fridge? Not that you could find a snack in Ray's fridge. I was
fully dressed, and I couldn't remember when I last stood unclothed in a
kitchen, my own or someone else's, but my point was still valid.

"Are you here, dear? It's me, Donald Donnie."

Of course it was.

"And me, dear. Loretta."

Again, shouldn't have come as a surprise. "We brought you some
brownies."

Brownies sounded all right.

"Come on in," I said. They were already making themselves comfortable on the sofa, but hey. "Do you want me to put on the tea?"

"We weren't sure if you were up to that, so we brought a Thermos
too."

"Mugs?" I said, wondering if I should be miffed about not being "up
to" making tea.

"Sure."

I hustled into the kitchen and located three mugs. Gussie hustled as
well, and the little calico cat joined them on the sofa. She had given the
leather an extra scratch or two to ready it for company.

"We didn't know, dear, what you had in the cupboard, so here's the
milk and sugar."

"You're too kind," I said, meaning it. Long minutes later, while they
were sipping strong, sweet tea and hoping for some juicy bit of gossip,
I chug-a-lugged the tea, inhaled a brownie or two, and threw myself on
their mercy. First, I came up with a bizarre story about my silly fiancé
losing his phone after an outing with some of "the boys." And then I
added that—by accident—he'd departed with the duffle bag containing
items I needed.

They were enthralled. I didn't give a rat's ass about Ray's reputation
as a sensible cop. Donald Donnie sounded thrilled when I asked if I
could rent their car to get me to Baddeck and back. "Jeez, Camilla. You
can borrow it. I'll give Loretta a ride to her sister Betty's place and come
back with it. Ten minutes. Ya can drop me off home on the way."

Astonishingly, Loretta had no issue with this arrangement, and I somehow failed to note my lack of a drivers' license. In return, I offered them

the tickets to the Louisburg dinner and concert so I could have a clear conscience and also not worry about wasting more than two hundred dollars. I hung on to the remaining tickets in case things sorted themselves out.

I hurried upstairs and threw yesterday's dirty duds and the pile of clean, folded clothes into two plastic bags, since I had no suitcase. I couldn't even lock Ray's door.

Donald Donnie was ebullient as he showed up beaming in the new white Accord. He opened the door, itching to go over the story again. "He's after losing his phone, is he? And him a policeman? Who'd of thought of that?" Donald Donnie's long phlegmy laugh disintegrated into a coughing fit. "When will ya be back?"

"Hard to say, Donald Donnie. I might have to stay overnight. I'd be glad to reimburse you, as I said before."

The smile vanished. "We're cousins. You think your father would charge me to use his car in an emergency?"

I had no idea. My father has always been a mystery to me, this past year even more so. Plus now, at ninety and getting care in the Perley and Rideau Veterans' Health Centre after a series of mini-strokes, he no longer drives. Still, he was a Cape Bretoner, so I had to assume he would have helped his cousin. "Sorry. I wasn't thinking. I'm grateful." I hardly recognized myself sweet-talking. The so-called sisters would have been proud.

"I'm happy to drive ya."

Drive me? Of course, that might be a good solution to the license problem. "What if we're not back in time for the concert?" I said.

"Loretta can take her cousin, Betty. She'll like that better anyways."

"And one more item," I said, glancing at Donald Donnie and then back to the smiling and panting Gussie, who had heard the word "drive." And to Mrs. Parnell's little calico cat, who appeared supremely uninvolved but was no doubt planning an escape. "Two, actually."

"Whatever your heart desires, dear."

Okay, so that was bizarre. "I'll need to arrange for the pets."

"We'll take them with us."

Before Donald Donnie could spot the insanity of his own suggestion, I propelled Gussie into the back seat, tucked the little cat into her snazzy box, and tossed the plastic bags with my remaining clothes into the trunk.

Donald Donnie sang out, "But you better put a warm jacket on, the temperature's after having dropped ten degrees."

He was right. I sensed a new chill in the air. But my puffy jacket and hat were with Ray. I dashed back to the house, picked up the collection of gifts from my sisters, and deposited them in the trunk. If worse came to worst, Donald Donnie would be happy to deliver them to our various relatives around the island. I'd give him a cut, of course.

I took the stairs two at a time and opened Ray's closet. He kept a few spare clothes for visits. I snatched up his old plaid flannel shirt and a down vest in faded blue. Ready to roll.

"You might want to open the window," I said with a smile as I sank into the passenger seat.

Lucky for me, Donald Donnie has a heart the size of the island. We stopped at the ATM at the bank on Charlotte Street, where I borrowed enough cash from him to ransom Ray's phone and address any other emergencies. "I'll pay you back as soon as I get my card from Ray," I assured him.

"Least I can do, Camilla. Loretta and I have always been fond of ya." I wondered if that would still be true after our trip.

The hour to Baddeck from Sydney stretched past an hour and a half between our slow departure and Donald Donnie's turtle-like driving. Through clenched teeth, I said, "We're on the Trans-Canada. What's the speed limit? A hundred?"

But Donald Donnie never did get the hint. Even with a steady stream of passing traffic, we plodded along at seventy klics.

By the time we got to Buns and Bagels in Baddeck, my back had started to spasm. In front of it was … no one. I got out of the car and checked around, glancing into the parked vehicles. A couple of kids skittered away when I tried to question them. A trio of silver-haired tourists shook their heads and asked if I spoke German. Finally, I stepped into Buns and Bagels. A happy server greeted me. I wanted to tell her to wipe the grin off her face, but sanity prevailed. "I'm looking for Trevor. He found my fiancé's phone."

Her smile faltered. "Trevor's not here."

CHAPTER NINE
Why not Ray?

❝Is he coming back?" I tried not to be distracted by the fragrant fresh baking and the scents of coffee and bacon.

Her lip quivered. "I don't know."

Obviously. "Where did he go?"

She shook her head a little too emphatically.

"Do you know where he lives?"

She hesitated. She knew Trevor all right. She was his mother or his sister or his elderly girlfriend. She didn't want to give him grief.

"I have a reward for him for finding the phone and contacting me. And a bonus if he shows up soon."

She shrugged. "He's gone home."

"What a shame. I had a hundred bucks for him."

"A hundred? The little bastard told me fifty."

"Do you know where I can find him? I need that phone."

"He's going over to the Co-op. Sammy Smith said he'd buy it for fifty. Said you were jerking him around, and he couldn't wait."

"Where's the Co-op?"

"Doesn't matter because I have the phone here. Sammy's going to get it from me."

"Let me guess. You gave him the fifty, and he couldn't wait to hit the road." Too many years as a Legal Aid lawyer will leave you with skills you wouldn't believe.

She nodded sadly. She had a lot more wrinkles when she wasn't smiling. I figured Trevor wiped the smile off her face a lot.

"You can give me the phone, and I'll give you the money you advanced him. We'll be even."

"But I need to give it to Sammy. It was promised."

"Well, that would work if the phone were yours or Trevor's, but it's my fiancé's. So I'll have it."

"I'm not going to give it to you. Trevor will be—"

I leaned in. "I don't give a crap about Trevor or Sammy. That phone doesn't belong to you. Put it in my hands right this minute, or I'm calling the cops."

She raised her chin. "Possession is nine-tenths of the law."

"In your dreams it is. You're extorting money for a phone stolen from a police detective. Let's see what that's nine tenths of."

"But I'm not extorting!"

"The hell you're not. I'm a lawyer, and I know the definition of extortion."

She leaned back, deflated. "Now I'm out fifty bucks."

I rustled out two twenties and a ten from Donald Donnie's ATM cash. "I promised him fifty and a bonus. I'll give you this, and you'll get the bonus when you tell me where Trevor is."

"I don't know where the little toe-rag got to."

My turn to shrug. "He saw my fiancé drop the phone when he got into some truck. If Trevor can give me some usable information, I'll give him a bonus too."

She said, "You mean the guy that jumped into the Silverado?"

I took a deep breath. "Description?"

"A Silverado." Obviously, she thought I was a fool.

"Colour?"

"Silver. I think."

"I don't suppose you saw a license plate?"

"I wouldn't remember a number."

"Nova Scotia plate?"

She squeezed her eyes shut and kept her mouth closed. I had begun to wonder if she'd gone to sleep when she said, "No. It wasn't."

"Your bonus is drying up."

She licked her lips. "I can't remember."

Behind me, Donald Donnie cleared his throat. I had forgotten about him.

I tried not to show my annoyance when I turned around.

By now, he was tapping me on the shoulder and beaming.

I said with a tight smile, "We need to get a handle on the license plate of the Silverado that picked up Ray, if her story's true."

"That's it, girl," Donald Donnie said, pulling at my arm.

"What's that supposed to mean?" Miss Formerly Smiley was having trouble with "if her story's true." She scowled. "You calling me and my son a liar?"

I managed not to say "I'm calling you both liars" before I gave in to Donald Donnie's relentless arm pulling. I kept in mind he had driven me here in a good and generous spirit, and two stinky animals were still residing in his vehicle.

"This here's Donnie Red MacIssac," he said as he dragged me toward a tall bald man with a vaguely biblical beard. The name told me it must have been red at one time.

I am so often at a loss around Donald Donnie. "Nice to meet you," I managed as Donnie Red, who should have been Donnie Giant Bald Yet Furry, nodded at me.

"Donnie Red remembers your father, Donald Big Joe MacPhee."

"Does he?" Donald Big Joe MacPhee? Unless I missed my guess, Big Joe had been my grandfather. That was a first for me. Of course, one would find far fewer Donald MacPhees in Ottawa, and the multigenerational distinction wouldn't have been necessary.

"I do," he said, a smile cracking his lined face. "Pleased to meetcha."

"Donnie Red says he saw your Ray get into a truck willingly."

"He did? How did you know it was Ray?"

"I knew Ray Deveau, eh," Donnie Red said, "years back when he were a cop in Sydney, new in the town, down from Cheticamp."

Good. At least it had been Ray in the truck and not some stranger who'd stolen his wallet and phone and left him to die in a ditch somewhere and then spent the money on a batch of drugs and was so high five minutes later he dropped the phone before taking off. This complex and worrying scenario had been lurking in the back of my mind. The fact Ray had gotten into the Silverado of his own will came as a relief, even though it made me mad as hell. *Get a grip on your temper, Camilla*, as my sisters like to say.

Never mind, I preferred anger to grief.

Donnie Red said, "Ray Deveau helped me out more than once."

The stories about Ray helping would be worth hearing, but I needed to focus. "Can you tell me what happened?"

"I seen Ray run and get in the truck, that's all."

"Oh. Did you also see the license plate?"

"I did."

"And…?

"New Brunswick plate. We see a few of them around here, but not that many."

"I don't suppose you got a number?"

"No reason to, was there?"

"I suppose not."

"At the time," he added.

"And did you see the driver?"

"Fella had a ball cap on, that's all I seen."

"Did you notice anything about the ball cap?"

Donnie Red scratched his bald dome and thought hard. "I wouldn't have noticed any of it, if I hadn't recognized Ray."

"Were they friendly? Glad to see each other?"

Now Donnie Red shuffled his large feet. "Hard to tell. Didn't seem too happy, neither of them."

"What makes you say that?"

"I heard a lot of yelling. It all happened right fast, ya know."

"And then?"

"The truck squealed away. Fella was drivin' like a maniac. Hard to believe with a cop next to you, isn't it?"

"Yes," I said, "it is."

Donald Donnie wasn't used to being the quiet one, He said, "And then Ray had dropped his little phone getting in, but Donnie Red didn't see that."

"I don't like them cell phones," he said.

"But you saw Trevor pick it up."

"He picked up somethin'. I never paid any attention because I was busy wonderin' what was going on with Ray Deveau. Strange, eh."

"That all?"

Donnie Red shook his red beard. "Nothin' more to tell."

"How about the kid?" I glanced over at Trevor's mother, who was doing her best to catch our conversation. I lowered my voice. "Any idea where he went afterwards?"

"Well, he was talkin' on the phone, and then he hung around for a while before he left. He's a little arsehole."

"Agreed." I'd been hoping that we'd find Trevor and he would succumb to the lure of cash and tell me what happened with Ray and the truck.

"Well, nice to meetcha. Say hello to your father from me."

Donnie Red shuffled back to the small wooden table by the window where I assumed Donald Donnie had found him. Donald Donnie followed. They engaged in a desultory conversation before Donnie Red stood up, stretched, and ambled out, letting the door bang behind him.

Fine.

I fiddled with Ray's phone. Who had called him? I was working my way through the call list when Donald Donnie put his hand on my elbow.

"Time to go, girl," he said, blinking dementedly.

"What's in your eye?"

He paused, "Could be a splinter. We'd better get to the car and the first-aid kit. Or find a walk-in clinic before I lose my vision." He pivoted and said goodbye to the waitress. "Thanks for all your help, dear."

I wasn't sure if that was sarcasm or Donald Donnie's insatiable sociability.

As for the waitress, she was standing—arms crossed over her ample chest—with an unreadable expression on her face.

I felt myself being frogmarched out the door. As has happened before with Donald Donnie, I was too astonished to refuse.

The minute we were out of sight of the café, he said, "Donnie Red thinks he knows where this Trevor lad is. He'll take us to him, but we didn't want that mother to know. She'd call him and warn him off."

Well, of course she would.

Donnie Red drove. Donald Donnie rode shotgun, and I sat in the back seat with Gussie and the little cat. It wasn't quite as awful as it sounds.

We prowled through Baddeck, eyes peeled for the duplicitous Trevor. On any other occasion, I would have been keen to be back to this delightful little town by the waters of Bras d'Or. I'd had a visit with the family when I was six or seven. I do remember it being somewhat marred by Edwina's need to turn every outing into an educational experience. Having the Alexander Graham Bell National Historic Site in town played right into her hands. Sometimes a kid wants to … I had a chuckle at the memory. I had taught her a lesson when I departed for my own little tour instead. Let's say it was a long drive back to Ottawa that year. Some days, I can still feel the frostbite on my ears.

Donald Donnie blathered on about relatives in Inverness, uncles in Mabou, cousins in Judique, and other sleep-inducing topics. Donnie Red's eyes should have grown heavy, but he kept nodding enthusiastically. What was it about the endless reciting of names that these people enjoyed?

Donald Donnie said, "Do you ever see Silver Dan MacLeod? No, no, b'y, I mean Black Dan MacLeod."

Donnie Red replied, "Black Dan? You mean Black Jimmy Dan from up Margaree way?"

I knew from long experience that this Dan MacLeod was someone who once had dark hair and probably a father named Jimmy. I just didn't care.

"Blah blah blah," Donnie was saying when I shrieked. "Stop!"

He clutched his chest, wounded. "We like to catch up on the relatives, girl. Not like youse snooty big city types."

"I mean stop the car!"

I hadn't meant for Donnie Red to slam on the brakes in the middle of the road. Gussie and the cat and I landed in a heap on the floor. Donald Donnie's head snapped.

"What?" he shrieked.

"Could have been Black—"

I cut in. "I just saw Ray's vehicle. Turn around and go back. After checking traffic first," I added not a moment too soon. "In fact, why don't

I get out here?"

The guy in the car behind Donald Donnie had New York State plates. He glared at Donnie Red and made the international symbol for crazy person who shouldn't be allowed to drive. I gave him the thumbs-up.

I galloped along the road and turned the corner, back the way we'd come. I screeched to a halt and stared at Ray's red Ford Escape.

No Ray, of course. He was off in some stupid truck, whether by choice or coercion remaining to be seen. I peered in to see if he'd left a note. I couldn't see one. In a fit of frustration, I pulled hard on the handle of the driver's side door and flew back as it swung wide. What was going on? Ray never left his car unlocked. I sniffed that week-old car. It still had traces of that new car smell, overlaid with elements of cat and dog, sweaty middle-aged man, and the faintest whiff of Hugo Boss.

I poked around the glove compartment. Ray always keeps a notebook and two pens. He often leaves me little notes. Never mind what they say. It's private. But this time I found nothing for me in the notebook. One pen remained. I checked to see if that all-important note had drifted to the floor or under one of the seats.

My fingers felt a lump wedged down on the left side of the driver's seat. I fished out Ray's key ring with the fob for the Escape.

I straightened up and banged my head on the door frame. How was it possible that the supremely sensible Ray Deveau had left the fob for his *new* vehicle in the car?

Was I dreaming?

But the fob was real. The throb in my skull where I'd hit the door frame was real too.

What the hell would make Ray abandon his car unlocked? In the back, I found the duffle bag and inside that my wallet, files and computer, abandoned in the vehicle belonging to the man I had been planning to spend my life with. Apropos of that was the wedding outfit that I had a sudden urge to set fire to.

Twenty-four hours earlier, I wouldn't have thought any of this was possible. But that was before I found out that nothing was what I thought it was, including me. The people I believed in and looked up to all my life had all been part of a lie. Why not Ray? I retrieved the menagerie and settled into his Escape—with the dog and the cat cozied up in the back seat—and pondered my next move. Several facts were now obvious: I had the duffle bag, a vehicle at my disposal, my driver's license, plus my credit and debit cards. I still had some cash, and that worked well as Donald Donnie chose that moment to puff up to the car. I insisted on paying him back on the spot. I swear he was disappointed.

"I'll be off. Um, thank you so much for helping me. If you hurry, you can make that concert in Louisburg with Loretta."

But Donald Donnie had inserted himself into the Escape. "Nah, Loretta and Betty would be ticked off if I showed up. So then I better help you find Ray," he said slyly. "It's not like you know your way around the island."

There's one main route. How hard could it be to find my way?

"Thanks, Donald Donnie. You've done more than enough. You and Loretta need your car."

He didn't try to hide his disappointment. "Where will ya go to?"

I still needed to figure that out.

Behind him, Donnie Red lurched forward and said in a stage whisper, "Been talking to a couple guys who thought they saw that Silverado at the Esso."

Donald Donnie sputtered. "Goin' where?"

Donnie Red's shoulders rose. "They heard them fellas talking about Sandy somebody. Kind of hard to make out."

"Last name?"

Donnie Red rubbed his nose and said, "I'll work on it."

Donald Donnie suggested, "Maybe MacDonald." I could hear the doubt in his voice.

"Could be MacMullin or MacNeil," Donnie Red offered.

So MacWhatever.

I said goodbye and thank you a few more times to make the point that I'd be moving on. But where? Finding a guy named Sandy in Cape Breton would be a bit like finding that one special snowflake in a blizzard. Never mind. Filled with foolish optimism, I waved and drove away. I made sure I was out of sight and began to analyze the new developments without the presence of the double-Donnie brain drain. I pulled over and made the call.

"You're like a dog with a bone," Mombourquette snapped when he answered. In the back seat, Gussie sat up with interest.

I resisted saying better than a rat in a trap.

"Listen, Leonard. Here's the latest: Ray abandoned his new vehicle, unlocked, in Baddeck."

"Unlocked?"

"Yes. With the key fob lying by the driver's seat."

"In Baddeck? Why Baddeck?"

"No idea. To my knowledge, he knows no one in Baddeck except a guy named Donnie Red."

"He wanted to get away from you. That ever cross your mind?"

"It has, actually. But any time he wants to get away from me, all he has to do is leave. He doesn't have to abandon his house or vehicle. Did I mention he jumped into a truck and took off? And he dropped his cell phone as he got in and kept going. That sound like Ray to you?"

Mombourquette always hated to agree with me, so there was silence.

I dislike silence. "All to say, I'd be relieved to find out it's some kind of assignment for the Ottawa force."

Mombourquette cleared his throat.

"Squeak up," I said.

"I don't know why I bother with you," he shot back.

"I get that, Lennie. Not like he's your friend or cousin."

"He's not."

"Last I looked he was your friend, and he's always going to be your cousin. What is the matter with you?"

"Knock it off. I mean, Ray's not working on a case for the Ottawa force."

"You sure? Maybe your reach isn't what it once was."

"I dug deep on this one, called in some favours. Ray Deveau is not on any official business for OPS."

"Crap."

"He won't be working undercover either. And no one would talk about it anyway. That's the whole point of undercover. But supposing he was, you'd be jeopardizing his safety."

"Consider this, if he was undercover, why would he ask me to come to Cape Breton with him in the first place?"

"He'd have to be out of his mind to go undercover with you in the picture. You'd blow everything sky-high."

"Thanks, Leonard. But what exactly would I be blowing sky-high?"

He ignored that. "More to the point, Ray's a familiar face. He was on the Cape Breton Regional Force for years. And we both grew up near Cheticamp."

"I know that." I made an effort to keep the impatience out of my voice.

"It would be hard for him to fly under the radar in any of those communities."

Even wobbly old Donnie Red knew Ray here in Baddeck. Mombourquette was right. Ray wasn't on some urgent last-minute official mission. And deep down I knew that if he had been, he would have found a way to let me know.

I was about to ask him about someone named Sandy MacThis or MacThat when Ray's second line beeped. Mrs. P. perhaps? Ray himself?

"I'll call you later, Leonard."

"What? You don't have to—"

I pressed FLASH to answer the incoming call.

"Holy shit, Ray. Where are you? All hell is breaking loose." The speaker sounded distraught, his voice thick and shaky. "Matty's dead, man. Kenny left a message. He's already dead."

"What? Who's dead?"

"Who's this?"

"It's Camilla. I need to find—"

Dial tone.

Who was Matty?

What did Ray have to do with his death?

CHAPTER TEN
All this and a budgie too

When my helpers rolled up again, I was still pounding the steering wheel. Donnie Red leaned toward the window and tapped himself on the chest. Donald Donnie pointed to him in case I hadn't noticed.

I started the car in order to lower the window. Some conveniences I don't get. Windows that need the engine turned on to work being among them.

"What is it?" I didn't want to talk to my new sidekicks. I needed to figure out who Matty was and what his death had to do with Ray. At least I had Ray's phone and his car and a description of Ray getting into the Silverado, so I really had no more need of the little creep, Trevor.

Donnie Red opened his mouth, and Donald Donnie cut him off, burbling with excitement. "Donnie Red's got news."

"Do you know someone named Matty?"

They both stared and slowly shook their heads.

"Fine, tell me what you have then."

"Go on, Donnie Red," Donald Donnie said.

I held up my hand to keep Donald Donnie from interjecting any more helpfulness.

Donnie Red said, "Might be nothin'."

"No problem." Except that my hair was about to catch fire.

"I might of remembered a part of that license number you asked about. It was sorta like the name of my old budgie. But only part of it."

I stayed calm. "What was it?"

"His name was Elfie, 'cause he was a little green fella."

I took a deep breath. "And the license plate part was ELF and then?"

"No."

I exhaled sharply. "What then?"

"FIE."

"It's better than a poke in the eye with a sharp stick," Donald Donnie shouted.

Marginally.

"Thank you, Donnie Red."

"Not enough to track him down," he said sadly. "I wish I could remember the numbers, but they didn't speak to me the way that FIE did."

"I understand."

"Except for the nine."

"There was a nine?"

"I've always liked nine. Some people say it's a mystical number."

I felt a throbbing in my temple.

"Glad you saw it. And was it next to the FIE?"

"Yes. One of them was."

"There were two nines?"

"It's not much, is it though?"

"It's plenty. So FIE9 something 9 something?"

"Well, when you put it like that, I'm not so sure."

"Let me make a call."

Mombourquette didn't sound happy to hear from me again. Of course, that had never bothered me before, and it didn't this time.

First the plate. "Breaking news, Leonard. The truck that Ray got into was a silver Silverado, New Brunswick plates FIE9 something 9 possibly. Any chance you can run that?"

"No, no chance I can run a plate. You forget that I'm retired." This was true and not the first time he'd reminded me.

"I bet you still have access."

"Not legally, and not without getting someone else in trouble. Why do you want it?"

"Witnesses," I almost said "witlessness"—also true, "saw Ray get into a silver Silverado with New Brunswick plates."

"Been through this, MacPhee."

"Point conceded, but the dropped phone, the abandoned car, the keys left behind, no message to anyone, all these facts add up to a suspicious circumstance."

"They'd laugh you out of the station if you went in with a story like that."

"Why don't you talk to one of the higher-ups?"

"If Ray did that to me, I'd be royally pissed off, and if I did that to Ray, he would be too."

I got it. I hadn't contacted Ray's supervisor because that would have been a much bigger betrayal. A partner saying she didn't know where her mate was revealed a lack of trust, communication, even a dying relationship.

But a friend who needed to get in touch. That might fly. "You could make up some kind of story. About wanting to meet up with him."

"Don't even think about it, MacPhee. Don't call again."

"Wait! Other news: someone named Matty is dead. Do you know who—?"

Fine. Hang up on me.

I'd confront Mombourquette about Matty the next time we had a friendly chat. Now, I had to get a move on to find Ray. If only I had some idea where to look.

CHAPTER ELEVEN
What next?

Time to think.

Logically, either Ray had gone off with someone he knew or someone he didn't know. If it was someone he knew, I'd have to figure out who and why. If it was someone he didn't know, I'd have discover why he'd go of his own volition.

Okay. Who did Ray know? A shorter list would have been the people he didn't know in Cape Breton. Even so, most of the people he would have known would be harmless. Neighbours, relatives, old friends. If Donnie Red was any example, even people he'd arrested were well disposed toward him. Had this dramatic departure grown from some less amiable criminal connection from his past, as Mrs. P. had suggested?

But the Silverado wasn't local. It was from New Brunswick.

Hang on. I smacked myself on the side of the head. Not the best idea, after the whack with the door frame and my history of mild coIncussions. I snatched Ray's notebook and added the number I had copied down from Ray's home phone. There was Pierre Forgeron with a 506 number. According to Dani, Ray's partner, Pierre had been an old colleague from school. Down East. That included New Brunswick. I had little to lose. I keyed in the number.

No answer. In fact, I understand enough French to get that the subscriber was unavailable. *L'abonné n'est pas disponible.*

Never mind. I knew who would be available.

"Ms. MacPhee! How splendid to hear from you again so soon. How is your search going?" Mrs. Parnell trumpeted into her speakerphone. I could imagine her reclining back in her leather chair with a tumbler of

Harvey's Bristol Cream in one hand. In the background, her medals from CWAC service in World War II would be displayed in shadow boxes on the wall.

"That's the problem, Mrs. P. The excellent Sergeant Deveau is still AWOL."

"Still? Not at all like him."

"But on the upside, I have my stuff back, no thanks to him."

"As you said before," she puffed. "Trouble afoot."

"And there's more. He was reported an hour away from Sydney getting into a truck with New Brunswick plates. He'd left his brand-new vehicle unlocked and the keys stuffed down the side of the seat."

"Not the new Escape, Ms. MacPhee! Curiouser and curiouser. Do you have the plate number?"

"A partial. FIE 9 something 9 or a variation on that. Not sure how reliable that witness is, but it's what we have. But a Pierre Forgeron, with a New Brunswick area code, called Ray at home in Sydney. And that phone number appears on his cell. Looks like a mobile. Can you find a link to a landline or an address?"

"Leave it with me, Ms. MacPhee."

"And I'm also trying to find someone named Sandy, unknown last name, somewhere on the island, but I think that's vague even for your quasi-magical powers."

"Never mind. It's quite extraordinarily dull in this place. Everyone's half in the grave. Plenty of gaga. I've been bored to death and back without you. Young Ferguson's tied up with this new venture of his, although I am thinking of investing a few thousand as a flutter."

"Don't forget to do your due diligence, because it is Alvin. By the way, your cat is fine."

She didn't respond to that, but then she never does. No wonder the little calico has been sleeping in my bed for so many years.

She intoned, "I have an old friend who thinks he owes me, and he still has connections *in situ*. I'll leave the plate challenge with him. What else can I do?"

That made me smile. I could imagine her surrounded by her high-end computer equipment and her speed dial set to contact her cadre of creaky spooks. She was still top of her game. I wanted to stop time and keep her like this forever.

"Ms. MacPhee?"

"This Pierre Forgeron was a cop; maybe he still is. Could be he's in some kind of trouble, couldn't walk the line, whatever. You talked about someone behind the scenes pulling strings. Can you link this Forgeron to trouble or to Ray? See where it takes you. Oh, and someone named Matty has died. I don't know where or when or how, but it's all connected."

Mrs. Parnell said, "On the double. I'll work on Pierre Forgeron and Matty. I'll see if anyone called Sandy or Alexander shows up in relation to them. Should I contact Young Ferguson?"

"Wouldn't hurt if you fill him in. I should have told Alvin about Ray's disappearance before this, but I was jangled already, and Alvin's obsession with his products could have sent me over the edge. Besides, he was researching the date on the tombstone issue." That reminded me to fill Mrs. P. in on that bit of drama.

She was silent as I mentioned the date at my mother's grave and the giant lie that my life appeared to have been.

As I ran out of words, she said, "We shall hope for an error on the stone, Ms. MacPhee. It certainly can happen. And if not, then I'll caution you that those were difficult times for thousands of girls, as I saw often during the war."

"This was long after the war."

"Don't delude yourself, Ms. MacPhee. Society hadn't changed in that way by the time you came along. We must not judge young women harshly. It was a terrible situation for anyone who found herself in an awkward position." I knew she was right, but I wasn't completely at home with the idea yet. She added, "Stiff upper lip and soldier on."

•••

I called Ashley first. She answered—bored as always—on the fifth ring.

"Oh, Camilla. You again. What do you want this time?" Me again? That meant she'd gotten my first message. I needed a source for Ray's old friends, so I tried to keep a smile in my voice.

"Excellent. You?"

I imagined some eye-rolling, if history is any gauge. "I'm good."

"And Brittany?"

A slight pause. "She's good too. We're just going out."

"Now I'm thinking about a party for your dad. A big one. I want people to send messages and all that."

What is it with people and long pauses? Finally: "Like where would this party be?"

"Sydney. He's in Cape Breton, and that would be handy for him and anyone he's still in touch with. You and Brittany could get down here pretty quickly for an important event like that." My jaw hurt from maintaining my phony smile. "Could you give me a list of his old friends and colleagues? And I'll get busy and follow up."

"Uh-huh. And what about Brittany and me, are you going to get in touch with us?"

"That's what I'm doing now, Ashley."

"I meant to invite to the party."

"I'm not sure what—"

"You haven't invited *us*."

"But I am inviting you both right now. You are the first people I've asked, *obviously*. I still need to work out the fine points, like where and when, but I'd welcome your suggestions."

"Sure, okay."

I couldn't imagine how this would go if we'd been informing the girls that we'd eloped. For a second I was almost grateful to Ray for running away.

"You'll be involved in the planning. I'll never forget that kitchen party you had at my house in Ottawa."

"When are you thinking of having this event?"

"Haven't decided, but it should be soon. Sometime this week, perhaps."

"Sydney is a five-hour drive for us. Don't you think we'd need a bit of notice for that? We have responsibilities, you know."

Responsibilities? I loved that load of steaming BS.

"Of course. Let's decide what the best time is for you and Ashley—"

"This is Ashley. What's the matter with you?"

"So sorry. I meant Brittany. I'm keyed up about the party—"

My second line started beeping. I couldn't tell who it was. "I've got to go. I'll call you back. In the meantime, think about the people we should invite to the party and the best timing for you and Brittany. And your partners."

"Fiancé."

"Right, *fiancé*, and Brittany's fiancé, of course.

"Boyfriend. Brittany doesn't have a fiancé."

In the background, I thought I heard someone screech, "Stop lording it over me all the time, you—"

"I have some names I want to run by you. I'll call you right back," I shouted, but they were having a lively discussion.

By the time I figured out how to access the second call, it had gone to message. Mrs. Parnell.

I called back and was surprised to get her voicemail. I left a message and kept going. I was feeling a bit lightheaded. Perhaps because I hadn't eaten for—I couldn't remember how long. Even so, I didn't feel like eating. Might never feel like eating again. But I knew Gussie and the little calico would have needs. I considered fishing out dinner for them, letting them pee on the grass and then sending them to Sydney with Donald Donnie. Loretta would fuss over them, and it would have the added benefit of making the Fergusons nervous. On the other hand, if I ended up home in Ottawa, I wouldn't be happy to have to drive back to Sydney to collect the menagerie.

Walking the dog might be useful. Gussie was thrilled to be offered a pit stop. The little calico managed to dodge me and her leash to slink under the car. Fifteen minutes later, she still hadn't reappeared. Donald Donnie left the Accord and waddled over to see what was going on.

I said, "The cat has gone into hiding. Perhaps it's contagious."

He waited, apparently thinking I'd have more to say on the matter.

He finally said, "Here kitty, kitty."

As if that would work.

I had a theory. "We should put some cat food close to the car to attract her and but far enough so she has to creep out. We'll totally ignore her until she emerges."

He blinked.

"I've been down this road before, Donald Donnie. Act as if you couldn't care less. First, we need some quality cat food, the kind that doesn't need a can opener." I produced two twenties and waved them. "And get some extra dog food, Gussie likes it all, but he gets IAMS gastrointestinal. You don't want to know why."

"Whatever you want, my girl. The Co-op's right around the corner."

"Tuna in a can with a tab or Fancy Feast, Friskies, Temptations, catnip. Any or all and a bag of food for Gussie."

"I'm on the case." Donald Donnie snatched the bills from my hand, got back into the Accord, and shot off to the store, less than a block away.

I leaned against the vehicle and waited for him or the little calico cat, whichever appeared first.

When Donald Donnie returned huffing with a can of tuna fish without a tab top but with a newly purchased can opener, a package of Fancy Feast, and a bag of Temptations Blissful Catnip Flavor Cat Treats, plus another plastic bag hanging on his wrist, I was staring out over the immense blue and glittering Big Bras d'Or Lake. But no time to enjoy the beauty of Baddeck today.

No cat so far, but Gussie was intrigued by the new food options.

"What about you, Camilla? Don't you need a bite?"

"I can't go anywhere until the cat is repatriated."

"I'll watch for the wee puss, and you go to and get yourself something to eat."

I was starving and had no idea where to go next. It made sense to take him up on it. I hustled up the road to Wong's Bras d'Or House and ordered chicken fried rice and egg rolls and a Coke to take out. Might as well go to hell in a handbasket.

The customers in Wong's watched me with interest, especially a group of five middle-aged couples. Cape Bretoners are friendly. They talk to strangers. They are interested in other people, observant. Perhaps one of them had noticed Ray get in the truck.

"Egg rolls are excellent here," a man said. That was good news, because I'd ordered four of them.

I forced my lips into a stiff smile and turned to the nearest diner, a pleasant fiftyish woman with crisp grey hair and dark-rimmed bifocals.

"Sorry to bother you, but I've missed out connecting with my fiancé. We're getting married this week and we're both a bit…" I stopped, chuckled, and let my audience draw its own conclusions. "I guess you could say we're overexcited. Anyway, I'm here with the dog and the cat and the car, and he's gone on with friends. I'm supposed to join them. And a guy is trying to reach him with a job offer. He needs the work. Time's running out, and I don't know what direction they went in. Sorry, but what is it with men?"

The five women thought that was the funniest story they'd ever heard. The men acted less amused. Perhaps they thought that my fiancé had made a run for it.

"His friend has a silver Silverado with New Brunswick plates. You didn't happen to see him, did you?"

A couple of the men exchanged glances, always a good sign. I added, "I'd call him or he'd call me, but he dropped his phone when he hopped in the truck." I waggled Ray's phone in one hand and mine in the other.

"Wouldn't he use one of his buddies' phones then?" said a grizzled fellow I took to be a veteran of the marital wars. I heard a murmur of agreement among the gents.

"He would if I he knew my number by heart, but he has it on speed-dial—I held up the phone as evidence—so he has to press 1. It's nice to be number one in his phone list." I pressed 1 on Ray's phone, and mine rang.

The ladies laughed long and hard.

I upped the ante. "I hope he doesn't miss out on that job offer. But there's always another job coming along. Right?"

That got a general stirring. This was Cape Breton, after all, and jobs were scarce.

"How do we know he wants you to find him?" a brave soul muttered.

"He asked me to marry him on ten separate occasions, but yes, maybe he didn't mean it."

The ladies got an extra kick out of that one. Two of them were wiping away tears of laughter.

I added, "And Ray Deveau is not a man to run away from trouble. He'll face right up to it. You can assume that if he wanted out, he'd tell me."

The men nodded, although one of them said *sotto voce,* "Bit risky that."

Someone else said, "Ray Deveau? Cop from Sydney?"

Oops. "Formerly Sydney," I said, deciding to play to the local card. "Now he's working in Ottawa, where we live together. I was born in Sydney. My father is Donald MacPhee, originally from Inverness County. We would like to come back here if that job pans out."

All eyes turned to the door as Donald Donnie made a breathless entrance.

Donald Donnie said, "And I'm Camilla's second cousin, once removed." I was glad he could remember the exact relationship, because I never could. He leaned in and whispered to me, "The c-a-t is back in the car." I wasn't sure why that was a secret, but Donald Donnie's presence and his vouching for me made all the difference. One of the men fiddled with his John Deere hat and said, "Them guys were driving toward the Trail. I heard Ingonish."

Another one piped up, "They filled up over to the Esso. I was there myself, and I heard them talkin' French."

French. That sounded right. "So, Ingonish. That's good news." With luck I could catch up with them, although they had a serious lead. I paid and snatched up my bag of take-out.

"That's where we're supposed to get married. He must have been confused. Thanks for the tip."

I squirted plum sauce onto of one of the egg rolls and gobbled it on my way out the door. It probably tasted pretty good. I didn't notice.

Donald Donnie skittered after me. "I'd better follow you in case you get in trouble."

I couldn't imagine worse trouble than navigating the Cabot Trail while worrying about Donald Donnie plunging to his death behind me. As it turned out, I had much more to worry about.

CHAPTER TWELVE
Why did you hang up on me?

❝The problem is, Donald Donnie, I need you here in Baddeck." Once again, I tried to channel my sisters' general-like qualities.

"You do? What for?"

Before he asked seventeen more questions, I said, "You need to find out who else was in that Silverado. Say nice stuff about my father and make sure everyone knows that Ray was head over heels about me."

Worry flooded his face.

I said, "Fine. Exaggerate if you have to. It's not a mortal sin. I'm going to see if I can catch that truck. I've wasted a ton of time already."

"But how will I let you know what I find out?"

"Call me?"

"On what? There's no phone booths around anymore."

"You don't have a cell phone?"

"Now, what would I be doing with one of them, my girl?"

"Okay, I have Ray's phone, so I'll leave you mine. Here's Ray's number on my contact list, so you can call me simply by pressing 1."

Donald Donnie stared at the phone as though I'd offered him a live snake. He did a little stress dance, waving his hands like a panicked cheerleader. "How would I begin to use it?"

"Ask one of those people in the café. Or find a kid, any kid." I said, jumping into the Escape. "Hang on, dog and cat. You're going for a ride."

"All right," he said, "but if you are giving me this—"

"Just temporary."

"I'd like to give you a present in return." He proudly opened the bag he'd been carrying and produced a baseball cap with motto *THE BEST GIRLS ARE FROM CAPE BRETON.*

I knew better than to argue.

"Was gonna be Loretta's lucky hat," he said.

I wasn't foolish enough to ask how a newly purchased baseball cap could be someone's lucky hat.

"Put it on and check in the wing mirror."

I didn't look any worse than anyone else would in the hat, so that was good enough for me.

"Thank you," I said and hit the gas.

In the rear-view mirror, Donald Donnie's round but forlorn figure receded. But that's the thing with extroverts—they recover quickly. He was lighting a smoke to cheer up. And someone was already ambling over to offer comfort.

•••

On my way out of Baddeck, I remembered that Mrs. P. hadn't returned my returned call. What if she'd been trying to reach me with the information about those phone numbers? Or the license plate?

Donald Donnie had my phone. What if she'd reached him expecting to find me? I was pretty sure Mrs. P. was up to any task, but Donald Donnie was another story. He might not have grasped how to answer the phone yet. I hated to waste time, but I pulled over anyway, just before the turn to the Cabot Trail. I had Mrs. P. on speed dial. She was number 2, after Ray and before Alvin, and it goes without saying before my sisters. I didn't have the foggiest what her actual phone number was. Of course, Ray didn't have Mrs. P.'s number on his phone. Or Alvin's. I contemplated calling my sisters, whose numbers I do remember, but I was angry at them for allowing me to live a delusion. I planned to deal that with once I settled Sergeant Ray Deveau's hash.

I crossed my fingers and called Donald Donnie.

At least there was cell reception.

He didn't answer. My call went to voicemail. If he couldn't answer the phone, he definitely wouldn't be able to figure out voicemail. I left the phone within reach on the passenger seat.

I tried Donald Donnie three more times. The phone went to voicemail after each attempt. Oh, well. Ray had Bluetooth in the Escape. I could answer and keep driving if Donald Donnie figured it out.

I squealed back onto the road, made the sharp left turn onto the Cabot Trail, and ignored the speed limit. Once you figure out your priorities, you have to stick to them. What's a white knuckle or two when you're chasing your man?

No sign of that silver Silverado. Of course, it would be long gone. I gasped as a shiny black Jeep Cherokee passed me in the face of oncoming traffic—an offence to which many of my former legal aid clients were partial.

The phone rang. It was not the right time to take my eyes off the traffic, what with the presence of lunatic drivers. Keeping my eyes on the road, I clicked a button on the steering wheel. The radio came on. I tried another. The windshield wipers answered that one.

Finally, I heard a distant and tinny hello.

"Ray?"

"It's not Ray, it's me."

"Who?" I could hardly check the number.

"Donald Donnie!"

"You sound like you're at the bottom of a well."

"So do you. These gadgets don't work so good."

"I'm glad you called. I need you to find a number for me."

"What?"

"On my phone. It's in my contacts. Simply press 2."

The line went dead.

"Not now, you nitwit," I muttered. Of course, I wasn't being fair to Donald Donnie, who had not asked to take charge of the phone, but this was no time for fairness.

Two minutes later, the phone rang again.

"It's Donald Donnie."

"Great."

"Why did you hang up on me?"

"You hung up on me."

"Oh. How did I do that?"

"Just wait until we *finish* talking, then hang up and please press that number '2' and tell Mrs. Parnell, whom you have met, I believe, to call me at this number."

"What number?"

"The one you called."

"Well, I didn't actually call it. I think I pressed one."

"Fine." I did my best to describe the steps for finding a contact number to Donald Donnie. "Got it?"

"I think so. It says Ray."

"Right. Check the number on the screen and copy it down. That's this number. Then give the number to Mrs. Parnell when you reach her."

"So, it's Violet, is it? Great. Always good to talk to her about the war." Donald Donnie was too young to have been in Mrs. Parnell's war, but that would never hold him back.

"Tell her she's calling Ray's cell phone."

"But—"

"Copy the number and give it to her."

"But I don't have her number."

"You're going to press 2 to reach her, like you pressed 1 to reach me. Don't think about it. Press."

Silence—possibly wounded feelings—unless we'd lost reception. Wouldn't have surprised me.

"Please and thank you, Donald Donnie." People can be so delicate.

"Fine. I'll do it."

Maybe I imagined the frostiness.

As the phone disconnected, I wondered if I might have messages. What if there was a message from Ray on my cell? He wouldn't call his phone to speak to me, because he didn't know I had it.

I contemplated giving Donald Donnie another remote lesson in elementary phone usage. But I barely knew how to get those messages myself. Mrs. Parnell could figure it out. I'd give her my password when I spoke to her next.

Maybe I needed to call Donald Donnie back and do some remedial training, but I decided to give him fifteen minutes and keep driving.

Priority one was to catch up with Ray.

But in the meantime, so many questions and no answers.

Who was the dangerous-looking hulk Ray had been arguing with outside Kiju's?

Who were all these UNKNOWN numbers?

Was one of them the mysterious Sandy in Ingonish?

What was Ray mixed up in?

CHAPTER THIRTEEN
What just happened?

According to Ray's partner, Dani, Pierre Forgeron was also a cop. So was Matty another of Ray's cop friends? Except for Ray, most cops seem to have nicknames for each other, Lennie, Dani, and so on. I hated nicknames and tuned them all out. Had I tuned out Matty?

Matty must have been important to Ray, because someone had called him to say Matty was dead.

Someone with a local accent that sounded vaguely familiar. After a while, you could feel you knew everyone in Cape Breton. And all their relatives, living and dead.

Getting lost in your thoughts isn't the best idea on the Cabot Trail. I'd been thinking hard and tuning out the explosion of fall colours, the scenic drive with few scattered houses, and the occasional bright hull of a Cape Island boat, out of the water for the season. I'd ignored the steep hills, dips, and sharp twists until the car veered off the road with a rough crunching onto the gravel shoulder. Gussie barked in disapproval, and both sounds brought me back to the necessity of paying attention. Sound number three: the phone ringing. I pulled over and stopped the car. Alvin was so agitated that I didn't even ask him how he knew to call Ray's phone. Perhaps Donald Donnie was a better assistant than I'd thought.

"Okay, calm down, Alvin. I understand why I might be upset after talking to my sisters, but how come you're the one hyperventilating? After all, they like you. Kind of."

"You suckered me into it. And your sisters are the scariest women ever."

"Hmm." I thought briefly of Lisa Marie Ferguson, Alvin's own sibling and surely a gold medalist in the scary woman category. "High praise indeed."

"Very funny. Edwina reamed me out over the phone. It was terrifying. I didn't even have a chance to use my cover story, and it was a good one."

"So, let's accept that they're formidable and frightening, but what did they tell you?"

"They didn't say a friggin' thing. Alexa wouldn't answer her phone, and your sister Donalda actually blocked my number."

"Huh. I wouldn't have thought she'd know how to do that, but if you say so. And then Edwina was angry at you?"

"She was first. And I'm not finished. Then Alexa's *husband* called me and accused me of harassment. Me! I hadn't even spoken to her, and anyway, how is it harassment to ask what year your mother died?"

"I may not have told you all the facts, Alvin."

"Right. He said I could be arrested! So once again you sent me into battle carrying a straw instead of a sword."

"Nice image, Alvin. Obviously, you've been spending quality time with Mrs. P. But Conn is full of it. You couldn't be arrested for asking that question or calling her once or even twice."

"And, because I'm still not finished, Camilla, *then*, Donalda's husband came over here and pounded on the door."

"Did you answer it?"

"Do I look crazy?"

"Well, I can't actually see you."

"Why don't you try a career in stand-up?"

"Sorry, Alvin. I shouldn't push you when you're…"

He sniffed.

"So tell me about Edwina. She's always been the tough one in the trio."

"Quartet."

"Trio."

"Weren't you four sisters, Camilla?"

"Maybe not, as it turns out."

"Lord thunderin' Jesus. What are you talking about?"

"Fine. I'll fill you in but first, what did Edwina say? Don't hold back. No date?"

"Insults. Apparently, I'm useless and, what's more, I'm a disgrace to my family." I heard the choke in his voice.

"Well, that was pushing the limit, even for Edwina."

"That was the beginning. Then she got really wound up."

"I am sorry, Alvin."

"You are?"

"Yes, I am. You shouldn't have had to put up with personal attacks, and unfair ones at that."

"It's not like you to apologize, Camilla. Especially twice." Alvin sounded more than a bit suspicious. "Have you been trying some new kind of medication?"

"People change. Especially when their worldview is shaken."

Alvin was strangely silent.

I said, "Are you there?"

"Has your worldview been shaken?"

"It has been, and in more ways than one." There was the whole Ray situation on top of the weirdness of my mother's impossible death date. Of course, I was starting to think of my "mother" with air quotes.

"Does their weird behaviour have to do with the date you wanted me to find out?"

"That's part of it."

"And that's what has your sisters turning psycho?"

"That's a good bet, Alvin."

"Considering what I went through, would you mind explaining?"

"Here's what I know: my mother's date of death is well before I was born."

"Before you were born? That's not—but didn't you tell me she died when you were a baby?"

"That's what I was told, but it turns out that the date on her gravestone is the year before I was born."

"That doesn't make sense. Oh! I see why you were hoping for a mistake on the monument."

"Exactly. If the date is correct, it explains why my father has looked at me strangely all my life and why my sisters were so much older and why I was so different from everyone in the family."

"That stuff's all true."

"Yes, and if I am not the daughter of Camilla and Donald MacPhee, who the hell am I?"

"They deceived you," Alvin breathed.

"All my life."

"Probably meant it kindly."

"Kindness is not a major character trait for my sisters."

"Right. They're pretty, um, well, you couldn't call them kind."

"Obsessive. Bossy. Controlling. Pick from any of those traits."

"Don't leave out savage."

"All to say, I'm not sure kindness was their motivation."

"What then?"

"I don't know, Alvin. If I knew what had happened, then I might know why they had to hide it and why Edwina's so angry and the other two are—"

"Hysterical."

"Exactly. What is there to be hysterical about? I'm well past forty."

"Actually, you're—"

"I'm not a child to be protected. None of it makes any sense. I need to find out what's going on."

"Don't count on me. I'm not going to be a target for them again."

"I understand, Alvin. But I have a right to know who I am. And I don't need to be protected."

"Maybe it's not you they're protecting."

That took a few seconds to sink in.

"Camilla?"

"That's it. They're not protecting me. It might be my father."

"And he's older and getting kind of fragile, isn't he? Sorry, I don't want to upset you more."

"I am well aware that my father is old and fragile."

"Who else could it be?"

"The mother, Alvin. It could be the real mother."

"And your father…?"

"My father, a young widower, lonely, bereft, had a relationship that resulted in me? Is that what you're suggesting?

"Lord thunderin—"

I thought about my father, respectable school principal, firm parent, faithful churchgoer. I knew a lot of duplicitous men, but I couldn't imagine him as one. "More likely some other explanation entirely."

I was finding it hard to breathe. Fortunately, I'd pulled over, or I might have gone off the road in a worse place.

Alvin said, "Oh, I have an idea. What if you belonged to another couple, unmarried, unable to raise a child, and then your father helped out by adopting you?"

"There would have been plenty of people around to adopt a baby girl at that time. People waited for years. The Children's Aid would never have given me to a single-parent family."

"Private adoption?"

That didn't feel like a MacPhee approach. "There's another possibility. *She* may still be alive."

If Alvin noticed I was unable to say my *real* mother, he didn't allude to it. My supposed mother had never felt real either. She'd been a bit like one of the more glamorous saints you learned about as a child. I used to imagine her sporting a little halo.

"How would you feel about that, Camilla?"

"I would feel as mad as hell. And I should tell you—."

Alvin yelped, "What now?"

"Ray has left me."

"Ray has left you?"

"Stop parroting me, Alvin."

"But Ray is … Ray."

"I thought that too, but it appears that Ray used to be Ray, and at this moment I have no idea who Ray is."

"Are you coming home?"

"No, I'm damn well not coming home. The man left me without most of my clothes, my laptop, my files and my wallet, and without an explanation. I am going to hound him to the ends of the earth so I can tell him what I think of him. Unless, of course, he's been kidnapped, and then I'd have to rescue him before I let him have it right between the eyes."

Alvin remained silent. His brain was probably exploding from all those revelations. "Are you driving without a license? Isn't that a—"

"Don't obsess." I felt if I told Alvin I'd recovered the clothes, computer, and wallet, it might weaken my case. I was glad I hadn't brought up the wedding gear.

"Camilla, you know I'll be here for you."

"What? You'll be where?"

"I'll be here for you. It's an expression meaning I've got your back. I can't believe you don't know that."

"Oh."

"Feel free to say thank-you."

"I appreciate it, Alvin." For a rocky minute, I'd thought that by "here" he meant in Cape Breton and possibly around the next killer curve of the Cabot Trail. I had more than enough to deal with already. "If you want, you can discuss this with Mrs. Parnell. She's in the loop."

"No secrets from our gal, Violet. Right."

"Absolutely. And she may be able to find out that date of death. You probably should steer clear of my sisters for a few years."

"I don't have a death wish, so yes."

"I've gotta go, Alvin. I'm in a serious situation here."

"Wait! Donald Donnie gave me this number. First tell me why your wacky old cousin has your phone."

"Because this is Ray's phone, and I may need Donald Donnie's help. He's not wacky, just … enthusiastic."

"Donald Donnie helping is hard to imagine. And why do you have Ray's phone?"

"He dropped it as he was making his getaway. Can you call Mrs. P. and make sure she had this number?"

"Manners."

Manners? Oh, right. "Please and thank you, Alvin. You know, Donald Donnie's good-natured, but I think he has issues with technology."

"He'll need to be good-natured, and who are you to talk about issues with technology?"

True enough. I hung up before we bounced along yet another bumpy conversational trail. I needed to get a grip on the business with Ray. The rest could wait, including my "mother."

•••

Getting to Ingonish involved actual driving before the fog became impenetrable and not squandering time in a parked vehicle. Fog is not good on twisty mountain roads with sheer drops to the sea. The occasional white crosses by the side of the road reinforced the message. Such a tricky drive and yet not a cop in place. Well, time to ignore the weather conditions and start using my brain, although that brain had gotten a bit foggy itself with my easy new comfortable life with Ray. Never mind, I still had a few grey cells left, and it was time to use them if I had any hope of finding the Silverado.

I hurtled through the thickening mist, mentally recapping what I knew and what I needed to know. I didn't know much, as it turned out, and I needed to ferret out plenty. It would have helped to learn exactly who had called to say that Matty was dead. Mrs. P. would get on that, even if Donald Donnie had been unable to handle the instructions on how to reach me. Alvin could call her if only to discuss the breaking news about Ray and my "mother."

Before I got going, I clicked on the number of the man who'd told me that Matty was dead. I redialled. Why hadn't I thought to do that before? I could have given Mrs. P. the number. Seriously, this situation had reduced me to a gibbering fool.

But REDIAL was brilliant.

"*It's Kenny. Leave a message.*" Huh. But whoever had called from that number had not been Kenny. Who the hell was Kenny? Again, the voice sounded vaguely familiar. Of course, it had that hint of Cape Breton, and I was surrounded by people who spoke like that.

Now this Kenny needed to be added to the unknown list. Apparently, Ray was familiar with him and someone they both knew was dead. Any gambler would say there was a good chance the caller and this death were somehow connected to Ray's disappearance.

Kenny wasn't a name I remembered from the Ottawa force, nor was the voice one I recognized as a regular or even occasional caller back home. Not that I paid all that much attention to Ray's calls, but he's an affable type, or he had been. He always told me who had called, and I usually pretended to be interested. That was our old life. This new reality left a lot to be desired.

To my knowledge, Ray had no close ties to Ingonish. Ray and Leonard Mombourquette had grown up outside Cheticamp, close to two hours away through Cape Breton Highlands National Park. So was Kenny connected to Cheticamp? Or to Ingonish and Sandy, whoever he was? And the newly dead Matty, what about him?

Had I made a big mistake by not questioning the "intel" from Wong's in Baddeck? After all, it was just some strangers in a restaurant talking about overhearing the men in the Silverado going to Ingonish. Not much to hang my hat on. Would the Silverado have blown right through Ingonish and over to Cheticamp? I thought there must have been a shorter route, but I wasn't sure.

I gobbled another rapidly chilling egg roll and scribbled down the telephone number from the list. It wasn't a private number and hadn't been blocked. This guy wasn't worried about Ray, and he was unaware that Ray had dropped his phone. Therefore, the caller couldn't have been in the Silverado. When I answered instead of Ray, he hung up instead of giving me a perfectly reasonable explanation. Panic? Now that was going to work against Kenny, whoever he was: friend, colleague, or informant.

Shortly after we got back on the road, Gussie uttered the heartrending howl that indicates he needs to pee. I pulled over once more, and while I kept one eye on Gussie on the side of the fogged-in road, I belatedly checked Ray's list of contacts. I didn't find a Matty, Matthew, Mathieu, or a Sandy or even an Alex or Alexander. No Kenny or Kenneth either. I scrolled slowly, searching for matches from his cell to the ones I'd copied from his home phone in Sydney.

No joy. There were Ottawa police names, family and friends—even my sisters—but no one whose numbers had recently appeared on his Sydney telephone or on his cell. That told me that Ray hadn't been in touch regularly with any of these people. Unlike me, he was diligent about keeping contact info up to date. Perhaps they hadn't even known his cell number, just the regular landline at his old home that was probably still listed in Canada411 under Carol Deveau. Surprising that he didn't add them to his cell phone contacts.

Kenny's tone of familiarity told me whatever was happening came from Ray's old life. Was his disappearance connected with his time on the Cape Breton force? Was Matty a cop? A crook? A victim?

I stayed long enough to figure out the Bluetooth and located the number for Wayne Nowicki in the contacts. He was a former colleague of Ray's, although Ray didn't think much of him. I bit the bullet and called.

"Start talkin." So not his work number for sure.

"This is Camilla MacPhee, Ray Deveau's, um, partner."

Silence on the other end.

"Ray's trying to reach someone named Matty."

"Yeah?" he said. Unlike Ray, he had a typical cop's voice, flat and uninflected.

"I hear he's dead."

"Who told you that?"

"I, um, overheard someone."

"Not Ray."

"No, not Ray. But I need to find out what this is about."

"You kidding me? None of your business."

"Have I mentioned I'm a lawyer?"

"Oh right, I'm shakin'. Tell you what, Carmella—"

"Camilla."

"If Ray needs information, tell him to call me. Right away."

"Sure. But—"

I was talking to empty air. Wayne Nowicki didn't want to tell me anything, but his reaction told me he was aware of Matty. Ray was involved with Matty somehow and—interestingly—that didn't come as surprise to this former colleague.

"Hurry up, Gussie. I haven't got all day."

With Gussie back in, I spun my wheels getting on the road and kept thinking.

The combination of our location and Wayne Nowicki's reaction convinced me that whatever was going on had to do with Cape Breton and Ray's time here. So why would that rat Leonard Mombourquette not be in the loop about that?

●●●

A half hour later, the call finally came in. With the Bluetooth, I was able to keep driving hands-free.

"Mrs. P.! Did Donald Donnie reach you?"

"Actually, I telephoned him. Young Ferguson informed me of the connection. Mr. MacDonald appears to be unaccountably flustered and yet at the same time proud of what he is doing to assist you."

"Well, here's my update. I've finally got a lead, aside from the Silverado travelling with Ray to parts unknown."

I imagined her leaning back in her recliner with a gleam in her eye. "Splendid. Out with it!"

"Well, it's good news and it's not."

"I await your pronouncements." I heard glee in her voice and possibly the splash of Harvey's Bristol Cream into her favourite cut-glass tumbler. No prissy sherry glasses for our Mrs. P.

She said, "No intel on Matty yet. Next I shall search Matty and Matthew in deaths, obits, disappearances, news reports, and more. I'll start with Nova Scotia and then go wide. Leave it with me. As for Pierre Forgeron, he's divorced and lives alone. His ex does not hold him in high regard, but there may be former colleagues. Stay tuned."

"There's more. I found out about Matty from a guy who thought he was calling Ray. This guy's name is Kenny, and here's his telephone number." I read it off to her. "As you know, 902 covers Nova Scotia and P.E.I. I need a last name and an address, and I'll track him down. I'm thinking Ingonish or even Cheticamp. Maybe Sydney. Sorry I didn't give you the number before."

"Not to worry. Expect a call when I have more. I'm away to the races, Ms. MacPhee."

I was smiling as she disconnected. Mrs. Parnell has that effect on me. But it didn't take long before I began to wonder how Matty died. Poor Matty—whoever he had been—was not merely dead, but *already* dead. Had people been expecting him to die? Expecting him to be killed? There was plenty to think about as I barrelled on through the fog.

I chewed on that until I noticed that gas gauge was at less than a quarter tank. How long that would last in this vehicle? It wasn't like Ray to let his tank go below half. Unlike me, Ray loves pumping gas, no matter what the weather. That is a weird personal trait, but it has always been convenient. If memory served, there were few fuel sources on this route. The velvety evergreens on the mountainside and stunning views on the other side—with potential sheer drops to the sea—were better negotiated with a full tank. I had to play the odds. Should I keep going or scuttle back to Baddeck for gas? I'm not the kind of woman who turns back, so that settled that. I did slow down, figuring that I'd conserve a bit of fuel that way.

"Cross your toes," I said glancing at the rear-view and smiling at my two passengers in the back seat. "We'll need a bit of luck with what's coming." Gussie's tail thumped. The little cat licked her paws to indicate supreme boredom.

Speaking of coming, what the hell?

A shiny black Jeep hovered right on my tail. He was too close for me to see his plates. I planned to give him the finger when he finally passed me.

At the first available opportunity, I swung onto the shoulder to let him by.

He gunned his engine and roared toward me. If he hit me, I'd be flying straight through the guardrail, with nowhere to go but the undertaker's.

CHAPTER FOURTEEN
And what do we have here?

I stood on the brake and braced for impact. Time slowed and at the same time sped up. I can't explain it.

An elderly Winnebago crested the hill as the Jeep slammed my bumper. Two white-haired people gawked, wide-eyed and open-mouthed, at the scene. The Winnebago pulled over. The Jeep reversed, made a startling U-turn, and roared off. I slumped, knowing the front bumper of Ray's new car was pressed against the metal barrier at the edge of the road. The rear bumper was probably in several pieces on the road. The racket inside the car was entirely due to my heart beating.

I waved a "thank you" to the couple in the motor home. They both put on their Tilley hats and took their chances crossing the road. They blinked at me from behind matching horn-rimmed glasses.

"Are you all right?" she said.

"Thank you," I said. "I think so."

"That man should be arrested," he blustered.

"I didn't see his face. It all happened so fast. I couldn't get his license plate either."

She said. "It was smeared with mud."

"Did you get a look at him?"

They shook their heads in unison. "He had a toque pulled down and sunglasses on. Imagine, with all this fog. No way to get a description."

"Right. Shiny car. Muddy license plate. No face."

He said. "Should we call the police?"

"No point. I can't wait around. But if you hear on the news that I've been killed or hurt, tell the cops about that black Jeep."

"But we don't know who you are," she said reasonably.

"My name is Camilla MacPhee. This car belongs to Sergeant Ray Deveau. Tell the police what, where, and when. That's all."

"But don't you think you should wait for them?"

"Nope, but thank you all the same."

He thrust a paper at me with their names and cellphone number. "In case you need witnesses," he said.

"Thank you, Harold and Grace," I said sincerely before I left them.

The road ahead was blessedly empty. So was the road behind. No shiny black Jeep. No rescuing seniors anywhere.

Eventually my heart rate resumed normal levels. I pulled over long enough to call my old nemesis again and put him on speakerphone. Desperation for sure, but Leonard Mombourquette was the only person I could think of who would know about Ray's former police contacts.

Elaine Ekstein picked up. "Ray?"

"It's Camilla. I need to talk to Leonard again. It's urgent."

"Oh, it's you, Camilla. Well, I'm not sure if he wants to talk right—"

In the background I could hear Leonard: "Especially not to MacPhee."

"Understood completely. Tell him that Matty's dead."

"Matty's dead?"

I could hear Mombourquette bellow "What?" He must have snatched the phone. "What are you talking about?"

"Matty's dead."

There was a long pause. Finally, "How do you know that?"

"Ray got the call. Mind you, Ray won't know that because, as I said, he's without his phone and in a Silverado, driving straight for trouble. Some guy named Kenny didn't want to talk to me."

I could hear Mombourquette breathing again, fast and stressed.

"So, Leonard, do you know who Matty was?"

"You have to let it go, MacPhee."

"Not happening. What about Kenny?"

"Let. It. Go."

"Oh, and by the way, I'm in Ray's vehicle and someone just tried to run me off the Trail and into the Atlantic.

"Who could blame them?"

"Laugh if you want, but all this stuff is connected."

"Did you get a plate?"

"It was a large black Jeep, so close that I couldn't see the plate. I'd be at the bottom of the sea now if a couple of seniors hadn't come out of nowhere. They said the plate was muddy."

"Turn around, go back to Sydney, and then come home. That's what Ray would want."

"I don't give a flying fig what Ray would want. I'm going to look him right in the eye and tell him what I think of his behaviour."

"Don't be stupid. This is turning out to be dangerous."

"Yeah, for Ray and for Matty. How about making it less dangerous and telling me what's going on?"

But he was gone. That conversation told me that Mombourquette knew who Matty was. He never asked who Kenny was. So, he knew that too.

But if anyone was going to be dangerous, it should be me. I fully intended to find Ray.

•••

As the fog lifted, the view was so spectacular I found myself mellowing, although the sun nearly blinded me. Ray's Ray-Bans were lying on the passenger seat, next to his phone charger. I slipped the sunglasses on.

When Alvin's call came in, I managed to be civil.

"You have an important message on your home phone."

I said patiently, "But I don't know how to access my home phone remotely. Remember? That's why I asked you."

Alvin said, "Are you driving?"

"Yes, I'm on the Cabot Trail."

"Lord thundering Jesus. You better pull over, and I'll explain to you how to retrieve it. I don't want to be responsible for you ending up in the ocean."

"I'm tired of pulling over. I'll call you when I get to Ingonish."

"You better hear this first, Camilla. Follow the prompts when you get into your system."

I grumbled about how I hated all this stuff, but as soon as I found a good spot, I pulled over and listened to Alvin lord it over me with instructions and passwords. He sounded like a swarm of buzzing bees.

Ray's voice hit me when I finally got into the system and pressed 1.

Camilla? I know you will get this eventually by some means. I need you to understand our relationship is over, and you need to accept it. I figure you'll be on your way back to Ottawa, and I'm sorry for the inconvenience. It wasn't meant to work, and I finally accepted that on our trip. I'm sorry if I hurt you. Hell, you're probably not hurt at all, just mad as a hornet. I can't help that. Move on with your life. Sting someone. I'll arrange to get my stuff when I'm back in Ottawa, if you haven't torched everything I own. As far as our shared property goes, I won't take advantage. But I'd like to get my CD collection back.

I laughed out loud. Now I knew for sure that Ray wasn't sincere. The entire message was calculated to turn me into a simmering silo of fury, flying back to Ottawa to immolate Ray's clothing on our dog-pee-stained front lawn and topping up the inferno by tossing in his CD collection. I would have already taken a hammer to that.

Now why would he want such an outcome? I tried to keep my eyes out for homicidal Jeeps as I worked out Ray's motivation. Then it hit me. Ray knew that I would go after him to find out what was going on and for the satisfaction of telling him off. So he was trying to make me furious enough to return home, where I wouldn't get into trouble, interfere, and/or get hurt. This would have been a risky strategy on his part, but it did explain that idiotic message.

My fingers loosened on the wheel. His disappearance was not connected to our planned elopement and the wedding that was his ridiculous idea anyway. It wasn't about me. There was a serious problem and at least one dead person.

Fine. I wanted to tell him to his face what I thought of him and his lack of trust. Mind you, I was already aware Ray was worried and distracted. Driving along, ignoring the view, I asked myself if Ray even knew he'd had my stuff. I thought back to the bedroom. I had just taken my small pile of clothes from the duffle and left them on the bed as

Ray lumbered into the room. Ray always finished what he started. He'd have assumed I'd unpacked, if he even gave it a moment's thought. That would go a long way to explaining why he would leave me without my computer, files, and wallet. Wedding dress too, of course, lest we forget.

That confirmed my nagging fear: Ray Deveau, who was always bailing me out of jams, must be in real trouble. And if he thought he could go put himself in danger without me sticking my nose in, he had a half-dozen more thinks coming.

"Nice try, jackass," I said. "You want to get me out of your hair, you'll have to be a little less blatant. I'll see you when you least expect it. Be very afraid."

Even though my world was somewhat topsy-turvy, my best bet was that Sandy MacSomething-or-other was expecting Ray to show up in Ingonish or vicinity, even as far away as Cheticamp, where he might actually be Alexandre MacQuelque-chose.

"What do you say?" I asked Gussie and Mrs. Parnell's cat. "You want to bet a week's treats on me finding this guy?

I had no takers, so I drove on.

Smokey was straight ahead and nearly straight up too.

On a day with less to worry about, I would have enjoyed the stunning autumn colours. After many dramatic driving moments on the steep road, I was approaching a curved look-off with a couple of parked cars and tourists taking selfies when Gussie barked. Although it hadn't been long, I have learned to let him out when this happens. I pulled over and glanced back to suffer a shock. How had I forgotten that Jeep?

My mouth hung open as the driver rammed the rear end of Ray's car. The shock of the impact took my breath away. I shoved the car into drive and stepped on the accelerator, yanking the steering wheel sharply left to avoid the guardrail. As the Jeep connected again, I felt a second shock. In the back seat, Gussie barked hysterically.

My attacker reversed. I used the time to accelerate and spin around in a one-eighty. Mr. Crazy Jeep may have damaged Ray's car, but he hadn't done his any good either. I needed to give him a taste of his own medicine before he killed me and my furry passengers. I swung in back of the Jeep, trying at the same time to catch a glimpse of the driver. All I saw was the toque and the sunglasses. Of course, I was hidden behind my own baseball cap and Ray-Bans.

But why was this lunatic attacking a stranger?

Wait. What if he wasn't attacking a stranger? What if he thought I was Ray?

Of course, now that he'd actually committed a serious crime, I didn't want to show him my face. I might not have been the person he was after, but I was a witness to his crime. I put the pedal to the metal and shot across the highway and back the way I'd come from. I needed to escape the look-off, the sheer drop, and the homicidal maniac.

The Jeep roared after me.

Where were Howard and Grace when I needed them? And who was this guy?

I could see him gaining in the rear-view. Around the next curve, a motorcycle rode into view. I leaned on the horn and flashed my lights. The Jeep did a U-ey and sped away. I pulled over, stopped and shook. Gussie howled. The motorcycle, a Harley, pulled up.

I considered getting out, but my legs had turned to mush. I worked to get my breathing under control as the biker stopped and dismounted. Was this guy my salvation, or was he somehow connected with the Jeep? With shaking hands, I used Ray's cell phone to call Mombourquette and left a message.

"Just so you know, Leonard, a Jeep crashed into Ray's car and tried to push it through a guardrail on Smokey. Second attack. I don't know if he was trying to do in Ray or me. A biker on a Harley just stopped. I'll send you his picture." I managed to snap a photo and press *send*. The biker was long and lean, bulked up a bit by black and maroon leathers. He strode toward me, taking off his helmet and swinging it a bit as he moved. I put the phone down by my side but left it on.

He bent down and leaned forward, face in the window. It was a nice enough face, framed by short silver hair and a bit of stubble on his chin. Deep lines indicated too many drinks and cigarettes. His eyes widened when he saw me. But then he grinned, showing good teeth. I forced a weak smile. "Thanks. I think you kept me from being killed."

He appeared to be in his early fifties. I put the motorcycle down to a midlife crisis.

"What went down?"

"Did you see the guy in that black Jeep? He tried to push me over the edge. I was trying to get away when you showed up."

The biker said, "Your rear end's banged up pretty good."

I produced a weak smile. "It's my former fiancé's rear end. He's not going to be happy."

I chose not to mention my former fiancé was a cop. For all I knew this guy was connected to the whole mess. He looked more like a high school teacher than a villain, but you never can tell.

He said, "The front of his vehicle would be damaged too. Probably going to slow him down. Any idea why he'd want to do this to your, um, former fiancé's ride?"

"I have no idea," I said truthfully. "As I said, not my car."

"Did you ever see him before?"

"He tried the same tactic a half hour ago. A tourist couple witnessed the attack, and he took off." I decided not to give their names or to mention the Winnebago, because—as I was learning—you never know.

"Hang on," he said. I hung on while he produced a cell and made a call. At the end, he bent down again. If he launched an attack, I could accelerate and get away while he was off his bike. I planned to travel in the opposite direction from my assailant. I didn't know what the route held, but I could find a side road to hide the car if worse came to worst. But he smiled, waved, and sauntered back to his bike.

"I'll keep an eye out. He won't be hard to spot with that banged-up front end. Did you call it in?"

"No time. I'll make a report in Ingonish. I think that guy might have been after the real owner. I'd rather not hang around, and it's not like the cops are going to be able to do much."

I gave myself a mental kicking for having talked about my fiancé. If my rescuer was involved, I'd given him a heads-up. I said, "I'm okay to drive. Thanks again."

"I'll keep an eye on you," he said. He had a nice voice, smooth and cool, like ice cream. "Got a number where I can reach you if I see the guy again?" You'd think he was asking for a date.

"You can call my friend. He's helping me."

"You mean the geezer back in Baddeck?"

Well, well. So, he'd observed me and Donald Donnie.

"Hey, doggie," he said. Gussie thumped his tail. Mind you, Gussie is no judge of character.

"That's my second cousin from Sydney. He drove me to Baddeck to get my boyfriend's car. He doesn't know him." Mainly I didn't want to be responsible for dragging Donald Donnie any deeper into this mess. He was an innocent—if somewhat annoying—bystander. "But here's a number you can call if you hear any news. Ask for Leonard. He's my ex-fiancé's oldest buddy. Tell him Camilla gave you the number." I tore a page from my notebook and checked the phone. I scrawled down Mombourquette's number. And if I didn't make it or Ray didn't, Leonard Mombourquette would use any information he had to follow up.

My rescuer squinted at the number. "I'll follow you."

"Appreciate it, but I'd be nervous, after what just happened with the Jeep. How about I follow you? I need a couple of minutes to calm down."

He shrugged, then chuckled. "Sure. Nice hat, by the way."

He slipped on his helmet, glanced back, and waved.

I thought hard. The Jeep had not been behind me when I left Baddeck. If the attacker was following Ray, how did he know where to find Ray's car? A black Jeep had passed me in the face of oncoming traffic not long after I got onto the Cabot Trail. Did the driver recognize the Escape?

The biker revved that big Harley engine. I started the Escape and waved back. As he idled at the edge of the road, a tourist bus rolled in and blocked his view of me. I was counting on that. I leapt out of the car and raced to the damaged rear end. I bent down and felt around under the bumper. Sure enough, my fingers encountered a small disc. As I suspected, a transponder. I gave it a yank. It wasn't only police who had access to these devices. Anyone could order one on the Internet. I once had a client whose abusive ex had placed one of those on her car. He showed up wherever she went until he finally snapped and tried to wring her neck. All to say, planting a tracking device was not so legal and not so innocent. Someone had wanted to get the jump on Ray, a seasoned cop with good instincts. Was that why Ray ditched the new baby and departed in such a hurry in the Silverado? But if so, why wouldn't he have notified the local cops instead of abandoning the car and keys?

My new best friend was still idling at the edge of the road, pretending to check out the misty view. I opened the back door of the car. The little calico must have been hiding under the seat, but Gussie was thrilled to get out for a health break. I made a big deal of parading him over to the edge of the cliff, bending slightly to pat him as I passed along the side of the bus. The transponder found a new home. As the bus was pulling out in the opposite direction, I figured this would slow my tracker down.

"Get a move on," I suggested to Gussie. "We've got places to be. Lives to save."

Back in the car, we eased out toward the highway. The biker swung gracefully onto the road and ploughed in front of us. I followed in his wake, keeping a watchful eye in the rear-view. No one was following us, and I hoped to make good time. First Ingonish. Then Cheticamp. I considered letting Alvin or even my brother-in-law know about the attack but settled on Mombourquette again. This time he picked up.

"What now, MacPhee?"

"Check your messages. For the second time in an hour, a guy in a Jeep rammed me right at a look-off. All to say, Ray's new car isn't a virgin anymore. But I wasn't supposed to be driving this car. If you remember, I found it with the keys in it. When that Jeep hit me, I was wearing a baseball cap, Ray's down vest with one of his plaid flannel shirts, and his sunglasses. If you don't care what happens to me, think about Ray. It might be him next time."

"Could it have been an accident?"

"Nope. I told you, he hit me more than once. He backed up and took another a run at me. If it hadn't been for a couple of seniors the first time and then this biker showing up, I'd be upside down and underwater. I love the Atlantic, but I never wanted to be breathing it in."

"Listen—"

"Before you make whatever annoying remark you are about to utter, let me add that I found a transponder planted under the Escape."

"Maybe that transponder was to track you?"

"Except no one knew I'd take Ray's car. If a kid hadn't found his phone, I would never have gone to Baddeck. It was a fluke that I found it."

"I wouldn't worry about it, MacPhee."

"I'm choosing to worry."

"Ray's a big boy. He can take care of himself. I think you should chill. Come home."

My head spun a bit. Mombourquette's reaction didn't make sense. Although he never minded giving me the gears, it wasn't like him not to care about Ray. Any fool could see the problem. And Mombourquette was no fool. Therefore, he was already aware. He was merely distracting me from Ray's whereabouts or activities. Pretty much the same tactic that Ray had employed when he "broke up" with me.

Although people accuse me of being stubborn, I can't hold a candle to Mombourquette when it comes to not budging, so I didn't bother to get flustered.

"Are you going to check out what I've been telling you, Lennie?"

"What part of chill don't you understand, MacPhee?" he said before disconnecting.

We were in a worse mess than I'd thought. Luckily, I had other options. I kept fretting over the transponder. Whoever had planted it had known that was Ray's vehicle and presumably that he would be in Baddeck. That was a head-scratcher. I was betting that the night before, even Ray hadn't known he'd be in Baddeck.

Action was called for. I called my own cell phone. My fingers were crossed that Donald Donnie could figure out how to answer and give me the number I needed next. Luckily, he was getting better.

I gave it fifteen minutes, and then I called Elaine Ekstein on her cell, since I could hardly reach her on Mombourquette's number again without giving myself away.

"Don't say my name," I said when she answered. "Pretend I'm a client and listen. Then decide if you're willing to help me."

"Sure, Jason," she said after a worrying pause. "What's happening?"

I filled her in on the story with Ray since Quebec City in case "Lennie" had kept her in the dark but leaving out my own story and the bit about my mother's grave; that would be a conversation for another time. Elaine was, after all, a social worker, and I wasn't in the mood to be social-worked.

She was uncharacteristically quiet, with a few "No, Jasons" that told me Mombourquette was in the room. I truly regretted ever having introduced them.

I finished with the two attacks on Ray's new car and the discovery of the transponder. "So, do you think that Lennie has an idea of what's going on and is refusing to help me?"

"Well, Jason. It's probably for your own good. There are people you shouldn't hang around with."

"Did he tell you?"

"Best you steer clear of those bad hats. You don't want to violate the terms of your probation."

"Is he planning to get involved?"

"That is correct. And you better believe it."

"Can't you fill me in?"

"I cannot do that, Jason. It would be unprofessional in the extreme."

"Sure. I get your misplaced loyalty, o friend of many years. Can you at least tell me if anyone besides me has contacted him recently on your home phone or his cell? I need numbers."

She sighed one of her huge and famous sighs. I could imagine her shaking that tousled red hair and rolling her large, overly expressive eyes.

"You are altogether too needy, Jason. But I will see what I can do."

"Great. I'll call back. When would be good?"

"Half an hour. But don't get your hopes up."

•••

The guy on the Harley was gone. I pulled back onto the highway, hoping to continue my way around the trail without encountering anyone murderous. When I glanced back into the misty gloom, I got yet another shock.

CHAPTER FIFTEEN
Just tell me what's happening

Donald Donnie MacDonald waved madly at me from a battered, multicoloured vehicle. That meant he was steering with one hand—or possibly none—as he wove around Smokey, inches from certain death. I pulled over onto the shoulder. Donald Donnie shuddered to a stop behind me and scampered up to my window.

"Wow. What happened to you? I bet Ray will be fit to be tied when he sees the rear end of his new—"

"I know Ray loves this car, and he won't be happy. Someone tried to run me off the road."

"I can't believe you wrecked Ray's—"

"To reiterate, I didn't 'wreck' it. Someone tried to kill me."

"Well then, my girl, I can help. Get a load of this baby!"

"You mean that—?"

"What else would I be meaning? Of course! I borrowed it from Loretta's second cousin's nephew, as long as I take good care of it. Loretta wanted the Accord back to get to that there concert of yours in Louisbourg. She got a friend to drive her to Baddeck to pick it up. I was kind of stuck until I made this arrangement. And I think you shouldn't be driving. Whoever took Ray might recognize this vehicle. Although it's pretty wrecked now, so they might not."

Who was he to talk? Donald Donnie had arrived in a Toyota Corolla from the Paleozoic period. It was a sickly shade of green except for one red and one yellow door, rust creeping up from the wheel wells, and plenty of Bondo for added interest. Also, who needs bumpers?

"You're after making yourself a target, my girl, if you know what I mean."

I did know what he meant. The person who'd tried to kill me had obviously considered the Escape a target. But he wouldn't necessarily know about the nephew's car of many colours. The question was, would he know about Donald Donnie? If he lived in Sydney, he might recognize him. On the other hand, in this particular car, Donald Donnie could have been any one of many older, pudgy men with twinkly eyes and a red nose and no hair who might have fallen on tough financial times. He could look even less like himself with the smallest of adjustments. But I couldn't leave Ray's damaged Escape in the look-off, and I suspected my attacker would be back to try again.

"So, what do you say?" Donald Donnie asked, his eyes shining.

"Not much to lose," I grumbled. "Let's find a place to hide Ray's car so it's not obvious. And we can give Gussie and Mrs. Parnell's cat a change of scenery in your, um, vehicle."

"You need a place to hide it. I know the perfect spot."

"'Course you do."

"You know, you're kinda pale, Camilla. You need a cup of coffee and a snack," Donald Donnie said. "That must have been a helluva shock."

The remaining spring roll and the chicken fried rice were now stone-cold and congealed, and my stomach was growling, but I said, "I'm all right."

"Well, I'm hungry, and also I'm no spring chicken."

I had to admit Donald Donnie was the colour of old grout. I hoped coffee and a snack would be enough.

"I know a little restaurant right up the road that's worth a stop. Best apple pie on the island. Practically in the middle of nowhere."

Perhaps his concern for my wellbeing was actually a hankering for apple pie. But I was hungry too. Apple pie sounded nutritious.

"All you need to do, Donald Donnie, is stay behind me on the road, close enough to see if anyone tries to run me off and yet far enough away to avoid running into me."

We rolled on, although the pace was slower because Donald Donnie was, as usual, well under the speed limit. Once I found a half-overgrown side road that offered the right amount of hiding place, I took off the baseball cap, corralled the cat and the dog, and joined Donald Donnie in the Toyota. Gussie barked with joy that we were all together again. The little cat gave us the silent treatment.

A few minutes later, after navigating the last twisty bits of road, we caught sight of Pearl's Pies and Prose, a roughly built café with a couple of rustic picnic tables in front. We parked the multicoloured wonder around the back behind a clump of trees, hoping for a little anonymity. The front door had weathered dark red paint. Someone had made a half-hearted attempt to scrub off a bit of graffiti that said *NO POETRY*.

Inside were four rickety wooden tables and an assortment of faded plastic garden chairs. Mass-market paperbacks with curling covers peered out from a bricks-and-board bookcase on one wall. The counter was presided over by a tiny soul with buzz-cut silver hair, sharp black eyes, and a raspy voice. For some reason she made me think of a badger. She wore a faded Grateful Dead T-shirt, an apron, and a faint dusting of flour. She wasn't a smiler.

I was thankful that Donald Donnie did not know either Pearl or the three denim-shirted locals in the café. I didn't think I could bear another conversation with a stranger, much less a dose of iambic pentameter.

The coffee smelled heavenly. I got black, no sugar for me, and a triple-triple for Donald Donnie. His next triple might be a bypass. The aroma of fresh pies was enticing. Donald Donnie had trouble choosing from apple, raspberry, blueberry, cherry, lemon meringue, and chocolate cream.

A teenager in frayed jeans slung low enough to display the Stanfield band on his jockeys leaned languidly against the counter, chatting. On second glance, he was probably early twenties, with a jaw that you could use to cut glass, black hair, and deep blue eyes, slightly unfocused. Even the backward baseball cap couldn't detract from his face. More than one girl would have fallen hard for that lad. I listened to him shoot the breeze, finding myself slightly hypnotized by the bright tattoo that ran up his bare arm. Who knew you could have a theme with a killer whale, roses, and Celtic crosses? I'd learned from some of my clients that these "sleeves" are pricy and painful. He didn't appear to be buying pie.

"So, yeah," he said, "Like last week I swapped the engine from Uncle

Hughie's old truck into my Saturn, eh. It's friggin' awesome. That baby'll go like a rocket."

Pearl kindly stifled a yawn.

I knew the type, a lost boy who could easily find himself in all kinds of trouble with the law. The kind of kid who'd get used by dealers and other lowlifes and would end up as collateral damage unless some young woman settled him down. I felt like giving him a bit of advice, but I knew it would be a waste of breath.

"Like, I'm here for the weekend, so let me know if ya want any pie deliveries, Gran. Glad to help."

"I'll call if I need ya, Cody." Her hands didn't pause as she cut strips from dough to make the lattice tops for the next batch of fruit pies. "You better come for dinner though."

"Okay then," he said.

"You need gas money?"

"Nah. Just filled up at the pump."

"Help yourself to coffee and pie."

Cody picked the largest piece of chocolate cream plus a hunk of coconut cream and made for the coffee station. He smiled the smile of a hungry boy who'd scored. Pearl's lips twitched. It softened her wizened face.

Cody shot us a speculative glance as he slouched by with his snack, maybe wondering if we needed a delivery.

As Donald Donnie finally settled on blueberry and lemon meringue, I hunched over my coffee and tried to figure out what exactly had happened. The odds were that someone wanted to kill Ray. Or stop him. Or wreck his vehicle. Back in Baddeck, Donnie Red had said he'd recognized Ray from his days on the Sydney force. He might not have been alone. People can hold serious grudges against cops. Despite the upbeat island personality, Cape Breton had its fair share of bad guys.

So how was that connected with Ray's hasty departure in the Silverado? A departure that may or may not have involved force or coercion. Evidence for voluntary departure was the message he'd left for me on our home phone: totally calculated to get me to leave Cape Breton in a flaming snit. Evidence for involuntary was leaving the car unlocked with the keys in it and not stopping to retrieve his phone.

What were the chances that one person could practically kidnap him and on the same day a different person would try to kill him? How was any of it connected with the Sandy Someone, Pierre Forgeron, and the mysterious Matty's death? And Kenny, of course, let's not forget Kenny.

I chewed my lower lip and worked on sorting that out while Donald Donnie slurped his triple-triple and smacked his lips over the pies, quiet as a freight train. Every time he opened his mouth to speak, I held up a hand to silence him.

"That's not nice, Camilla."

"I need to think."

At least then he went quiet, except for an injured sniff. I sat running possibilities through my mind. None of the possibilities made any sense.

The front door of the café jingled.

"Oh, no," Donald Donnie whispered.

"What?" I whirled to see.

"Don't stare," he mouthed.

"Well, it's a bit late to bring that up." I turned back to my coffee. "What's your problem?"

"That's Rita Susanne Kelly."

Wasn't that the same woman who was helping out my Auntie Annie? I was supposed to have a gift intended for her. Oops. Had I given it to Donald Donnie and Loretta? Or consumed it myself? Damn.

I had to ask. "And why is she a problem?"

"She's not a problem. She has plenty of problems of her own to deal—"

He blanched as a tall, angular woman ambled straight toward our table.

"Rita Susanne? Is that you? Lord love a duck, dear. I'd a known you anywheres."

Rita Susanne had tanned skin and the kind of deep wrinkles that told of smiling in the summer sun for fifty years. Her short brown hair was shot with silver. I liked her style, from the pale blue scrubs with Mickey Mouse on the top to the sturdy lime-green clogs on her feet and the whiff of baby powder, a scent I've always loved. God knows why. She had plenty of muscle too. She'd need it in her job.

She obviously didn't feel the cold, even in October. All to say, I felt overdressed in my plaid shirt and vest. Not to mention the not-so-lucky hat.

"Well, I hope you'd know me, Donald Donnie. It's only been two weeks since we saw each other."

"Ah, but I'm getting on, dear. Don't even buy unripe bananas anymore."

She managed a hearty laugh at the old joke, perhaps not a hundred percent sincere.

I sat back to ignore the banter when Donald Donnie had to go ruin the mood.

"So sorry for your troubles, dear."

A shadow passed over the cheerful face.

Donald Donnie fumbled for his words. "Loretta said she was talking to you just the other night in Sydney. I bet she knew just the right thing to say. Not like me, but I mean well."

Rita Susanne softened. "Indeed, Loretta did know the right thing to say. But thank you for your kind thoughts, Donald Donnie. That's what matters. And you know, we all do our best to cope when trouble comes knocking. Easy-peasy if you have the right attitude."

"Speaking of that, if you're talking to Loretta, dear, don't, um, be telling her that you saw me here."

A small furrow appeared between her eyebrows. She glanced at me. She put her hands on her broad hips. "And why would that be, Donald Donnie?"

I couldn't have her thinking Donald Donnie and I were an "item." I stuck out my hand. "Donald Donnie's my cousin, and he's helping me scout out my fiancé, who may have decided to back out of our wedding. I'd rather Loretta didn't know that part. A bit embarrassing."

She stared. "I'm sorry—?"

"You know what they say, men are like buses. There's always another one coming along shortly."

Donald Donnie said, "You don't have to hide your true feelings, Camilla."

"Trust me. I'm not hiding my true feelings, and my dominant emotion at the moment is pissed off."

He gasped and said, "Rita Susanne used to nurse at Cape Breton Regional when Loretta worked with her, until she took leave and moved back up here to Ingonish."

I barely avoided saying "And?" It wasn't always easy to follow his line of thought.

She chuckled. "I've heard the words 'pissed off' before."

I switched topics. "Do you live near here? By any chance did you see a silver Silverado with a couple of guys come by?"

She turned serious. "But shouldn't you let him go? Wait for the next bus, so to speak?"

"Nope. He's been after me to get married for years. And if he wants out, he damn well better tell me to my face."

"Makes sense. Sorry, I didn't notice a Silverado. But we have lots of pickups around here. They call them Fort Mac trucks. I'll keep my eyes open, though."

"Sure. What about a black Jeep? Did you happen to notice one of those?"

She blinked. "How many of these fellas do you have?"

I rustled up a reasonably convincing laugh. "This guy tried to run me off the road up on Smokey."

From behind the counter, Pearl watched our encounter, her inky eyes bright with interest.

Donald Donnie said, "Maybe not all Camilla's fault."

Not all my fault? Before I could glare at him, Rita Susanne gave me a hearty slap on the back. "You're having one hell of a day, my friend. I thought I did see a black Jeep go by like a bat out of hell less than an hour ago, but I had a lot on my mind, and I wasn't paying much attention. Pearl, give my friends each a slice of your finest for the road. I'll settle up with you tomorrow, along with these." She helped herself to a large coffee and snapped the lid on it. She picked up a pair of pie boxes and headed for the door.

I started to say, "No thanks, we're in a—"

Donald Donnie glowed. "Well, thank you, Rita Susanne."

Rita Susanne gave a nod—a wave would have been impossible with that load. "Give my love to Loretta. She's a grand girl." She glanced outside at Cody, who was enjoying a cigarette with his coffee, his pie container resting on the hood. She turned back and said to Pearl. "What's going to become of that lad?"

Pearl bristled. "Kid stuff. He'll grow out of it."

"I hope you're right, before he kills someone with one of his idiotic stunts." Rita Susanne strode to her zippy little green Fiesta, stopping briefly near Cody. From the expressions on both their faces, I assumed she'd just offered him a bit of life advice.

All that talk about Silverados and Jeeps and killing people had given me a pain in the rearus endus. I narrowed my eyes at Cody and speculated about what he'd been up to. Rita Susanne had definitely been referring to some transgression. B&E? Cooking meth? Mugging? Nah. Cody was not the type for mugging.

Donald Donnie decided on blueberry for the next round. Pearl waited for me with her silver eyebrows raised. I said, "My friend will have mine. Thanks."

Donald Donnie lit up. "Chocolate cream, in that case."

As Pearl cut his serving, she said to me, "And you should have a wee one yourself. After all, it's been paid for."

It would have been rude to refuse and, in fact, I was starving. With only cold Chinese food in my near future, I wasn't sure why I had refused earlier. I pointed to the apple pie, fresh out of the oven, judging by the wonderful aroma.

Pearl slipped a slice on a plate for me and thoughtfully added some French vanilla ice cream. "I thought I saw those guys go by earlier."

Donald Donnie said, "What guys?"

"The ones in the truck your friend was asking about." She nodded in my direction. "You sure you don't want to try another flavour too? I got a custard cream everyone's talking about. I can give you a sliver."

"Sure. Thanks a lot. Did you happen to notice where the truck was heading?"

"They were off toward Smokey in a jeazly hurry. Lucky they didn't kill no one."

"When was this?"

"Maybe half an hour ago. I'd just put that last batch of apple pies in the oven."

"Thanks. Good to know."

"You might catch up if they stop. Those big pickups go through gas like crazy," she said raspily.

"I'm counting on it."

I took my pie to the table to join Donald Donnie, who was making short work of the chocolate cream. I did overhear a bit of grumbling from some of the other customers about special treatment for people who come from away.

Donald Donnie puffed himself up and stated loudly that *he* had not come from away. I took the time to eat both slices of pie. They were not slivers. When the pies were finished and our faces wiped, I sauntered back to the counter.

"I'll do what Rita Susanne did and take a pie to go. That chocolate cream pie will do the trick." I had a pleasant vision of mashing it in Ray's face, but it would be a shame to waste such a treat on revenge. "Happy to pay," I added, fishing out my cash. I left enough for a tip.

Donald Donnie was sad to leave. The other customers gave us the stink-eye as we wandered out back to the car. Cody was gone.

"She was lying." We were still in the scrubby parking lot in back of Pearl's Pies.

"Who was?"

"Pearl."

"About what?" Donald Donnie's eyes were huge.

"No way did that truck zoom down the road a half hour earlier. I could not have failed to see it, even when the killer Jeep was ramming me. That Silverado was top of my fevered mind. So, no missing it. Hard to know why she lied without confronting her—"

"Oh Lord, Camilla. Don't be confronting her! Loretta will have my guts for garters if I get into an argument up here."

"You need to find out who she's connected to."

"I'll make some calls as soon as I catch my breath." He did a pretty good job of simulating a mild asthma attack as he started the car.

When we left, I couldn't resist a glance at the café. Pearl stood in the front door, arms crossed, watching us with what I imagined were flinty eyes. I waved merrily.

We sprayed a little gravel as we peeled out to pick up the Escape.

Donald Donnie said, "But I've been thinking. Pearl coulda made a mistake. Lots of people have trouble with directions. I think she was upset about her young lad."

"My fat fanny," I snapped. "You can't mistake Smokey."

Conversation lagged a bit after that. Fine with me. Donald Donnie had an idea of where we might leave the Escape. It was worth a try. He waited in the Toyota as I got back into Ray's car. When the phone rang, I answered breathlessly, thinking that Elaine would have a bit of news.

"Camilla? Is that you? What are you doing on Ray's phone?" My sister Edwina's voice nearly blew out my eardrum.

"More to the point, why are *you* calling Ray? How did you even get the number?"

"Don't try to change the subject."

"There is no subject. And I'm in a meeting. I'll call you back."

"You are not in a meeting, and you never call back."

"But this time I mean it."

"Two points, missy. First, you're the one who shouldn't be on Ray's phone. Men need their privacy. Second, I was calling Ray because *he* wouldn't lie to me about your intentions in going to Sydney."

I let the men need their privacy item slide. If my sister wanted to live in the Victorian age, she was welcome to it. She could put skirts on the piano legs while she was at it. "I have to go, Edwina."

"Your family put up with your first elopement. Now we are entitled to see you married properly in a decent dress and with suitable witnesses so that we don't have to be mortified in the parish."

"Entitled? Goodbye, Edwina."

"Yes, entitled, and if you won't think of me, think of Daddy. We should be attending your wedding and celebrating. We can make it a proper occasion instead of some furtive and slipshod affair. You cannot sneak off and get married down East like common criminals."

Furtive. Slipshod. Common criminals. I didn't get sucked in.

"I'm on Cape Smokey. Bad reception." I wasn't actually near Smokey, but no point in wasting the truth on Edwina. And speaking of the truth, I noticed she hadn't alluded to her treatment of Alvin over the "mother" issue. I knew that she wanted to talk to Ray about getting me off that topic. I didn't plan to mention our "mother" because I had enough to deal with and anyway, I didn't know yet if the date on the gravestone was an error. But the time would come.

"Yes, and speaking of receptions, you will need flowers and a cake and toasts, and you need to be wearing a decent dress. Not white, of course."

"No worries. I will not sneak off to marry Ray Deveau. I will not marry him under any circumstances, and let me assure you that I will no longer sully the family name by living in sin with him. You're cutting out, Edwina."

She was in the middle of an outraged squawk when I pressed *END*. It was the first time that I felt good since Ray took off. Except for the pie.

The phone rang again. I'd taken a chance with the previous call because Elaine was supposed to get back to me. Her phone also said *UNKNOWN NUMBER*, a privacy consideration required in her social work practice. Oh, well. I could always hang up on Edwina again if it came to that. I'd be paying the price for this whole trip for the rest of my life anyway.

But it was Elaine, whispering, "Leonard has stepped out to the garage."

"Did you get the numbers from his phone?"

"God help me. I can't believe I did this to the perfect man. Get your pen ready."

I didn't ruin the moment by laughing out loud at the notion of Leonard Mombourquette as the perfect man. More like the perfect mouse.

"Shoot." I pulled out my notebook and wrote fast as she reeled off the numbers. I recognized the 514 and the 902 numbers.

"They're talking to the same people, Elaine."

"Not surprising. They have a long history together, and they're related. And what about all the cop friends? Oops. He's coming back in. This call never happened."

She hung up before I could say "what call?"

I was kicking myself because I hadn't asked her about Pierre Forgeron and Sandy Somebody or Kenny Somebody Else before she hung up in my ear. I should have been grateful that I'd planted a little seed of suspicion. Elaine and Mombourquette had been most irritatingly besotted ever since they fell for each other. For a long time, I'd thought they played the happy game to annoy me, but after a few years I'd accepted it was real.

Now I needed to find a phone that wouldn't show as Ray's. I could call Elaine back, and she could once again pretend to talk to some imbecilic client. But what phone would that be? Didn't matter, because a few minutes later, she called me.

"Camilla?" Elaine was breathless, even for her.

"Oh course it's Camilla." I knew I had to be calm, but it was getting harder by the second.

"Leonard's gone," she wailed.

That was alarming. Elaine may induce wailing in others, but she's pretty steady herself.

"What do you mean?"

"What do you think I mean? He's gone! He left!"

Cautiously, I said, "Wasn't he just in the garage? Gone where?"

"I don't know. He booked a flight."

"Sit down."

"How do you know I'm standing up?"

"Put your head between your knees. And pull yourself together."

Time ticked by as Elaine pulled herself together.

"Okay," she said at last.

"That's better. Where's he gone?"

"He booked a flight to Halifax. I don't know where he's going after."

"Cape Breton," I said.

"Wouldn't he fly all the way?"

"Nah. The schedule's tricky. The next flight's probably not until ten tonight or so. It used to make Ray crazy. Leonard can fly to Halifax and drive faster."

"You think he'll drive to Sydney? But isn't that about five hours from Halifax?"

"Maybe four the way Lennie speeds."

"Oh my God! Those roads. I've seen pictures. Sheer drops!"

That was rich, Elaine worrying about Mombourquette's driving. Elaine was arguably the worst driver in the world. Sidewalks and streets were pretty much the same to her, and lanes of no concern. Still I wanted her to focus.

I said soothingly. "Don't worry about it. I doubt if he's going to Sydney. I think he knows where Ray is, and it's on the north of the island. Ingonish or beyond. Have you visited?"

"No. We were planning on it when—"

"Did Lennie ever mention anyone he knew in Ingonish?"

It was good that Elaine had never driven over Smokey.

"A colleague from the police force. I think."

"Would he visit this guy?"

"I don't think it was a close relationship. But they've been talking."

"What about a Pierre Forgeron? Somewhere in New Brunswick?"

"I'm all stressed. I can hardly think straight. No. I don't know anything about New Brunswick. Stop badgering me."

"Concentrate. So, Leonard's flying into Halifax airport and renting a car?"

"He bought a one-way ticket, Camilla! What does that mean? Ray left you. Do you think Leonard has—?"

"It means he doesn't know when he's coming back. He'll buy the return ticket when he does. Take another deep breath. Don't worry. He's not leaving you."

She shuddered. "Business class. Does that sound like Leonard?"

I snorted. "Are you kidding? The guy's as cheap as a ten-dollar suit."

"Frugal! Not cheap."

"He probably had no choice if he wanted to leave right away. Did he say what flight?"

"He said he was barely going to make it. He called a buddy to drive him to the airport with the siren on."

That was really bad. A cop can get into a lot of trouble doing that. Leonard was retired, but whoever helped him had taken one hell of a risk.

"Do you have the friend's name?"

"Don't try to bully me. He refused to say a word. I know about the ticket because he booked it with our credit card. I checked online."

Our credit card. How quaint was that?

"Can you check what kind of car he rented and from which company?"

"I don't know how to do that. Wouldn't he just pick one up when he arrives?"

"You can get to Halifax airport and find out that there's not a single car available. Leonard knows that. Then what would he do? Take a cab all around the Cabot Trail? Is there another credit card he could use?"

"Give me a minute," she said, sniffling.

I knew Mombourquette. It would be a mid-size or even a full-size sedan. He always loved those old Crown Vics the cops drove back in the day. So, a Buick or a Lincoln. But being Lennie, it would be from Budget or Thrifty. Or even Rent-a-Wreck.

"Got it," Elaine said.

"Great. Can you give me the rental company phone number?"

"Back off, Camilla!"

I tried to protest until I realized she was actually checking. I copied the info as she read it and said, "You're a true friend, Elaine, and I owe you."

After I hung up, I asked myself if she'd been crying. But that wouldn't be like Elaine.

Next, I checked the flight schedules into Halifax on Ray's phone. Air Canada's five thirty flight would be arriving at eight thirty, if all went well.

I consulted Google directions. Assuming Leonard's flight was on schedule and giving him enough time to pick up his car rental, it would take him about three hours to reach Cape Breton. Everyone had to cross the Canso Causeway to drive onto the island. Leonard should come barrelling over between ten thirty and eleven thirty. He did drive like a bat out of a bad place, but plenty could go wrong.

My money was on his destination being Ingonish, since that was where Ray and the Silverado were said to be heading, but he might choose Sydney or somewhere else instead. If I caught Mombourquette as he came off the causeway, I wouldn't need to guess what highway he'd take. Unlike me, he seemed to know what was going on. I planned to capitalize on that. I could be at the causeway in plenty of time. The entire day had unfolded in slow-mo anyway. It would be faster if I backtracked, but I saw no point in being early. I'd continue on the assumption that the Silverado would be in Ingonish or possibly Cheticamp. If I found it, I could save myself the aggro of intercepting Mombourquette.

Best to keep going while watching for the killer Jeep and the Silverado. Even if they'd gone to Cheticamp or one of the Acadian communities on the French shore of Cape Breton, I might catch up. Of course, I'd have to get the Toyota away from Donald Donnie.

I did a shoulder check from the passenger seat, since Donald Donnie had failed to do one from the driver's side. No Silverado. No Jeep.

We picked up Ray's car, and Donald Donnie and I drove convoy again. All we needed was a place to tuck the Escape, and we might even make it alive.

CHAPTER SIXTEEN
Fresh oatcakes at the hideout

Donald Donnie, it turned out, had a third cousin twice removed on his mother's side who lived in a farm near one of the various Ingonish communities. This was no relation to the guy who owned the Toyota. Other side of the family. This cousin would probably know who Ray was and also his friends. He might be able to tell us about the mysterious Sandy. With the fog gone, the late afternoon light added a pleasing golden haze to the brilliant red and sugar maple trees.

We bounced up a rutted access road to an older farmhouse with a cluster of outbuildings. Dark cedars fringed the edge of the lawn. A vintage dust-coloured Dodge Ram was parked outside the farmhouse. A collection of bumper stickers celebrated the island, including one for the Cape Breton Liberation Army and another promoting puffins. The house was a two-storey saltbox with fading blue paint on the clapboard. I opened the car window, and from the house I could hear a dog taking issue with our arrival.

"Be quiet, Brutus," a man bellowed.

I glanced around, assessing. What kind of person keeps a raging beast called Brutus? The place seemed to be in reasonable repair. Yes, the blue paint could do with a refresh, and the one-storey shed at the side was painted an even more faded blue, but the garden seemed well tended, with bright sunflowers waving cheerfully.

My sisters would have commented that the windows were clean. A large, newish red barn and two other weathered outbuildings stood near the edge of the lot. I parked the Escape out of sight on the far side of the barn. I finally forced myself to examine the rear of the vehicle. We were

in for thousands in repairs. The worst possible additional damage might
be a bit of chicken guano. I didn't spot any chickens.

The dog hadn't stopped barking, although his owner kept shouting.
Donald Donnie beckoned me back to his purely temporary car. He kept
explaining why this was a safe place. "You see, we can leave Ray's car
here without worrying because this here's Calum MacDonald's place,
and Calum's mother was—"

I held up a hand. Gussie barked joyfully.

I wasn't sure when I'd be back in Ray's new baby, so I made sure to
stuff his phone charger into my pocket. If Ray's phone quit, life would
get even worse. As I transferred the pets once again into the Corolla,
Gussie leaned in to nuzzle my ear and the calico cat clung to my lap. A
first. I staggered over with the duffle bag. And finally, in case we needed
them for bribes or rewards, I lugged the box with all the gifts from my
sisters.

"We'll let them know you're leaving the car here. Then where to?"
Donald Donnie said.

"Somewhere we can get some disguises."

"Disguises! That would be great. What do you have in mind?"

I'd been more or less kidding. "Given where we are, I'd say ball caps
and sunglasses. Denim shirts."

"Oh. But we already have those."

"Mine have been seen. Yours too. We need different ones. Pick up the
pace."

A tall, rangy man with weathered brown skin appeared from the side
door of the farmhouse and loped toward us. He had on muddy overalls
and a green John Deere cap. He smiled broadly. He had a mouthful of
even white teeth, a bit big for his mouth. It wasn't a smile you could
resist. I found myself smiling back. Ignoring the fact we'd been trespass-
ing, Donald Donnie introduced us to his cousin Calum, another Mac-
Donald. No doubt they went back to some Outer Hebridean island in the
eighteenth century. Calum had no problem with me leaving the Escape
behind until my fiancé "got back." "Sure. Leave her up behind the barn.
No trouble."

Donald Donnie kept alluding to a mysterious venture we were involved in. It sounded like we'd meet with Miss Moneypenny and Q any minute.

I shook Calum's callused hand and pointed at his quite ordinary ball cap. "Any idea where we can get a couple of hats like that? I'm worried about sunburn."

He was too polite to point out that this was fall in Cape Breton, and an hour earlier the fog had been thick as cotton batten. Sunstroke probably wasn't the biggest local problem.

"I probably got half a dozen of them. How many d'ya need?" As they say, don't ask, don't get. "Come on in the house for a bite. We'll see what we can find for ya."

Come in? *No, no, no.* We absolutely did not have the time to have a Cape Breton kitchen party while Ray was being kidnapped and/or murdered.

"I wouldn't say no to a cup a tea," Donald Donnie said.

"Yesss you would," I hissed at him like a black-and-white movie villain. "You just had a mountain of pie."

"Sure, that was a while back, and I would not say no to tea," he said, affronted.

I juggled the gift box so I could jab at his plaid shirt pocket. "We are in a hurry. And you had coffee at Pearl's. Do you want to explode and splatter all over the wall?"

"Simply a cup of tea, my girl. We're not inviting ourselves to dinner. Although…"

I decided to cut my losses and agree to tea, since I could use the facilities and Gussie needed a break. I figured the calico cat might have felt nature's call as well. I only ended up with one scratch when I hooked up her harness.

"We need to find out if he knows Pierre Forgeron or this Sandy person. Or Kenny," I said through clenched teeth. "You ask, because I don't want to talk about Ray and me and all that. I'll catch up when I've taken care of the animals." I took my time, and if you've ever walked a cat, you'll know you're not in charge of the schedule. Finally, the little calico was settled back in the Corolla, curled up on Donald Donnie's jacket, shedding briskly in three colours. The house dog continued to sound off about our arrival. Calum claimed that Brutus was eighty pounds, equal parts bad attitude and muscle.

Calum had a soft, round wife, Sherry, who acted happy to see us, even me, although we'd never met before, and Gussie, who she hadn't gotten a whiff of yet. Before Sherry came out of the house, wiping her hands on her apron, she'd hooked the large dog onto a chain. She had silver waves to her shoulders, a face that could grace a magazine cover, and her own teeth to smile with. Her outfit appeared to have come from Hippies R Us. I figured she was closing in on fifty, and those fifty years had been kind to her.

Brutus, mostly German Shepherd and unwelcoming, hurled himself to the end of his chain, snarling. Speaking of teeth, his looked like they'd been recently sharpened. Donald Donnie gulped and jumped back. "He's probably hungry."

"Don't be silly, Brutus," Sherry said as we entered the house. "Come in and sit down, please. Brutus has to learn some manners. We won't let you back in, you naughty boy, until you behave yourself."

Brutus made a big deal about settling down outside. He lay down, put his big head on his paws, and whined unconvincingly.

In the kitchen, I offered Sherry one of Edwina's prize jars of strawberry jam and took a seat on a wooden chair out of biting range in case Brutus propelled himself through the screen door. He howled.

Calum said, "Shut up, Brutus. These are guests."

Sherry said, "Be a good boy, Brutus." Even the dog was under the spell of her potent smile.

Her husband muttered about "that spoiled dog" and pointed to the door to the adjoining room. Brutus whined again. Sherry said, "He has to learn to be in company."

"He has to learn who's in charge," Calum said in his slow, calm voice.

I was voting with Calum on this one.

Sherry brought Brutus into the kitchen and steered him through the door. The big dog slumped through it, complaining as he went. Despite the flimsiness of the door and the disposition of the dog, I found myself relaxing. Donald Donnie lit up with relief.

Once the danger passed, I could admire the old-fashioned kitchen, with its farm sink, and the home-built daybed in the corner. Someone—I assumed Sherry—liked puffins. There were puffin photos and cartoons and a puffin cushion on the day bed. Two mixing bowls and some ingredients sat on the countertop, along with a wooden rolling pin and two sets of puffin salt and pepper shakers.

"Sorry 'bout that," Calum said. "He's a rescue and not used to us yet."

Sherry couldn't resist adding, "He needs humane treatment."

Donald Donnie said, "Well, this here's my second cousin, Camilla MacPhee. She's a liar from Ottawa."

"Lawyer," I stuck in quickly. "He means lawyer."

Donald Donnie quivered with laughter at his own lame joke.

"MacPhee from Sydney? So, who's your father?" Calum said, leaning forward with interest.

"Donald MacPhee," Donald Donnie said. "He ended up a bigwig in them schools up in Ottawa."

I shot him a disapproving look. "He became a high school principal. Of course, he's ninety now, so that was a while back."

"Ninety, is he?" Calum said with amazement.

"My heavens," Sherry said. "Isn't that grand."

I supposed it was, although my father's recall was lessening by the month, and he'd always had trouble remembering me. Of course, now I knew why. I smiled as sincerely as I could.

Alarm flitted across their faces. I guess my sincere smile still needed work.

"Well," Calum said, "did his people come from East Bay then?"

I shrugged. "Couldn't tell you."

Calum and Sherry raised their eyebrows. Donald Donnie flapped his hands in apparent alarm and tried to rescue the moment with a little genealogy. "Camilla's grandfather's family was from Inverness, and then they moved to Glace Bay to work in the mines. Those MacPhees worked in the mines, except for Donald, Camilla's father, who went off to St. F.X. on a scholarship. Her grandfather was Lauchie MacPhee. His mother was Mary Margaret MacDonald, a sister to my grandmother, Callista. This here Camilla's mother was also Camilla. She was a Gallivan from New Waterford."

It was enough to put you into a coma. I had picked up on the idea that I was an oddball by not knowing where my father was "from."

Unfortunately for me, Calum and Sherry enjoyed visitors. They'd forgotten their spat about the murderous new dog. The tea was strong enough to strip the finish off the antique pine dresser in the corner. I put plenty of milk in mine and added two teaspoons of sugar for added security.

All was quiet for a couple of minutes. I used the time to ponder why I didn't know where my father was from. It was never part of conversations when I was growing up.

Since I didn't want to be rude, I accepted a couple of traditional oatcakes. It hadn't been long since Pearl and her pies, but I decided it would be better to keep my strength up, since I didn't know what challenges we faced. Sherry opened the door and let Gussie into the kitchen. He fell in love with her immediately and parked himself by her feet.

While Donald Donnie babbled, I did the math about the trip to the causeway in the crumbling Toyota.

"Where are you off to then?" Sherry said.

"Visiting relatives," I said, accepting another oatcake. You could taste the butter and brown sugar in them. "These are wonderful."

She smiled and sauntered across the kitchen to turn on the oven, although it was already quite warm in the room. "Eat up. I'm just making more."

More?

"We're hunting for Ray Deveau," Donald Donnie said. "He's Camilla's fiancé, but he buggered off. Know him? He's about your age."

I shook my head frantically.

Sherry said, "Ray Deveau?"

I was bored with playing the betrayed woman. "I'll hand over his belongings before I fly back to Ottawa. That's why we need to leave his car here. It's a long and hilarious story how he lost it."

"Is he a Deveau from out by Cheticamp?" Calum wanted to know. Sherry stared off vacantly. Maybe she was still back at Ray losing his car.

I was proud that I could say yes.

"And is he related to the ones in Glace Bay?"

Donald Donnie said, "No connections in The Bay far as I know."

I pointed to my full mouth to indicate that I would have provided a family tree if only I hadn't gobbled the latest oatcake.

Sherry stood up and began sifting flour into the larger bowl. "I knew Ray Deveau from Cheticamp, way back."

"And you?" I asked Calum.

Calum scrunched his deeply tanned neck and admitted he wasn't sure. Sherry said, "Ray went to college with Frankie Kelly, honey." She flushed and then went back to sifting flour, adding salt and baking powder, simple ingredients that I recognized.

Donald Donnie's face fell again. "Och indeed, Frankie. Terrible news about poor Francis Xavier. I knew his mother. She was related to my Loretta on her father's side. She always had a weakness for the double names. Not the easiest fella, but they sure had a boatload of illness and trouble in that family. And now this."

Sherry nodded as if this was a normal conversation. She beat an egg and whisked in some vanilla and brown sugar. She cut in the butter with a metal pastry cutter, the type I remembered my sisters using. The egg, sugar, and vanilla mixture went into the bowl. I don't know why I was so fascinated, but I can't image baking without a recipe, or even with one. "Well," she said, "Frankie was always trouble for sure."

Calum and Donald Donnie nodded sagely. In seconds, Sherry picked up the rolling pin, scattered some flour onto it, and rolled out the dough, deftly cutting it into diamond shapes.

While I was oddly fascinated by Sherry's baking and the sight of her dropping the oatcakes on the baking sheet using a spatula, Donald Donnie was droning on about this and that. "We saw Rita Susanne today at the pie shop. I didn't know what to say about Francis Xavier. What do you say when the cancer's hit another member of a person's family? First the mother, then the father, and now Francis. How can she cope with that?" He sighed heavily and gazed into his mug of tea as though he expected to find answers.

This was my opening. I said, "Tell us about Pearl at the pie shop."

Sherry paused as she slid the baking tray into the hot oven. Donald Donnie's eyes popped. Calum frowned and scratched his chin. Gussie cocked his head at me too. Apparently, I was quite a unique specimen.

"I mean," I said, "she looks familiar. She must be related to someone I know, but I can't put my finger on who that might be."

"Pearl?" Sherry said. "What is her last name? I should know that. She's always just Pearl."

"Gouthro," Calum said.

"Oooh. One of the Arichat Gouthros?" Donald Donnie asked for no good reason.

Calum shrugged. "Been here forever as far as I know. She opened the shop a few years back, after her husband died."

Gouthro. I'd been hoping that it would be one of the names I was interested in learning more about. But I thought Gouthro might be French and could have meant another Cheticamp connection. Relatives? Friends? Could that be why Pearl lied about the truck?

"Does she have children?"

"Do you even know any Gouthros?" Donald Donnie asked me, forgetting whose side he was supposed to be on. I shot him a warning glance in case he asked for the names and ages of the imaginary Gouthros.

Calum said, "She had a son, but he died out West. Industrial accident in Fort Mac. She's just got the one grandson, I think."

I glanced at the clock and stared meaningfully at Donald Donnie. He didn't get the hint that it was time to go. But then I thought that these people might know who Sandy or Kenny were.

As I opened my mouth to ask, Sherry spoke over her shoulder, "Did she seem all right what with Frankie's situation and all?"

I said, "Who? Pearl?"

"Rita Susanne. She's Francis Xavier's sister," Donald Donnie said. "I thought you were aware of all that."

Sherry added, "Frankie was a police officer before he went on medical leave for…" She paused and blew her nose. "He was a bigwig."

"And now the big C.A.'s got him," Calum said with a slump of his shoulders. Things were starting to make a bit of sense, although in a sad way. This must have been why Donald Donnie had been so tongue-tied with Rita Susanne at Pearl's. The big C.A. can make people edgy.

Donald Donnie sighed. "Loretta tells me it's the end of the line for

Frankie, and here he's hardly fifty. He was such a star as a lad, smart, athletic, he had it all. Everyone had high hopes for him. The parents thought the sun shone out of his—of course, he had a grand career with the Mounties."

I didn't care about Francis and his sun-shiny rear end. "So, if this Frankie was a police officer, do you think he'd know Ray?" I said. "We should drop in on him."

You'd think I'd suggested an armed shoplifting spree.

"He's not seeing anybody, he's so terribly ill. Nothing but skin and bone. I doubt if he has more than a few days left," Sherry said with a catch in her voice. "Father Tim was called for last rites. Frankie won't see anyone."

Donald Donnie's eyes welled up. "The pain and the drugs were affecting his mind, Loretta said."

"Right. Well, this has been lovely." I did my best to infuse my voice with sincerity. "Do you mind if I use your—?"

Always choose indoor plumbing. It's a much better idea than hunkering behind a juniper in the woods.

"Down the hall. You can't miss it," Sherry said.

CHAPTER SEVENTEEN
Going undercover

While washing my hands with lavender-scented soap and wondering where exactly Sherry could have purchased that puffin soap dish, a beautiful, framed photo of a beach caught my eye, reminding me of a question I should have asked before.

Back in the kitchen, I said, "By the way, Ray might be visiting an old friend named Sandy here in Ingonish. Do you know who that would be?"

Sherry shook her silver tresses and laughed. "You're funny."

Calum grinned. "Sandy? We have lots of those around here. What's the last name? Beach?"

Defeated again, I asked about Kenny. I shrugged as everyone guffawed. Apparently there were wall-to-wall Kennys.

Sherry said, "You'd better take some oatcakes with you in case you want to have a little snack on the road. In a couple of minutes, you can have them fresh out of the oven."

We'd just finished hoovering the previous batch. "Oh, we don't—"

"You're a grand gal, Sherry. And you're a lucky man, Calum." Donald Donnie glanced admiringly at Sherry, although the hummingbird tattoo on her forearm seemed to catch him by surprise.

"And we're way behind." I would have made tracks without a word, but we did have Ray's car hidden on their property and I'm aware that politeness pays off.

As I reached the door, I heard a roar of an engine. A massive blue motorcycle shot up the hill, slowing to a stop in the front yard.

"Who's that?" Calum said.

Sherry shook her silver hair. "Better go see."

Donald Donnie said, "Is that the guy who showed up when they tried to run you off the road, Camilla?"

Calum's jaw dropped. Sherry's eyes widened.

I said, "Donald Donnie's a bit nervous because of an incident on the trail today. A Jeep nearly pushed me through the guardrail at one of the look-offs. I was driving Ray's vehicle, but no one knew that. A guy on a motorcycle intervened, but that was a Harley, black not blue. But this guy is another reason we needed to tuck away Ray's new car and travel in Donald Donnie's, um, vehicle."

They both stared. It was a lot to absorb in a short time.

I said, "Please don't discuss me or Donald Donnie or Ray with anyone."

"I'll see what he wants. Calum couldn't keep a secret to save his own life." Sherry pushed open the door, her hair gleaming in the late afternoon light. She was the perfect image of "nothing to see here."

Calum sputtered, "It should be me, being the man of the house."

"The man of the house can ride to the rescue if it doesn't go well," Sherry called back.

Calum turned to me, "Did you contact the police when that happened?"

I massaged the truth to fit my needs. "Trust me, I tried Ray's friends, his kids, his partner, and I called one of his old cop colleagues in Sydney."

He seemed so surprised that I added, "No one took it seriously."

Donald Donnie said, "I think Calum means when the Jeep rammed you, not the other, um, situation."

In fairness, until the Jeep tried to ram me, what could the police have done? And at this point, unless they were aware of what was going on, which I seriously doubted, they would slow me down.

Sherry positioned herself between the driveway and the path to the barn. Hoping we weren't visible through the window, I peered through the curtain and watched the hulking motorcycle rider gesturing. He'd left his dark blue helmet on, so I couldn't see his face.

Sherry kept shaking her head. Eventually she pointed down the road, in the direction we'd come from.

The biker leaned forward and spoke. She produced a spectacular shrug. They took each other's measure for way too long. It was like a scene from *High Noon*. Finally, just when I expected one of them to keel over dead, motorcycle guy revved his engine and peeled up the driveway toward the barn.

I gulped. "I sure hope he didn't spot the Escape."

What were the chances of a total stranger on a motorcycle showing up just after we arrived? It had to be connected to Ray and the attack on the Escape.

The rider made a tight turn in front of the barn. Sherry waved good-bye.

He nodded threateningly. A warning? Those dark full helmets could make anyone appear menacing. I found myself wanting one.

Beside me, Donald Donnie exhaled.

When Sherry opened the door again, we peppered her with questions. I felt I had the most pressing need. "Who was he?"

"I don't know. He was looking for his friend in a red Ford Escape."

I felt a tingle down my spine. "Good thing he didn't see it."

"Holy Mary." As Donald Donnie said it, a prayer.

"Did he ask about Donald Donnie's car?" What if he or someone else had noticed us together at Pearl's Pies?

"He did not. But he was no great conversationalist."

"Right. But he's seen it here."

Donald Donnie sank onto the wooden kitchen chair. "Camilla, we should…"

"You can take Gussie and the little cat back to Sydney. That might be best."

"I can't leave you by yourself to deal with…"

All three of us stared at Donald Donnie, a good talker, a friend to many, a loyal husband, but as a back-up gunslinger, a definite dud.

I said, "I'd never forgive myself if something happened and Loretta was left alone."

A crafty expression stole over his plump face. "She'd be fine. The house is paid off and the car too, and there's insurance. Plus, the death benefit."

"Stop talking like that," I snapped.

"The death benefit?" Sherry said.

Donald Donnie said. "It's why we pay taxes, isn't it?"

I suspected that Donald Donnie didn't pay too many taxes.

Calum scratched his chin. "What's going on?"

"You'd better tell us the whole story," Sherry said. "You've involved us. You said someone tried to run you off the road, and that biker knows where we live."

Reluctantly, I filled them in on the background.

Calum's squinty eyes widened. Sherry watched, lips pursed.

At the end, Calum smacked the tabletop. "Okay, this guy's been here, and you can't go riding around in either of those two cars. You'd be sittin' ducks."

"Right. But—"

"You'll be takin' one of our cars, won't they, Sherry?"

She nodded without giving it a moment's thought.

I said, "But what about you?"

"Don't worry. We've got a couple of beaters and the truck too," she answered with a shaky laugh. "We not as hard up as all that, you know."

I said, "If he came here, it's because he thought he might find us. He was probably on our tail. Therefore—" I held up my hand to forestall any arguments "—he could come back, and he could have friends with him, and I don't mean our friends."

"Speaking of friends," Sherry said, "isn't it time we all got going?"

Calum got to his feet. "Let me get you a couple of hats, like you asked. Then we'll tuck both your cars where no one will see them." He reached for my key fob, and Donald Donnie waddled after him, dangling his keys.

"Don't worry," Sherry said. "Calum will park them inside the barn behind the bales of hay, and he'll put tarps over them."

"So," I said, putting on the alarming yellow cap Calum had given me, "you sure you didn't recognize that guy on the bike?"

"Absolutely." She smiled.

As soon as the men returned, Sherry dropped both sets into what she called her junk drawer. "They'll be right here when you collect the cars again."

Five minutes later, Calum left. Donald Donnie was stretched out in the rear of Calum's dust-coloured Dodge Ram and covered with a green tarp, with a container of oatcakes to keep him calm.

Minutes later, Sherry followed. I lay on the back-seat floor of her Ford Focus, on top of her dark green rain jacket, huddling under a Cape Breton tartan wool blanket and clutching my own tin of fresh oatcakes. Apparently, the blanket had been a wedding present, and I knew I should have felt more grateful. Gussie and the little cat rode with me. They did a great job of raising the discomfort factor. I worried that I might forever associate the scent of oatcakes with the miasma of Gussie and my new cat scratches. To make matters worse, Gussie was chewing on one of Sherry's stuffed puffins.

All the bases were covered, and the duffle and the box with my sisters' gifts were now crammed into Sherry's trunk. If I had to trade any of it for help along the way, I was prepared

"Do you see anybody on the road?" I said from under the blanket, pushing away a tangled dog leash that must have been for Brutus.

"What do you mean?" Sherry said from the front seat.

I whipped off the blanket and reminded myself that this woman and her husband were helping us get past creepy motorcycle guy unobserved.

"It would help," I said, calmly, "if you described the people and cars you pass on the road."

"Oh right, and what about parked on the side of the road?"

"That too." The floor of the car was clean, but Gussie's presence was changing that. I kept my mind off what I was inhaling and on the problem at hand.

"Okay then," she said, cheerily peering from side to side. "But we would have missed quite a few."

Of course. "Did you notice the motorcyclist?"

"Which one?"

Seriously? "The one who rode up to the farm and spoke to you."

"Right. Him. We passed him parked by a tree and talking on a cell phone."

I sat bolt upright, inconveniencing the little calico cat. I said, "Ow."

"What happened?" Sherry actually turned around. That would have been startling even if we hadn't been clipping along on a road with hairpin turns.

"The cat happened. Where did you see him?"

"Who?"

"The biker."

"Oh, back a bit."

I tried not to sigh or grunt or swear under my breath. I've been told that these sounds—which I'm not generally aware of—irritate people. "And?"

"And I waved back, and that was it."

"Did he get back on his bike?"

"No, he was talking on the cell. Why? Are you still worried about him?"

"Of course I'm worried. Someone tried to kill me or Ray." Had she forgotten this elaborate charade that involved lying on car floors covered with blankets?

"I suppose he might have been telling someone to watch out for you. But no one can see you here."

"Do you think he'd have seen Calum's truck drive by?"

"Fly by, you mean," she said with a chuckle. "Calum has a heavy foot. But yes, I think he must have spotted the truck. The guy was just standing around."

"Waiting for me and for Donald Donnie, I bet. I wish I could get him to just take the animals and drive back to Sydney."

"Well, for heaven's sake, why doesn't he?"

"My guess is that he wants an adventure."

"And you?"

"All I need is answers, and I don't want Donald Donnie to be killed in the process."

Sherry's high-pitched laugh had a nervous edge. "Of course. I'm sure it will all turn out to be a big mistake."

Right.

"Thanks. I wouldn't want anything to happen to you or your husband either."

"Och, don't worry about us. Oops, I spoke too soon. Better get back under that blanket."

"Act normal," I mumbled from my tartan woollen prison. She slowed. The low rumble of a bike was loud enough.

Sherry's car quivered to a halt. After a few heart-stopping minutes, she opened the door and must have stepped out. I heard the door close. Her voice was distant. "Oh, hi again. Are you lost?" She issued another of her high-pitched laughs. "Of course, you couldn't be."

I heard half of the conversation because I was working hard to keep Gussie's mouth closed. As I was losing that battle, I thought to give him an oatcake. So much for barking. I heard a deep voice. "Heading in to Ingonish?"

Sherry said, "Calum got the idea to have a bite at The Seagull. Right. Great seafood. You should try it some time. What? Oh, he's gone on in his truck. We're planning to leave the Focus with a friend to fix the transmission. So, I'd better be on my way so I don't keep him waiting. No, I still haven't seen any kind of red Ford crossover."

He said, "Call me if you do."

"Sure. I still have your card." She finished with a nervous giggle.

Card? When did she get that? I closed my eyes to recall their encounter and tried to remember every second of it. It was a good distraction because my nose was itching.

"Okay then," Sherry called out gaily. A less interested person might have missed the little shake in her voice. "Enjoy your ride. Although it's beginning to rain already. As they say: if you don't like the weather around here, wait five minutes."

I kept the blanket on when she started the vehicle.

"Keep covered," she said. "He's right on my tail. I wouldn't want him to spot you."

Under the blanket, I wished that Gussie hadn't eaten those extra oatcakes back in the kitchen. If I ever caught up to Ray, a suitable penance for him might be a few hours under a dusty wool blanket with Gussie.

Sherry called out, "You can breathe again. He passed us."

"He did?"

"Yes, he's roared around the bend. I guess we're all right."

Ray's phone picked that minute to ring. I swiped. Mrs. Parnell's voice boomed. "Got your Sandy, I believe. That number belongs to a Kenneth Sutherland in Ingonish."

"Oh, but—"

"Bear with me. A bit of research shows that he has a brother, Alexander."

"Bingo!"

"Exactly. And wait, there's more."

"And?"

"Alexander, known as Sandy, is guess what?"

"Just tell me."

"Oh? Someone listening, Ms. MacPhee?"

"Exactly! What a shame. So close and yet so far away."

"At one point, Alexander Sutherland was a police officer in Halifax. Apparently, both brothers attended Holland College too. Around the same time as a certain person you are hunting for."

"Well, well."

"Should you need to pay a courtesy call you could find him at…" She rambled off an address. I was pretty sure I could remember it. I'd be dropping in to see the Sutherland brothers before I tried to intrude on poor Francis Kelly's misery.

I made a note to tell Mrs. P about him and see what the connection was, but, since Sherry could overhear, this was not the moment.

"That's too bad. I was hoping you'd have the information we needed. But thanks so much for trying."

"Nothing ventured. Nothing gained, Ms. MacPhee. Call when the coast is clear."

After I disconnected, I said to Sherry, "Another dead end. I'm beginning to give up hope."

"Sorry."

"I've had people all over trying to find connections." I met her eyes in the rear-view mirror.

She nibbled at her lower lip. "Connections?"

"Yes, interactions that would explain what's going on with Ray. No luck at all. So, is anyone else behind us?"

She squeaked and turned to stare. "What? Who would be behind us?"

"I don't know. Hard to tell from down here, but maybe whoever our friend on the Honda was talking with on his cell."

"Hadn't thought of that. But no one's behind us."

I opened the window and took a deep breath of lovely, dog-free Atlantic air. I got a few drops of rain with that breath.

"I'll keep an eye out in case. You have me worried," she said with a laugh.

I knew all about worry, and after the years I spent in court—so often fighting a losing battle—I was well practiced in keeping it out of my voice. Sherry had plenty of genuine anxiety in hers. She needed training in fake laughs, plus she was a lousy liar.

CHAPTER EIGHTEEN
Because you never know

I had watched that entire encounter with our warm-hearted hippie hostess and the menacing spectre on the blue bike. They hadn't been within reach of each other, in fact. That card had not fluttered through the air between them. No way was I sharing Mrs. Parnell's welcome information about the Sutherlands or other info with Sherry, including where I was planning on going.

"It's not far," she said brightly. "We're off to our friend Archie McCarthy's car yard for a bit. Like I told that guy, Calum helps Archie to do a bit of work every now and then. Archie may have a solution for you."

"Great."

We turned at a sharp angle and careened along a rough road. I speculated that Archie specialized in shocks. He must have blasted through a ton of them getting home every day.

Archie occupied a weathered A-frame on a hill with a fleet of disabled cars in the front yard and a million-dollar view of the beach and the lovely cold waves of the Atlantic. Calum's truck was parked next to a Subaru up on blocks and a Volkswagen bug that would have been better with an intact windshield.

We unfolded ourselves from the back seat, and Gussie shot out to pee on the bug's tires. At least it had tires.

Archie should have been Big Stainless-Steel Archie. He resembled a massive fridge. He had hands like hams, a shock of shiny grey hair, and a beard to match. He also had twinkly brown eyes and a snaggly smile.

Sherry cast sidelong glances at the various vehicles. I got the impression that she'd have loved to haul those cars away and plant a few nasturtiums in their place. Donald Donnie was already checking out each of the cars for obscure reasons of his own. I felt that needed to be discouraged quickly.

"Archie has a car for ya," Calum said.

"Thanks, but—"

Archie lifted a ham-like hand. "No charge. Unusual circumstances. Friend of friends, eh."

I assumed that meant Calum and Sherry. "Well, thank you."

"That way ya can drive off and no one will know it's you," Calum said with a flash of his too-big teeth.

My experience with the local culture was that everyone within a hundred miles would know, but I didn't wish to appear ungracious. "That's kind," I murmured.

They stared at me. Even Donald Donnie glanced up from his examination of a grimy Dodge Dart.

Too little, too late? What?

I dug deep. "It's amazing how generous everyone is around here. I can't believe that you would do that for me, a complete stranger."

Apparently that response was better. Everyone relaxed a bit.

"Are you sure?" I added in case the too-good-to-be-true deal evaporated.

"Aw, it's nothin'. Bring her back at some point." Archie pointed to a bright yellow Honda Civic with more rust than paint on it.

"Well," I said, "no trouble finding that in the parking lot. Is it a custom paint job?"

Everyone thought that was pretty funny. I made a show of joining in the laughter.

"Still rides pretty good if you don't go over sixty."

So much for a quick getaway.

"Hard to do around here with these roads," I grumbled.

"And the park speed limits," Sherry said.

"It's got a Resident's Pass in it so you can get back and forth through the park. Belonged to my uncle, but he died last week," Archie said. "Should come in handy."

"So, what happens now?"

Sherry chuckled. "Well, you and Donald Donnie will do what you need to. We'll leave my car here as part of the decoy and take the truck to the Seagull for dinner in case that guy shows up." She wrote a number on a piece of paper and handed it to me with a smile. "Call me anytime you need your vehicles back. Or even to let us know that you're all right."

I glanced at the number and slipped it into my jeans pocket. "Thank you. Sounds like a plan." And except for that big fat fib about the business card, it did.

Still, we waved goodbye with false smiles and the dog, the cat, the jars of jam, etc. (minus a couple I'd left with Archie) all ensconced in the yellow Civic with Donald Donnie and me. Calum and Sherry left first. As soon as they were out of sight, I thanked Archie, and we turned the other way. We needed to change our appearance, but there was nothing that could help in the duffle short of the wedding outfit.

"Stay in the car and make sure the dog and cat don't escape. They're starting to get restless, and I can't say I blame them." I used my firm voice.

"Why do *you* get to leave?" Donald Donnie whined.

"Trust me, it's better this way," I said as I bustled into the hardware store before it closed for the evening. Minutes later, I was back with a Styrofoam cooler that contained my disguise, a new ball cap (the camo design did not flatter), and a black bucket cap for Donald Donnie. We ditched the caps we had gotten from Calum. Into the cooler they went because we might need them again.

"I think I like yours better."

"It's a gift, Donald Donnie. Try liking the one I gave you."

"I guess."

In the cooler, I also had a green John Deere hoodie for me and a dark-green rain slicker, the only one that fit, because we hadn't packed rain gear in our duffle. Not sure what or if either of us had been thinking. But in the hardware store, I found a size XXL men's yellow slicker for Donald Donnie.

"I'll be like a big yellow whale in that."

"It doesn't matter what we look like as long as long as it's not ourselves. What's the point of having a different car if anyone can clearly see who we are?"

He said, "And anyways, what difference does it make what we look like as long as we're in this rust bucket?"

"We won't be in it long."

I made a big deal out of setting down my other purchases, including a large dog bowl. I filled it with fresh water from one of the plastic bottles I'd bought. The little cat turned up her nose at any attempts at appeasement, but Gussie was happy to make a big hairy deal over it. No one would notice the headgear and the jackets, just a happy dog and a decent human being.

That all being done, I pulled out of the Home Hardware parking lot and onto the road.

"This old beater sure does make a racket," Donald Donnie grumbled.

"No doubt we'll look back on it fondly," I said, wondering how he'd forgotten the Toyota of many colours. It wasn't long before I found a spot to park with easy access to the beach and the place I needed to be. I checked the time yet again. If my luck held, I could still get to the Canso Causeway before Leonard Mombourquette. It would be an intense drive but worth if it I could squeeze some truth out of the little rodent. Of course, if I got lucky, I'd find who and what I needed before I had to leave Ingonish. We exited with the dog and the cat (on leashes) being walked by Donald Donnie, and me lugging the newly purchased cooler. We staggered along and finally took shelter behind some rocks. The wind rose, the rain spit, and the sky turned an ominous charcoal.

It felt like the longest day ever.

"Make sure you stay here," I said. I slapped on the camo cap and pulled the green hoodie on over my clothes to guard against the drizzle. With the sound of Donald Donnie bleating at my back, I stuffed an assortment of my sisters' gifts into my pockets. I picked up the nearly forgotten chocolate cream pie in its box and struggled up over the dunes to the road leading to a beach house nearby. I kept out of sight behind trees. The guys guzzling beer on the deck wouldn't have observed a pride of lions prowling by. I reached the road and got a move on, keeping an eye on the traffic. Of course, my interest ran to large blue Honda motorcycles and black Jeeps.

At last those MacPhee relatives could start to pay off. I felt a grudging gratitude to my sisters for forcing me to carry all those jams and jellies. And I was glad I still had that pie from Pearl's.

•••

Auntie Annie MacNeil's home was just off the road and up a short driveway. The weathered clapboard was set off by a shiny yellow door and shutters and some bright orange mums in planters. There was a garage and a shed in the rear. A yellow table sat by the side of two yellow plastic Muskoka-style chairs, placed at neat angles on the front porch. I smiled at the sight of an older but pristine blue Volkswagen Golf parked near the gate.

I knocked on the yellow door and waited. I tried not to let myself glance nervously around, although I couldn't resist checking the time on Ray's phone. A tall white-haired lady finally inched her way to the door and opened it with a broad smile. She was a bit bent over and leaned on her cane. She regarded me with interest and a sparkle in her eyes. I hoped the sparkle meant she had a sense of humour, because she was going to need it. She had the same tall, lean frame as my father, and the white hair was strong and thick, formerly blonde like all the MacPhees. Her soft pink cable-knit pullover and crisply pressed slacks indicated that she still took pride in her appearance. She gave off the slightest scent of lily-of-the-valley. Very appealing.

I grasped her hand. "I'm Camilla from Ottawa and—"

"My heavens, dear, I know that!" She enveloped me in a hug. Although it was not like me, I didn't want that hug to end.

"Of course, dear. I've been expecting you." Ah yes, my sisters would have made sure of it. "I haven't seen you since you were a bitty child."

"Yes. And—"

"How is your father? We never seem to be able to talk anymore."

"He's um…" I couldn't bring myself to say that my father was vanishing into himself more each day, unlike Auntie Annie, who obviously had all her marbles.

"Och. A shame. I'd heard. Such a brilliant boy he was. But I guess it comes to us all. Old age, dear, it's not for sissies."

"So I'm told."

"You're not at all like your sisters then, are you, dear?" She turned and began to hobble into the interior of the house, beckoning me to follow her to the kitchen. It welcomed us with the scent of fresh baking. A cluster of large, well-tended jade plants added to the hominess. A day bed with a crocheted afghan seemed to suggest we stay a while. Did everyone have one of those in their kitchen? If so, I approved.

"No. I'm not like them, and Auntie Annie—?"

"Yes, dear?" I was relieved that I'd gotten her name right. I decided to spare her the family scandal I'd just uncovered.

"This pie is from me, not my, um, sisters. I'm not much of a baker, but I'm a good buyer."

She chuckled. "You didn't have to do that, dear."

"And I have some gifts for you from my sisters. Jams and jellies and preserves. Plus some homemade liqueur. They claim that Ontario straw-berries make the best jam. And they sent a jar for Rita Susanne Kelly. Maybe her brother will like it too." I unloaded my pockets and placed the goodies on the farm-style table.

"Jam for Rita Susanne? Isn't that grand. Well, she'll be glad of that when she comes back tonight. I remember those MacPhee lassies always were so competitive. Are they still trying to show one another up?"

I kept a straight face. "Sorry, but as much as I love discussing my sis-ters' eccentricities, I can't stay to talk. However, I do need your help."

She turned and lit up. "What do you need, dear? Cookies?"

Cookies? "No, I need shelter, and not for me. For my cousin, Donald Donnie MacDonald, and my cat and dog. Well, they're not actually mine, but—"

"Donald Donnie MacDonald? Married to Loretta?"

"Exactly."

"Bit of a loose cannon, that one."

I felt disloyal nodding.

"Indeed, but he has such a good heart, and he's my cousin too, of course," she said. Perhaps she sensed my ambivalence.

"Auntie Annie, my, um, fiancé, is in—"

"Now, that would be Ray Deveau, would it now?"

"Um, yes." How did these people know all about us, and I couldn't even remember even meeting them? "I believe he's in danger. I have to try to find him."

"Yes, dear." Nothing, it appeared, would surprise Auntie Annie.

"So, first I need to set up my laptop so I can charge the cell phone."

"There's a plug by the table," she said.

"Then I need to get to the causeway to meet Ray's cousin, Leonard Mombourquette, because Leonard knows what is going on."

"Indeed, both of them policemen."

Again, how?

"Yes. I need to make sure Ray's safe, so Leonard's my best bet."

"Oh, I remember them. Ray was a handsome lad, but poor Leonard…" She shook her head, no doubt recalling Mombourquette as a young rodent.

"I don't want anyone to know I'm going. No one at all, no matter how innocent they are. My sister told me you still have your car, although you're not driving. Is that right?"

"Indeed. I kept it because you just never know."

"Exactly. You never do know. Could I leave Donald Donnie and our small zoo and our car here and then borrow yours? That way anyone who is watching out for me won't recognize the car and anyone who's trying to keep me away from Ray will think I've given up—"

"And you're visiting me!"

"Yes."

"And you'll actually be off up the road to intercept Leonard Mombourquette."

"Exactly. To the causeway. I don't have that much time."

"You don't look much like your photographs, Camilla MacPhee. Perhaps it's that hat. Is it part of the plan?"

"It is." I wondered where she would have seen my photos but suspected my sisters.

"Well then, I'll get the keys and a snack you can take on the road."

"I'll be back in five minutes with Donald Donnie. I am grateful, but I don't need a snack."

"Of course you do. Be prepared. Isn't that what the boy scouts say?"

As she spoke, rain started to pound the roof and the porch.

She handed me the keys, and minutes later I hustled myself back to the beach and transferred Donald Donnie, the duffle bag, the remaining gifts, and the menagerie into the Golf. I left the rusty Civic tucked out of sight behind some spruce in case I needed it later. Auntie Annie was right about the Golf. I had to pump the brake, and the clutch was tricky, but I felt wonderfully incognito. I may have left some rubber on the road. We were back in no time.

Donald Donnie took Gussie and the little cat and trotted into Auntie Annie's, more than a bit sulky, but that soon switched to optimism because Auntie Annie had quite a bit of baking on hand. He was a bottomless pit, and she was in a sharing mood. I staggered in with the duffle bag and the remaining gifts. Auntie Annie offered me a space in her back closet for the duffle. I figured it was much safer than in whatever car we were driving. I was optimistic enough to assume that at some point I'd get back to my computer and case files. I'd also be able to put the still virgin wedding dress up on Kijiji.

By the time I'd finished, Gussie had made himself comfortable on the daybed in the kitchen. I moved to get him off, but apparently a pooch on the furniture was no problem for Auntie Annie. Soon the little calico cat settled in too. I joined them on the daybed with that cozy afghan. Auntie Annie had two plates of cake with two forks, all nicely wrapped in plastic and a plastic tub of cookies. She had packed up four sandwiches because, "You never know, Leonard Mombourquette may be hungry too." She'd included a battered Thermos of tea in the small picnic basket, covered with a garbage bag to keep it dry as far as the car. Getting to the door would be a slow process because of her arthritis. I was in the midst of a crisis, and it was barely dark, yet I wouldn't go hungry.

"True enough," I echoed, hopping on one foot and trying to escape without upsetting Auntie Annie with my rudeness and perhaps changing her mind about lending the Golf. It was all nicely surreal and would make a great tale to tell my few remaining friends at some point. But I needed to get the hell out of Ingonish and onto the road.

Donald Donnie reached for a piece of cake as I slithered out. Auntie Annie accompanied me to the door, and I leaned over and whispered a question as soon as Donald Donnie was out of hearing.

"The Sutherland boys, dear? Oh yes. Of course, I've known them since they were born."

"I'll need to speak to them. Sandy might be a friend of Ray's."

"At one time, I suppose. It's a sad enough story. He's a lovely boy, but he's fallen on hard times, that Sandy Sutherland. A little trouble with the bottle, they say. Every so often he ends up here with his brother, Kenny, until he pulls himself together. The visits are getting longer and more frequent." She sighed. "Such a burden for both of them."

"Do you know anyone named Matty in the community?"

"Not that I remember."

I reminded myself to be careful to ask the right question. "I should have said did anyone named Matty or Matthew die here lately?"

She thought hard. "No. People make sure I know who's died and who's been born in the area. I don't know anyone called Matty, dead or alive. Thank heavens."

Oh, well. I was hoping Sandy Sutherland would be sober enough to give me a clue about what was going on. "I hate to change the subject, but was this Sandy always a drinker?"

"He liked to party when they were all in school, I think. The last few years it's become more of a problem."

"Also, I was wondering if I should drop in to see Frankie Kelly tomorrow? Ray was at school with him too." I hoped that Mombourquette would resolve the mystery, but you always need a plan b.

"Now, that's a tragic situation with Francis Xavier. Best not to visit, dear. Rita Susanne has her hands full, and it's very stressful. He's not long for this world, and he's unconscious or hallucinating from the pain whenever he is awake. Father Tim says it won't be long now."

"Sounds awful."

"Life is unfair sometimes. I always got along with Francis, although he rubbed a lot of people the wrong way. He was brilliant, the apple of his parents' eyes. He had a big career in the RCMP, but I don't know much about it. He's been gone from here a long time and, except for their funerals, he didn't come back until he got sick. Wasn't one to keep up old friendships, I guess. I am closer to Rita Susanne. She manages to help me every day, even though she has her hands full with Francis and a large load of clients. I couldn't get by without her." She paused to chuckle. "I'm kind of tippy in the shower, and with these hands I can't do all I used to. She's overcome so much in her life, and she makes a big difference to me."

That reminded me that Auntie Annie knew everyone. "Tell me about Sherry and Calum MacDonald."

She chuckled. "No one ever imagined those two getting together. Back in the day, Sherry Gillis was the prettiest girl in these parts. A real beauty."

I smiled. "I can imagine."

"Och, indeed, she's still lovely. Calum was always … Calum. I don't know what brought them together, but Sherry was going out with Francis Kelly, pretty serious. Then he had an accident, and I guess she didn't stick with him through that. They were quite young at the time. Then she was a bit adrift for years afterwards. I don't want to speak badly of her, but you know what I mean."

"I think so."

"Time heals all wounds, as they say. After a couple of years, Sherry went to St. F. X. and got her B.Ed. She got a job teaching in Hawkesbury for a while, and one day Calum was in the picture. They seem happy enough, and I'd say she's grown into a good and kind person."

I changed approaches and asked, "Do you know Pearl at Pearl's Pies?"

"As well as anyone, I guess. I see you're after bringing one of her chocolate cream pies. I have my skills in the kitchen, but no one beats Pearl with pies."

"Do you know if she's connected with Sandy or Kenny?"

"I don't know of any special connection. Why do you ask? Is Pearl all right?"

"Just wondering. Is she related to anyone named Matthew? Son? Grandson?"

"Not that I know of. She's had her hands full with her only grandson, Cody. Rita Susanne says he's on road to ruin and tells me to keep my doors locked. Imagine!"

"I think he might have been at Pearl's when we bought our pies. A kid with tattoos?"

"Not a bad lad. Youngsters get off-track sometimes. Trouble in school, not enough to do. They can get in with the wrong crowd. It's not easy growing up without stable parents."

Sounded like half my clients.

"I think he said he was taking a course in Sydney."

"That's right. In my long experience, a fresh start and a bit of success is all it takes for a boy to turn around."

"Right." I knew from my practice that wasn't always enough. But good news when it was. I was still troubled by Pearl's lie about the direction that the Silverado had taken. Was Cody the reason? Was that because the cops might have reason to talk to him? Could he and his "trouble" be the key? I decided I would keep an eye out for the kid. And Pearl might be worth a revisit too. But for the moment, I had plenty of other places to go, people to see, and rodents to intercept.

Snacks in hand, Donald Donnie had tottered down to the door to make sure he wasn't missing any news.

"I think I'll drop in and see this Sandy tomorrow."

"You may not want to wait long, because if Sandy's on the sauce, he could be passed out or on his way to detox. You never know. You could always try talking to Kenny, although he tries to protect his brother."

"I'll come with you," Donald Donnie said, springing up with enthusiasm.

"Auntie Annie loves your company. Why not discuss all your mutual relatives? I'll be fine," I said before he thought of twenty reasons to join me.

I used Ray's cell phone to check on the status of the five thirty flight from Ottawa to Halifax and was thrilled that it had been delayed. I could use that time productively to check on the Sutherlands. With luck, I could avoid the long, dark dash to the causeway.

After a last pat for Gussie and a salute to the cat, it was finally time to hit the road.

Auntie Annie said, "My old Golf's not the most reliable ride. Did I mention the brakes are not what they once were? And the clutch tends to stick. Aside from that…"

"I didn't have any problems," I fibbed.

She was chuckling about the Golf as she opened the door. It nearly blew off the hinges. The earlier sunshine was long gone, replaced by tempestuous wind, and brutal rain had turned the driveway into a mudway.

"Oh my," she said. "This one is going to be a humdinger."

Iffy brakes or not, I was off into the gathering storm.

Donald Donnie suddenly loomed behind Auntie Annie and said something unintelligible with his mouth full. He thrust the size XXL yellow slicker at me. Easier to take it than argue with him.

"I'm glad to have it." I slipped it on, rolled up the extra-long sleeves, and bolted for the car. Auntie Annie continued to call out advice as I hopped in and entered the Sutherland brothers' street into the GPS on Ray's phone.

Dusk falls early in October, and with the rising gale the Cabot Trail lost its charm. The falling leaves made the road even more slippery, and those brakes really were lousy. I inched forward along the winding road toward the Sutherlands, hoping they'd have news about Ray. I reached the Cape Breton Highlands National Park again. Even though Auntie Annie's car had a current Resident's Pass, I pulled up at the wicket.

I tried a little chitchat with the attendant in the Parks Canada green uniform. "I'm trying to catch up with my friends. Don't suppose you saw them?"

She blinked like it had been a long day. "Um, quite a few people pass through here every—"

"They were a couple of middle-aged guys in a silver Silverado. New Brunswick plates. Easy to overlook for sure. Earlier this afternoon."

This time she shrugged. "I didn't notice."

Ray's face was the most memorable visage in the world for me. How could anyone not notice him? I tried not to scowl.

Maybe my non-scowl scared her. "I might have been on a break."

"Sure. Did you happen to notice my other friend? In a black Jeep with a banged-up front?"

She pursed her lips. "Was that your friend?"

Hmm. Promising.

"Anything but. In fact, that Jeep rammed into me, and I'd like to discuss it with the driver. I guess you did see it."

"Had a Resident's Pass, but it went back and forth a few times. You should get the police to handle it. The driver was a pretty aggressive type."

A Resident's Pass? That came as a surprise. It meant the Jeep was local. Or at least spent a lot of time in and out of the park. "For sure. But I'm pretty good in a fight. Was it passing this way the last time?"

"Yep. Are you doing errands for Mrs. MacNeil?"

Of course. You can't keep a low profile in these communities. I knew the Jeep had been traveling in the same direction I was, although it could be hours away by now. I'd be on the lookout for Mombourquette. He wouldn't know me in Auntie Annie's car, but I would recognize him.

The wipers barely kept the windshield clear of water and rogue leaves. I drove into the park, squinting through the rain, watching for Jeeps. Of course, there wasn't much chance that the Jeep was sitting waiting for me to drive along in Auntie Annie's Golf. The park attendant had said it had driven back and forth "a few times." Why? Searching for me? Stalking someone else? As far as the driver knew, I was Ray Deveau. I assumed he hadn't realized that Ray Deveau was with his friend Pierre Forgeron and the elusive Sandy and everyone was upset about Matty. I had Ray's phone. Did he already know that Matty was dead?

I crept along the road, pulling over every now and then to let some confident local speed by. Finally, on the far side of Ingonish Beach in what I figured was the village of Ingonish itself, the disembodied voice of the GPS croaked about recalculating. I slowed and then pulled off the road to assess. A yellow Mustang blew by me, and I'm pretty sure I got the finger. I'd arrived at the small street running off the main road and straggling up a hill. The GPS approved when I turned around, but apparently I wasn't going up that road after all, judging by the flashing lights, police cars, and ambulances.

CHAPTER NINETEEN
Make it snappy

I stared through the cluster of vehicles at an unadorned bungalow with a long, covered porch in the back. The Sutherland house was close to the road, halfway up the hill, and it would have a spectacular view when the weather was good, which, of course, it wasn't. By this time, cold rain had soaked the ground, spawning giant mud puddles and glare on the road. I sat tight in Auntie Annie's Golf and watched the Mounties at work. An ambulance stood with its lights still flashing. A cluster of figures had gathered around a small dark car, the centre of the drama. One officer was trying to secure a bright blue tarp that was about to blow away.

I pulled up the hood on the yellow slicker and climbed out of the car. I dodged a couple of speeding trucks and crossed the rain-slicked main road, deked through the soggy backyards of the first two houses on the other side, and hurried up the hill. My mind flicked back to Ray's caller saying "all hell is breaking loose." A wave of anxiety rose in my chest. Was this my own personal hell breaking loose? Who was that ambulance for?

One of the Mounties strode toward me. The yellow stripe on her pant leg seemed strangely upbeat. It matched the yellow on the band of her cap. She motioned me away from the car as another police vehicle arrived.

"What happened?" I said, pointing to the house, although clearly the action was all around the car, cordoned off with police tape. I could see that it was an older Kia sedan with Nova Scotia plates.

She glanced toward it before catching herself. "You'll have to step aside, ma'am."

I let the ma'am slide and stepped aside as she directed.

I said, "Is that the home of Sandy Sutherland?"

"Are you a family member?"

"No."

"Friend?"

"'Fraid not."

"One of the neighbours?"

"None of the above, Officer."

"And you're here in front of this particular house in Ingonish where you have no connection whatsoever because…?"

"I thought my partner might be going to meet Mr. Sutherland. What happened in the car?"

She didn't care for that. "Your partner's a friend of Mr. Sutherland?"

"He knows the brothers." I glanced toward the car. I thought I could see someone bent over the steering wheel. "Is that—?

Her eyelid flickered. If I judged that flicker correctly, it didn't bode well for Sandy.

"What made you think your partner would be coming to meet him?"

"I heard a message on his answering machine from Kenny Sutherland's number. I picked it up because I thought it was actually for me." Not quite true, but close enough. Although normally I don't care what people think of me, I hated the idea of this woman concluding I didn't trust Ray.

She kept the smirk to a minimum.

I shrugged. "Someone suggested he might be coming here."

"Huh. And you followed him to give him the message?"

"I'm touring the trail. I have some Celtic Colours concert tickets, but I was at loose ends today."

"Do you see your partner's car here?"

I'd worked long enough as a defence lawyer to know when someone was shaken up. That meant what had happened here had been hard for her.

Luckily, Ray's car was still hidden in the barn. I felt a rush of relief that I hadn't shared the information from Mrs. P. about the Sutherland brothers with Sherry and Calum, otherwise I might be wondering if they were responsible. I peered past the Mountie cars and ambulance. No sign of the Silverado. No dented black Jeep. "I don't see his car. I guess he didn't come this way after all. Although he could be with friends. They drive a silver Silverado. New Brunswick plates." I glanced around, trying to give the impression that I could have missed a Silverado somehow.

She clearly didn't want to watch whoever was in that car. "Do you know what business he would have had with the … with Mr. Suther-land?"

"I do not."

"The message didn't say?"

I decided was better to come out with it. "The message said: 'Are you still home? All hell is breaking loose.'"

"And was that Mr. Sutherland speaking?"

"No idea, but it was from his number."

"And you know that how?"

"Reverse phone number info." Of course it hadn't been, but I wasn't throwing Mrs. P under that particular bus.

Her upper lip curled. "You always do that to your partner's calls?"

"First time. And it does look like there's something bad here."

The Mountie and I stood in the downpour, staring at each other. I said, "I don't suppose there's any chance I could talk to Kenny Sutherland?"

"We'll want to talk to your partner. Do you think he's involved in this?"

"Of course not. He's a police officer."

"A police officer? Sandy Sutherland was too."

I already knew that, and she shouldn't have let on, but she'd chosen to bend the rules. I'm used to that. Use it in court all the time.

So Sandy Sutherland was dead.

First Matty.

Then Sandy.

Who would be next? Kenny? Ray? Pierre?

"We'll need a statement from you."

I smiled innocently and wished I'd had some boots to go with the slicker. No wonder she was so cool and confident. Those black lace-ups were probably waterproof unlike my squishy running shoes. "You want it here or at the station? Where is the station?"

There was a distinct splash as a dark SUV arrived and squealed to a halt. A man with a bag and a grim face got out and made for the house.

My Mountie turned to watch.

"Let's see your ID," she said.

"It's in my bag in the car. Give me a minute." I pointed in the wrong direction.

"Make it snappy." She turned toward the newcomer. I used the distraction to melt behind the first house and run like hell.

A woman thrust open the back door of the bungalow closest to the road. She stood under the overhang of her back porch, leaned against the wall, and lit a cigarette. Her curly hair was pulled into a high ponytail. As she inhaled deeply, I cleared my throat.

She jumped and shrieked, "Sweet Jesus!"

I moved closer, affecting my best Cape Breton accent, "What's going on up the road?"

"They won't tell us." I was close enough to see that she was pretty, late thirties, and her mascara had left dark tracks down her freckled cheeks.

She took another drag of her cigarette and said, "No wonder I can't quit. You want one?"

"Don't smoke, but I'm considering taking it up."

She managed a throaty laugh. "Good thinking."

I said, "By any chance, do you know where Sandy is?"

"Sandy. Oh my God." She covered her mouth and choked back a sob. "Sandy."

What about Kenny? Were there two people in that Kia? I'd seen what looked like one, but what if the other person was slumped over? What had happened?

"Sorry to upset you. You didn't happen to see a silver Silverado around here today? I am trying to find my friend. He knows both Sandy and his brother. I hope Kenny's okay."

She said, "Couple guys in a Silverado were here earlier, banging on the door at Sutherland's. No one I know. I guess nobody was home at

Kenny's at the time, although Sandy's car was in front of the house, and Kenny's motorcycle was around the side. I figured they'd gone for a walk on the beach." She didn't sound convinced about that. "Sandy always liked the beach."

She took a long drag. When she exhaled, the smoke eddied through the rain. The wind whipped her curly ponytail. "I heard Kenny found him and called 911."

"So Kenny's okay?"

"My husband's over with him. He's in shock."

"Okay, I'll go and—"

"Forget it. Nobody's getting in or out. My Brian has to stay until the police say. But he wouldn't leave Kenny anyway. He's wrecked over it. Carbon monoxide. Why would Sandy want to kill himself?" She stubbed out her cigarette.

I took a chance. "It's all pretty shocking so soon after Matty."

She shook her head. "Who's Matty?"

"Doesn't matter. Is Kenny's motorcycle blue? A Gold Wing?"

She shook her head. "Black. It's a Harley. Brian's pea-green with jealousy."

What were the chances that Kenny Sutherland had been my helpful new friend after the attack on the Escape? And had Kenny been expecting to see Ray instead of me? He had trained as a cop too. He'd asked if I'd "called it in."

"I have to go," she said and stepped back inside. The door banged behind her.

I needed to get out of the area before the Mounties started house-to-house interviews and I ran into "my" officer. Anyway, it was time to head for the causeway to intercept Mombourquette. His flight wouldn't be delayed forever.

As far as I could figure, Sandy Sutherland was dead in his car, probably from carbon monoxide, possibly his own choice, although I wasn't buying that.

Either Ray or Pierre had been banging on the door of the Sutherland house not long before the cops showed up. But when did Sandy die? Was Ray on site at the time? The body was visible from the car window after the tarp blew off. Had the car been under that blue tarp before that? If not, either Sandy wasn't dead at that point or Ray hadn't seen him. I wanted to wait for the neighbour, Brian, to be released from his vigil with Kenny Sutherland, but I had to make tracks.

Back inside Auntie Annie's car, I checked the rear-view and barely recognized my soggy self. Still, the yellow slicker would be easily identifiable. I took it off and slid it under the seat. Desperate times. Desperate measures.

I checked the status of Mombourquette's flight. A further delay was working in my favour, if that schedule was accurate. I decided to return to Auntie Annie's and hoped she had a clothes dryer, a spare pair of rubber boots, and a good source of gossip in the community. She'd know who else lived on that street. She could make a call and perhaps get some kind of information about what had happened.

As I shot past The Seagull, fantasizing about warm, dry clothes, I caught a glimpse of Calum's Dodge Ram in the lot. Sherry had said they were off to The Seagull for fish and chips, and I briefly considered turning around to ask if they'd heard what had happened to Sandy. But I was wet, cold, and grouchy. I nearly missed a big motivation. The Golf skidded crazily as I slammed on the crummy brakes.

A large blue Gold Wing was angled off at the edge of the parking lot. No driver in sight. Whoever he was, he had to be inside The Seagull. I told myself there was more than one Gold Wing in the world.

Only one way to find out.

CHAPTER TWENTY
I hate those questions

I was getting pretty good at U-turns, even on the slick roads.

I fished out the still-dripping yellow slicker and shivered as I slid it on. I saw no sign of the RCMP vehicles and the officer who might recognize me. My new quasi-disguise was not brilliant, but it would have to do. I parked out of sight of the restaurant. No point in being associated with Auntie Annie's Golf this early in the game.

I repeated the Gold Wing's plate number to myself as I dashed by and bounded up the steps toward the scent of seafood platters. Every seat was taken, with a line-up waiting to get in. Loud laughter and competing conversations swirled, as did the beer. By the cash, I dodged heaping platters being carried two at a time from the hectic kitchen. Out on the enclosed deck sat Sherry and Calum, warm and dry, each with a pint of beer. It was the perfect night for a seafood dinner with the rain beating on the roof. They were bent forward, their hands and mouths moving in intense conversation with a hulking guy in leathers. He sat with his back to the wall. I couldn't see his face because of some thoughtless people blocking my view, but there was no doubt in my mind it was the same rider. His huge hand rested comfortably on Sherry's forearm. Like old friends.

Great. What else had Sherry lied about? Ray's Escape and Donald Donnie's car of many shades were on their property. She'd asked me to call when we needed them back. What would they have in mind for us? Would the Gold Wing guy be waiting? Or would he show up conveniently as soon as we were blocked in? Would our cars have new transponders?

I asked for a takeaway menu and slipped out of view. My notebook page was rumpled with water, but it would do. Mrs. Parnell would probably be happy to help trace the plate. I waited until I was out of sight of The Seagull to phone. But I had no signal. Was it a dead zone, or had something disrupted the service?

I reached Auntie Annie's with my teeth chattering, having driven around more than a half-dozen downed branches. The skies opened again to mark my arrival. The wind snapped the yellow slicker.

Auntie Annie was thrilled to see me. She did have a dryer, circa 1970. I remembered the harvest gold from my sisters' stylish laundry rooms back in the day. She was prepared to do it all for me, but I couldn't have that.

Donald Donnie said, "That slicker didn't work at all. You should take it back for a refund. It's not like it suits either one of us."

"And it's noisy too. Who would have thought?"

"I'll see what I can dig up for you. After all, we had generations of fishermen in this house," Auntie Annie said, teetering off. I felt like introducing her to that other formidable ally, Mrs. P. Together, they could cope with any disaster.

"Donald Donnie," I said once Auntie Annie refused help and clumped slowly toward the rear of the house and her storage room. "Someone in the village is dead."

"What? Who? When?"

I held up a hand. I hate those questions.

"I'm pretty sure it's Sandy Sutherland."

"But—"

"Listen: Sherry and Calum were having dinner with the guy on the motorcycle."

"Does that mean we can't trust them?" he whispered, his eyes practically bugging out.

"Right."

"But the cars are at their farm."

"Correct."

He opened his mouth, but I shushed him. "Let me see if Auntie Annie can get us some information about what happened to Sandy Sutherland."

Auntie Annie came puffing back into the room. For me, she'd found a red flannel shirt and a pair of battered men's jeans—now in style because of the rips and frayed hem. She also brought a belt to hold them up. The outfit was completed with winter long johns and an orange hunting vest. I accepted the clothes with a chattery smile and inhaled her reassuring scent of lily-of-the-valley. I thought that things would have to be all right now.

"We can put your clothes in the dryer."

We all stared at my dripping jeans. They were muddy as well.

She said, "The washer and dryer will get a workout. You're shivering. You need to hurry into the hot shower to get rid of the chill. There's a hair dryer under the bathroom sink."

I hated to burden her with the news about Sandy. Maybe Donald Donnie could do it gently when I left.

The walls of the stairway were filled with family photos. On a better day, I might have enjoyed studying them. Was I reverting to my roots, whatever they were? I didn't have time to waste, so I was downstairs—with dry hair—in under fifteen minutes.

"Found you some rain boots that might fit," Auntie Annie said. "The boys' boots will be huge on you, but my granddaughter forgot these here last year when she visited with some friends. The wool socks are hers too. I made them myself from alpaca yarn, back when I could still manage to knit."

The pink rubber slip-on boots turned out to be my size. The daisy design running up the sides was the least of my problems. On the upside, the alpaca socks felt like a small chunk of heaven.

"You're the best, Auntie Annie."

"Wait until you see the bill." She chuckled.

As my own clothes whirled in the washer, I checked my cell and was glad of a signal. Of course, I had to leave a message with Mrs. Parnell about the plate number of the Gold Wing. I ended with "So, any word on Matty?"

I called Alvin to leave a similar message and was thrown off when he actually answered.

I repeated all the info about the license plates and the new developments and asked him to check in with Mrs. P.

"You must be especially tense, Camilla," he said.

Tense? What the hell did he expect?

"Because I have a product that could make all the difference to you. This will be life changing. It's an amazing bath soak called Green Tranquilli—"

"Gotta go, Alvin, I'm going to miss Mombourquette."

I didn't want any of Alvin's "life-changing" products, plus I had to make tracks.

"Or you could get a real energy boost with our Super Bath Bong!"

"Can't hear you because of the storm. I'll call back."

"Don't worry about your clothes. I know you're in quite a rush," Auntie Annie said when I prepared to dash out the back door and through the slashing sleets of rain to the car. She'd given me the yellow slicker, now dry, in a bag. She reminded me about the lunch she'd packed earlier and handed me another thermos of tea. "Just found this extra one."

Before braving the storm again, I bit the bullet and told Auntie Annie about Sandy Sutherland.

Her kind face crumpled, and she sagged against the wall. "Sad, that. I knew him since he was a lad." I wished that I could take back this news.

Donald Donnie put his arm around Auntie Annie. "Be careful, Camilla. It's turned into a real hurry-cane. Don't get blown off the road."

"I'll try not to."

"What can I do?"

"Get Auntie Annie talking more about Sherry and Calum and Pearl. Then suggest, subtly, that she might be able to find out what people are saying about Sandy Sutherland. But only if you think it won't upset her."

"Roger, over and out," he said, making no sense whatsoever. "Oh, and by the way, someone called Rabbit is trying to reach you. I told him you were busy."

Rabbit? Oh. Bunny Mayhew. Probably had a probation issue or a newly constructed alibi. My favourite client but the last person I needed on this night.

●●●

I had two and a half hours to catch Leonard Mombourquette as he came off the causeway. That included a lot of driving through a storm that was getting wilder. The mountain route through the Cape Breton highlands is as twisty as the road into Ingonish. I'd be buffeted by winds, and the hard rain would make it almost tough to navigate. I was banking on people staying off the roads.

Once I was away from Ingonish, our suspected villains, the police, and Donald Donnie's chatter, I could allow myself to think straight. A bit of solitude might help me figure out what was going on. There wasn't much chance that Sherry and Calum or the guy on the Gold Wing would find me on the way to the causeway.

I was crawling through the outskirts of Ingonish when Ray's cell rang. With no Bluetooth in Auntie Annie's Golf, the car swerved when I answered.

"Camilla," Alvin shrilled. "Where are you? What is going on? Why haven't you picked up?"

It appeared he wasn't upset about my abrupt departure. Good. No point in burning all my bridges.

"Lots of dead zones here."

"Where the hell are you?"

"Didn't I tell you I'm on my way to the causeway to intercept Mombourquette?"

"I thought you got cut off. Reports about that hurricane are all over the Internet. Why are you meeting Leonard there?"

"Not meeting. Intercepting. I'm not supposed to know he caught a flight to Halifax. And I know he's rented a car."

"But—"

I couldn't let myself be diverted. "Mombourquette knows what the hell is going on. And he wouldn't tell Elaine. But he'll damn well tell me when I catch him."

"I almost feel sorry for the guy," Alvin said. "Which is weird in itself."

"Don't feel sorry for him yet. Something dangerous is happening, and he's keeping it from me. Another guy is dead, a Sandy Sutherland, and he was in touch with Ray."

"Lord thunderin' Jesus. Are you on the Cabot Trail as we speak?"

"Yes," I said.

"Fine. Never mind about my business stuff."

"What?"

"Don't give it any thought. We'll have lots of time to work out the legal details later."

The line went dead.

Was this one of Alvin's passive aggressive stunts because I was slow to help with the business? I didn't like the sound of "legal details" in the same sentence as "we," but it wasn't the best time for a flat no. Still, as much as he got on my nerves, I almost wished Alvin were with me. Fact was, I could have done with another pair of hands and a few more eyes too. Plus someone to answer the phone. I gripped the steering wheel of Auntie Annie's car and thought longingly of my three-year-old Mazda3 back in Ottawa and even the Escape. Oh well. Thick blankets of fog drifted across the highway that was tough enough under ideal conditions.

I needed to get to the causeway in one piece, but it made sense to go through the highlands on the longer route through Cheticamp in case I spied the Silverado. A slim chance, but if I found Ray, I wouldn't need Mombourquette. Meanwhile, dangerous thoughts swirled in my brain, such as: what was going on with Sherry and Calum and the sinister guy on the blue Gold Wing? Were they connected with Ray's disappearance and the motley group of former classmates?

It was early evening, but so darkened by rain and fog, it might as well have been midnight.

I called Alvin back. "Can you track Mombourquette's flight for me?"

"Please and thanks, Camilla."

What a pain he could be. "Fine. Please and thanks, Alvin. It's the five thirty flight. It was supposed to get in at eight thirty. It left late. And I need know what he's driving. The cell service here is spotty, and it will probably get worse. Do it right away and call me back."

"Who was your servant last year?" Alvin hung up before I could respond by saying that he had been, although he never earned his salary.

Now I needed to grip the steering wheel and squint to see the road. Who knew finding your own lane could be so tricky? I eased about two feet forward, and the phone rang again.

Alvin said, "That flight has landed. Good luck."

Canso Causeway, here I come, pedal to the metal. Most of the communities ribboned along the Cabot Trail. I flew past lots of trucks, but no silver Silverados.

I smiled, remembering why I was aiming for the causeway. *Look out, Leonard, and prepare to spill your guts.*

•••

The Cape Breton highlands are awe-inspiring and more than a bit scary on a good day. Under normal circumstances, my jaw would be dropping at the sight of the forested valleys, rugged rock face, and the startling turns with sharp glimpses of azure water below. No two vistas were the same, and each one was more stunning than the last. But this was no good day. This was a very bad night. The Golf rocketed from side to side on the twisty and steep-sloped road as I fought the gale. I decide it was better not to be distracted by the scenery. I did wonder why people would choose to live in this remote area, although admittedly no one lived on the road right through the highest plateau in the park. The idea that this section of the Trail was uninhabited wasn't comforting as I wobbled along. At one point, it occurred to me that I must have been driving through that hellish bit of landscape where the spruce budworm had devastated a swath of forest. I shivered at the thought. It seemed suitably grim for this drive, but I was glad it was too dark to see the scarred and damaged trees. I could only hope the moose were hiding out somewhere until the weather cleared. *This had all better be good, Ray.* When I neared Cheticamp, every one of my muscles was tensed to the max, and it was time to start breathing properly again.

Cheticamp, a traditional Acadian fishing village, was usually welcoming with its cheerful white, red, and blue Acadian flags (complete with gold star) and the well-kept houses along the road, but tonight the residents had apparently hunkered down because of the storm. It looked like a major power outage was underway. There was not one miserable silver Silverado in sight. However, an open garage and convenience store with a noisy generator running beckoned. I stopped for gas and asked the proprietor and the one other customer about the truck. Had anyone seen it? Did anyone know Ray Deveau? That netted suspicious glances.

Perhaps I needed to refine my technique.

I tried smiling and bought three bags of salt-and-vinegar chips, not that it got me anywhere.

Back on the road and away from that bit of civilization, I made good time despite trees whipping like skipping ropes and new waterfalls shooting out from the hills when you least expected them. Frankly, the mudslides took a bit of getting used to. The old car rattled on through the hurry-cane.

CHAPTER TWENTY-ONE
And what do we have here?

I had already worked my way through the sandwiches, cookies, and tea that Auntie Annie had packed for me. The delicious ham on home-made whole wheat bread was just a memory. I'd eaten Mombourquette's too, figuring he didn't deserve them. The salt-and-vinegar chips were history, and I was no longer capable of smiling when the Golf crept through the dying storm into Port Hastings. My knuckles were probably going to remain permanently white.

Annie's car slipped easily into a small lay-by along the side of the road close to where vehicles rolled onto the island. When Leonard Mombourquette crossed the causeway, I would nab him. I stretched out my cramped fingers, worrying that the claw-like shape would be permanent.

Alvin answered when I called. I said, "What's he driving?"

"Hello to you too, Camilla. He's rented a Chrysler 300," said Alvin. "It took a bit of deception to find out."

"I don't even know what that is."

"Big car. Premium. Do you want to know the colour?"

"Not at all, Alvin. I'll follow all the cars coming on to the island until I figure it out. Of course I want to know the colour. I need to intercept him. Unless I've already missed him."

"You probably haven't. The flight didn't land until ten thirty. According to Google directions, it's two hours and eighteen minutes from the airport to where you are. Which normally would have meant you missed him."

"Right. Except that it must have taken him a bit of time to get the car, even with a booking, and then I'm sure the weather would have slowed him down."

"Red velvet." Alvin snickered. "That's the colour."

"That mouse is moving up in the world." It was a matter of time until Alvin got on my nerves, but I was sick of my own company.

Alvin said, "What are you doing?"

"Sitting here, watching and waiting and wishing I had another sandwich. Or a piece of pie."

"Let me fill you in on my campaign."

"What campaign?" I asked foolishly.

"Very funny. We are about to test our product line. You will flip when you see what else we're offering."

I'd already flipped when I heard what business he planned to get into. I muttered a noncommittal response. Just as well he didn't hear me say, "Who in their right mind?"

"We've got some soothing salves too. I will be doing all the package designs." I hoped he didn't practice by designing a frieze of five-leaved stylized plants on my living room walls in my absence. Stranger things have happened with Alvin and paint.

I smothered a yawn that actually made my eyelids ache. "Looking forward to seeing that, Alvin." Not.

"Do you think you could test the products, Camilla?"

In your dreams.

"I think I see him!"

"See who? Ray?"

"Mombourquette. Gotta go. I'll call you." Although hopefully not about testing a pile of idiotic cannabis-based personal products. Because that was never going to happen. It was more likely that I'd help by being Alvin's lawyer once he ran afoul of the law. And with the provinces managing cannabis regulations, how could he not?

Of course, Mombourquette was nowhere in sight. I waited, squirming irritably for another half hour. Visions of French fries danced in my head as I kept a sharp eye out for a red velvet—was that even a real colour?—Chrysler 300.

What if I'd missed him?

To be on the safe side, I called Donald Donnie and told him to watch for a crimson Chrysler around Ingonish.

"But I'm getting ready for bed, Camilla."

"Donald Donnie, you need to convince someone to drive you in the direction of the causeway. You'll need to keep your eyes open for that car. Find some guy in Ingonish and pay whatever is asked. I'll reimburse you."

"What would I do if I saw that red car?"

"Use your brain. Call me!"

I heard Donald Donnie bleating to someone, his voice getting higher by the syllable.

The next voice was calm but suffused with authority. "Camilla? This is Rita Susanne. Now look here, we are dealing with a raging storm. Trees are down everywhere. The roads are practically impassable. I'm only arriving at Auntie Annie's at this ridiculous hour, way past her bedtime. I don't know what you are going through, but please do not bully Donald Donnie into going out in this weather. I'll have to spend the night as it is. The visibility is zero. Even my poor brother will have to be on his own, so don't be crazy."

I blinked. Of course, she was right. I couldn't endanger anyone. I was losing my marbles over this.

"Tell him not to worry."

Her voice softened. "I will, but I'm glad I was late tonight. Otherwise who knows what might have happened to poor old Donald Donnie. You need to get a grip. Pull over and take shelter somewhere. Easy-peasy. Whatever you've gotten yourself involved with, it's not worth a life."

I spent the next half hour pondering my own craziness. I had no right to endanger anyone. Before I could castigate myself further, both the day and the night caught up with me, and I conked out. I slept deeply with my neck at an unnatural angle and produced a puddle of drool on my shirt.

My eyes snapped open at dawn. I glanced at my watch, feeling a sharp pain in my neck. I had slept for more than six hours in a small vehicle that smelled like stale potato chips.

For sure, I had fallen down on the job and allowed Mombourquette to slither by me to who-knows-where. But self-recrimination could come

later. The priority was finding a restroom and a place to wash up. A Tim
Hortons in Port Hawkesbury solved those problems and netted me a large
double-double and a breakfast sandwich plus ten chocolate glazed Timbits. Falling asleep on duty is hungry work. I wolfed it all.

The bad news was that I saw myself in the mirror in the small ladies'
room. Big mistake. Matted rain-flattened hair, drool on my red flannel
shirt. The battered men's jeans worn with oversized pink rubber boots
with flowers did not make a fashion statement, although I couldn't actually see the boots. Even early morning, I faced competition for a stall and
a sink. Two women waiting couldn't resist giving me the side-eye.

"What's not to love?" I said as I squeezed past them and left.

I went into the first open gas station, filled up the Golf, and bought
a toothbrush, toothpaste, a small hairbrush, a box of tissues. Too
bad I hadn't had all that at Tim's. I also snagged three more bags of
salt-and-vinegar chips.

I called Elaine, planning to bulldoze her into telling me where Leonard was.

"Calm down," I blurted as she shrieked a pile of gibberish.

"Don't tell me to calm down," she yelled. "You should know that
makes a person more agitated."

"You have a point. I hate it when people tell me to calm down. So why
are you shrieking?" I could almost see that uncontrolled red hair sticking
out in all directions.

"I can't reach Leonard. He promised he'd check in."

"Oh. When did he check in last?"

"When he got off the causeway. In Port something."

"Hastings. Or Hawkesbury. And that was it?"

She hiccupped and said, "Yes."

"Well, the reception's almost nonexistent as you get away from the
main communities. And we had a walloping storm last night."

"That's what I'm afraid of."

"I'm sure he's fine. But I'm driving toward—do you know where he's
going?"

"No! Why doesn't he call?"

"Tell you what, I'll call you if I find him parked anywhere."

"How will you know?"

Oops. A slip. I didn't want to reveal that we'd found out about the vehicle. "You want to tell me what he's driving?"

"I have no idea," she wailed.

"Never mind. I'll track him down."

Her voice rose. "You don't care about Leonard the way I do."

"No argument on that front."

"He could be dead. You've had a hurricane!"

Now the weather was my fault too? "According to the latest reports, it's been downgraded to the tail end of a tropical storm. Let's be accurate."

"That's it. I'm coming to Cape Breton."

"Cape Breton's a big place, and if you want to—"

"Do not condescend to me, Camilla! I am an intelligent woman. Do you think I can't find wherever he is trapped, alone, frightened?"

"Call me if you need directions."

"I hate sarcasm."

"You love sarcasm. Anyway, the cell service is lousy and even worse after tropical storms, but sooner or later you'll get me. If I find Leonard first, I'll put you out of your misery. If you find him, please let me know. Stay in touch. We have to work together if we're going to save anyone. If you can't reach me, try my Auntie Annie MacNeil in Ingonish. She'll know where I am, probably."

"What's the address?"

"I'd have to check. It's on the Cabot Trail."

Her voice went up again. "Be serious!"

"I am serious. Just ask anyone in Ingonish. They'll tell you. Let me know if you find the little—"

"I will not let you know," she yelled. "I hold you personally responsible for this and if anything happens to Leonard, I will finish you."

Elaine hung up in the finest social work tradition.

Finish me? I laughed out loud, and that cheered me up a bit. Now where was that slippery little rodent? I couldn't be sure, but I was betting he was somewhere between Cheticamp and Ingonish, the two places that I knew had some connection to him and Ray. I was well aware that I could have been completely wrong.

•••

The damage from the storm was severe, with crumbled road and rock-slides. The new waterfalls spouting enthusiastically from the mountain-sides told me how much rain I had driven through. The steep slopes still looked unstable, and piles of mud and rock blocked parts of the route. I got used to swerving and also to glancing up in case another load of rock was on its way down. The western coast was even more dramatic than the trip up from Baddeck, and it was much better in the day, if you didn't worry about the sides of mountains giving way. I was glad that the fog and rain had kept me in the dark about the perils. I drove by five aban-doned cars, all off the road, all badly damaged. None was a Chrysler 300. Not a red velvet sedan among them. Needless to say, no Silverados.

Work crews and huge yellow machines were out in full force. I tipped my head to view guys in hard hats rappelling down cliffs to deal with partially dislodged trees. I could have been wrong, but I bet those guys were having a pretty good time. The trip would have been fun if I hadn't been on a critical mission.

On an uninhabited and wooded stretch, I was distracted by the sight of three huge trees that had been blown over, leaving their vast root systems exposed. I went sailing by, noting that a portable toilet was already in place. I figured it was for the use of road crews. But it had been tipped at a forty-five-degree angle. That had been quite the wind. Something felt wrong about the trees back by the blue structure. It niggled at the back of my mind as I wrestled open my last bag of chips while steering with my elbows.

"Never go back. Always go forward," I told myself, gobbling a mouth-ful of chips.

"But," a small inner voice whined, "could that have been a glint of crimson in those woods? Possibly even red velvet? Or are you hallucinat-ing?

Damn.

I turned the car around and gave an apologetic wave to a guy in a Sub-aru wagon who leaned on his horn.

I drove slowly to where the three giant trees were. Sure enough, there was the rakishly tipped blue hut. I didn't see the glint of red. I passed the strange little scene and made another U-turn, more carefully this time. I crawled along the shoulder, peering into the gloomy evergreens.

There it was. From this direction, I could see the glimmer of metallic red behind a thick clump of spruce. I stopped the car, grabbed the cell phone, and got out. The shallow ditch was brimming with water from the storm. I squished through the ditch to the spongy ground on the other side. Auntie Annie's granddaughter's pink rubber boots came in handy. Who in their right mind would park in that spot? You could leave your car anywhere along this stretch of road. I made my way to the vehicle. It would be no picnic getting that Chrysler out. I glanced behind me and held up the phone. Do I even have to mention no signal? And not another vehicle in sight.

The air smelled of damp earth and rotting leaves, overlaid with the happier scent of cedar and spruce. But this was no school outing to enjoy nature. My heart hammered as I approached. I couldn't think of a single reason why Mombourquette would stick his pricey rental where it would take a tow-truck to remove it. The vision of Sandy Sutherland's car haunted my thoughts. I reached the door and tried to open it. "Leonard?"

The car was locked. I pressed my nose against the windows.

Empty.

No keys in the lock.

I shivered at the echo of Ray's disappearance. Had Mombourquette been kidnapped? Or joined some other co-conspirators?

I banged on the trunk in case someone had forced him into it. I yelled his name.

Not a sound from within. That could be good or bad, I thought.

I squished around to the front of the car. A glance at the fancy-schman-cy grill suggested it had collided with a tree. Or had it been hit? There was no shortage of deer and moose in the area, but either would have made for far more damage than that at any speed. A rock? Unlikely. A couple of saplings had been snapped. Would that have been enough? Visibility had been so bad, anyone could have driven off the road, snapping a few young trees. But where was Leonard?

In the back, a small, neat carry-on bag lay on the leather seat.

I squished back through the oozy bog to the highway. Had Mombourquette skidded off the road? Easy to do when you were tired. Could he have hit slippery debris from one of the mudslides? But where were the skid marks? Where was the mud for that matter? Had it washed away?

This was one of the few clear, flat stretches of road and pavement. What could have sent the Chrysler careening into the woods? A glossy black Jeep? An angry squirrel was the only witness.

What was that? Not a squirrel this time. A faint, echoing sound of drumming came from … where? Near but weirdly far away. Boom boom boommmm?

Sounded like somebody banging. The noise couldn't have been coming from the trunk, although I splashed back to double-check.

I peered around into the surrounding trees. Still nobody. But the noise continued.

Was it coming from deeper in the woods? No way was I checking that without allies. So the bottom line was this: I'd found a pricy rental abandoned by a retired detective, a guy who knew how to watch his back. A weird noise emanated from somewhere in the creepy woods. The hair on the back of my neck rose, and I fled back to the highway again, hoping to flag a passing vehicle.

"Leonard? Where the hell are you?" I yelled it this time. The drumming stopped. I waited and heard a muffled voice, tinny yet reverberating. I stepped to the right, and it diminished. "It's Camilla. Make as much noise as you can!"

Still tinny, the voice got a bit louder. It got even louder as I moved to the right toward the uprooted trees and the portable toilet.

I started to run. The racket came from the blue cabin, leaning at a forty-five-degree angle against an uprooted tree. As I approached, I saw that a large stick had been pushed through the lock holder. I struggled to pull it out, yelling, "Hang on and don't move. The structure could tip over, and you'll be stuck in it."

I couldn't make out his words, but that probably was just as well.

"Settle down, Leonard. Give me time. Unless you want to spend the day trapped."

The toilet went silent.

The stick was tightly wedged. "I need to get a tool from my car. Be calm. I will get you out."

If worse came to worse, I could always commandeer some of the workers from down the road. But Leonard would never recover from being rescued from an outhouse in Cape Breton.

Auntie Annie's tire iron did the trick after some hacking and yanking. When I finally pulled the door open and saw Leonard's expression, words failed me. I held out my hand, and he extricated himself with surprising dignity.

Whoa. Did that enclosure reek or what?

I gave him time to pace and to pick up a couple of handy rocks and hurl them at the portable. I learned a few French expressions not intended for polite company.

Finally, I had to ask, "So what happened?"

He did his best to achieve outraged dignity and came up short and stinky. "Did you do this, MacPhee? Because I will kill you."

"Are you insane? You think I locked you in this thing?"

"Why are you here then?"

"I'm trying to intercept you, doofus. I found out about your flight and what car you were driving. I went to head you off at the causeway."

His beady eyes narrowed. "You called me a doofus?"

"Total doofus." I didn't bring up the blue structure. "Anyway, I figured you'd be coming this way. I was waiting at a lay-by near the causeway, and, um, I fell asleep. I guess you shot by during the night."

"Someone must have followed me."

"Obviously. I didn't believe for a minute that you drove your car into a marshy spot in the woods and—"

He flushed pinkly. "What? Where's my rental?"

I pointed. "Behind those trees. What did you do that for? I thought you'd been killed." I stopped myself from saying, "Cat got your tongue?"

He sputtered, "For the record, I didn't park my rental in the woods. The storm was raging. I got out to use the—"

"Yes, of course."

"And I heard someone drive up. I thought it was weird because there was almost no one on the roads. Then I heard a noise at the door."

"Oh yeah, someone jammed a strong and stubborn stick into it."

"I couldn't get it open. And then I heard a vehicle revving outside. Then the friggin' box started to tip over."

"I think that might have been your rental doing the pushing, judging by the damage to the front of it."

Mombourquette's beady eyes bulged. I figured the notorious cheapskate and conceited driver had gone for the highest deductible.

"Well, compared to being dead like—"

"What?"

"It could be so much worse. You smell a little, and it must have been horrible, but—"

"Dead like who?"

"Sandy Sutherland."

Mombourquette steadied himself by clutching the nearest tree. He wiped his muddy hands on his stinky jacket.

"I thought you were going to keel over, Leonard."

"What happened to Sandy?"

"I don't know. People are suggesting suicide."

Mombourquette scowled. "No."

"I heard it was carbon monoxide. He was found in his car, and that's what people are saying." Okay, one person. "When I showed up, the cops weren't talking. I was thinking about calling Wayne Nowicki again to see what he knows. He used to be a colleague of Ray's. He's a surly SOB on the phone, anyway."

"Better stay away."

Mombourquette was ragged, bags under his eyes, drooping whiskers. That told me two things: he'd been up all night in unenviable outhouse solitary confinement, and Nowicki was definitely involved.

"I could have died," he said, flashing me an accusatory stare.

"Again, not my doing. Though I am sorry it happened to you, Leonard."

He wrinkled his pink nose.

"But I don't think they intended to kill you."

He opened his mouth, but I held up my hand. "Think about it. The bar was in the door. Someone would come by in—"

"The spring?"

"Nah. Before the end of day, someone on one of these work crews would have noticed that portable toilet tipped over."

"I could have frozen to death. It was damned cold."

"Your attacker didn't want you to die, but he didn't want you to get wherever you were going. Why would that be?"

"No goddam idea, MacPhee."

"Betting it has to do with whatever Ray is involved in and whoever Matty was and whoever is driving that Silverado and whoever Pierre Forgeron is. And what happened to Sandy et-friggin'-cetera. So, may I suggest enough bullshit already? Start talking."

"We need to get the car out first."

A vision of Stinky Mouse racing down the highway in his red velvet chariot flashed through my brain. "Talk first. Car second."

Mombourquette was shaking. If he lost consciousness from hypo-thermia, he'd be no use to me. "We need to get you somewhere to take a shower and get some clean clothes."

"Not important. I have to get the car out of the woods. MacPhee, you can never say a word about this to Elaine."

"We're friends, aren't we, Leonard? We'd say you had a slide during the storm."

"Don't talk to her about me at all. Or to anybody else." He would have been more menacing if his teeth hadn't clattered like castanets in a flamenco show. "Elaine c-c-c-c-can n-n-n-n-ever find out."

The chattering teeth worried me. Better get him warm and dry first. "No problem."

I was pretty sure that car wasn't coming without a fight, so I shrugged and led the way to the Chrysler. Mombourquette still had his keys in his pocket. In the car, he turned on the heat, and I tried holding my breath until the interior warmed to the point where I could open my window.

Without warning, Mombourquette gunned the motor. Obviously, the fumes had affected his thinking, because the wheels spun and dug them-selves deeper into the soft earth.

"Maybe if you push," he said.

As if. I knew absolutely he'd leave me covered with mud, but I was willing to fake it. Not hard to appear to push and struggle without actually putting any muscle into it. After a couple of minutes, Leonard caught on.

"You back up, I'll push," he yelled from the car.

Sadly for Mombourquette, that plan didn't work. That car was truly stuck in the mud.

"I suppose we should call roadside assistance. Ray insists that we each have memberships."

"We have no signal here. Do you think I would have spent the night in that hellhole if I could have reached someone?"

"Let's take my car and keep going until we have a signal. The tow trucks will be busy today because so many cars went off the road during the storm. While we're waiting, we can find a motel where you can take a shower. There will be someplace I can buy you some clean clothes."

"Not in Cheticamp. I don't want anyone knowing."

"I'll say you're my husband, Jim Smith. They don't need to see you."

His "okay" was subdued.

"But you are going to have to talk to me."

To my surprise and his, we hadn't driven that far when we once again had a signal and were able to use Mombourquette's phone to reach roadside assistance.

I put the phone on speaker. The dispatcher said, when we finally got through, "One and a half to two hours, if you're lucky."

CHAPTER TWENTY-TWO
At least he cleans up good

"You can't be serious?"

"One and a half to two hours," the dispatcher repeated with a yawn. "We had a storm, you know. Wild weather."

"Hours? Holy crap. We'll have to go somewhere to wait." I gave them Mombourquette's cell number and struck an agreement to be back in ninety minutes. Mombourquette was quiet as we got into Auntie Annie's car and drove slowly, watching for a motel. He still reeked. Must have been some powerful wave of splashback when that outhouse went over. I was going to owe Auntie Annie big-time after this. I said, "We have to talk about Ray."

"Not talking."

"Not your choice."

Mombourquette's paws tightened. "What part of I don't want to talk about it isn't clear?"

"Give it up."

Mombourquette drew himself up to his full height, not easy when you're belted into a passenger seat. "Look, Camilla, there's no easy way to do this, but you are right. It's past time I told you. Ray wants out. He feels trapped by the relationship. Could be a midlife crisis," he mused. "Maybe he's trying to find himself."

I said, "Didn't I just rescue you? You better tell me the truth."

"Ray decided he didn't want to be tied down to—"

"The old ball and chain?"

He shrugged. "It wasn't working out between you. You know what men are like, MacPhee."

"Sure, I know what men are like. Emotionally dishonest. Cowardly. Unstable."

"Right," said Mombourquette, looking a tad ambivalent.

"So that's it, eh."

"Mmm." Mombourquette reached over to give me what was probably a consoling pat on my shoulder. He was lucky I didn't stomp on his tail. "For the record, I'm sorry, MacPhee."

"Thanks," I said when I got myself under control.

No way would I get the information I needed from Mombourquette. "No matter how sleazy most men are, I guess I can count on you to be honest."

His eyes veered to the right again. "Glad I could help, MacPhee."

"Here's the thing, Leonard: I'd been having doubts myself about the relationship. You gave me what I needed. Now when I see Ray again, I'll break it off myself. And you know me, Leonard, when I make up my mind, I don't change it. I'll be sure to let him know that you helped me decide."

I watched Mombourquette's furry Adam's apple bob a bit after that. I pretended not to notice and continued to twist the knife. "This guy's been making the moves on me, and I've been putting him off because I wanted to be faithful to Ray. But I'm going to give him a call as soon as I get you settled. He'll probably drive down to get me. Thanks again. You're a good friend to both of us." I would have given him a hug, but he smelled like a septic tank. I added, "Now watch for a motel."

"It's October, for God's sake. They'll all be closed for the winter."

"Lots of people stayed open for Celtic Colours. Have faith." Of course, every motel or inn we passed for miles was either closed or *NO VACANCY*. Mombourquette sniffed each time we drove by one. Finally, I sighted a small group of log cabins, next to a two-storey home. West Wind Cabins had a *VACANCY* sign.

While Mombourquette scrunched out of sight, I rang the bell. I told a tall tale about a fall into an outhouse for my poor husband, Jim. The woman who answered the door stared at me with round blue eyes. She sported a white apron and had a great collection of freckles and bright red cheeks. She was the picture of a Campbell's soup kid. Like many people I'd met on this trip, she turned out to have a big heart. She also wore an X ring and that told me she'd graduated from St. Francis Xavier University in Antigonish, as my sisters had. I couldn't afford to get sidelined by a conversation about who knew whom, so I kept my mouth shut about that.

She introduced herself as Susan West. I said, "I need to rent a warm cabin and a hot shower. I'll pay the daily rate upfront, and I hope you can direct us to a self-service laundry."

"A self-service laundry? You'll not be finding one of those near here. But, oh, the poor man. I'll wash his clothes for him. Does he want to come in?"

"He does not. He's mortified."

"I get that. Let me open up Number Two. It has baseboard heat, dear, but it's quick. I'm sure I can find some of my husband's old clothes that he could put on after his hot shower. And don't worry. The hot water tank heats up in a flash."

Really, it seemed like everyone in the region would hand over their spare cars and their relatives' clothes without hesitation. "Oh, that's not nec—" But she was moving too fast. I hurried after her to Cabin Number Two without commenting on the coincidence of the name. "You have no idea how bad he smells."

"Our four boys are in fishing or farming. I know what bad smells like. What size is he?"

"He's a little mouse. My height. Quite a bit thinner. I hate to admit that."

"My Connor's old gear will fit him then. He's a wiry lad. He's off to Fort Mac again, and he's lucky I haven't been charging him storage."

I said, "We'll get them back to you."

"You have kids?"

"Um, no."

"Trust me, when they grow up, they leave all their junk behind. Been trying to get rid of some of this stuff for years."

Number Two was a pine-lined cabin with plaid décor. It smelled like pine too. Well, more like Pine-Sol. It was spotless, and the cabin and the hot water both heated up quickly. Susan returned with dry, warm clothing, not stylish, but serviceable, including a down jacket with a little tear in it, a fleece beanie and a pair of work gloves. Grey socks with two red stripes stuck jauntily out of beat-up work boots. Jackpot for Mombourquette. And she brought a large green garbage bag, some zippered plastic bags, and a pair of rubber gloves for me.

Leonard lurched into the bathroom and, from behind the safety of the door, tossed out his jeans, fleece, socks, and underwear in exchange for towels that Susan had actually warmed somehow. Using the rubber gloves, I got Leonard's keys and wallet from the jeans pocket, sealed them in a plastic bag, and dropped them into my baggy jeans pocket. I transferred the clothes to the garbage bag and hustled them over to the house, where Susan whipped them out of my hands and trotted them to the washer. She returned, smiling, washed her hands, and pushed coffee and chocolate layer cake with mocha frosting at me.

"Sorry, got to get back," I said, although I took a coffee for each of us. The olfactory fallout from the portable toilet incident had diminished my appetite, possibly for all time.

"Later then," she said. "You look like you've been through a war."

Back in Number Two, Mombourquette announced he was ready for his dry clothes. I had placed the stack of borrowed clothes on the small table by the front door of the cabin next to my car keys, and the stinky duds were safely in the laundry.

I smiled and sipped my coffee. Why had I turned down that cake? By now, my nose had gone on strike, and food was once again possible. We still had nearly an hour to wait for our tow truck.

"Got you a change, Leonard, but it'll cost you."

A squawk ensured.

"Tell me what's really going on with Ray and I'll pass you your clothes."

Silence.

I smirked because I had the upper hand. Seconds later, Mombourquette—soft, hairless, and pink except for the large white towel he was wrapped in—emerged from the bathroom. Let's say he wasn't happy. Oddly enough, he had a gleam in his eye. What did he have to gleam about? He was in my power.

Of course, that was before he flung the towel over my head. I yelped as he manhandled me into the bathroom. My coffee went flying. I fell into the shower, smacking my knee on a sharp metal edge before I had the presence of mind to pull off the towel. What a difference three seconds makes. I stumbled out, slipped on the wet floor, and whacked my shoulder on the door frame. I steadied myself and stared at Leonard Mombourquette's bare behind as he leapt across the frost-covered lawn with the pile of clothing in his arms.

After a stunned second, I dashed after him, bellowing. What was he doing? I could see Susan at her door. She appeared to be doubled over.

Mombourquette opened the driver's side of Annie's car. I laughed because I was gaining on him, and he didn't even have the car keys. But of course he did, because I had left them beside the clothes while I tried my unsuccessful bit of blackmail. I reached the car just as he got it in gear and swerved off down the driveway, still starkers as far as I could tell.

Susan couldn't stop laughing as she beckoned me inside.

"He stole the car," I bleated. "The little bastard."

When she regained her composure, Susan tried again with the coffee and cake. "So your husband did a runner?"

I really could have used something stronger at this point, a neat single malt, for instance. But it was morning, and I was faced with an impossible chase. At least the duffle was safe in the closet at Auntie Annie's and not at the mercy of a maddened mouse.

I reached for the coffee. "Actually, that was Leonard Mombourquette, from up the road, near Cheticamp. Sorry to deceive you, but he didn't want his name known, since he grew up not far from here. Pretty humiliating being locked in a tipped-over portable toilet, don't you think? Don't be shy about telling your friends."

She wiped a tear from each cheek and shook.

"That would be M-O-M-B-O-U-R-Q-U-E-T-T-E, Leonard. Recently retired as a detective sergeant with the Ottawa police," I said before caving and gobbling a large slice of cake. After all, I hadn't a hope in hell of catching up with him. When I finally finished, I added, "Ask around. I'm sure plenty of people will know him."

"Oh, priceless. Best thing ever."

"Uh-huh. I'll settle up for the room and the stolen objects and the mess in the bathroom."

"No charge for you."

"Oh no. We have to. I mean your bathroom in Number Two must be…"

She showed me her palm. "Your money's no good here."

"Thank you. I hate to be wasting your time, but I'm not going to be able to catch up with him, until I get his car. It is struck in a boggy area behind some…" My voice trailed off as it dawned on me that I had not rented that car, and that meant issues with me driving it.

"He sounds like more trouble than he's worth, if you don't mind me saying so, dear."

I snorted. "The trouble is—sorry if I didn't mention it earlier—that some people have died, and more people are likely to if I don't find him."

"Normally, I wouldn't believe a word of that, dear, but after today, with what I've just seen, well, it could be true. I bet there's more to this story than meets the eye. Tell you what, why don't we get in the truck and pull you out of that bog?"

I stopped myself before saying that I couldn't accept that, since it wasn't my rental. But I was mad as hell, and I still had the keys to the Chrysler and Leonard's wallet. No point in quibbling about the fine print. I put all legal and ethical issues out of my mind until a better time. After all, Leonard would need to find a place without witnesses to get dressed. He'd also need gas. Then he'd wish he had his wallet.

"I don't know how I can thank you, Susan."

How far behind was I in the chase? I had just watched a retired and naked police officer steal an old lady's car, so now the official phrase for the day was "anything goes."

Susan was more than a smiling face and an amazing baker. She could handle that big Dodge and phone emergencies too. On the way, I ran the names of all the key players by her in case she knew any of them. After all, Cape Bretoners got around. But she shook her head at Ray Deveau, Sandy and Kenny Sutherland and Pierre Forgeron, Matty whoever and, of course, Sherry and Calum. When we arrived, the rakish portable toilet got Susan laughing again.

She was able to attach chains to some part of the Chrysler and drag it to the road before you could say "car theft."

I called Donald Donnie and told him that Leonard Mombourquette had given me the slip, but I was on his tail. I told him to keep an eye out for the little rodent in about an hour. "Life-or-death situation," I said, not entirely sure if Donald Donnie had grasped the seriousness.

I turned back to Susan, my laughing salvation. I promised to stay in touch. She insisted on mailing Leonard's clean clothing home to him. She refused my twenties for postage and trouble. I smiled my biggest smile and wrote down his address, easily done, since it was also my good friend Elaine's address. Susan said that she'd have no trouble getting the postal code from the post office. I said, "Make sure to leave a note, sign it LOVE SUSAN, and maybe add a lipstick kiss if that's not too much trouble."

She chuckled. "Entirely my pleasure."

I pulled away in the rescued red velvet chariot. That reminded me to give Elaine a call.

"Not here yet?" I said when she answered her cell.

"How did you know I was coming?"

"Because I know you. And I'm well aware that you'll have no idea where you are going."

"I'm glad you called. So where am I going?"

"When you get to Cape Breton, take the Cabot Trail toward Cheticamp and stay in touch. I think you're going somewhere between Cheticamp and Ingonish."

"Where are *you* going?"

"Funny you should ask. I'm about an hour away from the causeway, and I'm pursuing the mouse of your dreams."

"Don't call him that. Wouldn't he have gotten farther?"

"He would have if he hadn't spent the night in an overturned outhouse and then stole some clothes and raced off over the frost-covered lawn stark naked."

After a brief silence, she said, "I don't believe you."

"Suit yourself."

"Is he all right?"

"He won't be when I catch him. You'd better find him and kill him first. Did I mention that he stole an old lady's car?"

"It must be something terrible to make Leonard behave like that."

"Well, yes, Elaine. People have died. And Leonard won't tell me what's going on and insists that Ray is through with me. I'm supposed to go home and forget about him."

Her answer was anyone's guess, because the signal was lost.

Oh, well.

I sped along, over the speed limit, because I figured the cops would be run ragged what with storm-related activities and writing up reports. I had to admit I enjoyed the smooth ride and the luxurious interior with heated steering wheel and seats.

I slowed when I went through the immaculate Acadian communities that dotted the trail. Neat homes, none in need of paint, and crisp un-adorned yards with well-kept lawns. I figured kids would be out playing, and I wasn't keen on running over any of them. I kept an eye out for the blue Golf.

Once outside those villages, I floored it. The Chrysler's powerful engine had the edge over Annie's bucket of bolts. I slowed again for the return through Cheticamp and stopped for gas. No one at the station had seen a Golf with the naked mouse. Again, I made sure to spell MOM-BOURQUETTE clearly.

Outside the village, the road turned away from the stunning coastline and wove inland before the slow climb into the highlands.

Leonard Mombourquette was still my best hope of discovering what the hell was going on with Ray, and I had to locate him. I kept on his tail—pun intended—with my foot to the floor and my heart in my mouth and other relevant clichés. The road curved, and below I could see Pleas-ant Bay. I hoped he hadn't gone in that direction, but my money was on Ingonish. I drove like lives depended on it, which they did. At last, I reached one of the magnificent crests and the look-off at the Aspy fault, a sight that had been invisible on my drive down. The astonishing scenery with swaths of red, gold, and deep green foliage carpeting the huge cre-vasse was nothing compared to the impact of seeing that cute little blue Golf parked at a jaunty angle.

I eased into park, pocketed the keys, and slung my bag across my body. I pussyfooted up to the door and wrenched it open, finding myself nose-to-nose with a worried rodent making a phone call. He'd been able to get dressed somehow, a blessing for both of us. But how had he kept his phone?

I grinned evilly. "Gotcha."

CHAPTER TWENTY-THREE
Fancy meeting you here

He answered with a raised middle finger. For the record, laughing at an angry, ostensibly dumped woman is never a good move.

I gestured again for him to open the door. I lurched forward while shouting that I intended to bump him with his shiny red rental. This was neither good driving etiquette nor in keeping with the Revised Statutes of Canada. But desperate times, desperate measures. I hopped back into the Chrysler and shot forward to within inches of the Golf. I didn't want to destroy Annie's car, and as for the rental, imagine the paperwork.

He opened the door, his little pink nose twitching in outrage, and yelled, "What the hell? How many laws did you break tonight, MacPhee?"

Right. Proud words from a man who had danced naked across the frosty grass to steal a car less than an hour earlier. I backed up slightly and sneered. "Not enough, or I'd already have the answers to my questions. Number one, what the hell is going on, Leonard?"

"Nothing."

"For nothing you left Elaine hanging in Ottawa and paid full fare for a last-minute flight to Halifax and then rented Red Velvet here?"

I stepped out of the Chrysler, and he scurried away from the Golf. We both peered over the vast canyon and moved away from a couple that was gazing at the spectacular view. An orange-and-green minivan stuffed with tourists arrived at that exact moment. They swarmed out and around us, chattering in what sounded like German or Swedish, although a few seemed to have British accents. We edged farther from them, but they stuck with us. They did a lot of pointing and exclaiming about the scenery. *Schmorgy borgy bor.*

"I'm not going to tell you," Mombourquette shouted at me. Several of the warmly dressed tourists pivoted to gawk at him. I thought they might be the British ones.

"Wrong," I mouthed. "So wrong."

"It's not your business."

"Lower your voice, Leonard. You're giving Canada a bad name. And it is completely my business." I sidled up to him and pointed out into the canyon so we could both pretend to be enjoying the natural phenomenon created by the earth's violent upheaval a gazillion years earlier.

"Whatever."

"Tell me what's going on and I'll leave you in peace, Leonard."

He closed his eyes and leaned against the railing. I kept still, the cat outside the mouse hole.

The tourists were quite excited about the grandeur of Aspy fault. Normally, I'd share their enthusiasm, but not today.

Mombourquette's mouth opened. I didn't hear what he said because someone was screaming. I whirled to see what was going on. A glossy black Jeep with a crumbled front end accelerated forward and squealed to a stop. It reversed fast and took a run at the Chrysler, mashing it into the guardrail with a horrendous crash. Tourists panicked and scattered, squawking in many languages. Everyone had their hands over their ears, so not much point in all that shouting. I admit to squawking and running in circles myself before getting a grip and staring at Leonard's luxury rental. No one would be getting into the driver's side any time soon. The tourists kept calling to each other and pointing. Every one of them captured the drama with a cell phone. The Jeep backed up and took a rush at the Golf. I wrestled out Ray's cell phone and took a photo of it. I couldn't see much of the driver because of the watch cap pulled low over his forehead. Where the watch cap ended, a pair of aviator sunglasses began. He must have noticed people taking photos, and this might not end well for him. Before he could finish the job on the defenseless Golf, the Jeep whipped backward and shot down the highway.

The tourists huddled together, chattering, and showing each other their screens. A few were still shrieking.

Hoping someone had a good picture, I went from one to another, asking. I wasn't sure what they said, and they didn't understand my hand signals. If they spoke English, it had deserted them.

Speaking of deserted, we were about to be stuck with two nonfunctioning cars. Mombourquette put our "discussion" on hold to see if either of them was salvageable. The Chrysler was more accessible. I hopped in before Mombourquette and turned it on with the fob. The front of the fancy red rental was pretty much an accordion, but hope springs eternal. As Mombourquette opened the passenger door, the engine turned over. But when I put it in reverse, the car wobbled badly and then tilted as the front wheel broke off.

Mombourquette hopped out and ran for the Golf, with me after him. "I am the one who borrowed this car, and I should be driving it." Mombourquette merely laughed and got in. I tugged at the door. As he reversed and swerved, the wheels did not fall off the Golf, a bonus on the Cabot Trail, but I lost my grip on the door. With the passenger door still hanging open, he gunned it down the road.

The Europeans were still having a party with their phones. I figured that meant more than a few videos. Everyone nodded yes when I suggested pursuing Mombourquette. What an added adventure for them! But the van driver kept shaking his head.

"I'll pay you," I shouted above the din. "I'll make it worth your while. I've been abandoned here. That man stole my car!"

"I can't chase criminals. Think of the liability," the van driver said with puffed-up dignity. Under normal circumstances, I'd say he had a point, but these weren't normal circumstances, so I kicked his tire.

A male voice at my side distracted me. "I'll take you, um, miss. Careful, you don't want to hurt your foot."

I turned to find a young guy with a backward baseball cap, an armful of tattoos and low-slung jeans. I recognized the outfit, the tattoos, and their owner from Pearl's Pies. He pointed to his Saturn and said, "Hop in." That was good enough for me. I settled into the passenger seat and said, "Did you see that Golf?"

"Yep."

"Can you catch up?"

"This baby can practically fly. I put an F-150 engine in it."

Unless I was mistaken, an F-150 was a truck. I remembered him bragging to Pearl about that.

He glanced at me. "Want to see what it can do?"

Speed would suit my purpose, even though we were still on the twisty trail with extra mud and rocks.

"Go for it." I tried to ignore the McDonalds cartons, empty Tim's cups, cigarette packages, and I hated to think what else. The interior smelled like last week's overflowing ashtray with a topping of dirty socks. So what? I had a ticket to ride.

"I'm Cody," the kid said with a surprisingly shy smile as he gave the accelerator a thrill. I tried not to be distracted by his tattoo or the fact he liked to drive one-handed. He was my current knight in shining armour.

"Camilla MacPhee." I didn't mention that I already knew who he was.

"Are you married to that guy, Camilla?"

"I'm not married to anyone. And I'm never going to be."

"That's how I feel," Cody's smile widened. "So where to, Camilla?"

"Follow that mouse."

"What? You mean the Golf? The guy you're not married to?"

"Yes. Although he's only one of many men I'm not married to, I'm especially not married to him."

"That's Auntie Annie MacNeil's car, no? I know her pretty well."

"It is. Auntie Annie lent it to me, and this guy stole it from under my nose."

"Hard to believe. At his age too."

Mombourquette wasn't that much older than me. I shot Cody a dirty look.

He said, "So what happened?"

"Did you see the Jeep ram the red car? Minutes ago."

"I got here and saw him tearing off and you chasing him and then you hopping up and down." He didn't bother to suppress the laugh.

"Do you know anybody with a black Jeep?"

His eyes widened. "Sure, but not anyone who would ram a car. Who are we after? The Jeep or the Golf?"

"We need the Golf. But if we see a banged-up Jeep, that'll become top priority."

"Yeah, sounds like he's a homicidal maniac. Was he targeting you and the guy you were—"

"He was, and before you ask, I don't know why."

"But who is he?"

"Watch the road!"

"It's all pretty weird."

I checked the phone to see if we had a signal. We did not.

"Did you call the cops?"

"I didn't."

"I don't like cops."

"Join the club."

I waggled the phone. "I need to call my friend. Then I'll try to reach my former assistant, a marijuana impresario."

"Are they in Ingonish?"

"Ottawa."

Silence from the driver's side.

After a welcome question-free period, I said, "I appreciate this lift, Cody. What brought you up to the Aspy fault?"

"Just checking out the performance of the new engine on all those turns."

"That reminds me, can you ease up a bit on the turns? I need to stay alive until we catch him."

"You make me think of my mum. She's always screaming too."

"I am not screaming," I said with great dignity.

"Any idea where he's going?"

"I don't know, but I need to find him before anyone else dies."

"Cool," Cody said.

It turned out Cody was home for the weekend after his first month at Nova Scotia Community College. "Taking automotive service and repair," he said. "In Sydney."

"And you already know how to change the engine in a car?"

"Coulda done that before I went. It's more than knowing how. You need your papers, don't you?"

I gazed out the window as the scenery shot by. Dizzying. Was Cody involved, or was his arrival a bit of luck?

"What do you do, Camilla?"

"I'm a lawyer."

"Well then, you understand."

I gawked at him. "What?"

"You can't just tell people you're a lawyer and start representing them. You need to have your papers. Right? Do you have your papers?"

"I take your point."

New topic needed. I decided to grill him about the good people of Ingonish. He knew Auntie Annie and Rita Susanne because of some complicated relationship that I couldn't sort out. Of course, Pearl was his grandmother. He knew Kenny Sutherland but not Sandy, although he'd heard that Sandy was dead. He said he didn't know Ray, Leonard, or Pierre Forgeron.

"They sound like more of the French side to me," he said.

He knew Sherry and Calum, or his mum did anyway, but no one called Matty.

As we seemed to have reception at this point, I decided to get a photo of Wayne Nowicki.

Google delivered a cluster of images, including one large familiar one. I knew where I'd seen him before. He'd been at Kiju's talking to Ray, on his motorcycle at Sherry and Calum's and at The Seagull, being way too cozy.

I waggled my phone under Cody's nose. "Do you know him? He's a cop in Sydney. But he's been hanging around here lately."

"Nowicki. He's a hardass."

I assumed if you were driving a car with an illegal truck engine, it could colour your viewpoint. "In what way?"

"Doesn't mind knocking people around."

"Really?"

Cody shrugged. "That's what I've heard. Never met him personally. You look like you've already had a pretty rough time. So be careful, you know."

"*I* look like I've had a rough time? Please keep your eyes on the road."

"I don't mean to be ignorant, but have you been on a pig farm?"

I nodded. "Worse."

He said, "If you have a shower and get clean clothes and maybe some antibiotic cream for your face, you'll be ... um."

I took control of the rear-view to check my face. Sure enough, I'd had an abrasion or two. Must have been those branches behind the portable toilet. Until that point, I hadn't felt much, but those scratches had started to sting. My knee and shoulder were throbbing too. I owed Mombourquette for knocking me against the shower when he made his naked escape. Now, everything started to hurt like hell.

Despite the lull in the conversation, we made amazing time back to Ingonish without sighting Auntie Annie's vehicle or a damaged black Jeep.

As we shot past The Seagull, I said, "I'll buy you a fisherman's platter if I get where I'm going alive."

"Deal." Even with the deal, Cody didn't change his driving style at all. In his defense, I *was* still alive. Hard to know how, though.

We were well over the speed limit as we rocketed through Ingonish. Cody slowed as we neared the park entrance. He had a Resident's Pass. He waved at the attendant.

Not long after, we passed the Liquor Commission, and Cody commented on a couple of trucks parked. Of course, this kid loved vehicles. What was wrong with me? If anyone would notice Ray in the truck, it was Cody.

"Don't suppose you happened to notice a silver Silverado around here lately?"

"Sure. Lotta people bought trucks while they were working in Fort Mac, eh."

"Right. This one was silver, and it had New Brunswick plates."

"That one. Yep."

"You saw it?"

Again with the eyes off the road. "Sure did."

"I'm after one of the guys in that truck. Matter of life and death."

"Who are they?"

"One of them was Ray Deveau."

"I don't know him. Told you that, and I didn't see any guys. There wasn't anybody inside it. I seen a truck like that at Hughie's. Might have been the same one."

My heart rate shot up. "Who's Hughie? Where does he—? Hang on! Isn't that Auntie Annie's Golf up ahead?"

"Jeez, it is. Let me catch him."

"No! Don't let him see us."

"Why not? He doesn't know me."

"He'll recognize me!"

"I got a beanie in the back. Pull it on."

Nestled in the piles of Big Mac wrappers, cold leftover fries, empty Keith's cans—and other objects I didn't want to examine too closely—was the beanie. I didn't want to reach back into the debris, but I knew the hat could help.

"I got sunglasses too. In the glove compartment."

I slipped on the beanie and the sunglasses and convinced Cody not to ride on the Golf's bumper. I made a point of not smirking. No point in blowing my cover.

"You look like my little brother. That's pretty funny."

"Laugh away."

"Because before you put on the beanie, you reminded me of my mum."

"I have never reminded anyone of their mother."

He shrugged. "If you say so."

"You were telling me where you saw the guys in the Silverado."

"Nope. Saw the truck in the garage."

"Fine. You said it was at Hughie's, but I don't know—"

"Hey, your guy is turning up that road. Isn't that Sherry and Calum's place? My mum knows them."

"Pull over. Don't go up yet."

"Why not? You want to catch him or not?" With great reluctance, Cody pulled onto the soft shoulder before the driveway.

"I need to see who he's with first. Park here for a minute. I'll take a look through the trees. Stay put."

He lit a roach and said, "I'm not goin' anywheres."

I was thankful he hadn't smoked that before our harrowing ride. I hopped out and tiptoed behind the dark cedars fringing the side of the road. I turned and called back. "Leave the window open in case I have to call for help. I'll be right back."

"Sure, man. Wait, what do you mean, call for help?"

Through the trees I could see Mombourquette waving his paws at Calum. Calum stood resolutely with his own arms crossed as Mombourquette kept leaping in the air with rage—unless that was panic. Brutus responded by barking and surging to the end of his chain, apparently wishing to rid the world of Mombourquette. No one noticed me.

I slunk back into the trees and found a thick copse of evergreens to hide in. I was close enough to see and hear them clearly and, with luck, to figure out what was going on. But I heard no talk of Silverado. No black Jeep. And nothing else useful.

CHAPTER TWENTY-FOUR
Have I got a treat for you!

Calum and Mombourquette slunk into the house, glancing over their shoulders. They brought Brutus with them. Excellent. That would work in my favour. The kitchen window was open, but their voices were drowned out by the frantic dog. I was pretty sure Brutus was barking at me, but I had to get closer to hear what they were plotting.

Even from the trees I could hear Mombourquette yelling, "Can you not shut that creature up?"

That was followed by Calum yelling back. The back door opened again, and Sherry ejected Brutus and hooked him onto his chain.

I hurried back to Cody's car and snatched the half-eaten bag of French fries I had spied in the back seat. "Don't go anywhere," I said before hoofing it back to the house.

"Whatever you say, man."

Brutus stopped barking and sniffed the air as I inched forward.

"Hey, old buddy," I said softly, tossing a handful of the cold and fatty fries in the opposite direction. He lunged for them joyfully. Too bad he was back to me in under a minute. Luckily, I still had plenty left. I doled them out and strained to hear through the window. My instincts told me that Mombourquette, Sherry, and Calum were not killers. But they were implicated somehow. I tossed the nearly empty bag of fries as far as I could, and Brutus raced for it, stretching the chain to the limit.

"But do you know where Ray and Pierre are?" Sherry was asking.

"I don't, but we have to find them before it's too late."

"What about that Camilla? Is she still blundering around?"

"I ditched Camilla at the Aspy fault. Don't worry. She'll be on a plane home soon."

Maybe not, Lennie.

Everyone took that moment to stop raising their voices, and the stupid dog decided to growl at me for another mouthful.

"Shh," I said.

The idiot barked.

Sherry called out, "What is it, Brutus?"

"Never mind the goddam dog, Sherry. He can't answer you. Chill out. You're jumpier than he is."

"Do you blame me?"

"We won't get anywhere if we panic," Calum grumbled.

Sherry yelled, "We have to get the hell out of here before we're dead too."

Whoa! I didn't see that coming.

Brutus chose that moment to growl. No gratitude at all, that dog. I never thought I'd be glad to hear the roar of a motorcycle, but this case was different. Luckily, the hound turned his attention to the newcomer. I scrambled onto a metal trashcan and then up to the shed roof. My knee and shoulder gave me grief, and the new scrapes on my shins would have to heal along with them.

I might have been shocked enough to fall off the shed if I hadn't already known about the connection between Nowicki and Calum and Sherry. Soon everyone was yelling: the big cop, Calum, Sherry, and Mombourquette. Brutus helped by barking ferociously. Calum bellowed, and the dog went silent.

Sherry and the motorcycle guy reappeared and stood by the back door in an intense conversation. Calum was inside, settling Brutus into his time-out room.

I lay flat and kept out of sight, but my position on the shed roof would have taken some explaining. I caught snatches of words.

The motorcycle guy called out. "Get moving," and left with a roar of his powerful engine.

Crap. Get moving where?

Sherry and Calum made for their truck, followed by Mombourquette, who scurried to the Golf. I prayed they wouldn't spot me, but they never

looked back, just turned left onto the road. Mind you, Brutus was howling, and if Sherry had turned to look, I'd have been visible. But she was
busy crying in the passenger side of the truck. Calum peeled off down
the driveway, followed by the little rat. I jumped from the roof, twisting
my ankle slightly, and speed-limped through the woods to Cody's car,
swearing all the way.

Then I really had something to swear about.

As I should have anticipated, Cody was gone, spooked perhaps by
the cop, Nowicki. I sneaked back to the barn where the cars were hidden. Donald Donnie's car was in front of Ray's, blocking it. The two
front tires were flat, with gaping cuts on the rubber. Ray's tires had been
slashed too. Oh well, we were pretty much out of gas anyway. And so
much for trusting Sherry and Calum.

I had no way to catch up to Nowicki's bike, Calum and Sherry in the
truck, or even Mombourquette in Auntie Annie's car. But they wouldn't
be worried about me. As far as anyone knew, I was mid-temper-tantrum
at the Aspy fault.

I caught sight of Sherry's Focus with its distinctive *Hug a Puffin Today* bumper sticker. I reminded myself I had already stolen one car today,
however briefly and unsuccessfully. But might as well be hanged for
a sheep as a lamb, as they say. Of course, the keys were probably with
Sherry, unless they were in the drawer where she'd tossed my fob and
Donald Donnie's keys.

I dashed to the farmhouse. The back door was unlocked. Technically,
that made what I was about to do "unlawful entering" but not *breaking*
and entering. I could—if I found myself before a judge—make the case
that my keys were in the house and I had every expectation that Sherry
and Calum would have welcomed me. After all, hadn't they left the door
unlocked?

Stranger cases had succeeded before the bench. Making off with
Sherry's car would turn out to be a totally different kettle of legal fish. I
went straight for the drawer and ignored Brutus's heartbreaking howls.
I whipped it open to find a collection of keys and fobs. I rummaged
through typical junk drawer clutter and snatched up the fob for the Focus.
I dashed for the open door. Sherry would notice that someone had rum-

maged through the drawer, but then, of course, she'd also see that the car was missing.

Brutus was busy heaving his weight against the door. *Thump. Thump. Thump.*

"Sorry, Brutus," I said. "They'll let you out when the time is right."

The Focus purred like the little calico when presented with a dish of tuna. I eased it onto the uneven driveway.

As I reached the bottom, I slammed on the brakes. I closed my eyes and imagined the junk drawer. What was in it? Batteries. Safety pins. Rubber bands. Bills and envelopes. Sherry even had a couple of Celtic Colours tickets for the next night in Mabou. Was that it? Was I reacting to a reminder of concerts that were to have been part of my cancelled honeymoon?

I heard a vehicle coming just in time to put the car in park and duck down. Peering up cautiously, I reacted with horror to the black Jeep with the damaged grill. The driver—still with the hat pulled low—left the engine idling and raced into the house. Seconds later, he exploded through the door, Brutus right after him. He leapt into the Jeep and slammed the door. Lucky for me, the rain had washed off enough of the mud to make the plate visible. And the Jeep had been just parked long enough for me to memorize it. I broke another law and called Mrs. Parnell as I drove one-handed.

I left a message with the plate number and a précis of what had happened to me since we'd last spoken. I left the same message for Alvin. Then I floored it. For years, I'd attempted to talk sense into my criminal clients, and now look at me. I shot toward Ingonish, the same direction Sherry and Calum, the Golf, the Gold Wing, and now the Jeep had gone. Quite the parade.

I tried to recall the contents of the drawer because I couldn't return to check. Brutus was patrolling by the door. The drawer. Keys. What had my subconscious observed in the clutter? Wait. An envelope!

A taupe envelope had been tucked in that drawer. The type you'd find with trendy greeting cards that cost eight dollars a pop. I'd seen the twin to that taupe envelope behind Ray's bed after he disappeared. Two thick high-quality taupe envelopes made a strange coincidence. Coincidence often indicates a real connection.

I needed to get back to the farmhouse. I told myself it would take a minute and I would catch up with them. I didn't want to be close enough to be seen in Sherry's car anyway. I drove the Focus right up to the steps. Brutus was prowling around, hungry and annoyed. He hurled himself toward me and stopped. Of course, he was smart enough to know it was Sherry's car. He danced in excited circles, huge tail wagging. But it wouldn't be long before he got a whiff of me, the great imposter. I jumped from the car, keeping the driver's side door open to block him. I took the steps two at a time. Brutus was on to my little trick in seconds. Darn that sense of smell. I barely got the back door shut in time. He snarled and hurled himself at the door. I apparently didn't do much good as I shouted, "Hey, Brutus. Good doggie. I'll have a treat for you."

I took his response to mean: *I'm going to rip you to shreds with my teeth.*

One bit of good news: this envelope had a note inside. I prayed it would be worth delaying my chase. I stuck the envelope in my pocket and crossed to the fridge. Brutus was going to be in for a treat. But why was he so quiet all of a sudden?

I peered out the window at the step. No Brutus. Excellent, unless he was hiding ready to spring at me.

But it was worse: the murderous beast was waiting in the Focus.

I prayed for steak. No such luck. But I located a package of hamburger. Turned out I was a food thief as well. When this was over, I was going to have to rethink my entire value system. Fumbling, I shaped the hamburger into small patties and rewrapped all but one in the brown paper.

In case Brutus finished me off, I made the choice to check the note in the envelope. I would have hated to go to my grave not knowing.

The envelope was addressed to Sherry. It had been neatly slit. A folded note remained inside. I unfolded it and stared at the crisp block letters written with what must be a superfine Sharpie.

OCTOBER 2

FOR YOUR CRUEL ACTIONS, YOU WILL NOW PAY THE FINAL
PRICE.

YOU HAD A CHOICE. SOMEONE HAD NONE.

OTHERS HAVE PAID THE PRICE AND MORE WILL PAY.

IT'S YOUR TURN.

TOO LATE TO MAKE AMENDS.

PUT YOUR AFFAIRS IN ORDER.

Creepy. Over the top, even. Was it a childish prank? But the panic that
Sherry, Calum, and even Nowicki showed indicated it was no joke.

I refolded the note, inserted it in the envelope, and slipped it back in
the drawer. They hadn't taken it with them. Why not? Had they called
the police? Was that why Nowicki had shown up? Was he merely an old
friend arriving to warn of an ominous threat? But why had Sherry pretended not to know Nowicki? And just how did Mombourquette fit in?

Had Ray received a similar note about cruel actions and paying the
price? My mouth was dry. I "borrowed" a can of Diet Coke from my
hosts. One more small crime to add to my spree. I snapped off the tab
and drank out of the can.

Taking the car was essential and appropriate, given that our vehicles
had been disabled, but stealing food struck me as sinking to a new low.
Still, since Brutus had all those sharp teeth, it had to be done. I slipped
twenty dollars onto the counter to pay for the life-saving meat and the
pop. That included a tip.

I needed to find out what the creepy note meant. The envelope had
been addressed to Sherry Gillis, not MacDonald, so this must have to do
with her past.

I had more reason to catch Sherry and Calum and demand the truth
before the guy in the Jeep tracked down his next victim.

I presented Brutus with the first patty. He went for it, and I eased into
the driver's seat. It was time to hit the road. I kept the Focus to the speed
limit, even though it had the pep to go faster. Next to me, my new sidekick was happily licking his chops. The supply of hamburger dwindled,
and I worried what would happen when I ran out. To test the waters, I

reached out and scratched his ears. "We're in the car, Brutus. Going for a drive." That always got Gussie mellowed out. Of course, gentle Gussie was not likely to sink a pointed canine into a vein. But indeed, Brutus and I seemed to have reached an accord.

We bombed along, scanning the sides of the road, checking for familiar vehicles. The Silverado, the Jeep, and Auntie Annie's Golf could have been anywhere.

"We'll find them, Brutus," I said firmly.

"We'll rip their throats out," Brutus answered in my imagination.

"First we'll ask them about the note, partner."

Brutus stared gravely at the road. I took that as a yes.

"Let's find Sherry and Calum." The large tail found room to thump, even in this tiny car. With the Resident's Pass in the Focus, I waved my way through the park entrance, hoping the attendant didn't notice me in Cody's beanie and sunglasses driving Sherry's no doubt familiar car.

A few minutes later, I glanced to the left as we shot by Auntie Annie's. I felt a flush of guilt about her car. I would have to replace it, and who knew what else I'd be liable for. It would take me a while to dig myself out of this financial hole. Probably a year in the heart of Europe would have been a cheaper option.

"Hindsight," I said out loud.

Brutus nodded.

I slowed passing The Seagull. The parking lot held dozens of cars, and the place was obviously hopping. I saw none of the vehicles I was hoping for.

The day had gotten away from me. I took off the sunglasses as the light was dimming. Brutus actually yawned. I know that can be a sign of anxiety in a dog, and I hoped Brutus was merely sleepy.

Scanning each passing property, I barrelled through the rapidly darkening evening. October may be beautiful, but the shorter days remind us that winter is on its way. It was hard to see, even if I knew where to look. But I had no better plan than to drive back and forth along the coast searching for clues.

A slow, steady drizzle started. How could there be any rain left after the previous night's storm? Approaching headlights made for a dangerous glare.

I slowed and swore at the first sign of flashing lights. Cars were lining the road on both sides. Was it a traffic stop? Not so good when I was driving a car that didn't belong to me. I pulled over.

"Excuse me, Brutus," I said, and opened the glove compartment. I switched on the interior light and dumped out a box of tissues, a can of Coke, a wool hat, painkillers and even a pair of binoculars. Sherry probably used them to spot puffins. I rummaged farther back and located her manual. I held it by the spine and shook it. Sure enough, a plastic card holder with the registration and insurance papers fell out. I slipped them into my pocket. If questioned, I'd say that my car had been disabled, and so I'd borrowed my friend, Sherry's.

Squinting into the darkness, I could see cell phone flashlights and people out wandering around in the rain. The Mounties were on site. One officer stood in the middle of the highway, apparently trying to keep order on the dark road.

I reached into the back seat and dragged Sherry's green rain jacket into the front. I ditched the beanie and slipped on the jacket. I picked up the binoculars that had fallen to the floor and slowly eased out of the car. "Stay, Brutus."

Brutus did not care for the wet weather. As I exited, he crawled over to the driver's seat and settled down with a giant sigh.

I hunched my shoulders and ambled forward. A thirtyish couple leaned against their vehicle. He had his arms wrapped around her and was stroking her long, dark hair. Rivulets of rain ran down their faces.

"What's happening?" I said interrupting their moment.

They both stared at me, glazed. I felt a sharp pain in my gut. "Is it some kind of accident?"

She sobbed and burrowed closer into his chest.

"How long ago?"

"They won't say."

Please don't let it be Ray. Whatever he was up to, I'd forgive him if he was alive. I moved forward toward a buzz of conversation. The whoop of a siren sounded behind me. I shifted from the centre of the road to the side, and an ambulance rolled forward, blaring whenever some fool blundered in front of it.

The side of the road with the overhanging evergreen branches worked well to let me gain ground.

"Sorry," I said, nudging a bystander out of the way. "I have to know it's not my fiancé. He didn't come back today." People edged aside, and I got closer.

The Mounties had set up flares and stretched yellow caution tape off on the right side of the road to hold back onlookers and protect the scene. A young RCMP officer was being firm with a couple of excited locals. It wasn't the woman I'd encountered at the Sutherlands, but I knew I wouldn't get past that tape.

I felt turmoil swirling in the growing crowd, and I was sure the officers could too. I climbed onto a large flat rock with a clear view, raised the binoculars, and peered at the muddy Dodge Ram, tilted and smashed into the rocks. I could make out the puffin bumper stickers and even the large one with the Cape Breton Liberation Army. It didn't seem funny anymore. I felt my throat closing. The passenger's side window was open. The airbags had deployed, so it was hard to see inside. I could make out two people. The driver's head was bent at a nasty angle, but I recognized Calum's cap. The passenger was hunched over, her arm hanging limply from the open window. The binoculars were powerful enough for me to reveal a veil of silver hair and a hummingbird tattoo.

My legs turned to rubber, and my hands shook. My stomach heaved. I slipped down and slumped against the rock.

"Are you okay?" A woman with a kind face bent down to check. She offered me a tissue from the wad she was carrying.

"Yes. They weren't so lucky."

She blew her nose. "People are saying they're both dead."

CHAPTER TWENTY-FIVE
A bad night for a swim

Twenty feet away, Nowicki was leaning against the guardrail, his helmet tucked under his arm despite the rain. The big cop was weeping openly. Many of the people gathered near the crash scene were distraught. But I trusted Nowicki as far as I could throw his bike. Were these crocodile tears? From the way he handled that bike, he'd been furious when he tore out of the driveway at the farm. Was that fury aimed at Sherry and Calum? Had he driven them off the road? Or had it been that bleepin' Jeep?

He'd been ahead but could Nowicki have waited for the right moment, turned and blocked the road so that Calum would have no choice but to swerve into the rocks?

Possible but unlikely. Dangerous for the biker and hard to stage with slippery roads. Although I wasn't ready to give up on Nowicki as brutish murderer, I didn't see how he could have pulled it off. And I knew firsthand that the driver of the black Jeep was fully capable of slamming into another vehicle and coming back to try to finish the job. Even so, Nowicki was involved. Somehow.

His blubbering didn't convince me. I've seen too much contrived emotion on the witness stand.

Was he an accomplice? I'd once been part of case where an accessory had planted what looked like a dead body in the road, and the victim had panicked, swerved and ended up dead in a ravine, all while his new widow had a perfect alibi.

Justice did not prevail in that case. Would it in this?

I glanced back and saw other vehicles, pickups mostly, parked on the shoulder of the road. They shielded the Focus from view. At least fifty people milled around, crying and hugging and smoking. One guy was drinking from a can of Keith's.

I hustled closer to Nowicki. "Did you kill them?" I said from a safe enough distance.

He jerked up and glanced around, finally settling on me. He wiped his face. "What?"

"Did you kill them?"

It belated occurred to me that Nowicki was a cop and almost certainly would know the officers at the scene. Very unwise of you, Camilla, as Alvin and others liked to say.

The hood of Sherry's rain jacket hid my face and hair. I ramped up my new Cape Breton accent.

He yelled, "Why would I kill them? Who the hell are you?"

"You're mixed up in this, and I have proof."

"What goddam proof?"

I was counting on him thinking that I was a slightly deranged local with a chip on my shoulder. "What were you looking for at their farm?"

He lurched forward. "How do—?"

"Better get your story straight. Even if your buddies are across the road—" I pointed toward the cluster of police vehicles "—murder is murder."

He studied me with narrowed eyes, trying to place me. He moved quickly for a big man, and I skipped backward, keeping out of his reach. I continued the barrage of questions. "Were they going to meet Leonard Mombourquette or Ray Deveau? And what's your involvement in this murder spree?" I'd almost let down my guard when he lunged for me. I leaped back.

Lucky for me, he slipped on the wet mud. I ducked down and wove in and out of the crowd and raced for the Focus. I whipped off the raincoat and stuck it in the back seat. I opened the driver's side door after offering a few confident words of greeting to Brutus. He lifted his head, yawned, and returned to the passenger seat.

Without wasting a minute, I backed the Focus off the shoulder and onto the road. I joined the other cars making U-turns to head away from the disaster.

The cops would be locating witnesses, and it was a good time to leave. My hands shook as I clutched the steering wheel. I couldn't unsee the image of Sherry's still, white arm.

I drove back to Auntie Annie's to dry off and calm down. Sherry and Calum were dead, Nowicki was weeping, and Mombourquette and Ray were still unaccounted for. Of course, Cody was somewhere. Was he involved too? Brutus whined as I found myself shaking violently. I was about to pull over and fiddle with the heat and the defroster when the distinctive flash of red and blue lights in the distance caught my attention.

Police. Make that more police. Were they on their way to join their colleagues up the road? The flashing roof lights didn't appear to be getting any closer. That was an unpleasant complication. If the officers were from nearby or knew the area, chances were they'd know Sherry. They'd probably recognize her car with the puffin bumper and window stickers. And they'd possibly know Brutus.

This new criminal career was catching up with me. My fingerprints would be all over the kitchen and the car. Plus I'd dognapped Brutus. Anyone in their right mind would consider me a suspect. I pulled off the road and into the driveway of the first house without lights. If the police already had a reason to consider this a double homicide rather than an accident, they'd be very interested in finding witnesses.

It was time to hoof it. Auntie Annie's wasn't all that far. The Focus would be located soon enough. Who except the people involved would know where Sherry and Calum were going? I used my flannel shirt to wipe my fingerprints from the steering wheel, door, and glove compartment. Of course, a forensic examination would reveal traces of me. I could explain that. After all, Sherry had given me a lift. But Sherry would never have left Brutus alone in the car, so I couldn't either. Although Brutus was now on my team, I worried about his reaction to other people.

If confronted, I could always say I'd been visiting Sherry and Calum and became alarmed when I heard about the accident and decided to take the dog and go check it out. But we lawyers like to tell our clients: keep it simple. Don't make up stories if you encounter the cops. It's easy for the police to check and hard for the suspect to remember fibs invented in a panic. I didn't want to stay on the road and have Wayne Nowicki run me down with his big bike. That left the beach. I wasn't keen to stumble along the rocky shoreline, full of surprise pools and slippery sand. I was already drenched, and the Atlantic in October is not what you'd call hospitable. Still, what choice did I have?

I reached into the back seat for the dog leash. "You will have to behave, Brutus, because we are going for a walk on the beach, and we do not, repeat, do not, want to attract attention."

I suppose like all dogs he heard "blah blah blah," but "walk" rang a bell.

I hooked up Brutus, and we slunk into the darkness. The beach was far better than the alternatives. I needed to locate the path we had taken to Auntie's Annie's earlier. Brutus was in his element, standing tall, sniffing the salt air, revelling in the whole scene, making joyful dashes forward to catch the waves. Of course, he didn't know his people were dead.

As the rain began to taper off, the water glittered. The ocean always seems so appealing, but I wasn't fooled. The water temperature in October would be enough to kill you in fifteen minutes. I could probably swim faster, but I wouldn't last long enough to get far.

I kept trying the cell phone in case I got a signal. I almost shrieked with joy when I found three bars. That was like winning Chase the Ace!

By the light of the screen, I called Mombourquette. It went straight to voice mail. "Sherry and Calum are dead, I repeat, dead. Wayne Nowicki is skulking around, and he's involved in all this. You and Ray should stop playing games before someone else dies. I know about the letters. Call me."

Next Elaine. To my surprise, she picked up. I said, "Do not interrupt. Your lover-boy is in grave danger. Two bodies have been found, and they are people who met with Leonard. You must tell him to contact me."

"I'm on it," she said.

Next, Alvin. I'd kept moving while I was talking, not the smartest decision. The three beautiful bars vanished as I reached his voice mail. "People have been killed," I blurted before the signal died.

"Let's go, Brutus," I said, picking up the pace. "Auntie Annie will have a nice dry house. And she has a landline as well as a strong cell signal."

Brutus didn't care. He wanted those tantalizing waves. I tugged on the leash without success. He was eighty pounds of muscle, and I was more like a strand of overcooked pasta by that point. I lost control of the leash, and Brutus dashed off, dancing on the rough sand and running into and out of the surf.

"Food, Brutus. Let's go get some food."

He lurched forward in my direction, joyful. I was far from happy but felt a small measure of hope. Of course, that was before the rock slammed into my back.

I pitched forward, hands shooting out to break my fall. Rough-edged stones scraped my palms. I needed to—but I got a sharp push and grazed my forehead against a boulder. I was dazed and confused by my fall and stunned by the blow. It took me many long seconds to understand that I was now being rolled toward the edge of the water, buffeted by stones and scratched by sand. I gasped in shock when I hit the frigid water. I squirmed and fought, but someone was kneeling on my back, holding my face under the cold Atlantic.

CHAPTER TWENTY-SIX
Getting there is not half the fun

I pictured my sisters when they learned I'd been stupid enough to freeze to death in the ocean. And Ray. Ray's face was just out of reach. Thinking of Ray gave me a shot of adrenaline. I went limp, then heaved myself up, knocking my attacker off.

Over my gasping for breath, I heard snarling, barking, and a scream of pain. I sat back on my feet and fought to get air into my lungs. I keeled over, righted myself, and crawled out of the water. Brutus's snout nudged my face, and I felt the attentions of his large, rough tongue. I tried to say, "Good dog. There's a steak in your future."

Brutus whined and turned to the edge where the beach met the thick cedars. A dark blur disappeared behind the trees.

I wobbled to my feet, clutching the dog's collar to steady myself.

"We need to get out of here, Brutus." He must have liked hearing his name because he leaned his full weight against my legs. I suppose he meant it as a gesture of solidarity, but it knocked me over again, and then I had to put up with the nudging snout. "I'm good," I insisted, getting onto all fours and then crawling toward the nearest boulder to hoist myself up. "Why don't we get you a bite to eat?"

I wasn't sure if Brutus understood as my teeth clattered like my father's ancient Underwood. But he trotted forward. I latched on to his collar again, and it offered me some momentum. I was glad to know that if my stealthy attacker returned, Brutus had my back, my front, and probably my sides. Of course, a dangerous human would have no trouble finding a weapon to take out the dog and then me. Lob a few well-chosen rocks, and hypothermia would take care of the rest.

We needed to get back on the road. Some kind local would stop and help us.

We found a path from the beach and took cover behind the pines on the edge. Brutus liked the trip more than I did. Stumps and sharp rocks gave me a few more abrasions, but the pain reminded me I was alive. Brutus was also good to talk to. He didn't interrupt, and he left me with the feeling that I had at least one friend in the world.

We burst out onto the road with a strangled gasp from me and a bark from my hero. I hoped our attacker wasn't still lurking about to hear.

I tried to flag down the first few cars while Brutus lunged and howled. We staggered on in what I hoped was the direction of Auntie Annie's. My brain felt foggy and my limbs moved in slow motion. After the fifth car drove on the wrong side of the road to avoid us, I tied Brutus out of sight and entreated him to shut the hell up. Then I stood in the road and waved my arms as much as I could. A battered green pickup slowed and stopped. The grizzled driver gawked at my filthy, torn clothes and the bloody scrapes on my face and hands. "What's the other guy look like?"

"He'll be worse if I ever find out who he is." I was surprised he could understand me.

"You want me to get you to the nearest hospital? Our local clinic's closed now."

"If I can get a drive to my Auntie Annie MacNeil, that will be great."

"I know Annie MacNeil. Hop in."

As he was unscratched and unbitten and was wearing dry clothes, I figured he hadn't tried to kill me on the beach.

"Thanks. I have this dog with me. I can put him in the back and ride with him too. I don't want to wreck your truck."

"Suit yourself," he said. "We're not goin' far."

Brutus and I huddled in the open back of the pickup for the few minutes it took to pull into the driveway at Auntie Annie's. I stroked Brutus's wet fur and apologized for misjudging his character earlier. I thought he said thanks for all the goodies. I kept the leash tight, just in case we weren't as friendly as I wanted to believe. I could no longer open my eyes when we stopped. Our anonymous driver tried to give me a little shake, but Brutus did not care for that. My Good Samaritan tried shouting, "We're here, dear. At your Auntie Annie's."

I couldn't stand up or move at all. "Let me sleep."

In the distance, banging and shouting. Then dogs barking and then a skunky whiff of cannabis, followed by, "Lord thunderin' Jesus, Camilla. What have you done?" Then "Can anyone control this friggin' dog?"

Why was Alvin here? Had I died and gone to hell? I could imagine no other explanation. But in case I was alive and merely hallucinating, I said, "Brutus is a good boy. Saved my life." My hands were closed tight on his leash, frozen into position. "He's hungry. Throw a burger into the shed and he'll go."

My rescuer snorted. "Annie won't have no burgers."

I opened my eyes to see Auntie Annie's worried face. I took comfort in the bright blue eyes that matched her sweater and her faint lily-of-the-valley scent. It would all be okay now. Her soft, fluty voice whispered, "I have some shepherd's pie. Let's give it a try."

My tongue was thick and slow. "He's Sherry's dog. Sherry's dead. And Calum."

"What's she saying?"

Alvin said, "I can't tell, but she's freezing. We need to get her warmed up. Stat!"

Stat? I loved that. I couldn't manage to answer. *Atta boy*, I thought. *Stat! Ha ha ha. I don't know how you got here, Alvin, but I can almost forgive you for the time you painted all those murals in my house.*

Was that Brutus being enticed away? I heard shouts of *come and get it*. Then someone pried my fingers from the leather leash and the barking stopped.

I don't know how many people bundled me into the warm farmhouse. Alvin was shouting orders, an oddity in itself. Apparently, he knew that you could heat blankets in a clothes dryer.

My reluctant driver muttered, "I better call 911."

Then Rita Susanne's calm, in-charge voice felt like the warm soft blanket I was wrapped in. And Auntie Annie murmuring felt like all the hot tea, oatcakes, shortbread, and chowder you could ever want. Pies too. Rita Susanne said to the driver, "All the emergency services are under stress because of a bad accident tonight. My friends in the RCMP are telling people to stay off the roads because of the storm. You should get home before it's too late. I don't know why Camilla went out in this weather, but don't worry. We'll take care of her. Thank you."

I felt myself lifted and delivered to a soft bed. My freezing clothes were removed, and more toasty warm blankets surrounded me. Rita Susanne patted my icy shoulder, and I relaxed. There's something about the smell of baby powder that apparently combats near-death experiences. "You were lucky. You could have died. I'm glad I was able to get here for Annie's evening meds. I'm not sure she could have handled all this."

Before long, she returned with some herbal tea. "Drink it. It will help warm you." I felt far away as I watched her strong, capable hands adjust the pillows and blankets, sit me up, and close my hand around the mug. I took comfort in her scrubs with the owl pattern. Mmm. Owl. Wisdom.

My eyes didn't want to stay open, and that didn't go well with the tea. "Come on, Camilla. You can do it, easy-peasy," she instructed.

I did my best. Someone was trying to call Rita Susanne away. *No. Don't go. Don't leave me here.*

I was even glad to hear Alvin. Had he barged into the room? "Well, I'm calling 911, although heaven help them if they try to deal with you, Camilla."

I tried to say, "Hey, watch it," but went out like a light.

•••

My right eye opened a slit. Light? Morning? I lay under a heavy weight of blankets, tangled in some unfamiliar garment, struggling to remember something urgent. But what?

Next to me, Gussie added to the warmth that had seeped back into my body. Gussie's essential aroma was my first clue that I was still alive, unless that smell was part of the hell scenario. Gussie gave me a look that told me he knew about Brutus. The little calico cat reached out and swatted my nose. That would teach me to cheat on my pets. Alvin continued on guard in the yellow-painted rocking chair, like some evil pot-dispensing Ma Bates. A nightmare? His nine visible earrings glinted ominously.

"What are you doing here?" I said.

"Right, *thank you*, Alvin. Thank you for blowing out your savings to get a flight from Ottawa to Halifax and then finally getting Ingonish to tilt at windmills with the most ungrateful Camilla MacPhee. Thank you, Alvin, for saving my life."

"But Brutus saved my life."

"And you can save his by getting him to stop barking."

"I suppose he can't come in."

"Are you insane? He did his best to attack us. Fangs, frothing, the whole shebang. I thought I'd need to climb a tree. And he doesn't like Gussie either."

"What are you doing here, Alvin?"

"After your hysterical calls yesterday—"

"Never hysterical."

"Overly dramatic then. I knew you were in trouble."

"Was that when I told you my fiancé had absconded with my computer, clothing, cash, and the car by any chance, and someone was trying to kill us? Did I add in my overly dramatic way that was the afternoon when I discovered my mother was not my mother? Or that the bodies are starting to pile up? Or was it one of the times that Jeep tried to push me over a cliff into the sea?"

"Fine, you may have had your reasons."

"You bet. How did you get here?"

"Irritability. That's one of the symptoms of hypothermia. I googled it."

I glanced toward the window where all indications were that it was day, foggy and misty, but day. "Last night was hypothermia, Alvin. Not sure what this is."

"Told you. Flew."

One of the unassailable truths of Alvin's life is that he would never have the price of a plane ticket burning a hole in his pocket. I was pretty sure that any savings he claimed to have were tied up in his harebrained pot scheme.

I said, "Let me guess."

"Fine, Violet made it happen."

Of course, we could always count on Mrs. Violet Parnell to come through in a crunch.

"She found a flight for me yesterday morning and lined up a driver in Halifax. She's still a whiz on the computer, and she's also still got the connections."

"And deep pockets."

"Right. She paid the guy to wait for me because the flight was late. In the middle of a major business campaign that's a big deal for me, as you can imagine. Therefore—"

"Thank you. I didn't know you were coming."

"Lord thundering Jesus, I kept calling. You didn't answer."

"The cell reception was crappy. That reminds me, where's Ray's phone?"

"No idea."

"But how did you know I was at Auntie Annie's?"

"You can thank Donald Donnie for that. He stayed in touch with Violet. You left him high and dry, may I add."

"You may not add, Alvin," I snapped, struggling out of bed and hunting for my clothes. I was wearing a voluminous cream flannelette nightie with faded pink roses.

"Whoa," Alvin said, eyes wide.

"Don't start. I need my clothes."

"I agree. They're in the laundry room. They must be dry by now."

"The phone will be with them. Can you go get it? Please and thanks. I hope it didn't get washed or dried."

Alvin's face was chalkier and his nose a bit beakier than usual as he leaned forward. "You should lie down. I'll get your clothes if you promise to settle."

"I have things to do." I rose to my feet, wobbled, and was overcome by a wave of dizziness. I slid, boneless, to the floor, lessening the dignity of my words.

"Okay, don't move." Alvin loped through the door.

"I'll move if I goddam well want to," I said from the rag rug. "I'm taking a break."

Alvin was back in what seemed like hours but according to the cuckoo clock on the wall was just over three minutes. He brought my clean clothes, dry, folded, and smelling of dryer sheets. My bag was slung over his bony shoulder. "No phone anywhere to be found. I even called the number."

I struggled up off the floor and said, "I must have lost it on the beach. I have to go back. We need that phone."

He shook his head, causing the ponytail to flip back and forth. "It would be ruined on the beach in the rain, but don't worry, Donald Donnie said you were clutching it when they brought you in, raving."

"Donald Donnie was raving?"

"You were quite delirious."

I couldn't imagine myself delirious.

"It must be here somewhere. Slipped behind a cushion or caught in the blanket. Maybe Gussie's lying on it."

"I'll go hunt around. You should get back in bed, Camilla. Can you even get dressed by yourself?"

Was I in some alternate reality where Alvin Ferguson would help me put on my underwear? I thought not. "Find Ray's phone."

"Memory loss is a symptom of hyperthermia. And I hope you didn't also give yourself another friggin' concussion, Camilla. You know how long it took you to recover after the last couple."

We both hoped that. But I was feeling a bit more stable as I got out of the nightie and into my clothes. My bag had survived my trip, and I found my small hairbrush and toothbrush. I sat on the bed and made a plan. First, fix myself up enough so I wouldn't scare the locals and then get going. But where?

The foggy notions I'd woken up with hovered just out of mental reach. My top priority was to find Ray before a murderer did. Leonard too. I tried to gather my scattered memories and make sense of them. Cody could help. Who was Cody again? I worried about that before I remembered that Cody was the kid who'd been kind enough to rescue me from the Aspy look-off and take me to Calum and Sherry's farm. Mind you, he'd abandoned me. Had he mentioned the Silverado as we were pulling up? It had been seen out by Hughie's place, whatever that meant. I needed to find out who and where Hughie was, stat, as Alvin would say.

I made my way down the stairs on my bum. Gussie followed me, nudging my back and neck and adding a layer of new danger to the descent. I teetered into the warm and fragrant kitchen. Rita Susanne had already finished her morning care routine with Auntie Annie. Despite today's cheerful butterfly scrubs, she wore a stern expression. A lively discussion was underway around the table. The gist of it was that Auntie Annie couldn't be waiting on the crowd of us as we were all able-bodied and shouldn't be allowed (and I quote) to sponge off her.

Auntie Annie, a vision in her mint-green knitted pullover, straightened her back. "Very kind of you, Rita Susanne, but I still make my own decisions under my roof."

What a role model!

At the sight of me, swaying with admiration for Auntie Annie, Donald Donnie gasped. Rita Susanne rushed forward to steady me while Auntie Annie hobbled over and gripped my hands. Alvin continued searching for the cell phone, already a slight skunky haze about him. Never mind, I ignored that and Donald Donnie's old tobacco smell and instead chose to inhale Auntie Annie's lily-of-the-valley scent and Rita Susanne's reassuring baby powder aroma.

I needed to tell Auntie Annie about her car. Best to face the music right away.

"Auntie Annie, you were kind enough to lend me your car, and now it's been stolen and banged up too. Leonard Mombourquette stole it from me. I will cover the damage, of course. I am so sorry."

"Och, that's an old wreck, dear. Not worth ten dollars. I don't even drive anymore. We're glad you're alive. We were scared to death, weren't we, Donald Donnie?"

"Right scared indeed, dear."

Another memory surged forward "And Calum and Sherry are—"

Twin tears trickled down her wrinkled cheeks. "Both gone. We know. People are saying they died when their truck swerved off the road and hit those boulders. Terrible accident."

"Murder," I said.

"What, dear?"

"Not an accident. The same person who killed Sandy Sutherland killed them."

"But everyone is saying that Sandy committed suicide, God forgive him. Don't people put a hose into their cars when they want to end their lives? Carbon monoxide? Surely, it couldn't be murder. Not here. Not three people in our community." Auntie Annie's voice faded out, and she sank back onto the day bed and clutched the crocheted afghan.

Donald Donnie said, "What about Loretta's cousin's car, Camilla? And Ray's?"

I struggled to remember through the haze. "They're still at the farm-house, but the tires are flat. I'm afraid I took Sherry's Focus to follow them, but—"

Auntie Annie and Donald Donnie tilted forward.

I closed my eyes and tried to reconstruct. "I drove through Ingonish trying to catch up with Wayne Nowicki, Sherry, and Calum. When I came upon them, I saw the truck against the rocks—"

Auntie Annie made the sign of the cross.

Donald Donnie's eyes filled.

CHAPTER TWENTY-SEVEN
The thing is: he saved my life

"Wayne Nowicki was parked near the wreckage. I tried to get away without leading him back here." At this point, the images got murky again. "I abandoned Sherry's car and found a passage down to the beach with Brutus to avoid him. Where is Brutus anyway?"

Donald Donnie said, "He's locked in the shed, dear. Some people are terrified of him. Even Rita Susanne is nervous around him, and she's tougher than nails."

Oh, boy. Poor Brutus.

Donald Donnie puffed out his chest to show that he wasn't part of the terrified group. "Your animals are not keen on him either."

They weren't my animals, technically. "The thing is, he saved my life."

Donald Donnie put on his bravest face. "Of course, the poor doggie. I'll give him a sandwich or even a tea biscuit. Auntie Annie made some yesterday to go with our soup."

Auntie Annie said, "But they're better the same day. I could make a fresh batch."

Rita Susanne bustled into the room from somewhere and got her bossy on. "I won't have you exhausting yourself for that animal or these—"

I said, "Brutus won't mind yesterday's tea biscuits. Ten or twelve of them?"

Gussie moaned in case we forgot about him when it was tea biscuit time.

Alvin said, "Never mind the tea biscuits and the dog. Back to your story. What happened next, Camilla? Then we'll see about the Hound of the Baskervilles.”

"Someone chased after me on the beach. It must have been Wayne Nowicki. He hit my back with a rock and knocked me down. I hit my head on a boulder, and then he rolled me into the surf and held my face under the water.”

Auntie Annie gasped. "But he's a policeman.”

"Yes. But not the first bad one.”

"Well, he's the first bad one around here,” she said with her hands on her hips.

Was that true? Most of the people involved in this chase were police, and someone had killed at least one of them. What could they have done to make themselves targets of a murderer?

Rita Susanne frowned. "He's a bit of a bully, but he's still a respectable police officer. I don't want to doubt you, Camilla, but it's highly unlikely. You probably have a concussion, and that's messing with your thinking.”

Alvin said, "She's famous for them.”

She ignored Alvin. "And you were hypothermic. That also clouds a person's thinking.”

"My money's on Nowicki. I need to know where he is.”

She crossed her beefy arms and regarded me with a prison matron expression. "You must stay quiet until you get to the health center for a scan. Concussions can do a lot of damage. Wait until the doctor clears you.”

"But I—”

"Lord thundering Jesus, Camilla. Get your friggin' head examined.”

Rita Susanne stepped forward. "I'll be glad to drive you. I'll just let my other patients know I'll be a bit late.”

I raised my hand to silence everyone. "Don't leave your patients for me. Alvin can take me, but Sherry, Calum, and Sandy Sutherland are dead. I'm not going anywhere before someone tells me how these people are connected and what they have to do with Ray Deveau.”

Rita Susanne exhaled. "I gather you saw the accident?”

"I saw the aftermath of two murders. That was no accident.”

Rita Susanne put her arms around Auntie Annie's shoulders. She shot me a look that told me not to upset her patient. Having been born a MacPhee, of course Auntie Annie was far stronger than her nurse gave her credit for.

Rita Susanne said, "That must have been awful for you, Camilla."

I blinked. It had been awful for Sherry and Calum.

She added, "Didn't your first husband die in a car accident?"

"My only husband was killed by a drunk driver," I said.

Donald Donnie couldn't stop himself from blurting out, "And that driver never paid the price for it."

"No punishment would have brought Paul back." Even as I said it, the old familiar ripple of rage crept through my mind and heart. I could see my anger mirrored on everyone's face, even sweet little Auntie Annie's.

"It's the worst situation in the world," Rita Susanne said, "never to have justice."

Auntie Annie nodded. "Awful. That's what I was thinking."

Right now, the worst thing in the world was that I might lose Ray to some maniac. So, before Donald Donnie and Alvin could climb on board the last train to Must Be Awful, I said, "I want to find out whatever links Sherry and Calum, Ray Deveau, Pierre Forgeron, Leonard Mombour- quette, Sandy Sutherland and Matty."

Rita Susanne said, "Not much to tell. They all grew up in the region, like thousands of other people. I know Ray lives in Ontario now, but he was in Cape Breton for most of his life. I think Leonard Mombourquette is in Ottawa. No idea about Pierre Forgeron. New Brunswick, maybe? Sandy was living in Halifax and having trouble staying off the drink. It seems like a random collection of people from the north of Cape Breton to me."

Except that the four of them were police officers about the same age, I thought. As was Wayne Nowicki. "Can you think of some criminal they would have been arrested who might hold them responsible? Might be plotting revenge?"

Auntie Annie's jaw dropped.

Donald Donnie opened his big mouth. "Is that a bit far-fetched?"

Rita Susanne said, "Well, for starters, I never heard they all worked together. Did they?"

I said, "Ray and Wayne Nowicki did. And Ray and Leonard."

Alvin couldn't resist his two cents. "That's not much to go on, Camilla."

"Whose side are you on? Ray is missing. People are dead. I've been attacked three times. Far-fetched but true. What *would* be enough to go on? Any case that comes to mind? Some business that involves Wayne Nowicki? Everyone knows him."

Alvin muttered, "Not me."

The phone in Donald Donnie's hand rang with my old familiar ringtone. Donald Donnie stared at it before answering and not taking his eyes from my face. I resisted the itch to snatch it from him, mainly because he was out of reach. "Yes, she's here. She almost died, so help me. She was clinging to life when we dragged her into the house. What? Hypothermia. And could be a concussion. She's pretty scratched up too. What? Oh sure, she's right here." He handed me my own phone. "It's for you."

"Ms. MacPhee!" The familiar bellow was like a symphony to my sore ears.

"Mrs. P." I couldn't keep the grin off my face.

She said, "What are you getting up to? Do I have to fly down to set things right?"

A vision of my friend in her nineties setting things right kept me smiling. For sure, she'd get into the cockpit on whatever plane she commandeered, regulations or not.

"I found some newspaper articles, some old and some not-so," she said. "Are you ready?'

I wasn't. My back hurt like the devil, and my head was spinning. Not good. "I need to rest. I'll take the phone upstairs again, if that's okay."

"Let me know when you're all set."

I turned to the group in the kitchen and said, "I'll chat with Mrs. Parnell until I feel better."

Donald Donnie was bleating about needing the phone as I navigated the steps. Alvin, to my surprise, came along with me. "Just to make sure you don't tumble down the stairs and make a lot of trouble for everyone." He came in handy more than once on the endless one-storey journey.

I plunked myself on my unmade bed, causing a bit more whirling.

Alvin said, "I'll get you some tea and toast. That might help. Do you even know when you ate last?"

I shooed him away, closed my eyes, and listened to what Mrs. P. had found.

"I found the death notice for a Matthew Quinn, aged fifty-one. Isn't that the same age as Sergeant Deveau? At any rate, this Mr. Quinn died three weeks ago in Baddeck. Do you think that could be your Matty?"

"The timing's right. But—"

"Wait for the next part. Then I researched that name, as I believe you wanted."

I listened as she topped up yet another celebratory cut-glass tumbler of Harvey's Bristol Cream. Mrs. P. was on a roll. I hope she didn't light up a Benson & Hedges and set off the sprinkler system.

"This wasn't easy," she said. "But I have an acquaintance who knows her way around old local newspapers and databases, not important why, and she was bored out of her mind by retirement. Are you ready?"

"Yes."

"It was thirty years ago this month."

"Thirty years!"

"That is correct. Thirty years this month. A young man from northern Cape Breton was critically injured in an accident and not expected to live. His name was Matthew Quinn."

"The same one?"

"Be patient, Ms. MacPhee. The lad was a promising student and an athlete studying at what is now known as Atlantic Police Academy on Prince Edward Island. He was home for the Thanksgiving weekend and had been out with friends."

"What happened?"

"It doesn't say. Just that weather and fog might have been factors in the accident."

"Not surprising."

"It must be the same man who died three weeks ago in Baddeck. That's the trouble with those wretched accidents when someone isn't killed outright. The person can linger on in terrible condition and no one pays much attention. Saw it many times after the war. The so-called lucky ones who made it home and were never the same. Invisible and tragic, but that is a discussion for another time. To make a long story short, Matthew Quinn was left quadriplegic and lived in a care facility. After rooting around, I learned that his parents died a few years after."

"That's horrible."

"And all too common."

"But we could talk to someone at that facility and—"

"I've had trouble reaching them, although that may be because of the storm. I'll keep calling them and see what turns up. I'll get back to you. I read between the lines in the reports that someone else was also injured."

"Who?"

"It doesn't say, but I'll keep digging."

This accident with Matthew Quinn couldn't be a coincidence. Ray would have been at Holland College thirty years ago. Unless I missed my guess, Pierre Forgeron would have been too. Who else? Sandy? Kenny? Ray Nowicki?

"You're the best, Mrs. P. Let me know. You'll have to call me on my own phone until further notice because I misplaced Ray's cell last night."

"I assumed there was trouble when you didn't respond. Quite a time you're having. But rest assured, I'm still on the case."

"Thanks a lot for sending Alvin, Mrs. P. I'll pay you back."

"Indeed you will not. You can't take it with you, as they say, and I like to spend on worthwhile projects while I'm on this earth. The least I could do. And how is Young Ferguson?"

"Irritating enough to take my mind off my bruises."

"Excellent. We each bring our own skills to the battlefield."

Talking with Mrs. P. had given me a shot of energy. Once again, I descended stair by stair on my behind to view a lot of action going on. Gussie was thrilled to see me, although I'd only been out of the room about five minutes. The calico joined me on the day bed and got her ears scratched for that. The rumble of the contented cat soothed me. If the animals had been resenting me, they'd gotten over it.

Auntie Annie had made steel-cut oatmeal for everyone. A bowl of brown sugar and a pitcher of thick cream were waiting on the table for it. Rita Susanne was worrying that all this cooking after the drama of the night before would exhaust her patient. "Please, sit down, Auntie Annie. I'll clean up. You've had way too much excitement."

Auntie Annie had had enough of that. She bristled. "I need more excitement in my life, Rita Susanne, not less. You're not a hundred percent yourself this morning. And I still make my own decisions."

Rita Susanne had the grace to blush. She rubbed her thigh. "I apologize, Auntie Annie. I pulled a muscle over at Mrs. Tommy Brown's place, and it's quite painful. I'm just not myself. And now we're hearing all this terrible news."

Auntie Annie patted her shoulder. "Everyone's on edge with the storm and the deaths. Terrible. And poor you, dealing with Frankie too."

Rita Susanne's eyes welled up. It couldn't have been easy needing to be strong for everyone.

Donald Donnie changed the topic by bleating, "I like Annie's oatmeal with lots of brown sugar and cream. Loretta always mixes it with skim milk and no sugar. It's not the same."

Auntie Annie chuckled. "Alvin told me he'd rather eat crushed glass than oatmeal, but after he's tried mine, he might convert."

Alvin said, "I'll give it a try if you'd be willing to help me beta-test my new products because—"

"She would not be willing," I snapped.

"I don't know what that means, but I'd be happy to help you, Alvin."

"No, you wouldn't," I said firmly.

"Oh dear, I saved some oatmeal for you, Camilla, so you'll get your strength back."

"I'll say yes to your oatmeal. And I'll enjoy watching Alvin survive the experience. I'll have a cup of coffee to kick-start my day before I hear any talk of eating."

Rita Susanne stopped fussing about and glared at me. "You'd better sit quietly. I'd avoid coffee if I were you. I'm making tea."

I exercised my right of self-determination. "I'll be much better when we find the other phone."

Alvin kept sulking about my refusal to let Auntie Annie get sucked into the wonderful world of pot products. "Maybe your phone washed out to sea."

I wasn't the only one worried. Donald Donnie wasn't happy about not having my phone either. It hadn't taken him long to get addicted. "But you know, dear, I do need to stay in touch with Loretta. She'll be getting worried about her cousin's car."

Auntie Annie chuckled. "I can't believe how people can't get through the day without those foolish phones."

She had a point. Much as I hate constant harassment via my cell phone on a normal day, I couldn't cope without it in this situation. Now I desperately needed Ray's.

Rita Susanne busied herself preheating the old Brown Betty teapot and then tossing four Red Rose tea bags into it. She glared at me again. "You have to be careful. Your system has had a shock. And you got an awful chill last night. You'll end up with pneumonia if you're not careful. I brought Auntie Annie some organic unpasteurized honey from my friends' apiary, and that's the best for you. Wards off sore throats and builds immunity. It will do you the world of good in your tea."

I hate honey, but as Mrs. Parnell liked to say, that was not a hill I'd choose to die on.

Donald Donnie said, "That's a great idea. I'd like some of that honey tea. Can we heat up them tea biscuits from yesterday and serve them with your homemade strawberry jam?"

Rita Susanne wasn't having any of that. "Loretta told me you were supposed to be on a diet, Donald Donnie. Because you know what they say, if you don't watch your weight, everyone else will."

Donald Donnie muttered about vitamin C in strawberry jam.

Alvin got in on it. "What about molasses cookies? Are they good for you too?"

"For sure they are," Auntie Annie said with a merry cackle. "I'll get you some."

"For me too. I'm looking after my health," Donald Donnie chimed in with a wheeze.

It seemed that tea must steep for seven minutes in that household. It was the colour of licorice and about as thick by the time it was poured.

Rita Susanne brought me an oversized mug with a map of Cape Breton Island on it. "Joke all you want. I won't say those cookies have medical benefits, but Auntie Annie's molasses cookies can't be beat. Better for you than tea biscuits and jam." I could see she wasn't going to take on Auntie Annie, who was living a long life on a diet rich in tea biscuits and strawberry jam. I protested as Rita Susanne stirred extra honey into my giant mug. When she turned to boss Donald Donnie around, I tipped the tea into one of the jade plants.

Rita Susanne just missed that. "How was the tea, Camilla? I bet you're already getting the benefits of that honey."

"I guzzled it." I picked up the empty mug to show her and tried to muster a grateful smile. She'd refilled it before I could find a polite way to protest. Donald Donnie was rubbing his back and moaning about the humidity. Auntie Annie said, "Tell me about it. Everything hurts in this damp weather!"

"I hear you," I said, putting down the mug to massage my sore knee.

"We're all getting old," Rita Susanne said, rubbing her thigh. I should have warned her.

Alvin leapt into sales mode. "I have a great deal for you! My Fuzzy Buzzy Anti-Ache Cream will free you from your pain. I need testers."

"What are you talking about?" Rita Susanne said. I had a feeling that she would not be in favour of Alvin's products, since they would not have passed through any Health Canada approval process. With all her friends in the police, we didn't need any more complications.

I shot him a warning glance. "Did someone say molasses cookies?" I asked.

At least the molasses cookies were calming. For about five minutes, we shared a bit of normal interaction before Rita Susanne resumed what she described as a "crazy day." I thought I'd cornered the market on crazy days, but I had competition.

She said, "I have to drop in on a few extra people today. Everyone's so upset about … the storm and…" She didn't say the three deaths, but we understood the meaning. "Of course, I have to check in on my brother, and one of my other patients is not far from Black Brook, so I'll take a peek on the beach for your phone, Camilla. Let's hope the salt water didn't ruin it. And I'll call the health centre and make sure they'll see you today." She gave Alvin a look that no one would argue with.

Donald Donnie said, "Och, we're all so sorry about Frankie. You're a saint, my girl."

"Not much of a saint, but whatever his faults—and they are many—I am his sister, and I have to make sure he gets the care he deserves. I'll be back soon. You may not be aware, Camilla, but no one here got much sleep last night after your misadventure. Promise me you will all take it easy today."

She backed out the door, and we remained on our best behaviour until she reached her car. She waved once more before climbing into her bright green Fiesta. I said, "I thought she'd never leave. I'd kill for a cup of coffee. Strong and black. No honey within two feet of it."

Alvin said with his mouth full of molasses cookie, "I'll make it. You sit tight, Camilla. Violet said I have to take good care of you."

"Rita Susanne means well. I'll warm up the tea biscuits. Donald Donnie, get the jam from the larder," Auntie Annie chirped

Everyone else wanted the paint-stripper tea.

"I'll have your tea, Camilla. Shame to waste that organic honey," Donald Donnie said, snatching my mug and glowing like a kid on Christmas morning.

"I'm drinking mine," Alvin said, sliding his mug out of Donald Donnie's reach. "I'm making a pot of coffee for Godzilla, I mean Camilla."

Turned out that Auntie Annie had an entire package of dark-roast beans, still with the vacuum seal, and a French press left over from a granddaughter's visit. She had a coffee grinder too. Alvin soon had that grinder shrieking. If it hadn't been for everything at stake, it would have been a terrific little party.

Once I had two mugs of dark roast blasting through my system, it didn't take long to feel steady again. Alvin bullied me into taking a couple of Advil, so that eased the rock-in-the-back problem. It was time for me to get the lead out. First, I needed a bit of information. "Do you remember an accident that paralyzed a boy named Matthew Quinn, Auntie Annie?"

"Oh, that's the Matty you were asking about. Must be thirty years ago. Och, that was a bad accident, but at least nobody died, unless I'm wrong. I don't remember much about it." She stared sadly at us. "Usually, it's what happened today that I can't recall, and thirty years ago would be clear as day. You could ask me about my childhood. I'd be fine with those memories. I got into plenty of mischief, but your father was always perfect."

Not always, I thought. "Don't worry about it, Auntie Annie. It was just a thought."

"After all you've been through, I was wanting to help you out a bit." She reached over and squeezed my hand with her own thin, blue-veined one.

"Tell me, Auntie Annie. Do you know anyone named Hughie?"

She brightened. "Hughie? We have plenty of Hughs and Hughies around here."

Right. "Do you think that a Hughie or Hugh might be connected with the accident that injured Matthew Quinn?"

"I don't recall any Hughie being involved. Why?"

"Well, the young guy who rescued me up at Aspy Fault might have seen the truck that Ray was travelling in at Hughie's place, but I don't know who Hughie is."

"What's this young fellow's name, dear?"

"Cody. He knows you."

"Ah yes, Cody Campbell. Pearl Gouthro's grandson. A good lad at heart despite the wee scrap of trouble he's been in."

I figured she was right. My legal aid senses had already alerted me that Cody would have had a brush or two with the law.

Auntie Annie sipped her tea and put it down. "He'll be talking about Hughie Williams who used to go out with Cody's mother. Now she's a gal who's never settled down."

I thought back and remembered that Cody said, "I call him my Uncle Hughie."

"That'd be the one. Unless he was thinking of Hughie MacLean down the other way. He was a cousin to Cody's father. And I can think of one more that's connected to him on his possible father's side."

I couldn't get side-tracked with the idea of "possible" father. "This is great. I knew you could help. Do you have a map somewhere?"

Alvin said. "In fact, I had my driver stop to get one on my way here.

Thought I might need it."

"Good work. Now, Auntie Annie, can you mark any Hughies you know on the map for me?"

A shadow crossed her kind and wrinkled face. "Oh dear, are you sure? You're supposed to rest. Rita Susanne will have kittens."

"She's a would-be general like my sisters, and I don't do what they say either."

Auntie Annie nodded. "You're cut from a different bolt of cloth from those girls, for sure."

Alvin cut in, "But you do have to take it easy, Camilla."

"I can sleep long enough when I'm dead. I need to find Ray Deveau before he joins the crowd at the funeral home."

Alvin's eyes widened. "Whoa. Show some respect, Camilla. People are—"

"We need to get going, Alvin. Are you in or out?"

"What about me?" Donald Donnie said with a strawberry jammy yawn. "I need to get out and get some exercise."

Alvin said, "Nobody should go."

CHAPTER TWENTY-EIGHT
When all around are sleeping

It couldn't hurt to have Donald Donnie keep me company. Alvin was being useful at Auntie Annie's, and I still had access to Sherry's car. A bit risky, but at least its tires hadn't been slashed. Donald Donnie talked me into handing back my cell phone.

In spite of his giant and insulting yawn, Alvin put up a spirited resistance to our departure until I said, "Remember you are here to help, and on Mrs. P.'s nickel at that."

"To think I was up all night because of you," he sputtered. "So ungrateful."

When Donald Donnie and I left, I was sporting my new-to-me jeans and plaid shirt, still warm from the dryer. Instead of the baseball cap or Cody's extra beanie, Auntie Annie had found me a charcoal knit toque that didn't do me any favours except to turn me into a different person. The huge yellow rain slicker could have belonged to anyone.

She said, "You know there is one other thing that I thought of. Probably silly but…"

"Great," I said. "We've got to get to Hughie's place because Ray's missing truck was seen on that property. As soon as I'm back, I'd love to have that talk."

Donald Donnie had the urge to drive, for my own good. "You're not yourself yet, Camilla. You know that."

"Fine. I'll be the navigator. Do what I say and don't talk."

Donald Donnie sniffed. "That's not nice, Camilla. We worried all night because of you." Everyone except Auntie Annie blamed their lack of sleep on me.

"My head is throbbing. I might have a bit of a concussion, so I'm not responsible for my behaviour. Wait a minute. Do you hear that howling? The other animals will be fine, but we should take Brutus. He has no supporters here, and things could go off the rails in a heartbeat."

Before I could cough up any more clichés, I hopped out. Brutus was overjoyed to see me. I sent Donald Donnie back to the house to get a snack to endear himself to the big dog. He was back in less than a minute. I wouldn't have made molasses cookies my first choice, but they seemed to do the trick. Brutus settled down in the back, ready to see what else the day would bring, his tail thumping on the seat. I would have felt a bit guilty leaving Gussie and the little cat, but they were being spoiled rotten.

We drove through Ingonish until we located the street where the first Hughie might be. We bumped off the main road—that hurt—and onto a straight dirt track that continued through some scraggly spruce. We reached the end of the road and checked. No Silverado.

A woman, smoking, scowling, and walking a scrawny dog, stared at us. Donald Donnie turned the car around and opened his window. "That's one awful cold wind."

She nodded. "Miserable."

I called out. "Right. Have you seen a silver Silverado with New Brunswick plates pass this way?"

The dog barked. Brutus responded. She blew a cloud of smoke and stepped back as I shushed my protector. "No. Been quiet since the storm."

A faint wail of sirens sounded in the distance. "Except for all the sirens."

I thanked her. Time for the second X on the map. Donald Donnie's eyes were heavy. We swerved off the road and shot straight for the ditch. That reminded me way too much of Calum and Sherry. I yanked the wheel and swore at him.

"No driving with your eyes closed. You'll have to move to the passenger side. I know all that sugar today has made you groggy, and you were up all night because of me, but I'm not grateful enough to let you get me killed."

"But you're the navigator," he yawned. He was already nodding off. I struggled to get him out of the car to switch places, and within seconds he was snoring, mouth open.

Number two Hughie was much farther along, well past Neil's Harbour. Despite the wind, it was a picture-perfect day for a drive. Fluffy cumulus clouds dotted the dazzling blue sky. The sea glittered. White-capped waves hurled themselves against the beaches. October at its finest, except for the wind near the shore.

This Hughie lived in a more isolated spot, down a longer and bumpier driveway. No sign of a truck, but there were outbuildings. People can hide a lot behind and in barns and garages. A couple of small boys in bright blue jackets were kicking the life out of a soccer ball in the front yard and ignoring the elaborate play structure in the background.

They raced to the car, probably because they'd been told not to talk to strangers. "What's wrong with him?" one of them said, pointing to Donald Donnie, now drooling on the upholstery.

"He missed his bedtime. I'm trying to find my friend's truck. It's a Silverado with a couple of men in it. It's from New Brunswick. Have you seen it?"

They shook their heads. I could tell they were disappointed. You can count on kids. They were probably cooking up a suitable fib when their mother came out of the house, wiping her hands on the backside of her jeans and shooting me a suspicious look.

I waved and shouted, "Sorry, wrong address!"

We were on our way to Hughie number three, all the way back through the various Ingonishes and out the other side. Third time's supposed to be a charm.

We passed Pearl's Pies. I thought about asking for her help, until I remembered her lie about the truck.

This third location was a bit more out of the way. I missed the hairpin turn and had to make a U-ey. The spruce-lined side road almost doubled back on itself, climbing the steep hillside as it went. Who would want to live here? What would it be like in winter?

"This is it," I said, but Donald Donnie slept on.

I gave him a nudge, but he slid sideways into the passenger-side door.

I shook him and yelled into his ear. "Wake up. I need your help."

Oh, well. Best to do a little reconnaissance by myself. Unlike the two previous "Hughie" residences, this one was out of sight of other houses. I slipped from the car. I decided that Brutus should come with me. Just in case.

"Quiet," I said. "And there's a hamburger in your future."

Over the scent of cedar and spruce, I caught a whiff of wood fire. I scrambled up the hill through the brush until I spied the lazy drift of smoke from the chimney of a beautiful post-and-beam log home with a red steel roof and huge front windows.

A porch ran the width of the house, and a pea gravel driveway made a wide semicircle in front. The smoke told me that someone was on the property.

I instructed Brutus to be quiet if he ever wanted another treat.

I squatted by the edge of the woods and checked my surroundings. No sign of anybody, but a motorcycle was angled off to the side on the pea-gravel drive. I knew that bike. Wayne Nowicki was here, his big blue Gold Wing right in sight. He wasn't expecting us, but our chances of overcoming him were slight.

Was the Silverado really in the garage, as Cody had said? Did the hulking cop have Ray?

That was the big question. I crept through the trees around the periphery of the property. Some major landscaping activity was underway on the grounds. A Bobcat hunkered next to a gaping hole in the ground, ready to move the pile of dirt on the edge. I figured a swimming pool was in the works. Hughie must have hit the big-time in Fort Mac.

I bent over and scurried so that Wayne Nowicki wouldn't spot me if he stuck his large, ugly nose out one of those windows. On the back of the property was the garage, made for at least three vehicles, no doubt trucks. The structure was almost as large as the house. The massive door was closed, and even if I figured out how to open it, I would be visible from the house. I knew from several trials that garages can hold a lot of interesting stuff besides cars. On the far side of the building, I found a window and peered in. Was that dark shadow a truck? Moving closer, I could make out the silver Silverado in the middle of the garage. The passenger door was still open. Next to it was Auntie Annie's beat-up Golf. The kicker was the black Jeep parked in front of the big door.

Calling the police was out of the question. I wouldn't get far suggesting that one of their own was a threat. I wouldn't put it past Nowicki to finger me in the crash that killed Sherry and Calum. Had he taken Hughie prisoner too? Or was Hughie part of whatever was going on? If so, where was his vehicle? Or was that the Jeep?

Even if I did have a plan, which I did not, I needed to alert someone to the fact I was at Hughie's and that Nowicki, the Silverado, and the Golf were here too. Of course, Donald Donnie had the sole remaining phone. So, back to the car.

"Let's run, Brutus, but remember, quiet!"

Brutus complied, and we went over the hill and back toward the road, slipping and sliding on wet leaves and soft ground. While checking over my shoulder, I smacked into a low branch. I landed flat on the ground with an "ooof," the breath knocked out of me. I let the leash go. Brutus couldn't believe his good fortune. Free at last!

"Brutus, come back." I had to whisper because I couldn't afford to shout. Wayne Nowicki would recognize Brutus. I pleaded with Brutus's retreating backside. "It's for your own good."

But Brutus was in the wind. He didn't give a flying for the only person who cared about him.

I struggled to my feet, head swimming, and wobbled back to the car. I was now wearing a nice outer layer of forest floor. I limped forward, trying to catch sight of Brutus. In the passenger seat, Donald Donnie slept on, his face now squashed up against the window of Sherry's Focus, a thin trickle of drool making its way down his chin. I knocked on the glass. I tried swearing. Donald Donnie was not waking up.

"Bloody hell," I said, hoping it wasn't some medical condition we'd need to deal with. "What is it with men and dogs?"

At least the phone was still clutched in his pudgy hand. I snatched it and checked that it was set to vibrate before making my calls. No response at Auntie Annie's. Alvin did not answer his cell either. How much trouble was it to pick up the friggin' phone? I left intense messages.

Even Mrs. P. went straight to voice mail.

Fine. My team was not available. The police were off-limits. But the Silverado had turned up at Hughie's place. Wayne Nowicki was parked by the house. I'd never forgive myself for wasting time if it meant someone else ended up dead.

Hoping that Brutus didn't bark a greeting, I hurried back toward the garage. I'd now broken enough laws to understand how some of my former clients decided they had little to lose by one more spree.

I heaved a large rock through the side window of the garage and used a cedar branch to clear away the shards of glass. I tucked my hands into my sleeves, and I tumbled through the opening, avoiding hitting my thick skull on a mountain bike. Hughie had all the toys for boys.

I sniffed the air in and around the truck, not sure why. Pierre must have been heavy smoker, judging by the smell of stale tobacco. I couldn't detect any of Ray's Hugo Boss and swore to myself that I would never tease him about it again if he stayed alive. There was another smell too. What was it? Before I could figure it out, my eye caught a taupe envelope in the driver's side door pocket. Inside, I found the same message that Sherry had received. I noticed a thin line of dark red on the dash. It ended in a smear. I instructed myself to keep calm.

The rest of the garage was immaculate, except for drag marks on the floor leading to the closed main door. Had someone been hauled out of the structure? Ray? Pierre? Or Mombourquette? Dead or alive? No way to know. I glanced around. Under normal circumstances, Ray would have loved this garage. Tools and supplies hung from a pristine storage system: a spare battery, some clean jars, rags and car cleaning equipment, a few cans of paint, brushes, rollers, a tarp, box cutter, turpentine, the usual. A small fridge was humming. Opened, it revealed shelves of bottled water. Near the entrance sat a whopping yellow generator and an oversized red gas container. On the shelf was a pair of powerful torches. This guy was prepared for anything.

So Ray was here, dead or alive. Mombourquette too. And Pierre Forgeron. The black Jeep looked like it had been through the wars. Of course, Wayne Nowicki would have a collaborator. He'd been following Sherry and Calum the last time I saw the Jeep, and I'd seen him with his bike soon after the crash. Was Hughie his accomplice? Or was he the mastermind? Although I had no signal, I took a picture of the Jeep's plate and texted it to Mrs. Parnell. Alvin insists you can text with no bars at all. Nothing to lose by trying.

Action time. The side door was bolted from the inside. At least I didn't have to climb through the broken window again. A small victory, but I faced a bigger battle.

Either Hughie or Nowicki must have captured Ray, Mombourquette, and Pierre Forgeron, all trained police officers. Ray never carried a weapon off-duty, and he didn't know he'd need one when we left on this turbulent trip. Elaine had told me that Leonard Mombourquette no longer owned a weapon. These guys knew they were being pursued and yet somehow they had let down their guard and been captured. What chance did I have with my entire team asleep or ignoring the phone? I could pass for a scary Sasquatch, and that might buy me two minutes as the villains stared in confusion.

I considered racing to the middle of the road to stop traffic and get assistance. But who in their right mind would fall for such a tale from a Sasquatchy come-from-away? Especially the part about a rogue Cape Breton cop.

Back in the woods, I searched for a spot where my cell phone might work. At the top of the hill, three bars appeared. Although it had to do with fewer trees blocking the signal, it felt like a miracle. So much for miracles; Alvin and Auntie Annie still did not answer. I left a message on Alvin's cell and an identical one on Auntie Annie's answering machine. I worried that Alvin had convinced Auntie Annie to beta-test his weed products. I tried Mrs. Parnell again and left a message outlining what was happening and where. I reminded her to do her magic with the license plate I'd texted earlier. I spelled Wayne Nowicki's name. "I believe he has Ray and Leonard Mombourquette and Pierre Forgeron. Maybe others. And he has a collaborator, probably the owner of the black Jeep. Find him and you find the murderer. This place belongs to a Hughie Williams, no other information about him besides the address and the fact he has worked in Alberta."

As soon as I disconnected, the phone vibrated again. Mrs. Parnell was breathless. I started from the beginning. "I'm going in," I said when I finished.

"Ms. MacPhee, may I suggest you reconsider. Remember that discretion is the better part of valour."

"No choice. I think Nowicki and Hughie Williams are going to kill Ray and Leonard and Pierre."

"Give me a few minutes to call you back. I have an old pal standing by to do whatever needs doing. I've already sent on the plate number. And in the meantime, who else could help? You need reinforcements. Perhaps a diversionary tactic?"

"Right. Find out who owns that Jeep ASAP, Mrs. P. And if our situation goes belly-up, at least you can ensure the truth comes out."

"Understood, but I'd like to avoid that at all costs."

"And thank you for everything."

"Take care, Ms. MacPhee. One always needs to hope for the best and prepare for the worst. I'll make that urgent call." Mrs. P. might be in her nineties, but she still had a mind like a general and a bevy of much younger friends from her days working for "the government" in some below-the-radar capacity.

I called 911 and yelled into the phone. "Fire! Fire at Hughie Williams' place. The house is going up, and I think people are trapped. I can hear them screaming!"

"Ma'am? I need an address."

"Hold on!" I ran down the hill, reached the car, opened the car door, and snatched up the paper with the addresses for the three Hughies. I read it out, babbling that I was a tourist and had seen the smoke. I gave my name as Mary MacDonald. Of course, I was calling from my own cell phone, and that might haunt me in the end.

The dispatcher sounded less than calm, a feeling I knew well. "We'll get them there as soon as we can," she said. "We have another big fire going. With the storm and accidents and unconscious people, our first responders have been working night and day."

When I raised my voice, she said, "We can't be in two places at once. Do not go into the building—"

I disconnected. I was dealing with criminals, and it was time to think like one. I felt grateful for every single crooked dimwit who'd ever sat across from me in the Regional Detention Centre.

Donald Donnie slumbered on. Troubling, but his snores sounded healthy enough, so not an additional emergency.

As I scuttled back up the hill through the trees, I felt the cell vibrate. Mrs. Parnell trumpeted, "The Jeep belongs to a Francis Xavier Kelly, with an address on the Cabot Trail."

"What? Not Hughie? It can't be Francis Kelly. He's dying. How would he—?"

My mind raced. What did I really know about Frankie? Could he be the perpetrator? Exhibit A: his banged-up Jeep was parked in the garage. Had he been on a murderous rampage on the roads? Did Frankie harbour a grudge against Ray and the others? Maybe his illness was a ruse. Could he have deceived everyone, including his sister, about his state of health? Stranger things had happened.

Mrs. P. said, "My sources tell me that Francis Kelly worked on undercover operations early in his career. Very successful outcomes, it seems."

"Huh."

"He showed a talent for deceit and a certain ruthlessness. And something else germane to your quest: Francis Kelly was injured in the same accident that left your Matty paraplegic."

"He's not *my* Matty."

She ignored that. "Although, unlike Matthew Quinn, Francis recovered and went on to have a good career in the RCMP. Respected, but as far as I can discern, not well liked." That matched what I knew.

I said, "What if Frankie was responsible for the accident and needed to keep that quiet, and after all these years, Matty was going to spill the beans? Could ruin the rest of a big career."

"Likely the accident and the recent events are linked somehow."

"Ray and the others were also friends at police college." I recalled Sandy Sutherland's shaky voice when he called to announce that Matty was dead. "They were upset to hear about Matty's death, although you say it happened a few weeks ago and they were just learning about it. What if Francis Kelly needs to silence them because they've made the connection?"

"Makes perfect sense." Mrs. Parnell inhaled.

"Auntie Annie had wanted to talk about something, but I had to cut her off to get to Hughie's. Maybe it had been about Francis Kelly. But how would Hugh Williams fit in?"

"I'm working on it."

The black Jeep meant that Frankie was mostly likely nearby. I had to get moving. I said goodbye and hightailed it back through the woods, crossed the driveway out of sight, and climbed up through the treed ravine on the other side, coming out at the back of the house.

Maybe I watch too many action movies, because I paused to rub forest dirt all over my pasty white face. Camouflage. The toque helped me to disappear. I sidled up to a window and peered into a bedroom with wide plank floors, neatly made double bed, plaid quilt, and pine furniture. The door was closed. Fine, not the only window in the world. I moved to the left. This one looked into the kitchen area of a huge open-concept living space. The kitchen area featured a sparkling stainless double fridge and a professional-style stove. A trio of cast iron frying pans hung on the wall by a raised granite-topped counter separating the kitchen from the living area. Just past that, a massive stone fireplace was flanked by a U-shaped seating arrangement of three large, handsome sofas in cognac leather. A vast raw-edge wooden coffee table sat in the middle of the U. There wasn't much else in the room, a pine console table near the front door. Beyond the farthest sofa, I glimpsed black boots splayed on the floor. Ray? Ray hadn't brought his boots on this trip. Mombourquette hadn't been wearing his. Pierre Forgeron?

Looking for better sightlines. I checked around the corner and found a garden door leading from the side deck to the kitchen. The door was locked.

Adrenaline coursing through my veins, my heart thundering, I scrunched down and peered through the glass door. Would I be seen and dispatched before I could help Ray? Wayne Nowicki was a formidable opponent, and Frankie might turn out to be even more dangerous. Then there was Hughie. Was I up to it? I shifted to the other side of the window, even if it made me more visible from the inside. I took a chance and grabbed a chair from the patio set and stood on it. What I saw made my stomach lurch.

Ray was propped up against the far wall, under one of the two huge front windows. His legs were stretched out on the floor, ankles bound with something white. Plastic ties? There are ways to get out of duct tape, but if you were restrained with those ties, you were SOL. His arms were behind him, and I figured they were secured too. That must have been agonizing, but at least he was alive. I exhaled. I hadn't even realized I'd been holding my breath.

Next to Ray, Mombourquette was curled in the fetal position. From what I could see, he was also bound. They both needed medical help. Where were the fire trucks?

CHAPTER TWENTY-NINE
Not quite what it looks like

Mrs. P. called back. "We have confirmed that your Hugh Williams of Ingonish is in Alberta as we speak."

"That calls for a rethink."

"So it appears, Ms. MacPhee."

Out on the wide front veranda, a shadow moved back and forth ready to do … what? Nothing good. I reminded myself about Sherry, Calum, and Sandy. Whatever else, Hughie Williams wasn't Nowicki's accomplice, or vice versa.

I hightailed it back to the garage, keeping out of sight. A vague thought nagged at the outskirts of my memory—something that didn't make sense. As every minute counted, I let that thought go and hurried through the unlocked side door of the garage, gathering what I needed. I dumped camping gear from a canvas bag, keeping the rope and safety matches. I added a half-dozen folded blue rags. In a shiny red standing tool chest, I located a chisel for my kit. Next, plastic ties and a box cutter. I emptied five plastic water bottles and popped them in. I slung the strap over my shoulder, tucked the axe under my arm, and picked up the gas can.

I thanked my most reckless client ever for the idea. Daniel "Hell Boy" Hellman was serving ten hard years in Millhaven for a rampage that involved a small bank, a large explosion, and a difference of opinion with a loans officer. Until that moment, I didn't have much use for Hell Boy.

I raced back through the woods, and crouched low, I hunkered down in a tiny clearing close to the house. I filled two bottles with gasoline and stuffed the rags into them. Then I dipped the rope into the gas canister. I tiptoed back and peered into the garden door again to make sure everyone was still in the same place. Was I wrong, or had Ray moved a bit closer to the right? The splayed feet in the black boots hadn't moved. I was thirty feet from Ray, and yet we might have been on different planets for all the good it did. I pressed my face up to the window. His eyes widened. He looked to the right. Then back to me and then back to the right again. Was he trying to warn me? He managed to look as innocent as a baby. Hm. Something about babies bothered me.

Baby powder! That was what I'd smelled in the truck.

The irritating and saintly Rita Susanne's signature scent. So many little things started to make sense. Of course, she must in cahoots with Nowicki and her brother. No wonder she'd told me I was wrong about him, blaming it on my nonexistent concussion. Rita Susanne knew all the players, dead and alive. She had history with them.

She always knew where I was going because of Auntie Annie. Thanks to my meddling sisters, she would have known about Ray too. No problem finding out I was chasing Mombourquette and then intercepting us at Aspy. I had even described the red velvet Chrysler to Donald Donnie. After Calum and Sherry were killed, she must have seen me in Sherry's car. Easy to track me to the beach. She was strong enough to roll me into the water and hold my head under. After Brutus came to the rescue, she would have changed at home and rushed back to Auntie Annie's, claiming the weather made her late. She'd been so concerned when I showed up, and yet she'd made excuses for not calling 911. In the morning, she'd been rubbing her leg and complaining about a pulled muscle, when the damage would have been from Brutus's sharp teeth. No big surprise she hated Brutus, and it was mutual.

How could I have missed all that?

As for my team, Donald Donnie was unconscious in the car, and no one was answering at Auntie Annie's. My money was on the "honey" tea and Rita Susanne's easy access to drugs through her work. Ray and Mombourquette were in grave danger, but so was almost everyone else I cared about.

I ducked down and made straight for Nowicki's big bike. Using the chisel, I pried open the gas tank and inserted the rope. I hotfooted it to the back of the house and lit the end of the rope. Then I grabbed one of the bottles, dashed to the other side, lit the rag, and fired it into a pile of logs stacked on the pea gravel. Reckless perhaps, but the only strategy I'd been able to come up with, given the absence of first responders. The woods were still soggy from the storm, and that gravel would contain any flames, but still I hoped that I wouldn't set fire to Ingonish. And surely the fire department must be on its way. What the hell did it take to get a bit of attention in this place?

I took a deep breath. As the Gold Wing went boom—metal flying everywhere—I used the axe to smash the garden window. I didn't bother to clear the edges of the glass. I hurtled through. I was still airborne when the significance of the black boots sunk in. Wayne Nowicki lay behind the farthest sofa, a red-stained iron poker next to his motionless body.

Rita Susanne leaned out the window, turning her gaze from the flaming remains of the Gold Wing toward the burning logs on the opposite curve of the drive. She'd missed my entrance. My feet hit the ground, and I stumbled forward, carrying the axe.

She looked capable as always in her butterfly scrubs and lime-green clogs, although she held what experience told me was a Smith and Wesson of the type used by the RCMP. The light glinted off the steel top of the weapon. Was she helping her brother? Of course, how else could she not have known he was faking?

Mrs. Parnell had nailed it. Someone had been pulling strings all along, manipulating all of us, and that someone had been Rita Susanne.

"Police," I yelled. "Hands on your head. Down on the floor. Get down! Get down now."

We've all seen that "get down" tactic on television, where I can assure you it works for two minutes. Rita Susanne dropped the Smith and Wesson, raised her hands, and sank to her knees. "Down, get down," I yelled. She lay on the floor, and I held the handle of the axe to her back, hoping she'd think it was the barrel of a weapon. I booted the gun out of her reach, but unfortunately out of mine too. With one hand, I reached into my pocket and pulled out the box cutter, flicking the blade up. I tossed it toward Ray, who bumped his way toward it on his behind. I prayed he would find a way to use it to cut the ties.

I yelled out to my unseen and nonexistent backup, "The suspect is Rita Susanne Kelly. Armed and dangerous." I searched around for the plastic ties that bound her prisoners. Several ties lay on the pine console, next to a pair of hypodermic needles and out of reach. I also spotted a baton and canister of pepper spray, probably from Nowicki's work equipment but all too far away. It wasn't worth the risk to get the ties. I couldn't have subdued Rita Susanne solo in any case. On the breakfast bar, I eyed another handgun that looked like a 9 mil Glock to me. It bothered me that I knew these things. This one must have been Nowicki's service weapon. If I raced across the room to reach it, Rita Susanne could get the upper hand. I yelled to my pretend backup again, "What the hell are you waiting for?"

I was still processing the idea that she could be a killer. The sensible figure, the strong hands, the kind smile, all wrong. A toque and some sunglasses had convinced me a man was after me. My own tricks, and yet I'd fallen for them.

Off in the corner, the boots shifted. I could see Wayne Nowicki raising himself to his elbows. I was distracted just long enough. Rita Susanne must have figured she had little to lose. She reared back and leapt to her feet, knocking me over. That was the same ploy I'd used during the beach attack. The axe flew out of my hands. She reached for it, grabbing it by the handle. "You had me fooled for a while. Now I can see it's just you, without a weapon."

Why hadn't I knocked her out with the axe handle when I had the chance?

"And the look of you," she said. "You're—"

I scrambled back toward the table. "So I'm a Sasquatch. I'll do better in future."

She advanced. "You don't have a future. If you had just kept your nose in your own business, you wouldn't need to die now."

I steadied my voice. "How do you plan to get rid of all of us? You've lost your weapon. You'll have quite a few bodies to dispose of, and we will all be missed."

Her eyes flicked toward the front window and the Bobcat by the hole at the edge of the lawn. She turned back to me and twisted her lips.

So, not a fancy swimming pool.

A grave.

My only hope was to stall until the first responders got there. "Imagine if you had killed Ray and dumped him in that pit, I would never have known what happened to him." Of course, that was for Ray's benefit, but I did need to drag out the conversation.

"Listen, since you have the axe and I'm unarmed, you are most likely going to succeed. Why not tell me why all this is happening?"

Maybe I came across as a deranged forest creature, but she was no picture herself. Her hair stood up in tufts, her face was red and blotched, and blood stained her butterfly scrubs and capris. Blood on her hands, in every sense.

"Clever of you to get them all here."

She smiled. "That was beautiful! I used Sandy Sutherland's phone to text Pierre and tell him that Frankie had escaped to Hughie Williams' place. Everyone knew Hughie from back in the day. He and Frankie were always tight. Sandy was already dead, but no one knew it yet."

"Did you track them all with transponders?"

"Easy-peasy to get trackers online and simple to install them."

"But Ray's Escape must have been in Sydney when you put the tracker on."

She shrugged. "It's only an hour and a half from here, and I knew you were arriving that evening. Your sisters gave Annie a call to expect you. I figured the transponder would let me track Ray Deveau until the time was right."

"And then you trapped him and Pierre."

She looked pleased with herself. "I texted them to park in the garage. They drove right in and I got them. Once again, easy-peasy."

"You had a weapon?"

"I had syringes with tranquillizers, and I had Frankie's service weapon. By the way, I don't think Ray is in any shape to do anything with that. He'll be in agony with his circulation returning. Where was I? Right, Francis foolishly hung on to that gun. Not supposed to, you know. He probably thought he might need to protect himself from me." Her laugh sent shivers down my spine. So much for Francis being a co-conspirator.

"And Nowicki? Did you text him?"

"He must have seen me coming here. I could hear the big motorcycle a mile off. I was waiting behind the front door with the poker when he kicked his way in. He had quite an arsenal of weapons. Very useful. I could have shot him, but I wanted it to last a bit longer."

Keep her talking. "I imagine once the Jeep was banged up, you kept it here out of sight and then picked it up when you needed it."

"Bit of a nuisance driving back and forth and switching cars, but I made it work."

"But why did you dope Donald Donnie? He obviously cares about you. He has a heart condition, and who knows what harm those drugs you slipped him will do."

She sneered. "He's a lot better off than in the pit with the rest of you, and he is guilty of being an idiot."

"And what did poor Auntie Annie ever do to you?" Not to mention Alvin.

"It was just an ordinary sedative in their tea. They'll be groggy, that's all. But if they are collateral damage, so be it."

I felt a buzz of rage. I scanned the room seeking a weapon. "That tea was meant for me, wasn't it?"

"I needed to knock you out and let me get the job done. I don't know how you avoided that."

Before I could say "thank the jade plant," she lunged at me. I dodged around the console table, wishing I'd planned this part better. A slight movement behind Rita Susanne caught my attention. Nowicki was inching forward.

I stopped with the table between me and Rita Susanne. I held up my hand. "I feel entitled to an explanation." Of course, that was a ridiculous strategy. I kept eye contact so she wouldn't turn and spot Wayne. "What did any of them ever do to you?"

She sneered. "Aside from ruining my life, you mean?"

"How did they do that?" Criminals often believe they've been hard done by. They feel entitled to perpetrate evil because of some real or imagined slight. The guy who beats his wife, the racist who spray-paints a mosque, the embezzler who makes off with retirees' life savings: it's all okay because someone once gave them a dirty look. The worse the crime, the more absurd the narrative that they've been wronged and therefore justified.

I kept the contempt off my face.

"We were going to be married," she said.

I blinked. "I'm sorry?"

"Matty was coming back for me that night he went off the road. He was critically injured. My own brother, Francis, was in the same car, and he was hurt too. For years I thought it was Matty's fault. We wanted to wait until he finished police college. I was going to continue my nursing degree, and then when he was working, we'd have a good start. But it took a year before Francis recovered, and he was all my parents could think about. Francis, Francis, bloody Francis all the time. No one cared about what I had lost. I had so much to handle that summer, I ended up with a breakdown."

I didn't dare let my eyes leave hers. I kept my mouth shut and nodded to draw her out. It's a technique that often succeeded with my clients, like pressing an ON switch.

"And you didn't go back to school?"

"Hang on," she said with a grin and dashed the few feet to the breakfast bar. Before I could get from behind the console, she had dropped the axe and snatched up the 9 mil from the counter.

"Where were we?" she said, aiming the gun at me. "Oh yes, school. Obviously, I couldn't, could I?"

My mouth was still hanging open.

She said, "Francis was in traction for months, broken femur, tibia, you name it. My mother couldn't cope with his care. My father couldn't manage the farm on his own. Francis had so many bills and treatments not covered by Medicare. Physiotherapy. Equipment. Drugs. My parents put their savings into helping him recover. They took out a loan against the property. Our family had no money left for my studies. I switched to the practical nurse's training. If it wasn't for Francis, I'd have a husband and an amazing career instead of helping little old ladies take their showers and remember their pills."

I decided against mentioning student loans. Or that many practical nurses found great careers. Rita Susanne wanted sympathy, an ally. How could she think that I, Ray's partner, would agree with what she was doing? Yet I'd seen this type of narcissistic reasoning before.

"And Matty woke up, but he never got better. I couldn't leave him. No one knew him like I did."

"And then he died three weeks ago." Was that what had tipped Rita Susanne over the edge?

Her face contorted. "All those years, Matty was fading away. Even with all the advances in medical care, there was never any sign of that beautiful boy. Just the shell of his body, weakening over time."

"I'm sorry for that great loss, Rita Susanne."

"Francis is dying," she said cheerfully.

"I'm sorry about that too."

She sneered. "Don't be. We never got along."

Another sympathetic nod from me.

"He bullied his way back into my home, expecting me to put my life on hold *again*. He told me that Matty never wanted to get married. He claimed I'd thrown myself at him. Francis said there was another girl in P.E.I. that Matty was crazy about. He claimed the boy I loved wanted to leave without saying goodbye and 'setting me off.' Setting me off! Like I was a bomb or something. He said Matty had confided in his police college friends, and everyone supported his decision. They all laughed behind my back and joked that I was trying to trap Matty. All of them! Even Frankie's girlfriend, Sherry."

In that moment, other comments made sense: remarks about Rita Susanne getting her life together, changing. What had she been like before? Easily "set off"? I wished I'd discovered that bit of history earlier. She kept talking.

"Think of it! Frankie recovered completely, thanks to me, and in time passed the RCMP physical. He shot up the ladder in the force." Her voice shook with rage.

She waved the hand that held the Glock. "Back in *my* house, Frankie told me it was my fault. He said Matty swerved to avoid me, and that's when the car went over the bridge." She swiped at her dripping nose.

"Francis told me to stop deceiving myself. Imagine! He ruined my life, and now he wanted me to blame myself. I couldn't let him get away with it anymore."

I could have tried to defend Frankie Kelly, but that wouldn't fly with his demented sister in her role as judge, jury, and executioner. "Perhaps he was suffering from his disease when he told you that."

She snorted. "He didn't suffer enough, if you ask me. He's definitely making up for it now. He'll be the last one to go, and he will know everyone involved died because of him."

"But do any of them know what this is all about?"

"Sure they do. Sherry wormed her way in to see Frankie one day when I was extra-busy with my patients. He must have held back on his sedatives so he could make sense if anyone came by. He's very sneaky that way. I had warned him that if he told anyone, I would have to kill them. He put Sherry in danger. But he also played right into my hands, and that gave me the idea to make the whole lot of them pay. I sent them letters. I used his phone to text Sherry and that idiot Wayne Nowicki and say that if anyone tried to see Francis, I would kill him immediately. And Matty too. So that they didn't doubt my intentions, I made sure that Matty died. I knew that they would reach out to the others, and everyone would try to help Frankie. Frankie was the bait, and Matty was the proof that I meant business. It's easy to use a pillow on someone with breathing difficulties. No one at the facility figured it out, but *they* knew." She pointed to Ray and glanced out the window. Luckily, she didn't turn to Nowicki.

I struggled to compose myself. "And Sherry and Calum? You mean they were both involved?"

She shrugged. "Sherry was Frankie's girlfriend, but she didn't have what it took to care for him while he healed. Calum came later. He had nothing to do with any of it, but I could never get the stupid woman alone. I thought about burning down their house, but they rescued that miserable dog, and it set up a racket anytime I got close. She had only herself to blame."

Oh, Brutus, you did your best to save your people.

"The thing is, I wanted to see their faces when they died. I needed them all to understand why."

"You ran their truck off the road."

Her sly smile sent shivers up and down my arms.

"Fitting, don't you think? A truck hitting the rocks. Now we're three down."

"But some of us are innocent. Calum was. Leonard Mombourquette merely tried to help his friend. Isn't it bad enough you trapped him in an outhouse?"

Her lips twitched. "You can take the blame for that. I wouldn't have known he was coming, but you told Auntie Annie you planned to intercept him at the causeway. I passed you snoring away while you waited, then I spotted him. I turned around and followed, biding my time for the right opportunity. The fool decided to stop at the portable toilet. Poetic justice if you ask me. It was a bit of fun using his own car to tip over that thing. Then when Donald Donnie told me that you were in pursuit of Leonard Mombourquette with him driving Annie's Golf and you in that Chrysler, I nearly got a double-header at Aspy."

Wayne continued to slither forward, leaving a wide smear of dark blood on the floor behind him. I felt rather than saw Ray move. Without taking her eyes off me, Rita Susanne said, "And next these three, one by one."

I tried again, "But really Leonard wasn't involved."

"Don't be stupid, Camilla. Leonard would never keep his mouth shut. Hang on! Are you playing for time?" She shot Leonard a pitiless glance. He was unconscious and lucky to miss it. She turned just long enough for me to lift the console table and hurl it toward her with all my strength. The force of the table knocked her to the floor. Wayne picked up the iron poker.

As she tried to stand up, Nowicki whacked her on the back of the knees. The Glock flew out of her hand and skidded across the floor. Before I could get to it, Rita Susanne snatched up the gun again, whirled and fired. Nowicki grunted and keeled over.

I slid across the floor and grabbed the Smith and Wesson. I trained it on Rita Susanne and yelled to Ray to check Mombourquette. Rita Susanne must have concluded I would have trouble shooting her. Her next words chilled me.

"I practiced shooting, you know. I knew I'd need a weapon to over-come them."

Unlike Rita Susanne, I had never practiced. Could I shoot her to save Ray and the others? Where the hell was the fire department?

I said, "So what have you done with Pierre Forgeron?"

She smirked. "Didn't take the time to check the pit?"

My stomach turned. "He's dead?"

"Should be by now."

I didn't doubt her ability to drag an unconscious man that distance. She heaved heavy and immobile people into bed and baths regularly. Probably didn't even get out of breath.

She said, "He was the worst. I know he was responsible for what hap-pened to Matty."

Ray croaked, "Pierre had nothing to do with it."

"He was always giving Matty a hard time. He would have bullied him into leaving, and that's what caused the accident."

Ray said, "There was no bullying and there was no accident. There was only you flinging yourself in front of the car to stop Matty from leaving—"

She shrieked. "He wanted to marry me. You hated that idea. You are all responsible for his death."

"He was worried about your obsessive crush. He asked for our help."

I wanted Ray to shut up before she shot him point-blank. All right, shooting might not have been among my skills, but my ability to stall at trial was legendary.

"You can't believe you'll get away with this, Rita Susanne." It was a blatant appeal to her ego.

"But I will. Hughie's gone for the entire month, got a business deal going in Alberta. His new holding tank arrives next week, and it will get placed in that pit on top of you all. He trusts me to keep an eye on the work. I nursed his mother, the old harpy, and left him free to go west. No one will ever dig up the earth at the bottom. You will just disappear. People will assume any odour is from the septic settling. You will be dead when you go in, Camilla, because you are not complicit, merely meddling. But the others will have a slower end when I cover them up."

So much to react to. "I'm impressed you can drive a Bobcat."

That brought out another vile smirk. "I'm a very capable person, even though I was deprived of chances. On the farm, I knew more about the machinery than the golden boy did."

"Plenty can go wrong with your plan."

"I don't think so. I intend to live happily knowing they've all paid the price." When she turned to gloat over her victims, I inched forward. Could I make it before she killed another one of us? It would have to be me or Leonard, since the others were intended to suffocate in the pit. As she narrowed her eyes at Leonard, I glimpsed a movement in the kitchen behind her. I raised my voice. "I'm pleading with you. Leonard's innocent. He needs a doctor. You can't—"

I had her attention.

"I'm going to finish what I started. Then I'll go on to live my own life at last. I'm Francis's heir. I'll get his house and investments. With him gone, I can sell the farm too. There are people who want to build country homes on the property. I'll be laughing all the way to the bank."

Ray said, "I'm sorry, Camilla. I tried to keep you out of it."

Everyone loves somebody else's conflict, so I decided I had nothing to lose by creating some. "Why the hell didn't you just call the police?"

"Because we had no proof, just a wild-ass story about a popular member of the community. They all know her up here. She's cared for many local families and even helped some of the officers. She built her credibility, told them that Frankie was suffering delusions as a result of his medications, a common enough phenomenon. Frankie convinced Sherry no one would believe him even if he had been an RCMP officer. She had systematically destroyed his reputation. Sandy confirmed that. He'd talked to people at the local detachment and even in Sydney, and they all believed that Frankie had lost his mind because of his disease."

"But Sherry believed him."

"Sherry knew how Rita Susanne was even before the accident. None of us doubted that she was dangerous. We were attempting to get Frankie out before it was too late. We thought we could deal with her afterwards."

"And you tried to stop her from killing Matty too?"

"Yes, we only found out in Baddeck that Matty was already dead. Sandy Sutherland was boozed up so his brother, Kenny, met up with us to check on him, just in case. The people at the care home said that Matty had died a couple of weeks ago from natural causes, but we knew she was behind it. I let Nowicki know, and we all tore off for Ingonish."

"Did Kenny stay behind you and Pierre?"

"Yeah, he wanted to get some details about Matty's death, so we took off. Sandy was panicking."

"Kenny must have called him, and then Sandy called your cell, but by that time it was my cell. I took your Escape, I'm afraid."

"Oh yeah. She found that out afterwards. She kept me in the loop every time she attacked you." His voice cracked.

"Kenny saved my life on the trail, and I am grateful. It's terrible about his brother, but I'm glad she didn't get Kenny as well."

Rita Susanne cackled. "Don't get ahead of yourself. That Kenny's another meddler who knows too much."

Ray hung his head. "I am sorry you got involved. I was trying to keep you safe."

I snapped. "Why couldn't you tell me the truth?"

"Because you would have barged in and made a bad situation worse. Maybe got Frankie killed."

"I haven't done that." But of course, I had. Barging is my signature move.

"I thought you might be killed. You might drag in other people. I just wanted you safe at home."

Other people. Was Mombourquette's fate down to me? Could I have stopped this psychopath in her search for revenge?

"I'm sorry, Ray. I *have* made it worse." We were having a long chat while at the mercy of a murderer. What sense did that make? I glanced at Rita Susanne, who was enjoying our sorrowful final scene. She chuckled. "Such drama. You figured it out, too little and too late." She pointed the gun at Ray. "Time to take a walk outside. We both know your girlfriend won't have the guts or skill to stop me, but I'll shoot her if have to."

I aimed the gun.

But behind Rita Susanne, a game-changer was about to unfold. A shrieking neon green shape landed on Rita Susanne's back, yanking her hair and punching. Her weapon clattered to the floor. I lunged for it. Rita Susanne collapsed, recoiling under punches and kicks. All I could see was the blur of Elaine Ekstein's green shirt and red curls. Elaine continued to scream as she pummelled the cowering nurse. A hank of Rita Susanne's hair seemed tangled in Elaine's fist. I kicked the gun toward Ray, who had succeeded in freeing himself. He managed to pick it up with shaking hands, but we had no way to stop Rita Susanne without putting Elaine in the line of fire.

Rita Susanne flipped Elaine over and attempted to get the gun when a cast-iron frying pan slammed into the back of her head. Rita Susanne dropped, limp, to the floor. Cody stood behind her, eyes wide, the heavy black pan hanging from his hand.

After moment's stunned silence, Elaine leapt onto Rita Susanne again, squeezing her throat. I yelled, "Leave her, Elaine. She's unconscious. I don't want to defend you in a murder trial."

"She tried to kill him. And you!"

I slumped against the counter in relief. "Yeah well, she's out of commission now. Go to Leonard." Elaine staggered across the floor and scooped up Mombourquette like a stuffed toy. She let out a heart-rending wail.

I said, "I'm sure he's alive. She has access to a ton of sedatives. Try to get him awake and talking."

Cody had started shaking. "I hope I'm not going to go to prison over this," he whispered.

I said, "Not much chance of that. But why are you here?"

"I went to Mrs. Annie MacNeil's place to see if you'd got back. I felt like a dick for ditching you when the cop showed up at Calum and Sherry's place, but cops make me nervous, and they don't always play by the rules."

"Don't I know it."

"Anyways, this lady, Elaine, was already banging on the door. I went right in, because I know Auntie Annie pretty well. But she was asleep on the daybed, and I couldn't wake her up. And some guy with a bunch of earrings and a leather jacket was dead to the world on the floor." Poor

Alvin. Cody pointed at Elaine. "She said he worked for you. We called 911 on the house phone.

"Elaine told me I had to take her wherever you were because it was a matter of life and death. I figured you might have come here because we'd been talking about that Silverado in the garage. She pried that all out of me, but anyway, she paid me pretty good for my trouble. When we got to the foot of Hughie's driveway, we seen that old guy passed out in the car. Couldn't wake him up either. Then we heard the explosion, and we seen the burnt-out motorcycle and we knew that was bad. We called 911 again, for all the good it did. We snuck around back and found the broken glass on the deck. We could see you and these guys and we both heard Rita Susanne talking about killing everyone." He gestured toward Elaine again. "She went right for her. I thought they might kill each other, then I saw them frying pans on the wall. I didn't have a choice except to whack Rita Susanne. That won't be good for me. People knew that she was always giving me a hard time, and I couldn't stand her."

"You saved the lives of three police officers." I hoped to hell that was true. Ray was alive, but I wasn't sure about the others. "We will all back you up, so you shouldn't be charged. I'm glad you didn't come in the front door."

"It was Brutus who warned me. He's that dog that Calum and Sherry rescued. I got a way with dogs. Anyways, he was dancing around like crazy and heading for the back of the house. That's why we came around that way."

I said, "Brutus must have been trying to reach me. That's his second save from Rita Susanne. Poor guy. What's going to happen to him now?"

"He's not going back to the shelter, that's for sure," Cody said defiantly. "I won't let that happen." At that moment, I felt the world had turned for Cody. Of course, I would never let Brutus go to any pound. Gussie and the cat would have had to cope.

I took the ties and secured Rita Susanne's hands and feet, trying not to recoil. "You did what had to be done. Cody. In my eyes, you are a hero. At least one cop will swear to that."

Ray stood, rubbing his wrists and swaying. "Camilla's right. I don't know who you are, but you saved our lives."

Cody, white as a squirt of toothpaste, said, "But do you think I killed her? She's—I never hit anyone before." He shoved me aside, pushed through the front door, and threw up in the bushes.

Elaine shouted, "Leonard needs medical attention." She had returned to her human shape, and her voice was working just fine.

I shook myself. Of course, he needed help. Why were we standing around talking? Shock? "What about Nowicki? He was in a bad shape even before she shot him."

A faint voice said, "I plan to live long enough to see that bitch locked up forever." Nowicki's eyes closed.

I located Rita Susanne's phone. I dialled 911 to get an ambulance for Leonard, Wayne, and even Rita Susanne. I hoped that the dispatcher would see Rita Susanne's name and give the call priority. "It's Rita Susanne Kelly calling from Hughie Williams' place. We have three people with life-threatening injuries. You are already aware of this fire, and you need to stop dicking around and get your first responders here unless you want to find yourself testifying in front of a coroner's jury."

Rita Susanne didn't move. I hoped for his own sake that Cody hadn't killed her. I knew that she needed medical aid quickly, and we would have to help her, no matter what.

Ray said, "Listen!"

In the distance, we heard the welcome sound of sirens, getting closer. Police? Fire? Ambulance? We needed them all.

Ray and I stumbled toward each other. My legs were like jelly after the adrenaline faded. He pulled me to him. "Camilla, when will you learn to mind your own goddam business?"

I buried my face in his chest and muttered, "Not happening, and if you ever pull another stunt like this, I will learn to shoot." We held on to each other. Rita Susanne had blood on her hands, but we were going to make it against all odds.

Ray said, "If only we could have saved Pierre."

I jerked back. "Maybe it's not too late."

He shook his head. "Could he actually be alive after all this time?"

Only one way to find out. I was already through the door, running as fast as my jellylike legs would let me. We passed Cody on the front steps with his head in his hands. I staggered toward the pit and I could hear Ray struggling behind me. He must have been in agony after being bound all that time. Inside the pit was a mount of dirt. A shovel lay on the ground.

Ray picked up the shovel, and I fell to my knees, scraping at the earth with my bare hands to reach Pierre Forgeron.

Cody loped up behind us and joined in, scooping away soil. We worked until a pale face appeared.

Cody kept whispering. "What is going on here?"

"Please be alive," I whispered.

Ray was beyond words, brushing the dirt from Pierre's face. I felt for a pulse and found it, faint, but real.

Ray found the strength to begin CPR and kept shouting, "Pierre!"

It seemed like forever before Pierre's eyelids flickered slightly.

"He's alive," Cody said.

"Yes," Ray said. "Whoever you are, thank you."

I said, "He's Cody, and remember that."

We stumbled out of the way as the paramedics took over reviving Pierre, while Ray, his face like chalk, filled them in on what had happened.

I said to anyone who would listen, "We need to check on Francis Kelly."

The paramedics had their hands full. The police were bound to show up, and then there'd be no getting away before statements had been taken. It was now-or-never, steal a vehicle and go. But Ray had also been listening. "We'll call 911 again from the Kelly house."

"No way. You stay. You need medical help."

"Don't start, Camilla. Francis's life is the priority."

"Fine. Mind if we borrow your car, Cody? They'll want to take your statement."

His eyes widened in panic. "They'll arrest me?"

Ray said, "Just statements. Nowicki will vouch for you, and so will I. We need to give statements too, but we'll be back before they sort anything out."

"Nowicki's unconscious with the paramedics. You guys look like crap.

I better drive you," Cody said.

On the way, I asked why Ray and Nowicki had been arguing in Sydney. It had been one of the reasons I hadn't trusted the big cop. Ray said, "Frankie told Sherry that Rita Susanne planned to kill him with an overdose if police responded to accusations from his friends. I argued for calling them anyway, but Wayne was convinced that someone would warn her if there was a report, and Frankie would be toast. People liked Rita Susanne, but Frankie didn't make a lot of friends in the RCMP. I hear he changed since we were students together. Ambition or power or whatever. In the end, Pierre and I tried to get here in time to save him and Matty. But of course, we found out we were way too late for Matty."

"You were shaken up by that news."

He nodded.

"That why you forgot your key fob in your new car and dropped your phone?"

"When we learned that Matty had already died, we just raced to get to Ingonish. Pierre was livid that we'd wasted time meeting in Baddeck to check on Matty. Frankie was our priority."

"Let's hope we're in time now."

●●●

The Kelly farm was quiet, dark, and eerie. My heart thundered as we opened the door, calling Frankie's name. Ray found his old friend in the main floor bedroom in the back of the house. The lights were off, no radio or television played, and the blinds were closed. There was no visitor's chair, no bedside table. Nothing on the walls to distract or cheer. A stash of pill bottles huddled on a shelf on the far side of the room, along with a few vials and syringes. The room reeked of sickness and despair.

Francis Kelly's eyelids fluttered when we entered. His eyes were huge and haunted, his body skeletal, cheeks sunken. His hair hung in lank strands. Ray crouched down and clutched his old friend's claw-like hand. I felt overcome and turned to fling open the window. Let the evil out.

Ray said, "They stopped her, Frankie."

Frankie's voice was so weak, we both learned forward. "Thank

God. She told me when she killed Sandy…" He closed his eyes again and shuddered. "And then Sherry and Calum. Poor Matty too. I'm so drugged, I can't think straight anymore."

I said, "But how did this happen?"

"I'd had successful cancer surgery, but I thought I'd come home to recover and Rita Susanne would help me. I had no clue what a monster she'd turned into. She told people my cancer was inoperable—terminal—and claimed I refused to see anyone. She taunted me about that. I don't know when I ate last. I can't even stand up."

Ray ran his free hand over his face. "We'll get you help. Won't be long."

"She was so full of hate. My own sister. She said that today she would bury you and Pierre alive at Hughie's place, and it was all my fault."

"We are okay. And we know none of it's your doing."

The dark eyes widened, and Frankie turned to stare in terror at the door. "Can she get to me, Ray?"

"Not anymore. You'll be good from now on."

While Ray reassured Francis Kelly, I called 911 yet again.

For some reason, my head kept spinning.

CHAPTER THIRTY
Who let you in?

The medical centre in Neil's Harbour had never been through such a night. But then the staff was new to the MacPhee clan. I was supposed to lie quietly in case my spinning head meant I had another of my famous concussions. I don't know who spilled the beans on that front. Muttered discussions were taking place about whether I should be transported to the Cape Breton Regional Hospital. Pierre Forgeron and Wayne Nowicki had been whisked away to ICU in Sydney, although Nowicki was conscious and wouldn't stay off his phone. Ray's injuries were less serious, and Mombourquette was supposed to be fine, if somewhat groggy. Elaine was fussing over him. Ray was with me. We're not fussers.

It took a while to learn that Rita Susanne had also been airlifted to ICU, her condition critical, the outlook bleak. Although Cody would be relieved, it would be worse for her if she recovered. But she was not to be underestimated and remained under police guard in Sydney.

The place was abuzz about Rita Susanne, everyone from medical staff to RCMP shaking their heads. Of course, it didn't take long for people to start saying there was always something a bit off about her. A stubborn few claimed they didn't believe a word of it.

Cody had suffered a post-disaster panic attack and was also being checked at the medical centre. His grandmother, Pearl, kept patting his hand and telling everyone how proud she was. A lot of pies were waiting for Cody. Donald Donnie, never out of earshot, looked wistful as he listened.

After a while, Pearl approached me, head down, and spoke in her raspy voice, "I am sorry for lying to you about the Silverado. I recognized Ray Deveau from years ago when he was a cop. I'm always worried about my Cody getting into scraps, and that Rita Susanne was on his case all the time for no reason. She'd already told the Mounties to keep an eye on him. She was just vicious, and I thought she'd try to stick it to him with Ray Deveau too. I didn't want you to mention seeing Cody in case. I guess I was being paranoid."

"We all should have been more paranoid, considering. Did you have any idea that Ray would end up at Hughie's place?"

She sighed. "No clue at all, but maybe if I'd told you the truth, it wouldn't have happened."

"Don't worry. I knew you were lying, so it didn't change our plans. And for the record, Cody is going to be fine."

Pearl passed Auntie Annie in the doorway. Auntie Annie had survived what she called "the third degree by that little doctor." She showed no signs of having been drugged and still gave off that reassuring scent of lily-of-the-valley. "I'm sorry, dear, that I wasn't more on the ball. I'd started to wonder about Rita Susanne and Francis Kelly and all that background. Rita Susanne was a very troubled girl back in the day, but then she turned her life around, and it seemed disloyal to talk about it. Every now and then, you could still see little signs. I'd felt sorry for her because of her parents and Francis, and now him being sick again. If I'd told you my concerns, maybe she could have been stopped earlier."

"You tried. I was in a hurry to get to Hughie's. I thought we could discuss whatever it was later. Not your fault." I squeezed her hand.

"I wish I'd told someone. But I liked Rita Susanne, and she was a huge help. Then every now and then you'd get a tiny glimpse of the girl she used to be."

"Rita Susanne had everyone in the community—except Cody and Pearl—under her spell."

"You're right there. She got herself involved in some of the families. A couple of times she even took some of Pearl's pies to the detachment. She said it was to thank them for their service to the community!"

"What could you have said? No one could have imagined what she got up to."

Auntie Annie sighed. "It's hard to believe such evil actions from a woman working with vulnerable people. I feel shaken to my very bones."

Another doctor arrived, and Auntie Annie was gently ushered out by a nurse. I was subjected to quite boring and unnecessary tests. Every jab and poke hurt like hell. "While you're nosing around, how about a pain-killer for my knee and shoulder? They got banged up this week." The doctor, who seemed younger than Cody—eighteen tops—remained calm throughout, and I drifted off.

•••

My eyes popped open when I sensed a chill in the room. Three blonde heads loomed over me like a trio of bad hallucinations.

"Double, double toil, and trouble," I said under my breath.

"Watch your mouth, missy," Edwina snapped.

Fire burn and cauldron bubble.

I said, "This is place of refuge. I need to be stress-free."

"We're here for you," Edwina said. If the clinic employed a security guard on-site, I imagined she had him hog-tied in the supply cupboard.

Alexa's voice quavered. "We care about you. We were worried to death."

Donalda added, "Even if you can be impossible, we *are* family. We rushed to get flights from Ottawa."

"About that family notion," I said, keeping one eye open. "We really must talk."

Apprehension flickered from face to face to face. Despite being so worried, they'd all taken time to apply their make-up. And not a hair out of place.

I propped myself up on my elbow. "You see, I visited Resurrection graveyard in Sydney. I may be impossible. I may even have a concussion, but I'm pretty good with dates. You have two minutes to tell me the truth or—"

Alexa began to sob.

"Never mind the waterworks. Tell me who I am, and we'll see what we can do to repair our relationship that was entirely built on lies."

Edwina said, "Not *entirely* built on lies."

"Sure. Entirely built on alternative facts then. Which one of you was it?"

Donalda and Edwina switched from stunned to offended. Alexa moved to tears, fresh mascara streaking her cheeks. As far as I could tell, they weren't even faking.

Donalda drew herself up to her full height and said, "What do you think we are?

"It happens in the best of families. Girls will be girls. Out with it."

Alexa sounded like a strangled duck. "It wasn't … any of us."

"Fine. I get it. A lonely widower meets a congenial woman and… Why couldn't he have married her?"

This was too much for Edwina. "Daddy would never have done that." I suspected she was right.

In that case, if none of my sisters was my mother, and my father wasn't my father, what other surprises were in store?

"If it wasn't any of you upstanding and honest MacPhees, who was it?"

They exchanged glances. To my surprise, Alexa showed a bit of spine. "We don't know."

"Do."

"Don't."

"Was I found in a basket on the doorstep?"

"You were born to someone Daddy knew, but not a—"

"Tell the whole truth."

"The poor girl was in a difficult situation. It was just as we were moving to Ottawa. We took you to Ottawa, where no one knew us. She planned to come for you when she got her situation sorted out, and no one at home needed to know."

"You know I love euphemisms. Who is she?"

"We really don't know. Daddy never said."

"Pull the other one."

"We have no reason to lie. And we have no idea who she was."

"Was?"

"Yes, that's it. She never came for you. We believe she died."

I didn't see that coming. "What happened to her?"

Edwina took the lead. "Daddy never told us anything. He had promised to keep her secret. And by then, we all felt you were ours."

Our father, always the intelligent, high-minded educator, had been slipping into dementia, complicated by mini-strokes. His memories were vanishing, along with most of his nouns.

"You mean now *I'll* never know."

I appreciated their guilty looks.

I said, "Must be documents."

Edwina shook her head. "We packed up everything when Daddy went into the Perley. We found nothing about your background."

"Hang on. My birth certificate would have her name."

"It didn't. It listed Mum and Daddy as your parents."

"But that's not—well, I can't believe Daddy would have gone along with that."

Again, glances exchanged.

"He didn't," Edwina said. "It seems your birth mother somehow managed to register you under their names."

"I doubt that is possible."

She shrugged. "Daddy said it was."

That would be something to check out when I got out of health centre hell, but it explained a lot, such as why I had a birth certificate without an adoption process.

"Did Auntie Annie know?"

Three heads shook. Edwina said, "No one knew."

Donalda squared her shoulders. "Most adoptees never find out about their birth-parents. You must let it go because—" The toddler doctor returned, cutting off Donalda mid-protest. He shooed the three of them away, leaving me with a throbbing in my temple and a gaping void in my history. Why had my father allowed this to happen?

Alexa tiptoed back a couple of minutes later. She stood silent, eyes brimming. She whispered, "Sorry."

CHAPTER THIRTY-ONE
No flowers, no speeches, no toasts

In case anyone has forgotten, I had a clear plan for a simple wedding, with no fuss and no extra people, the opposite of all our MacPhee family functions. It was to be Ray and me, the nearest available officiant, and two witnesses as required by law, no need to have met them before. No flowers, no speeches, no toasts. No drama.

Barring a second storm, we had committed to the beach in front of our honeymoon cottage, with the backup being the large front room of the big B&B overlooking the sand and sea. We had a sunny mid-October day, with the ocean glittering blue and silver and the last blaze of red and gold on the trees. The breeze ruffled the skirt of my red dress, and the cold sand squeezed into my sandals and between my toes.

We were perishingly cold.

I gazed at Ray and tried to ignore the gathering crowd when someone thrust a bunch of flowers into my arms. It was an imposing bouquet of the type I never would have selected, and it could only have come from Edwina, now standing on the edge of the gathering, flaring her nostrils triumphantly. Next to her, Donalda was convulsed over her husband's latest practical joke, and Alexa was getting ready to blubber. "Grant me strength," I muttered to myself.

Ashley and Brittany huddled off to the other side, tall, slender, and elegant in slinky dresses but sporting the kind of thunderous expressions reserved for custody battles. Word had it that Ashley felt "scooped" by the wedding, since she had a fiancé, and Brittany felt diminished by Ashley, since she only had a boyfriend. They were careful not to mingle with the generals on my side.

My sisters were responsible for the long row of tables with fluttering white tablecloths that stretched along the grassy lawn between the rows of cottages above the beach. The white plastic chairs had been prettied up with garlands of fall leaves. I knew the tablecloths were extra sheets from the B&B, but they were perfect. We'd managed a last-minute plan to have seafood chowder and homemade rolls (from Auntie Annie) and blueberry pie (from Pearl). My sisters upped the ante with seafood platters, appetizers, and a wedding cake. I mean, really.

Alvin had pilfered old-fashioned green and sea-blue dishes. Mason jars with fall leaves added a bit of zing. I later learned Alvin had made favours, tried up in organza and swirled with green ribbons. I tried not to dwell on anyone later experiencing the miracle of Buzzy Bath Bomb.

Leonard Mombourquette positioned himself next to Elaine, reluctantly prepared to officially witness our union. He'd cleaned up pretty good, considering his brush with death. And for all her Nordic and Celtic origins, Elaine made a fashion statement in an ankle-length African tribal print dress.

Ray and I waited as Cody paraded along the boardwalk with Auntie Annie on one arm and his grandmother, Pearl, on the other. Maybe it was my imagination, but I thought he held himself with a touch of pride. Brutus brought up at the rear, on his best behaviour, no doubt because Cody had adopted him.

Ray had told me earlier that the investigation could go on for months, but it was unlikely Cody would face charges for stopping Rita Susanne, although at least one of the local officers had been pushing for that. Her malignant influence lingered on. We'd heard that Francis Kelly's condition was slightly improved, but Rita Susanne had a lot of damage to her brain and was unlikely to recover. Wayne Nowicki had brought us that update. He made quite a sight, leg in a cast, arm in a sling, vast green and purple bruises blooming over his face. His last comment about Rita Susanne was, "If she so much as twitches, charges are going to land on her like a ten-ton boulder."

As I pondered that, Donald Donnie and Loretta arrived like dignitaries. Family of the bride and friend of the groom, Donald Donnie was heard to say. Donnie Red must have been Donald Donnie's plus two. Perhaps this was a reward for his help in Baddeck. I wasn't sure how much of a reward a wedding on a windy beach in October would be. Gussie accompanied the three of them. The cat had chosen to boycott, and I got that.

Some busybody had set up folding canvas chairs for the ceremony, close to the grassy edge so the "guests" didn't need to stumble over the large stones on the beach.

I would have been happier if it hadn't turned out that Wayne Nowicki was a licensed officiant. I had tuned out the long boring story of how and why. Seemed he was full of gratitude because I'd saved his life.

Word had spread throughout the community, and we could see strangers taking up places on the lawn, carrying camp chairs or blankets, and passing around bottles of Moosehead.

Since the ceremony had already been hijacked by my sisters, in addition to Cody, Pearl, and Auntie Annie, I had invited Susan West, owner of the West Wind Cabins and my rescuer. She said she wouldn't miss it for the world, itching to glimpse Leonard with his clothes on and to get a gander at the guy who almost got away. She brought her husband, since he hadn't believed a word and needed to see for himself. Next to the young doctor from the clinic, I noticed Kenny Sutherland looking still handsome but understandably bereft. He was chatting with Archie McCarthy. Apparently, they were both grateful to us for stopping Rita Susanne. I was grateful to them too: Archie for the old Civic and Kenny for saving me from Rita Susanne in the Jeep. I'd been able to reach Harold and Grace, who turned their Winnebago around at Canso to join the party. I could spot their Tilley hats bobbing in the crowd.

By now, we were nearly thirty for the ceremony that was supposed to be the two of us, the witnesses, and the officiant.

But where was Alvin? What jackassy endeavour had dragged him away from early morning? A murmur arose from the sand dunes, and I turned to spot his swaying ponytail, his leather-jacketed arm supporting the beaming Mrs. Parnell, in full military regalia, a brimming tumbler of Harvey's Bristol Cream in one hand. A thin trail of smoke wafted from the cigarette holder in her other.

"Wouldn't miss it for the world. Congratulations to you and Sergeant Deveau on a valiant effort and excellent post-conflict détente."

I said, "Thank you. I'm so glad you are here." For some reason, my cheeks felt damp.

"I wish you both much happiness, Ms. MacPhee."

Happiness? I supposed that might be possible. If I didn't let myself flash back to the deaths of Sherry and Calum, two people I had known and liked. If I didn't ponder the fates of Sandy Sutherland and Matty, who were innocent as well. If I didn't dwell on the damage to Ray and Leonard, the injuries that kept Pierre Forgeron in hospital. If I didn't think about what Francis Kelly had suffered. If my knee and shoulder didn't throb quite so much. And if my family hadn't lied to me all my life.

Never mind. I had a sneaking suspicion that bliss was overrated.

To my surprise, the ceremony went off without a hitch. I tossed my unwanted bouquet when the "guests" least expected it, and Alvin shot up to catch the ridiculous thing. Interpret that how you will. I swear that Donald Donnie tried to body-check him out of the way to catch it himself. Alvin bowed and offered the flowers to Mrs. P. Touching. The small crowd murmured in approval.

I nudged Ray. "No way any of these people are coming on our honeymoon. So I hope you have a new plan. The last one almost got us killed."

He put his arms around me. "I think we should get busy and find out who you are. I thought tests with the big DNA sites would make a good wedding present for you."

"DNA tests? Thanks for not making it anything girly. I can spit in a bottle as well as anyone."

"No question about that. We just have to be prepared to cope with whatever you find out."

I leaned farther into that hug. "Sure thing. After what we've been through here, it should be a piece of cake."

"I doubt it will be a piece of cake, but whatever turns up, we'll deal with it together. At least it won't be boring."

At that moment, boring sounded good, but just for once, I decided not to put up a fight.

Camilla's Favourite Traditional Oatcakes

2 ½ cups oatmeal
1 cup brown sugar
1 cup unbleached white flour
1 tsp each pure vanilla extract, salt, baking soda
1 cup butter
1 large egg, beaten

Preheat oven to 350 degrees

Combine dry ingredients and then cut in butter. This is easy if you have a pastry cutter. Add vanilla and egg and mix well. You can chill the dough before rolling. It makes it easier and you can keep chilled until you are 'ready to roll'.

Roll out to about ¼ inch thickness on a floured surface and cut into shapes.

Bake at 350 for ten minutes.

Acknowledgements

I had the good fortune to grow up in Cape Breton with its magnificent scenery, lively storytellers, wonderful music and enduring friendships. I have especially happy memories of the annual summer trips to Ingonish with our friends the McCanns, the Fritzes and the MacDonalds. The idyllic days were always punctuated by our chorus of screams as our long-suffering dad navigated the steep roads around Cape Smokey, avoiding the sheer drops to the Atlantic and later by our shrieks as we were smacked by waves on Ingonish Beach. As teenagers camping in Ingonish we were even noisier and less well behaved but the less said about that the better.

It was a shame to toss in a bit of murder to muddy those coastal waters, but, you know, that's what happens when your mind works the way mine does.

I tried to do justice to the beauty of the Cabot Trail, the warm nature of the people of Cape Breton and the humour that permeates the population of the island, but that's a tall order. I have taken a few liberties with roads, restaurants, accommodations and buildings on the trail and in Baddeck, but all those look-offs are real as is the outhouse. I hope every reader gets to try the trip.

Like all books, this one owes much to many people. My brother, John Merchant, brought his keen insights into an earlier draft of You Light Up My Death. He and my brother-in-law Alan Kent Chavez accompanied us as we toured the trail for recreation and research through notable storms and cooking challenges.

I must give an appreciative shout-out to my Cape Breton cousins for making our recent visits so much fun and to Viola Doncaster for wrangling them to gatherings. Speaking of cousins, special thanks to Barbara MacKinnon and Gerard MacKinnon for their important catches in the last draft and to Cathy and Shane MacKenzie for support and very useful information.

Throughout the series, I have benefitted from many legal discussions with my friend Janet MacEachen. Camilla doesn't always take Janet's wise counsel, but what can you do?

It has been a treat to work with Allister Thompson again. Allister edited the six previous Camilla MacPhee books as well as the Fiona Silk books. He remains unflappable in spite of everything that Camilla throws at him. Alex Zych's excellent proofreading has saved me from certain mortification. Thanks to Ron Corbett, friend, colleague and publisher, for welcoming Camilla and me to Ottawa Press and Publishing, and to Terry Tyo and Patti Moran for making it all work.

The cover photo was taken on our last visit by my husband, Giulio Maffini, one of a million supportive things he's done over the years, including trips around the trail with more stops than he ever wanted. Thanks also to my son-in-law Nick Fairbank https://badduck.ca/ for the cover design.

I am grateful to Linda Wiken for help with this and every book I have written. Thanks also to eagle-eyed early readers Barbara Fradkin and Mara Taracievicz Arno for their very insightful comments. Despite their tendency to bump people off in quantity, mystery writers are inclined to be funny, collegial and full of useful information. Writer friends Brenda Chapman, Vicki Delany, Robin Harlick and Mike Martin can always be counted on to keep spirits up.

Finally, many real dogs and cats have enriched our lives and given texture to books. Gussie and Mrs. Parnell's little calico cat and the new-comer Brutus are channeling some of the traits of my beloved pets. They give Camilla something to take care of, a reason to go out in the rain, to own a first aid kit and to take her mind off murder now and then.

Oh and by the way, this is work of fiction, so none of the characters are real or in any way related to you, me or any of our friends, cowork-ers or neighbours. Rather they are figments of my fevered imagination. Naturally, any errors are entirely my own.

Last but definitely not least, here's a heartfelt salute to the many readers, librarians and booksellers who have been so supportive of the Camilla books over the years.

Mary Jane Maffini

Lapsed librarian and former co-owner of Prime Crime Mystery Bookstore in Ottawa, Mary Jane Maffini is the author of twenty mysteries in three and a half series. MJ was born in Sydney, Nova Scotia and holds a BA (Hons) and an MLS from Dalhousie. Apparently, she made a fair amount of noise in her years as a professional librarian.

The seven Camilla MacPhee mysteries are set in Ottawa, with occasional side trips to Cape Breton, and feature the lawyer and crotchety investigator, her peculiar family, quirky friends and the world's worst office assistant, Alvin Ferguson, plus some random and inconvenient pets.

The two Fiona Silk capers, focusing on a failed romance writer and very reluctant sleuth, take place in a quaint village in West Quebec.

MJ's Charlotte Adams professional organizer mysteries have recently been optioned for television. The series has been reissued by Beyond the Page Publishing in 2021 and a sixth Charlotte book, Death Plans a Perfect Trip, arrived in 2022.

She is a charter member of The Ladies Killing Circle and has stories in all seven of the group's anthologies.

As Victoria Abbott, she collaborated on the five book collector mysteries (Berkley Prime Crime) with her daughter, Victoria. Book Four, The Marsh Madness, won the 2015 Bony Blithe for mysteries that make us smile.

In addition to the Crime Writers of Canada's Derrick Murdoch Award, MJ holds three Crime Writers of Canada awards for crime shorts and an Agatha award (Malice Domestic) for best short story. The Busy Woman's Guide to Murder (Charlotte Adams mystery # 5) won the 2012 Romantic Times award for Amateur Sleuth.

MJ lives and plots in Manotick, Ontario with a pair of miniature dachshunds at her feet. Her husband sleeps with one eye open.